THE

CURSED

WISH

PAULINE S. FLYNN

Published by Pauline S. Flynn in 2023

Copyright © Pauline S. Flynn 2023
Map Illustration by Pauline S. Flynn
Cover design by fantasybookdesign.com, copyrights owned by Pauline S. Flynn

This is a work of fiction. Names, characters, places, and incidents are either products of the author's imagination or are used fictitiously. Any resemblance to actual events, locales, or persons, living or dead, is entirely coincidental.

ISBN: 978-1-66640-620-7

Trigger/Content Warnings

T. C. W. <u>includes</u> references to:

- Parental Death

- Anxiety / Depression

- Violence / Self-Harming / Suicide

- Sexual Intent / Implication

As such, the *above elements* may be triggering to

certain readers.

Contents

Eat that cake, buy that thing you probably don't need
or take that day off.
You only have one life, and this is it.

THE CURSED WISH

PAULINE S FLYNN

PROLOGUE

A large hand gently closed the hardback of a book, concealing the last few pages within. "And they lived happily ever after... The end." Setting the weighty tome on his lap, a man smiled at the old tale.

"What happened to the bad man, Daddy?" a little girl with bright red hair and intense eyes questioned.

Regarding her with that same smile, the man answered, "Prince Warrick vanquished him."

"But why?"

The father laughed and placed the book on the edge of the white bedside table. Which was currently housing many little dolls, some dressed, others with pens all over their faces. Their synthetic hair was matted and knotted, a mess of their once pristine selves. Reaching back, he tucked the culprit of those crimes in.

"Because that's what heroes do, Kai. They take out the bad guy and save the day."

Kai blinked her big, blue eyes, her face twisted with confusion. "But maybe... maybe that man was lonely in his ice kingdom and wanted a friend. Why else would he keep causing trouble? Maybe he wanted someone to love him, too."

Her father chuckled some more, and his head shook at her child-like response. "Have you been listening to the story these last few nights, birthday girl?"

Her curious gaze sparkled like twinkling stars as the spinning disco light from her bedroom ceiling reflected in them, those stars jumping like little bouncing balls as she nodded quickly.

Her father released a sigh of resignation. "Maybe you're still too young to comprehend the plot." He nodded, pushing a tress of his daughter's hair behind an ear. "I'll let you keep this book since it's still, technically, your birthday. *The Cursed Rose* is a classic story, great for amateur fantasy readers. When you're older and understand, then we'll revisit this question. You can tell me then why the bad man kept causing trouble."

Kai smiled wide. "Okay, Daddy!" Seemingly happy with his response.

Her father leaned over and placed a kiss on her forehead. "Get some sleep. I heard from the birdies that someone's going to the fair tomorrow with Grandpa." He leaned back and brushed his masculine nose against her small button one a few times.

Kai spilt with giggles as a mischievous glint flared in her eyes. "Daddy can talk to birdies?"

"Loves his books and his gardens..." a woman interrupted, leaning in the doorway to the room.

She had been lovingly watching the two similar goofballs inside it, twiddling with a few strands of long, red hair that she had pulled over an exposed shoulder.

"I think your Daddy thinks he's a princess, too. Just like the ones in your cartoons."

"Babe," the man said, turning a playful glare at the woman.

"That means Mommy is the hero." Kai shot up in bed. "She's Prince Charming!"

The redhead in the doorway winked at her daughter. "The strongest of them all," she proclaimed.

Kai beamed, eyes going between her dressed-up parents. "So, we're going to live happily ever after, too?"

Her mother stepped into the room finally. The silk-green fabric of her dress shined in various shades from the lights bouncing off it. "Forever, and ever." She reached out, gently grabbing Kai from the back of her head, and kissed her petite forehead. "Goodnight, sweet dreams, I love you, God bless you... See you in the morning."

Kai closed her eyes, enjoying how her mother's words brushed against her skin.

Her father rose from the bed, straightening his suit. Hands tweaked the black tie against his chest, ridding it of potential creases. "You be good for Grandpa tonight. Go to bed, and no faffing about." His eyes gave Kai a knowing look. "If you cause him troubles, there'll be no fair tomorrow, little lady. Understand?"

"Yes, Daddy!" Kai giggled, wiggling herself back into her spot. All while her mother re-tucked her in, ensuring the thick quilt was securely stuffed under Kai's sides.

"Good girl." Her father fixed his collar and went to the flowery pink door. "We won't be gone long. Goodnight, Princess." He waited by that exit, a hand hovering over a light switch that matched the flowery pattern of the door.

His wife whispered something into his daughter's ear, too quiet for him to hear. But both his girls grinned ear to ear like the Cheshire cat at whatever was said. It made the man shake his head as a grin of his own twitched at the mischievous pair.

Her mother slowly swaggered towards the doorway, linking arms with her father, unaware of the little girl who watched them like a hawk.

Kai shouted, "Have fun!" As they switched off the light and blew her one last kiss. "Goodnight, Mommy. Goodnight, Daddy. See you in the morning."

Twelve Years Later

Chapter One

K ai Redsi lifted her head, making eye contact with the olive-toned face sat across. "Huh?" She hardly registered the individual's words.

Stace's features twisted, and her brown eyes rolled. "C'mon Kai, we hardly hang out anymore, and when we do, you always have your nose in your phone!" A hand reached over with cat-like speed, swiping the mobile device. "The least you can do is put this away!"

Kai blinked her icy blues, grumbling as she stared at her empty hands, "Didn't know you were taking ninja classes as well."

Stace caught only a snip bit of that as the coffee shop bustled with noise from the staff shouting names for the orders.

People lined up at a teller behind the girls, some impatiently waiting for their turn, others chatting in the queue. The different areas of people conversing raised the surrounding volume to a hard-to-hear-yourself-talk level. The shop's muggy air carried heavy aromas of coffee and freshly baked goods, appeasing the noise with mouth-watering temptations. The enclosed walls displayed stock images a typical coffee shop would use for aesthetics, giving the chain store an Americanised vibe.

Stace laughed at Kai's scrunched-up features, putting her friend's phone into her overly-priced, white Chanel bag on the bench. "Seriously, girl, what's up with you?"

Elbows found the streaky tabletop as Kai ran her fingers through her yellow hair. "I'm sorry..." she started, "these assignments have me stressed out." Kai tugged at those bleached ends as a chesty sigh slipped out. "Urghh... I keep refreshing my emails, praying I passed them."

Stace picked up the Starbucks cup from the table and sipped her iced coffee, listening to her friend rattle on about school.

When Kai had finished rambling, Stace placed her cup down, leaned over, and voiced her opinion. She raised her tone slightly so Kai could hear her over the business's commotion, "All you ever do is study or work. Take one night off for once and stop worrying about everything," she suggested.

Kai physically bit her tongue, holding back the nasty retort she felt sprang to mind. She had a sneaky suspicion Stace would say that and didn't expect her to understand. Kai knew it would be unfair to lash out at her for it.

Stace Williams didn't have to work to make ends meet or to apply for loans to further her studies. With her father owning many of the pubs and several significant corporations across London and her mom, Tracy, a housing real estate agent, she and her older brother lived secure lives.

They were well-off.

Meanwhile, Kai Redsi and her humble background meant she needed to work hard to have anything in her life - that was her own.

Kai needed to persistently study to pass these last few months left with her classes so she could earn a decent salary and not have to work at one of Mr Williams' pubs.

She also didn't want to rely on her grandfather, who solely lived off his pension. Who was also more than kind when handing out his pennies to his other six granddaughters.

Her mood soured with that thought as Kai remembered her argument with her older cousin, Adella.

Unlike them, Kai's parents were gone. She found it disgusting how her cousins preyed on their grandfather for coins when they couldn't acquire them from their parents. None of them visited much growing up or even called to chat, for that matter. She found it appalling that they had no issue sending him text messages for a *few pounds* here and there for whatever stupid or selfish reason they had at the time.

"What's wrong with your face?"

Kai shook her head, shaking away the building opinions in her mind. "Sorry Stace... I spaced out again..." She smiled bleakly at her best friend, wondering why this rich kid still bothered hanging out with someone poor like her, anyway. "You were saying something about a party last week?"

"Oh my god, yes!" Brown irises began to sparkle as Stace drew in a deep breath. "So, I heard from Francesca that Finn and Olivia were seen hooking up at that party last night!" Stace's face lit up, spilling the juicy gossip.

Long, red lashes fluttered as Kai physically fought the eye roll. Her voice began, hoping she didn't come across as disinterested, "Finn and Olivia? As in, Mr Know-It-All from engineering? And wanna be queen of the theatre, right?"

Stace vigorously nods. "That's not even the surface of it." Her head became animated as it bobbed along with her words, "That night, she was then seen messing around with Mr Godrick's son, too."

Kai was mid-sip with her straw, going over her mental database of these people Stace had told her about and choked on the iced caramel coffee. She coughed; some liquid travelled up her nose and stung the nasal cavity. "The engineering professor's son?!?!" she managed to say through her coughing fit.

Black eyebrows went high, and Stace's head nodded one last time. "What. A. Slag." She then sipped from her straw, wetting her lips to begin her rant.

It was Kai's turn, listening to Stace harp on about her hatred for Olivia again. Since their first year, Stace and Olivia have had some rich-kid rivalry, the real reason unknown.

Kai ran into Stace during one of the infamous insult battles when she attended a college party. Slowly, Kai attempted to leave the hissing students loitering by the makeshift bar — who looked ready to launch at each other — when someone latched onto her arm.

Stace had marched up to the red-haired stranger, attempting to sneak away, linked with her and left in a huff. She dragged a stunned, constantly blinking Kai along with her.

With no idea who the short, feisty Italian girl was, Kai had no choice but to play along. She listened to Stace's drunk babble as they waited for a bus on that cold curb, unable to remove her arm from the Italian girl's almighty grip.

Since that fateful night, their friendship blossomed over the five years of attending The Imperial College.

At some point, the girls got up and left the coffee shop. They made their way towards the pickup point where their friendship kicked off; strolling down the busy London streets, the girls weaved around the crowds of folks passing on the concrete sidewalks.

Luckily, the red, double-decker vehicle was pulling in just as they neared.

They hopped onto it, heading for Kai's small, stupidly expensive apartment. Stace was running Kai up to speed with the tea going on in her massive friendship circles the whole time. She went on and on about who was dating and who Stace thought she fancied. Her gossip rendered off to gushing over guys and then immediately following with rants over those same men.

With Kai busy working almost every night, she hardly had the time to accompany Stace to parties anymore, so she barely knew who these people were.

Kai believed this was the typical life of a college student. You either worked too much or partied too much. There was no in-between.

As Stace was the partier, Kai was the busy working bee, the ying to her yang.

Tonight was Kai's one night off before working another nine straight shifts. It was exhausting, to say the least, but she didn't mind. Kai couldn't forget some of her regular customers, who tipped her generously when there were a few too many cocktails in the evening.

Their tips paid for her wants, while her wages paid for her needs. It was them who basically helped Kai scrape by the last five years.

"Urg, I just wish I could meet my Mr Right!" Stace complained, hopping off the bus. "Like seriously, where have all the good men gone?" She sulked, observing the rain that started to soak into her jacket. The flimsy coat appeared spotty with each new drop.

Kai laughed at her complaints, skipping off the last wet step onto the curb. She zipped up her grey raincoat, replying to Stace, "One minute, you say you don't need a man, then the next, you're looking for them." She dug into her bag, finding her apartment keys as her fingers brushed miscellaneous objects within. "Stop searching, and maybe the right one will find you." Kai smiled at her friend, flicking her head to walk the last few yards to their destination.

They safely arrived at Kai's residence, escaping the dreary weather outside. Stace continued to moan as they ascended the elevator and paced down the long, windowless corridor to Kai's unit.

The apartment was small, the living room and kitchen open-spaced as they walked in from the white entrance. The walls of Kai's expensive unit were a faded peppermint green, giving the space a welcoming feeling. Straight across the room, adjacent to the door, was a big window with blinds, filling the living quarters with as much light as the weather allowed. The second white door - close to that window was her single bedroom, just beside Kai's twenty-inch Samsung TV.

When the entrance opened, Stace threw her bag across the space, successfully landing it on Kai's second-hand couch. "The only good man is a written one... and even then, you can't have them!" She pouted her lips, plopping down next to her discarded bag.

Her whining ceased, and she picked up one of the many books scattered across the coffee table, distracted by it. "Damn, this book has seen better days," she laughed, examining all its wear and tear.

Kai had just hung their coats up at the cosy entrance and made her way to the metal kettle just a few feet from the front door. "What has?" she asked, turning. Kai leaned over her tiny soapstone island, which smelt of lemon cleaner, and squinted at the book in Stace's palms. "Oh, The Cursed Rose! I adore that novel."

A chuckle released from Stace as she continued to survey the book. "I remember you bringing this to lunch back in our first year. I bet you could recite every line from this." Laughing even more, she opened the novel and stopped on a page. Her finger skimmed the first line it landed on. "Prince Warrick sent his horse galloping desperately to the Frozen Lands to save his princess." Her voice raised dramatically, reading the next, "His heart pounded violently. His mind was in chaos. He swore to the heavens that he'd save Princess Scarlett from that demon's clutches and wed her! He would love her freely, and with her by his side, he would protect her with his dying breath!"

Kai burst into giggles as she finished making two cups of steaming tea. "I know it's cheesy, but it's better than some of the dark stories you carry around."

Stace sat straighter. "Dark? They're crime novels!"

"How To Get Away With Murder – or what was the one you finished last month?"

"Oh, that was My Sister, The Serial killer." Stace pursed her glossy lips. "I enjoyed that one, and I think you would too if you gave it a go."

Kai placed the cups on the handmade, industrial coffee table her grandfather passed over, joining Stace on the single couch. "Your brother would text me, asking if he should be worried. I told him to sleep with one eye open, just in case."

Stace picked up her tea and blew at it, leaving the book on her lap. "This book is a prime example of what I was saying earlier... It's not fair. Even the spoiled Scarlett could get a man, so why can't I at least keep one?" She flicked a finger and closed the novel, looking over the other textbooks piled on the table.

Excluding the tattered storybook — Kai's coffee table accumulated a fair bit of studying material for entrepreneurs. Even her small, crooked bookshelf by the largest window in the apartment—was filled with studying journals. Only a handful of non-related books filled a shelf, along with small ornaments.

"You're too good for the men in this city. Don't waste your time on them," Kai offered lightly, sipping her milky tea.

Stace pouted again. "You're just saying that to make me feel better..." The sparkle in her eyes dimmed as she frowned at the book. "Cheating, lying bastards, the lot of them," she hissed.

Kai reached with a feather-like touch to Stace's arm, hoping to comfort her friend. "Don't say that because I mean it. You're too good for the grimy guys around here. You'll find your prince charming when you least expect it." Kai then picked up the novel with her free hand and brought it to her lap. "Just promise me he isn't going to be some closet serial killer…" she said, as her head shook.

The girls laughed together, and that glow returned to Stace's features. "Oh, I nearly forgot! Johnny boy is throwing a small get-together at the bar!"

Kai nodded, glad Stace didn't stay down too long. "I heard. It makes me glad, for once, that I'm not working tonight." She placed her tea down, flicking the book open. Her attention skimmed over the feathers that underlined the chapter heading.

"Sooooo, let's go!"

Kai gave her a pointed glance.

Stace urged, "C'mon, live a little!"

An exhausted sigh slipped from Kai's lips, closing the book in her hands. "You complain I'm either working or studying too much, and the one night off, you want me to go to work?"

A negotiating tone answered as Stace shot up to her feet, "You're not working. We're partying. Drinks are on my dad!" She giggled as she skipped towards Kai's bedroom. "C'mon, I'll do your makeup."

Kai found herself sitting between two stinking blokes that reeked of body odour. She did her best to listen as they bragged about *knowing* the owner of the Tavern. Her gaze fell back onto her best friend as she rolled her eyes, not amused with their fabricated stories.

Stace flicked her long dark hair over her shoulder by the illuminated bar as she flirted with Kai's colleague, Stephen.

Stephen smiled that boy-next-door grin, listening to whatever Stace was talking about. His head slowly nodded as he wiped the inside of the pint glass, briefly looking away. His eyes met Kai's, and that smile exploded.

Kai bit back the chuckle, wondering if and when he'd reveal his preferences for the same gender. She silently warned him, 'She'll keep you there all night.'

With the way his lean frame shook and those curls upon his head bounced Kai believed that he found her words amusing. It looked like he was laughing, but she couldn't hear it over the two goons she was sandwiched between.

"What's a gorgeous thing like you doing here alone?"

Kai turned her attention back to goon number one, Alex. He was the biggest of the two and the most talkative.

"I'm here with Scottie's daughter," she explained over the live music band.

Alex gave her a confused look, his arm still slung over the back of the booth's rest. A finger now and again flicked her hair, brushing against her shoulder.

Kai decided to be merciful with him and stop their little game, here and now. "Scottie? The owner of this Tavern? You know, the one you said you're chummy with. He's also my boss. I work here!" She didn't bother holding back her laughter this time as goons one and two awkwardly shuffled away from the table - fleeing with their tails between their legs.

As she shook her head, laughing still, she observed all the new faces tonight. So many people gathered around the tables, many peers from her school. Her attention clashed with another in a corner as she skimmed past the youngest-looking group.

An older woman stared intensely. She stirred her drink repeatedly with the black paper straw the pub provided for their customers.

Kai offered her an awkward smile, her hand coming off from protecting the top of her drink. Her gaze dashed away, sipping from the straw as she pretended the group by the stairs was more interesting.

She dared to peep back, wondering after a couple of seconds if that woman was still watching.

"That was odd..." she mumbled to herself. Discovering that she was gone, the previous spot she sat— emptied. Only a glass filled with ice remained at that table. The straw was bent, hanging over the rim.

Stace slid into the booth with a pout, and Kai turned just in time to see it. Brushing off that strange moment, she explained to her friend, "He's gay."

Stace granted her a mean look, those dark, groomed eyebrows coming together at her glabella. "Of course, you bloody knew!"

Kai laughed even more, right in her face. Coming into work as a customer for once was strange, but Kai had to admit she was enjoying herself.

CHAPTER TWO

Morning came far too quickly; Kai slammed her extended limb down on the side table, unthinkingly trying to find her phone. The mobile's alarm was blaring an awful chime, throbbing her head.

She regretted staying up late with Stace, only having three hours of sleep before classes would start. Kai dragged her sorry state out of bed, sluggishly getting ready. She didn't know how she would get through the day and work till three in the morning.

She groaned, throwing on a pair of ripped, faded jeans, and tucked her clean, white shirt into it. Kai grabbed one of the many scrunchies scattered across the dresser, throwing her hair into a messy bun. Quickly spraying her hair with a sea salt spray, she hoped to get away with one more day without washing it.

To add salt to the wound, it was pouring outside yet again. "Can't we just have one solid week of no rain!" she cried out, then aggressively pulled the raincoat off the back of her apartment's door.

Kai was soaked when she got on the bus and still had to walk after getting off at the next stop. The rain slipped down her neck and saturated her white top; the bra she had rashly chosen this morning showed through the sodden material. She grumbled and shivered, making her way to the first lesson, opting to keep her coat on.

"Did you hear about that boy, Charlie?" a girl asked in a nasal voice.

Kai was settling into her seat when she overheard the three girls behind. She pulled her textbooks out, pretending she was preoccupied — listening to the recent update on the resident student.

Girl number two exclaimed, "Can't believe they finally found him!" her tone of astonishment.

A few weeks ago, a young man named Charlie Flounder had just vanished from medicine classes. At first, many of his classmates thought he was skipping, but then the school contacted his family – assuming Charlie had dropped out - when his attendance was highlighted by one of the professors.

Only his family had not seen or spoken to him in weeks. The family then filed a missing person's report.

The whole campus erupted with gossip; police and detectives crawled the school following the report as they took statements.

As worrying as the news was for some students, Stace had a field day; she believed the college had a killer on the loose. The crazy girl was ecstatic that something 'juicy' was unfolding. Kai tried to reason with her, telling her friend, 'She read too many of those novels.'

Regardless, Stace ran around for days, gathering statements from fellow peers. She discovered a rumour surfaced as well about a girl from a nearby college, also missing.

Coincidently, around the time Charlie disappeared.

The nasal girl spoke again, "I'm glad that CCTV footage confirmed him entering his mate's flat and was able to find him and that girl... I wonder what happened, overdose maybe?"

Girl number three spoke up finally, her voice higher pitched than the other two, "No. There was no evidence of substances in the apartment or their systems. Hopefully, they wake up soon. It's a miracle they haven't died being out that long. With no medical assistance, mind you."

Kai shook her head as she prayed that they were all right. She didn't know either of them but sympathised with both families.

Her sympathy caused her mind to drift in and out during the long day, thinking about her relatives. Her parents, to be exact. On her final break between classes, Kai stepped outside and retrieved her mobile device. She mindlessly kicked litter and little stones in her path as she walked around the college's structure.

The rain continued to pour from the heavens as Kai decided to tuck herself into a dry alcove and called the first number saved.

The phone rang four times before it was picked up. "Hello?" an older voice called out on the other line.

"Hey, Gramps. It's me, Kai."

Her grandfather chuckled, "I know, you little brat. How's my little business lady doing? I was thinking, I wish I could hear your beautiful voice and poof - you called!"

Kai smiled and gently held the phone to her ear. Her grandfather immediately rattled off about his hobbies as he normally did when she called. She listened to him talk about his usual days in the garden, something he and her father had in common. Rambling on about the new sprouts, he spoke about how his back ached from pulling out all the little weeds that tried to invade it.

"But that's enough about me, pet. How are you? How are classes going?"

Kai sighed in thought — she preferred it when he did the chattering. "The usual, Gramps. Stressing my head off about grades, waiting for results on things, you know."

Her grandfather chuckled on the other end. "I told you... Karma does its circles. All that hustling and bustling you caused your parents, now you're getting a taste of your medicine! You were such an unruly child. Perhaps this will teach you to slow down a bit."

Her grandfather shot off with another one of his stories, which differed greatly from Kai's memory.

Without interrupting, Kai allowed her grandfather to walk down memory lane. A never-ending sadness washed over her heart, drowning her, as she listened to his carefree tone.

"You're awfully quiet... Tell Grandpa, what's wrong?"

Kai's bottom lip shook, but she quickly sucked it in. Her eyes darted off to the dark skies, searching for some distraction. "I just miss them so much..." she squeezed out.

A hum answered her, "As do I, dear, as do I." His tone calmed, and that enthusiasm in his voice waned, "Not a day passes that I don't think of them... They would have been so proud of you for chasing your dreams. I'm proud of you, too, and I miss your company. Terribly."

Kai couldn't keep the tear from falling, aggressively swiping away the lone rebel off her cold cheek. "I-Uh... I've been saving some of my tips, planning to take a trip back... Is it alright if I come to visit on my next break?"

Her grandfather made a weird scoffing sound, and the speaker at Kai's ear made an awful noise. "Of course, my girl! You needn't ever have to ask. This is your home. The door will always be open for you."

Kai had survived the rest of her classes and was now three hours into her work shift. Slowly, she idled, doing her job.

Mondays were always on the quieter side; usually, only the regulars came in. Kai waited for the evening to pick up; she needed a heavier workload to stay awake.

"There's our singing lass!"

Kai's spirits lifted watching three well-dressed, round-bellied men waltz through the front doors.

"Gentleman!" she said, her tone carried like a tune. "The usual, I presume?" Kai winked at the leading man, pausing as she reached for the whiskey behind. The wall beyond the bar was a colourful sea of bottles, and the many shelves were lined with several liquors and spirits.

"You're too good to us, lassie!" Brodie claimed, winking back.

Brodie Murray was Kai's friendliest regular, usually in Monday through Thursday, dressed to the nines. His short, greying hair was always sleeked back, his right pocket bulging from his overly stuffed wallet. The two other gentlemen flagging him were *business partners*, or so she was told.

They had been customers at The George Tavern for years. Long before Kai was legally able to set foot in a pub.

"Tell me, girl, why have you ruined that beautiful head of hair?" the gentleman to Brodie's right spoke up, Jimmy.

That's all Kai knew him as. He spoke a little less than Brodie, usually saying whatever came straight to mind, with no filter. His hair was similar to Mr Murray's, always styled back.

Kai poured their drinks, barely glancing at Jimmy. "I was tired of that crazy red shine, wanted a change."

Tommy, the last fellow, watched Kai as usual. Never speaking a word. The man was the only one who wore a hat, a fedora. Usually in black or grey, complimenting his already dark suit. He appeared younger than his boisterous mates, just in the face.

"Here you go, that'll be twenty-four, seventy-five." Kai pushed the drinks across the bar, careful not to spill the liquor over the sides.

Jimmy gave Kai thirty, shoving the notes over with a frown. "Keep the change, and get that hair sorted. Why bother ruining the natural beauty you were born with!" he spat out. He wobbled off to their usual spot, grumbling under his breath.

"Never mind him, lass. Your life, your choices." Brodie winked again and followed his mate to a seat.

Carefully gripping the remaining glass, Tommy was the last to linger. His eyes stared off at the liquor inside, that hat slightly tilted forward. "Who was it?"

Kai was putting the money into the register as she paused in alarm at Tommy's deep voice. It was rare for him to speak - to her anyway.

The man peered up, a dull shine in his dark eyes as he watched her from the rim of the hat. "Was it a boy?"

Kai slowly closed the register drawer. A customer service smile twitched into place as she quickly schooled her features. "I'm sorry, I didn't quite catch that?" her pitch raised higher, hoping to mask her surprise.

Tommy's gaze drifted back to his drink but remained leaning against the bar. "Your eyes lost that spark when you spoke about your hair," he pointed out. "So, tell your uncle Tom. Who made you dislike it so much?"

"I – uh..." Kai stammered. "I'm reminded of me mam... every time I look in the mirror."

Tommy's dark eyes rose and narrowed as they surveyed hers. "Not on good terms, I take it?"

She shook her head stiffly, swallowing quietly. "She died... her and my father were killed when I was young... by a drunk driver... The hair reminds me of her too much."

She didn't like talking about it, but her gut screamed. She was confident this man wouldn't leave it alone until she told him the truth, and he was satisfied with whatever she offered.

He nodded, pushing off the bar, still questioning, "And what of the drunk driver?"

Kai squeezed the rag she had picked up, attempting to work as she wiped the counter down. "He got off lightly..." Her attention focused on doing circles as she pretended to clean off imaginary spills. "Too lightly, in my opinion..." she added.

Tommy said no more, his head leisurely inclined. He twisted, beginning to walk over to his two mates, who were laughing about something between them.

Kai let off a shaky breath, wiping down the bar top for the last time. Tommy's chilled-out demeanour had shifted almost menacingly. There was something dangerous about his tone and how his body moved. She felt like a mobster was interrogating her and would have been killed on the spot if he didn't get what he wanted.

She preferred when that man paid her no mind.

"I'm sorry."

Kai nearly leapt out of her skin as Stephen suddenly appeared behind her by the black mini fridge.

"I didn't know your parents had passed, and so tragically..." His eyes were full of pity, and those lips twitched downwards. "When, if you don't mind me asking?"

"I had just turned ten... It was a long time ago," she said as she offered her colleague a tight smile.

Stephen gasped and quickly pulled Kai into a big embrace. His warm hand rubbed her back soothingly while he whispered his condolences.

Kai had to excuse herself, taking a break earlier than usual to breathe in some fresh air. Admittedly, it was to escape the pitiful stares of the others inside, and Stephen's all too touchy attempts to make her feel better.

She didn't like hearing 'I'm sorry' or the looks people gave her when they heard about her parents.

What Kai wanted was for the pain in her heart to stop. She wanted to be able to do something and not have the rug pulled out from under her when it evoked a memory. She wanted to forget about all the depressing crap that came after and how stressful and irritating her everyday life had become since then, too.

The air outside cooled Kai's heated body, and goosebumps rose like a tiny army of bumps all along her arms as the chill kissed her exposed skin. She inhaled deeply through her nose, allowing the bite from the cold concrete to nip her.

"You poor... poor girl."

Kai's frosty blues blinked at that old voice, then enlarged as she recognised who spoke.

The woman who was staring at her last night.

She didn't hear or see the individual appear next to her outside, sitting on the curb a metre from where she had plopped down.

Kai spied her surroundings, the usually busy street - quiet. Not a single car or person passed. The intersection of lights was all on red; the only company other than them was the litter lining some of the streets. She stood slowly and regarded the stranger, whose head was tilted watching.

That same intense stare made Kai's skin crawl.

"I'm sorry... Do, Do I know you?" Kai asked, recalling her steps back to the front door. Just in case she needed to run for it.

The woman's head twisted, looking across the road. Her dark hair was dull, with streaks of grey throughout it. She was dressed strangely, a knitted cardigan loosely hung over her shoulders, covering the design of her attire. "I apologise, child... I couldn't help but overhear your story and came outside to see if you were alright."

Kai's rapidly beating heart paused, kicking herself for being paranoid. "Well, thank you. And I'm sorry you had to hear that. Not the time and place to unload such private affairs." She reached and scratched the back of her neck.

The woman twisted her head, angling it back towards Kai. "Has anyone ever told you that you have a lovely voice... You could probably tell the most sinister story ever written, and people would listen. Mesmerised by you." She smiled after her mysterious words and crow's feet appeared beside her eyes.

Kai smiled back in an attempt at pleasantries. "Uh, thank you?" *What a strange woman*, she thought to herself.

There was a moment of silence as the stranger tried to stand, fumbling over her feet. With an exasperated sigh, she carefully sat back down with a grunt.

Kai extended her hand, remembering how often her grandfather had trouble getting up from low places. "Here," she offered.

After aiding the lady, Kai focused on the woman's slightly hunched back. A momentum of lumps piqued her curiosity; that knitted cardigan did nothing to hide how bony the stranger's spine was. Her eyes found Kai's, and Kai quickly darted away, embarrassed for blatantly staring.

"This is what you get for many years of writing with bad posture," the woman said, patting herself.

This intrigued Kai as she asked, "Writing?"

A tenebrous wave fleeted through the woman's features, making the shadows around her eyes and nose appear darker. "Yes, writing. I'm an author. I've been scoping out these old pubs to get inspired for a new story."

"No way!?" Kai's embarrassment shifted as excitement took its place. "That's so cool. I've never met an author before! What kind of work do you do?

What do you write?"

The woman dismissively waved her hand, heading towards the entrance. "Just some fantasy stuff you youngsters wouldn't be interested in."

A genuine smile graced Kai's face, hearing her preferred genre. "I love fantasy. My favourite novel is The Cursed Rose by E. R. Sula. I don't know if you've ever heard of it; not many people have," she laughed, eager to know more.

The woman's steps hesitated and stopped completely. "That old thing?" She twisted back to Kai, a grey eyebrow raised. "I wrote that when I was just starting…"

CHAPTER THREE

K ai became as still as stone. "Wait, your E. R. Sula?! Oh my god, hi, hello!" A feeling of star-struck hit her like a bolt of lightning, and many emotions erupted in its wake.

"Just call me Vanessa. My pen name was also something a very young, inexperienced version of myself chose and regretted."

Kai followed Vanessa inside, gushing, "What inspired you to write? Oh, more importantly, it goes without saying that I love your work! I swear, every time I reread your novel, it's like I discover something new. Like it wasn't ever there before!" Kai was red in the cheeks as she pursued the author to that quiet little corner.

Vanessa just smiled, allowing the youngster to carry on.

"Honestly, thank you. My dad gave me that book when I was young. It's been my go-to read when I need a little pick me up!" she huffed and puffed excitedly.

"Not only is your voice pleasing to listen to, but so are your words." Vanessa perched her chin on a hand, and that same intense stare assumed those aged features. "Is your tongue coated in sugar?"

With that, embarrassment poured over Kai like a bucket of water. "Oh my god... I'm so sorry. That was very unprofessional of me."

"No, no, child." Vanessa waved her other hand. A strange metallic ring with a massive dark gemstone twinkled, catching the ceiling's chrome downlights. "It is always nice when an author hears how their story has touched another. Whether it be one or two souls, that's always enough."

Kai smiled in thanks at the woman's kind gesture to overlook her having a moment. She couldn't wait to text Stace about this.

"Is there anything I can get you?" Kai glanced at the empty glass. "Perhaps another drink?"

Vanessa nodded in reply, and Kai promptly pulled herself together, collecting the glass.

All night, Kai found her eyes lured over to Vanessa's spot. She surveyed the writer as she continuously stared out the window, stirring her drink. Even as Kai fleeted around the tavern, serving other customers, she checked to see if the author was still there.

Vanessa left an hour before she knocked off, thanking Kai for the lovely words as the woman wandered out the front doors.

Kai texted Stace three whole paragraphs that early morning, telling her about her encounter while she walked home. When she skipped through the entrance of her apartment, Kai rushed to find the book—deciding to bring it with her tomorrow and see if she could get Vanessa to sign it.

This was the closest one to her heart of all the celebrities Kai had met working in that pub. She picked up The Cursed Rose and took it to her room, skimming through the story.

The esteemed kingdom of Rosethorne was a place Kai would dream of growing up. A story about a beautiful princess and a handsome prince overcoming the trials and tribulations the antagonist threw them through.

She placed the novel on her nightstand beside the bed and plugged her phone in to charge. Kai laid onto the stiff mattress, her fleecy duvet just what she needed as she fell into a blissful sleep.

Kai dreamt about the kingdom and meeting all the cliché written characters. She fantasised about twirling in a fancy, overly puffed-out gown on a dance floor with the story's prince charming.

Her father's voice narrated the dreamy tale, taking her through the scenes.

A luxurious ballroom materialised, with all the noble lords and ladies enclosing the spacious area. Kai was at the centre of the moment, swaying with the handsome male lead, Warrick. It was like every other dream Kai had envisioned, giving her a warm and fuzzy feeling inside.

Just like the book did every time she read it.

The act built to its climax as Warrick led Kai around the room, heaps of fabric swished and swayed like ruffling flags. The guests awed and oohed the scene, and a clock developed a ticking momentum somewhere close by.

It echoed softly at first, building with each of Kai's elegant steps. Many of those in attendance observed around, their attention yanked from the dancers. That clock then chimed, overpowering the beautiful stringed instruments that cascaded in the hall.

It chimed on and on, immobilising Kai's moving rhythm.

Kai awoke from her glamorous dream to that exact chime — her mobile's alarm rang out in the tiny room.

For once, she found she didn't want to hide her head under the feather-stuffed pillow but was excited for the day. She was a bullet as she rushed through the apartment, readying for school.

Excitement and anticipation coursed through every inch of her.

The day blew by swiftly like the windy winter weather. Kai practically skipped from the bus stop to work, throwing everyone who passed by a lovely smile, her arms swung at her sides or waved at the customers within the pub.

"Good evening, Redsi!"

Kai was coming through the door to the locker room after ascending the private stairs to the second floor. Her excitement was dampened as she realised who was on shift.

A tall, wide-shouldered man who was getting his uniform on.

"Evening..." her voice grumbled, "Humperdink."

Kai couldn't stand Zachary Hunderwink. An obnoxious womaniser who believed he was God's gift to women.

Not only did she work with him, but she also attended three classes he did at the college. Kai usually narrowly avoided him and his group's path most days as she scampered out the exits first.

She had forgotten he returned today from one of his many far-away family holidays.

When he finished, the sandy blonde leaned against the metal lockers, carefully scoping out Kai, who was quietly retrieving her apron from her own locker. He could tell she was trying to ignore his presence, so he gouged for a reaction. "Hi Zac, welcome back! We missed you!"

She finally turned to him with that mocking voice, her face of distaste. She was staring at him like he had three eyes and massive horns.

He continued, "Seriously, Redsi, you can't even pretend to be happy to see me?"

Kai batted her lashes and mocked his tone, "Hi Zac, wish you never came back! We sure didn't miss you!"

Zachary pushed thick, short hair to a side, and a show-stopping smile climbed his lean cheeks. "I missed you too, Redsi." Utterly unbothered by her predictable attitude.

Kai didn't bother wasting any more words. Slipping past his massive frame, she headed back towards the stairs. She really couldn't think of anything worse than starting her shift with small talk with *him*.

"See, you've dyed your hair in my absence." Her colleague prowled behind attentively. "Missed me that much that you're going for my vibe?"

Kai knew he was trying to instigate an argument - she repeated mentally not to lower herself to his level. She had witnessed it on multiple occasions in class and watched as he grandstanded fellow peers for some favourable reaction when they paid him no mind.

It was as if the man couldn't survive without having someone — *mainly girls* — fawn over him.

"Oh, c'mon, Redsi, I even brought you back a souvenir!"

A dark blur swiftly stepped in front of Kai and forestalled her from going any further down. A strong waft of men's aftershave evaded her nose, leather and something else she couldn't put her finger on. It nearly made her choke.

Zac dug into his left trouser pocket and pulled out his fist. His middle finger showcased.

"Wow…" Kai clapped her hands dramatically. "So original." She brushed past him again and practically shoved him into the wall with a bony elbow jab.

"I'M KIDDING!" A large hand gripped Kai's bicep, forcing her still with a gentle tug. "Here, Redsi, learn to take a joke." Zachary engulfed her puny hand and shoved something abruptly into her palm. He then marched away towards the bar without further explanation, the tips of his ears red.

Kai carefully examined the item, noticing it was a small silver pendant. She wondered if she should chuck it at him or toss it into the bin in plain sight for him to discover.

The last thing she needed was gossip spreading or her owing him any favours because of it.

Stuffing it into her trouser pocket, Kai decided to leave it be for now and quickly headed to her spot by the register. "Thanks," was all she said as she shuffled behind Zac, immediately reviewing the notes left by the cash register.

"It's a wishing charm," he began, "When you tie the bracelet, and the thread runs thin, eventually snapping, your wishes will come true." Zac delayed his movements, watching his co-worker tuck her hair behind an ear, fully submerged in her job.

Her gaze skimmed the notes held in her small hands; that other hand froze, keeping the hair behind the ear.

"Though you don't have to wait that long, just say the words Redsi and

I'll make it happen."

Kai raised her eyes from the note to him, a red eyebrow raised.

Zachary continued, a crooked smile tugged at his corners, "Say, I wish Zac would take me out. Just so happens, I'm free Friday night." He winked at her, escaping for the back of the kitchen before that flying foot could reach him.

The evening began just as abruptly as his appearance, and as much as Kai disliked Zachary at school, she couldn't complain too much about the guy at work.

Zachary always brought more customers in with his shifts, texting folks about specials or sharing the tavern's posts on his social platforms. He told his massive following to 'Come on down', which meant her pockets would be loaded with tips from all the people brought in.

The pub was so busy that she hardly saw the corner from the heads blocking her line of sight.

"Waiting for someone?" Zac chirped in next to her ear, reaching for a bottle as she was.

Kai ignored him and slipped away to a healthy distance, carrying out her customers' orders. Her attention was trained on pouring the correct amount of vodka into the cocktail shaker.

"You're looking for Redsi; she's just over there."

She whipped her head over to Zac to see who he was speaking with, causing some liquor to pour over the side. Finding that there was no one, the man just stood, arms crossed, observing her.

A bottle of whiskey was tucked under a bulging bicep as his head shook at Kai. "Seriously? You are waiting for someone, aren't you?" Zachary used that mocking tone again, his big nose scrunched up, "A *boyfriend?*" He laughed like he had caught her in some act.

Oh, how she wished she could have smashed the bottle of vodka over his head. "Yes. My boyfriend." Kai turned back, completely done with Zachary's shit.

Missing as his face dropped with her retort.

The evening carried on; Kai could not even take her break at the usual time. So many young girls and some blokes crowded the bar, and orders persistently delayed her. She slipped through the herd, heading to the tables her regulars usually sat at, ensuring they weren't neglected.

"Zachary sure gets this place lively, doesn't he?" Brodie howled, sliding the empties so Kai could collect them.

She grinned her customer service smile, placing their new drinks down. *Sure, he got the place lively. But usually, when there aren't enough bartenders and servers to manage the place,* Kai complained silently. Her eyes drifted over one more time to the corner.

Finding the red bench around the small circular table empty.

Did I miss her? She dejectedly returned to the counter to begin washing the stacked sink piled with deserted glasses.

Two-thirty stroked the clock without Kai realising. The crowds slowly dwindled, giving her time to clean up properly, busting tables. As the last of the folks started swaying out of the bar, Kai scanned every head leaving, hoping to catch Vanessa among them.

Zachary called to her from the sink, "Boyfriend pulled a no-show?" He was doing his round of the dishes now, the last round as they closed.

Kai went over, locking the door. She observed the dark and quiet streets beyond the glass panels riddled with stickers for the place. She couldn't tell if the skies were going to piss down or not. It was too dark to decipher what kind of clouds they were.

"What are you on about?" She turned, throwing the wet rag over a shoulder. The damp sensation felt cool against her heated skin, even with a thin cotton t-shirt between them. She couldn't wait to get home and have a cold shower. The bar always became too warm and humid when the floods of folks came.

"You said earlier that you were waiting on your boyfriend." Zac didn't bother looking up, sluicing off the cups.

Kai placed the cleaning bottles under the bar and put the rag on the side. Her voice mocked Zac's earlier one, "Learn to take a joke." She grabbed a clean dish towel and dried off the pint glasses with soapy residue, waiting.

Zachary's thick eyebrows rose, his motions pausing from rinsing. "Oh, so she can make jokes, can she? You surprise me every day, Redsi." Smiling at her, his deep blue eyes shimmered. "So, who were you waiting for then?" he tried again.

Kai placed the glasses in their respective places when they were dried appropriately, with no streaks left behind. "An author I met last night. I kinda hoped she'd turn up."

They spoke no more, carrying on with their designated tasks.

Once the clock struck three, Kai slipped out the back as Zachary called out again, "Hey, Redsi!"

She had just positioned her keys between her knuckles, readying for her walk home. The scent of rain permeated the chilly air.

Zac quickly caught up, side shuffling as she walked. "I'll give you a lift."

Kai paused, shaking her head. A funny look took over her feminine features. "Thanks for the offer, but I'm fine. I've got two feet and a heartbeat. I can walk."

"It's three in the morning, Redsi. My mother would kill me if she knew I let a girl walk home alone at this hour." Zachary pulled his jean jacket around himself, his large arms finding the sleeves over his head. "Seriously, she'd fucken batter me."

Kai wanted to say, *how's that my problem?* But she had to admit that tonight was exhausting, which was partially Zachary's fault. As she contemplated, the concrete started becoming spotted. Little droplets magically appeared around them at a steady pace.

"Awe shit…" *I don't have my coat.* Kai wanted to physically face-palm herself for leaving it behind. She bit her lip, sizing Zac up. "Actually…" Awkwardly backtracking on her words. "Do you mind… giving me a lift?"

Zachary smiled wide, all his straight, white teeth on display. Flicking his square jaw back in the direction she had just walked, he shifted that way.

Kai whispered a thank you as she quietly followed.

Her coworker made large strides towards one of the last vehicles parked in the back of the dark pub, noticing his approach to a white BMW.

Kai mumbled, "New car, huh." More to herself than anyone else.

Zachary smirked, throwing her a smouldering look. "You noticed? It's a Four Series Gran Coupe, and it drives smoothly." His hand slid above the car's sleek top - droplets of rain smeared from the action.

She nodded slowly, keeping her face as neutral as possible so she didn't come off as a bitch. Kai was thankful she didn't have to spend thirty minutes walking home in the rain, but she really couldn't care less what kind of car it was. "Coolio," she offered, not knowing what else to say.

Once she got inside the warm vehicle, her sense of smell was immediately assaulted by his black cherry car freshener. The fragrance was so overbearing she swore she could taste it in the back of her throat every time she swallowed. Her finger hovered over the window button, ready to roll it down once he started the engine.

The vehicle rocked slightly from Zachary's drop, plopping himself into the leather driver's seat. "Bought it just before our family went on holiday. Your seated backside is the second to sit inside, next to me," he started the engine, mindlessly chatting away.

Kai tuned him out, cranking the window down a smidge. Her nose angled up, letting the cool air blow into her face.

She stared at the darkened shops pass by her side of the vehicle, thinking about anything other than how awkward this was—or panicking about what rumours might surface tomorrow.

Zachary was relentless — his baritone voice continued to talk and talk, even though Kai remained silent as the grave.

Before she knew it, Zachary pulled up to a familiar curb. Bushes surrounded the bottom floor of some of the balcony units, the lobby light casting out onto the slightly slopped sidewalk. An untouched newspaper stand was displayed within the lit lobby, just by the silver mailboxes that lined one of the walls. She gripped the keys tighter into a fist as her head turned robotically to him. "I... didn't give you my address."

He sheepishly rubbed his palms onto his trouser legs, cheeks flushed. "I once dropped Stace off here after that crazy frat party... That's how I know where you live."

Kai recalled the night Stace rocked up to her place, a complete mess of her usual put-together self. When she asked her bestie how she got there, the woman merely grumbled before breaking down into tears, heartbroken about her ex-boyfriend cheating on her.

"Uh, well… thanks." She reached for the handle, stepped out of the car, and quickly raced for the building's front doors. The rain decided to pelt down the moment she was out of the vehicle's shelter.

"W-Wait! Redsi!"

Kai huffed out, turning back to regard Zachary. She pulled her sweater over, covering her head.

Zachary had rolled the passenger window down, leaning over to speak through it. "Goodnight. See you tomorrow!"

Kai offered a firm nod, shouting her farewell and another thank you as she fled inside, ready for her bed.

CHAPTER FOUR

Kai woke to the sound of someone relentlessly ringing her — hours before she needed to be up for her first class at nine. The chorus of 'Rich Bitch by Bankrol Hayden' blasted on and on next to her head.

She answered the phone, her voice still heavy with sleep, "Bitch, you better have a valid reason for waking me."

Stace shouted on the other line, "KAI, YOU WHOREEE!"

"Listen." Her best friend's shout woke Kai up wholly. "Lower your voice and talk to me normally. Or else I'm hanging up."

Laughter squealed, "Girl, I thought you hated Mr. Humperdink!?"

Kai rubbed her face and attempted to sit up, wondering why Stace was bringing him up first thing in the morning. "What are you-"

"Someone saw Zac drop you off last night!" Stace cuts Kai off, still screaming into the phone, disregarding the warning. Howling even more now, Stace wheezed, "You're about to be the luckiest and unluckiest girl on campus!"

Grumbling, Kai sat up finally and scratched her dishevelled head. "All he did was drop me off after our shift. Nothing happened. I still very much dislike the guy."

"Well!!!" Stace proceeded to deafen her. Spilling the gossip that had started to spread like wildfire as Kai readied for the day.

"We're not dating," Kai explained to her over loudspeaker, her voice muffled. "People have nothing better to do." She rolled her eyes, spitting the mouthful of toothpaste into the white sink.

Stace was enjoying this gossip highlight far too much to Kai's liking. She continued to hound Kai with her opinion, "Girl, just fuck him! Then you can tell me if he's a shower or a grower! I'll shoot my shot after!"

Kai countered, "As much as I may dislike him, using someone for something as superficial as *that* isn't my cup of tea." She debated with herself whether she should ditch classes for one day. Hiding away from the evil stares and nasty remarks she knew were bound to happen, with all the gossip now flying.

"Fuck your morals, Kai. Listen to me, fuck your morals, and fuck Zachary Hunderwink!"

Kai smiled, listening to her crazy best friend.

Stace was a terrible influence in her life, but she wouldn't have it any other way. Her personality might have been too much for some, but Kai loved the carefree girl for who she was.

Kai appreciated all the smiles Stace brought to her face.

As she got ready for the day, she carried her phone around still on loudspeaker, letting her friend bumble about Zachary's insane body features. How his abs looked sculpted from stone, or how sweat glistened off his firm, broad shoulders when he'd be in the nearby gym, working out.

"Then, you fuck him!" Kai shouted, gathering her textbooks up. "You're the interested party, not me!"

Stace made a weird noise on the other side. Her words inaudible. Kai imagined she was probably pouting her thick lips right about now, maybe even staring at herself in a mirror, watching herself sulk.

The line cleared up, and Stace giggled into the phone. "I think it's safe to say, girl, we all know who he is pining after."

Kai ceased all movements with a decision made.

Kai was curled up on her sofa, wrapped in a knitted red throw her grandfather made for her birthday. Reading The Cursed Rose.

Tiny drums echoed inside her apartment as rain pelted the window. Kai had just passed Eros's dramatic entrance, appearing with the flapping of giant black wings. She was so absorbed in the story that she didn't hear her phone vibrating on the arm of the couch. It mingled with the drumming of rain, creating an orchestra of white noise inside the unit.

She gasped for the millionth time, reading the part where Warrick is hurt protecting Scarlett when loud knocks came from her door, yanking her back from her imagination. She picked up her neglected phone to check the time and noticed all the missed calls.

"Shit…"

The knocking resounds again, and Stace's voice shouts with it, "BITCH, I KNOW YOU'RE IN THERE!"

Kai shuffled off the couch, holding the quilt around her like a cape draped at her shoulders. With great haste, she opened the door, greeted by a wet and miserable face.

Stace barged her way in, looking like a drowned cat. Her hours of makeup washed off in patches, her mascara smeared under those frowning eyes. "You know how many people have contacted me today about you?!"

Kai closed the unit door, locking it. "Which is why I suggested you come over and just hang out with me instead." She shuffled next to the kettle, popping it on with a flick. "Don't act like you didn't slightly enjoy the attention you got." She heard a little snicker following her words and twisted her neck back to her angry visitor.

Stace was checking herself in the mirror on the back of Kai's apartment door. "Well… maybe a bit." She swivelled her hips back and forth, flowering out her little black skirt. Stace's wet coat had just been discarded on the floor behind, creating a puddle inside the unit.

Kai leaned back into the counter, shaking her head at her friend's quick mood shifts. She raised her phone in her free hand and began swiping away the notifications that riddled her lock screen.

One notification caught her attention: an email she had been waiting for.

Kai gasped, sucking in a sharp breath, which caught Stace's attention, pulling her away from checking herself out.

Stace noticed that Kai's usual pale complexion had gone ghostly. "What's wrong?" she inquired, observing how Kai's eyes scanned whatever she was reading.

A cracking voice responded to Stace, "I failed the one written assignment." Kai slid down the cupboard, her head immediately gone between her knees. Her arms came up and caged her skull, hiding herself away.

Stace rushed forward, dropping to her knees beside Kai. "It's just one assignment. You still have two others you're waiting on; don't lose faith." Her forehead rested on the side of Kai's arm, and began rubbing against the quilt's fabric like a cat. "If all else fails, I'll speak to my dad," she started, trying to console her. "He thinks you're a star employee. I'm sure he'd give you a great job with one of his corporate companies!"

Kai ground her teeth as a ringing began in her ears.

She didn't want charity; she wanted to make her way up independently and accomplish things. Not because someone else pulled strings for her.

After soothing each other for the afternoon, Stace and Kai said their goodbyes and boarded their separate buses. Kai was looking forward to a busy night as she sat quietly brooding on the bus. She needed the distraction to drown out the words of failure that her mind constantly harassed her with.

She arrived at the pub in a blur, hardly registering her surroundings, her eyes glued to the floor. As she stepped through the pub's front doors and raised her head to follow the path for the stairs, her line of sight collided with expecting eyes.

Zachary had a smile plastered on his cheeks, stepping off the steps and looking her way. Her brooding turned fierce like an ugly monster, ready to rear its head.

She didn't want to deal with him either…

"There she is."

Kai's attention snapped away, whip lashing to the side. Vanessa was sitting in the same corner, her chin perched in a hand.

"Miss Vanessa!?" She stepped sideways, hands patting down her bag. *Shit* – Kai was alarmed by the lack of firmness she had forgotten to pack.

"Tell me, darling, why do you have such sad eyes this evening?" Vanessa's head tilted, stirring her rum and coke with her other hand.

Kai sighed, reminding herself to avoid making the same unprofessional mistake twice. "The usual… unfortunately." She offered Vanessa a tight smile and cleared her throat. "I'm glad to see you again."

Vanessa grinned, whispering, "And I, you."

Kai's eyes flickered to the clock above the bar, and she swiftly excused herself. She scampered for her locker, noticing she had already wasted minutes into her shift.

Kai didn't fancy listening to Stace's father reprimand her after learning what Stace had told her.

She needed to continue her committed work ethic and *stay* in his graces. Swallowing her pride, Kai mentally accepted Stace's offer. If all else failed, she'd at least have a prospect with Scottie's company.

When she returned, Vanessa had already gone. Her seat and glass emptied. With clenched teeth, Kai sighed a frustrated growl. Her mood took another dip as she tightened her apron with a deadly grip behind her back.

It seemed nothing was going to go her way today.

She threw herself into her job and ignored the side glances Zachary would give her, deciding she would leave as quickly as possible tonight and keep a very healthy distance away from him.

She only prayed that the exaggerated rumours would disappear by doing so.

The bar was packed, and another live band sang over the crowd of buzzed customers. Kai busted tables almost all night as the clock dwindled to the last call, trekking back and forth with tubs of empties on her hip.

She tried to overlook the glares from the girls tonight, scowling at her for simply doing her tasks. As she collected dishes from a nearby table, Kai inconspicuously glanced, investigating the faces of the ones who seemed to watch her the most.

She recognised a few of their faces, the girls who threw themselves at Zachary's friend group. They were all in attendance this evening; some even sat in the laps of Zac's best mates.

He's all yours, ladies. Kai collected the last of the glasses with a shake of her head and returned to the bar. Just as she was about to slip behind, something hard jabbed her side, nudging her painfully forward.

"Watch out!" Zachary quickly grabbed a stumbling Kai by the hips, appearing like a knight in dark armour, keeping her from falling.

Kai stared on in horror as all the pint glasses in that tub shattered to the floor before them, the pain in her side no longer relevant as a growing pressure bloomed in her chest.

"Oi, you!" Zachary was shouting at someone, "There's the door, get the fuck out!"

Mortified, Kai wiggled out of Zac's grip, fleeing for the back. She started searching for the broom, hoping to stop the erratic beat of her heart and burning cheeks. Her chest constricted that strange way, getting tighter and tighter as she frantically searched.

Stephen rushed after her when he noticed the commotion. "Are you alright?"

Kai couldn't hear his voice. Her breaths came in quickly, each more challenging to take, disorientating her.

"Oh girl, sit down!" Stephen gently grabbed her trembling arms and guided her to a crate by the back exit. "Slow your breathing and relax." His hand found her back with slow, steady circles.

The glasses shattering to the floor threw Kai into a mental world war.

All her frustrations and worries broke her pretend front. She began to sob as Stephen cooed, trying to calm her down.

"It's just a bad day, luv, not a bad life..." his gentle voice whispered to her.

Kai knew in her heart that Stephen was trying to be helpful, but her soul was screaming, shattering with disagreement like those pint glasses.

Her life had always been bad — it had always been one thing after another, threatening to snuff out any bit of joy in her. When she started to have hope, some minor inconvenience would jab her, sparking a landslide of more significant issues.

"Is she hurt?"

Zachary's voice joined in at some point, but the tears would not stop. Kai wished not to be there at all, wishing with all her crumbling heart to be somewhere far away or someone else altogether.

After the incident, the supervisor, Josey, found Kai unfit to serve customers, permitting her to go home early. Conversations happened all around, but Kai's thoughts were elsewhere.

Stephen offered to call one of her friends, worried about her leaving alone. Zachary negotiated to drive Kai, as Stephen agreed to cover until he could return. Kai waited until Zachary sought permission, and Stephen returned to the front to attend to the customers. Slipping through the back when everyone was preoccupied.

Kai didn't want anyone's help, charity, or pity. So, she disappeared, just wanting to be left alone.

She stumbled down the streets, mindlessly staring off at anything. Her mind ran a thousand miles a minute; intrusive thoughts shot into her like bullets— an onslaught of memories she forced down, reminding her how pathetic she was.

She waited for the painful reminders of her parents to start spiralling like they always did when she was at her lowest.

"You poor unfortunate soul..."

Kai wobbled to a stop; her stare dragged to that voice.

Vanessa stalked out from the shadows of an alleyway between two closed shops. Kai noted that she had changed from her outfit in the bar earlier. She was again dressed in all dark clothes, that same shawl around her shoulders, and some scarf wrapped around her head, securing her hair back.

Something seemed off about Vanessa.

Kai didn't know if it was her emotions making her paranoid or perhaps her anxiety. She tried to keep her voice steady, "H-Hello again, Vanessa." Easing a slow and stable breath into her lungs.

The woman shuffled near Kai and stopped with her hands behind her back. "What troubles you, child?"

Kai didn't know if she opened her mouth; her head suddenly felt light. The streetlights behind Kai flared momentarily as they quickly dimmed and went out individually. The streets around were eerily quiet. Even the skies paused from their usual weather, waiting.

She could hear the words ramble forth as the dark area seemed to sway, but she was too exhausted to care.

Vanessa watched her keenly, and her stare darted around Kai's face. "You wish to be somewhere far, far away?" A weird shadow moved inside the author's irises as she spoke, squinting, "Or live a different life entirely?"

Kai tried to step back, away from the woman, as she witnessed the weird phenomenon. A shadow whirled outside Vanessa's pupils, something much darker and more sinister. It sent a cold, slithering shiver down Kai's spine and locked her in her place.

"What if I told you... you could?" Vanessa's words started coming out in breathy shots, excitedly shuffling closer, "What if I told you wishes can come true, and all you had to do was pay a little price..."

CHAPTER FIVE

Kai couldn't quite remember how she got home. Vanessa's words echoed inside her skull, drowning out the other thoughts that plagued her. She sat on her sofa, blankly staring off at nothing in particular. Her phone flashed on the arm of the couch from the text notifications accumulating on the screen—the time nearly at midnight.

She tried to recall the conversation she had with Vanessa.

"What do you mean?"

The woman smiled, not the smile Kai was used to or familiar with. This smile was different, with some other meaning behind it.

Vanessa extended her hand, showing a weird marking at the centre of her palm—a faded circle etched into the flesh—a clock. "I've had all my wishes come true... and you could, too. It's a small ask for hefty rewards. If you're sceptical, why don't you try something small? Make a judgement for yourself. Try wishing for my autograph, perhaps, in your book." Her fingers curled into a fist, and that hand retracted.

Kai couldn't quite believe the nonsense she was hearing or how the woman knew what she wanted from her to begin with. She couldn't remember if she had asked for the author's autograph. Yet, another part of her cried for her to try, to hear more...

"How," she asked, unsure.

Kai's stare trailed to the book. '*Try something small?*' She mentally repeated Vanessa's words.

Picking up the novel, she got off the couch and sat back down in a clear space on the laminate floor.

'*Meditate, clear your mind and focus on your intention. Open your heart and wish with all your soul, then repeat these words.*' Kai crossed her legs, going over the instructions she was given.

Something painfully dug into her thigh as her legs interweaved. She reached, digging out the silver four-leafed clover attached to black thread from her work trousers. Realising the souvenir Zachary had given her was still in them.

She frowned at it and tossed the tacky thing to the couch. Reaching for the coffee table next, Kai grabbed one of the many pens off it, trying to draw that symbol Vanessa had shown.

She laid that palm onto the book, reciting Vanessa's words, "Good cess on me..."

A wave of silliness washed over her, making Kai pause.

It doesn't hurt to try. That voice inside her head argued. *The worst that could happen is nothing. And you'll still be living this frustrating, depressing life!*

She huffed, shaking all thoughts away, attempting to try with seriousness.

"Good cess on me. My wish take me. May I only prosper." The words began to flow clearly from Kai's lips, "The first drop of happiness quenches my heart — may it boil into my bones. May the flesh never rot and fall away putrid before my very eyes. May I fade into nothing, like snow in summer, to be born anew. May I be blessed in the sight of thy great mother and loved by my fellow people. May I be made in thy image, only with happiness and fulfilment. May thy mother's blessing rest on my weary soul and keep me. This, I wish."

Kai waited for a second and peeked from her tightly closed lids. She hesitantly opened the book, witnessing no magical autograph inside the hardcover.

Sighing in disappointment, Kai closed the novel. Blue ink from her sweaty palm caught her attention. "No, no, no!" She hastily jumped up, rushing to the bathroom to wash the pen off.

She felt very gullible and naive for listening to that crazy old goat. For believing, for even a fraction of a second, that something would happen.

Aggressively scrubbing the blue pen, she cursed at herself. *You're twenty-two years old, Kai, and still delusional for childish shit!*

She wiped her hands clean and dry on her pant legs, stomping to the novel on the floor to check it over. Fortunately, only a bit of pen got on the red battered cover. Blue ink smeared and smudged near the golden title, turning the area slightly purple from the colour clash.

The highs and lows of the day hit Kai like a wrecking ball, and her shoulders slumped over. She was exhausted with it all *and* herself.

She plodded to her room; her heels dragged against the floors. Putting her phone and novel on the side, Kai sat on the edge of her medium-high bed.

At least, tonight, she'd have a somewhat of an earlier night. She tried to find the silver lining for today as she stripped off her work uniform and fell back.

"I had a fucken panic attack," Kai complained over the phone, talking to Stace as she got ready in the morning.

Her best friend sighed deeply—her microphone made a strange noise. "Girl, maybe we should go on a holiday. You clearly need a break from everything."

Kai's attention rolled. "I wish. I'm going to head back to Ireland next month to visit Gramps, in any case. I need all the money I can get for that. Besides, it sounds like he could use some company... genuine company." She squinted at her reflection, suddenly straying away from the phone. "For crying out loud!"

Stace's voice cried out, "What, what's wrong?"

Kai poked at her scalp, moving the hair around. "My roots are coming in badly!"

The girls talked on the phone while Kai went to the bus stop.

"Are you going to be okay in classes today? You've got three of them with Mr Lover Boy."

Kai's face twisted. "God... don't remind me... I was trying *not* to think about that." She shook her head, boarding the waiting bus.

Showing the driver her bus pass, she quickly claimed the closest seat to the door. The area was humid from all the warm bodies inside; the windows fogged up. Some of the glass panels had drawings, one a smiley face, another a heart with initials. Continuing to survey out those windows, her eyes settled on a familiar hunched-back woman, smiling.

Kai froze, and Stace's words faded away.

She swore she could see Vanessa standing near the bus stop's booth, smiling that same creepy grin. Her hand raised, that marking thick and black now, unlike last night. She squinted, thinking she could see the hands on that clock spinning around uncontrollably.

"Kai – hellooooo? Earth to Kai?"

Kai blinked; the woman was gone when those eyes opened.

"Hey, you're freaking me out today!"

"Uh, sorry, Stace." Kai pulled the phone back to her ear, which had drifted away. She observed the street, extending her neck and bobbing her head, seeing if she could spy that woman.

Stace suggested, "Maybe you should just take another day, call the reception and say you have diarrhoea and sickness."

Kai couldn't see Vanessa at all. The only old folks that stood around were others waiting to board another bus. She took a deep and shaky breath, realising her heart was thumping in her throat.

"No. I need to pull my head out of my ass and work harder..." She began telling Stace of her plan, accepting her offer about working for Mr Williams if all else failed.

The bus pulled over after Kai hit the button mid-conversation. Signalling the driver, she was the next stop.

She gathered her things, still senselessly talking to Stace, phone crammed into the crook of her neck, "Do you fancy making a trip with me?" Adjusting the bag on the other shoulder. "I can show you where I grew up. I heard the house is up for sale again. We could go scope it out," Kai said, offering the driver a polite nod.

She stepped off at the stop as a slow, drizzling rain sprayed the area, and her hand reached to pull up her hood.

"Do you think your grandpa would mind you bringing a plus one?"

Kai went to open her mouth to reply to Stace when her vision started to darken around the edges. Her head began to feel woozy with it.

Weakly, she stumbled, bones melting into jelly. She twisted her hips at the last second as Stace's voice fell away. Her back slammed onto the concrete sidewalk as murmurs and gasps resounded.

The wind was knocked from her lungs as she tried to gobble down the air. Many dark faces appeared above, all blurred as the darkness crept closer, devouring her vision.

All but one.

Vanessa stood behind the tenebrific figures with a pompous look of triumph. "I forgot to mention one teentsy-tiny thing..." No one else there seemed to notice the woman as her skin started to wrinkle with her words, and her image transformed into someone completely different. Her face was limp, eyes hollow and lifeless. "... Tick tock, tick tock, finish the condition before the chiming from the clock!"

Kai was helpless, screaming internally for someone to help, as she fell unconscious.

CHAPTER SIX

A clock's tick echoed as a stream of bright lights agitated Kai's eyelids. She tried swatting away the assaulting causes, her body heavy as she rolled over to a side. A grumble released from deep within her chest, fleeing from that light, too.

Fingers dug into hard and rough material; the scent of earth filled her nostrils. She peeled apart her glued eyelids, confronted with bits of straw and grey shards of stone wedged into the ground. Her fingers flexed, feeling the raw, earthy material.

The area was loud, and that ticking faded away as noises of all sorts reverberated to her location.

"GET YOUR PAPERS! YOUR WEEKLY GOSSIP OUT NOW!" Somebody was shouting, followed by sounds of metal pinging and horses neighing.

Kai lifted her head, and the muscles in her neck strained, causing her to tremble with what little strength she had. She was laid out on a dirt path, no longer on the sidewalk at the bus stop. No cars, traffic lights or bikes passed by. No people rushed around the concrete city to get where they were going.

Stationed before her very eyes were grey stone walls that reached high above trees and a rusty iron portcullis. A young boy shouted at the entry, waving around a rolled-up newspaper tied with string. Further inwards, beyond that gate, various types of stalls lined the streets on almost white cobblestone.

Kai tried to sit up, distracted by thick strands of red hair that fell into her face.

What the hell? She wondered, *what happened to my bleached hair?* Pushing back the strands, she sat up on her pained backside. Her thoughts scrambled in every direction, from her hair to the enclosed scenery.

"Goodness me!"

Kai glimpsed at the little voice behind, painstakingly slow.

A child in a strange old dress was staring at her wide-eyed. Her pink-coloured irises were on full display, a colour Kai had never seen before.

"Are you alright, Miss?" The little girl rapidly blinked. Kai noticed a wicker basket hanging off her little arm. Stems and leaves spilt over the sides of the basket.

Kai attempted to open her mouth, but no sounds projected from her throat. Her lips just moved with the inaudible words.

"Is something the matter, dear?" Another woman approached from behind the little girl and noticed Kai on the ground. "Oh dear, are you alright, Miss?" She was identical in facial features to the child, wearing white bonnets and thick brunette hair tucked away. Stray, curly strands peeked out from under the cap, and her dress was almost identical to the little girl. Only hers was much cleaner.

The child turned without warning, grabbed the woman's clean skirting, and tugged at it. "Mommy, I think Miss has fallen and hurt herself! Look, look, her forehead is bleeding!" A small dirty finger was jabbing out towards the fallen stranger.

Kai reached up with those squealing words and felt warm liquid; the area where she made contact stung. As she brought her hand down, Kai noticed dirt and blood riddled her fingers – some even under her long fingernails.

"Are you hurt anywhere else?" that woman spoke again, stepping nearer to Kai for a closer inspection. "Oh dear, that's a nasty bump. Come, let's get it cleaned up so it doesn't get infected." A hand extends and waits to assist.

Kai was confused, accepting that bronzed hand with her somewhat cleaner one. She tried to offer her thanks, but still, no words tumbled out from her lips.

Fingers curled around; the lady's callused thumb rested on Kai's hand. The stranger attempted to help Kai with a gentle hoist, only for Kai to stumble over herself, nearly pulling the woman down.

Kai looked down, curious about what she had stepped on. She realised she was no longer in her high-waist denim jeans or her tucked-in Harry Styles tee-shirt. The shoes on her feet were some slippers, barely offering support like her white vans. The tacky footwear she was wearing had stepped on a god-awful, dirtied tan skirt.

"Lynn, rush home and get some clean water ready. We'll carefully follow behind you," the aiding stranger instructed the child.

With the woman's support, Kai wobbled away from the stoned fortress. Steadily following the direction, Lynn darted off.

The dirt path descended slightly, and as they cautiously walked, the staggering trees began to clear, a village appearing beyond them.

Not a single telephone pole or anything to show modern technology. There were no tall buildings or modern-day structures, but many little wooden homes were clustered tightly together. Kai hissed as her head throbbed, observing the medieval civilisation they approached.

The woman squeezed her hand in an attempt to comfort her. "Not far, dear. My home is the second one, conveniently close to the inner wall."

Inner wall?

Kai had no idea what she was talking about; just as she was thinking, she caught sight of another massive wall —this one, far into the distance, stretching all around. It disappeared into the trees and hillsides to her left and right.

Where the hell are we? she thought. Rapidly, Kai blinked, wondering if she had hit her head a little too hard and was now delusional.

A man with a shovel wiped his sweaty brow and paused from digging. "Back so soon, Margaret?!" he shouted towards the women, his voice quite mature, laced with a heavy accent.

"Not quite, Jerry. Miss here, had quite the tumble. Going to clean her wound up and be on my way!" the woman aiding Kai shouted back to that man.

Kai still surveyed the surroundings, noting fields of vegetation. Several men and women worked these fields with tools in their bare hands. No trackers or farming vehicles to assist them. Some horses pulled wagons, and strange iron equipment laid above the ground.

In the distance, beyond that elongated stone wall, were miles and miles of green lands and forestry. This nearby civilisation had no tarmac roads, service stations, or utility poles. A never-ending blue sky stretched on for ages, thickening and darkening towards the mountain range that was faintly visible far beyond the endless green lands.

"Careful now," Margaret said, her grip around Kai's waist became firmer. "Don't need any more bumps."

The women approached a little wooden porch lined with yellow clay flowerpots. Little bushes of flowers erupted from those pots, bright orange banksias. The house was no bigger than a small condo with a faded yellow door and yellow-rimmed windows brightening up the outdated thing.

"Mind your step."

Kai lifted her wobbling limbs as she entered Margaret's home. The inside of the house was smaller than Kai's apartment but pleasant. As she inhaled through her nose, her senses awoke by the aroma of herbs and spices. Various plants were drying from the ceiling brackets, hung by twisted rope threads. A narrow stairwell to Kai's left went up to a second floor. The wall she could see from her location, going up those narrow stairs, was covered with dried-out bouquets.

"Sit here." Margaret pulled out one of the three chairs at a small circular table a few feet from the entry. She let go of Kai once she was seated and shuffled off quickly.

Lynn came charging through the still-opened door, a wooden bucket sloshing liquid, some spilt over the sides. "Got the water!" she announced. Her two petite hands struggled as she held onto the rope handle, her knuckles pale.

Kai was confused by the people's strange accents, accustomed to hearing different dialects of the London accentuation.

These weren't remotely close.

She attempted to ask what they were, wondering what was wrong with her throat as she could not speak. Her hands rubbed and pulled the neck muscles in the area, which felt quite sore, even to the touch.

"Here, drink this!" Lynn shoved a wooden mug nearly into Kai's face. The little girl's cheeks were rosy, darkening that already bronzed skin as she examined their new guest.

Kai mouthed a 'thank you' to her before downing the cup.

Lynn's head tilted as her voice squeaked, "Your hair is so bright!"

The cup knocked on the table, making an unpleasant sound. Kai smiled tightly at the child and swallowed the lukewarm liquid. It had a very earthy taste, very different to her apartment's treated tap water. She tasted the residue left behind on her tongue as bits of grit-like sand could be felt along the surface of it.

"Here we go..." Margaret returned from rushing around the tiny home, appearing from another doorway that led out somewhere. A basket of rags and concealed tubs gathered between her arms. "This may sting a bit, but we must thoroughly clean that wound. I need to assess it to see if you need a couple of stitches."

"Mommy, doesn't her hair look like the princess's?!" Lynn jumped up excitedly, snatching handfuls of Kai's hair up.

"Lynn!" Margaret began telling off the child for her rude manners, mortified over her behaviour.

Kai tugged on Margaret's sleeve to gain the woman's attention, unbothered by the child's actions. She gestured her hands next, trying to explain what truly bothered her.

Lynn took off running with Kai's distraction and shouted over a shoulder, "I think she wants something to write with!?"

Margaret shook her head at the fleeing child and regarded the stranger with a questioning look. "Is there something wrong with your throat, dear?"

Kai nodded, her mouth opening. Awful gurgling sounds replaced what Kai's tone of voice should have been. Not a single coherent word was formed.

Margeret's fingers gently touched Kai's small, pointed chin. "Open wide, please. Let me see the back of your throat."

Listening, Kai dropped her jaw wide, giving the woman more space so she could examine it.

Many humming sounds came from Margeret as she tilted Kai's head to different angles. "It looks quite red and tender... I'm afraid I don't have anything here to aid that. Drink lots of fluids and rest your voice. It should be back to normal in some time." She then turned to treating Kai's forehead, prioritising the gash.

The sound of pattering feet shook the wooden floorboards. Lynn barrelled her way back, a quill and parchment paper flapped in her hands. She placed the items on the table before Kai, her face beaming excitedly.

Kai stared at the funny-looking feather, wondering what she was to do with it. *Does this town not have pens?*

As if Lynn could hear her thoughts, she dunked the silver-pointy end of the item into a tiny tub of ink that she had placed down, too. She was scribbling next on the paper, circles and squares sketched out. Eyebrows rose, Lynn's eyes twinkled with a mischievous glint peering up.

Still giggling, she offered the quill to the red-haired lady, who silently observed.

Presenting another tight smile, Kai took the quill from Lynn's tiny hands. The item felt foreign and wasn't nearly as firm as the pencil or pen she was used to. She dipped the tip into the ink, just as Lynn had shown, wondering if it was enough to write. Trying her best, the muscles in Kai's hand spasmed with nerves. Her usual neat writing was messy, as some ink pooled on the first letter.

where am I?

She pushed the parchment paper over for the little girl to read.

Lynn giggled some more, turning to look up at her mother. "Mommy, I think something is wrong with this Miss's head!"

Margaret glanced over the paper, her face concerned as she read the three words. Pausing with an open tub of ointment, she asked the stranger hesitantly, "Oh dear... uh... Do you, at least, know your name?"

Kai picked up the quill and wrote once more.

Kai Redsi.

A dainty sound nudged past her thin lips as the woman gasped. Her eyes widened at Kai, looking her up and down. "You are a lady of title?"

Lynn began next to the table, her arms shot up. "I knew it, I knew it! Maybe she's related to the princess!!"

"Settle down, Lynn..." Margaret frowned at the child. "I do apologise for my lack of hosting manners and shabby abode, Lady Redsi." She began to move, a leg tucked behind the other, a slight dip to the movements.

Kai baulked back in bewilderment at the ancient greeting she had only ever seen displayed on TV — no one curtsied anymore.

Margaret was still inclined downwards, hands gracefully holding her skirt. Her friendly way of addressing Kai changed as she spoke formally, "Once I clean you up, my lady, I'll escort you back toward the inner wall. Let us see if we can find the rest of your company."

CHAPTER SEVEN

Margaret was assisting Kai up that hill, retracing her steps to where she had fallen over. She grew more concerned over Kai's delirious state, reminding the lady to take it easy as they walked together so she wouldn't hurt herself further by accident.

Kai's attention was constantly shooting around, taking in the foreign place. Her theories progressed, wondering if these people were like the tribes that lived far away, hidden from civilisation. Much like those articles she had stumbled upon once on her Facebook newsfeed, assuming she was somewhere relatively remote, considering she still hadn't seen one piece of modern technology. Her mind tried to understand it all as she attentively walked with the aiding stranger.

The women entered the inner wall through the portcullis, passing a child trying to give out papers.

Even the boy's clothing was odd. His shirt was discoloured, tucked into his tied-up trousers, a rope keeping them from falling. The loose-fitted trousers were sewn in different coloured patches near his knees. Big green eyes sparkled as he took off his grey flat cap, bowing respectfully to the woman passing by.

Kai's eyes nearly launched from her sockets to what beheld her after the boy.

For it wasn't the stalls packed with shoppers - dressed in seventeenth-century fashion or the variety of fancy carriages pulled by magnificent horses, nor the more prominent, brighter buildings lined with small triangular flags of different colours streamed along those structures.

What had her flabbergasted was the massive, white castle beyond the bustling, well-kept town. She swallowed down the awful noise she nearly released, ogling at the fairy-tale-type castle.

Giant crimson flags flapped upon a breeze, a golden symbol at their centre. White towers with gleaming golden roofs shot high into the blue sky, and armoured men marched those lookouts. Even more armoured men carried long sticks along the castle's white walls.

Kai assimilated, *a renaissance fair?*

It was the only rational way to explain all this strangeness. That, or this, was by far one of the strangest dreams she had ever had. It was too vivid and almost organically natural, with no sense to it at all.

"Can you see your company?" Margaret spoke up, bringing Kai back from her space out.

Kai peered left and right, shaking her head. She pointed towards a wooden bench that caught her attention. All this was beginning to make her head spin and her stomach flop; she just wanted to sit down and gain her bearings.

Margaret was ever so patient and kind, guiding Kai to that bench. "Wait here, my lady. I will ask around. I'm sure your company must be looking for you." The stranger swiftly scuffled off; her modest dress - compared to others - swayed with her departure.

She stopped folks who would listen nearby, questioning them as she discreetly pointed towards the stranger, resting.

Kai's head was down, her hands supporting her throbbing skull. *What the hell is going on?* She stared at the pathetic slippers on her feet, feeling lost, frustrated and disoriented.

I was on my way to school, wasn't I?

She tried racking her memory, but a fog clouded it from recalling anything further than stepping off the bus and falling. She could briefly see in her mind a phone in her hand, a foggy picture on the screen. Then that fog sweeps in, muddling the rest of it up. Kai's mind drifted, thinking about class.

She wondered if her professors were having fits because she hadn't called to excuse herself. She would be in trouble if she were still in bed, dreaming. Her mind spiralled further as she thought about the steadily dropping grades if she didn't get to class and do the assignments.

She couldn't afford to get another student loan and retake the classes should she fail them.

"Lady Redsi?"

Kai's head rose, and two more strangers were at Margaret's side.

The woman who had spoken wore a blindfold; her skin was brown with undertones like the sun was dancing beneath her complexion. She had thick, dark hair plaited back and a thin headband matching her blindfold, keeping her hair still. She was dressed in some maid attire, that white apron giving it away.

Kai's squint drags, following the arm. The woman's rich, Sepia-coloured hand was tightly latched on to an individual beside her. A man guiding her, Kai presumed.

That man was so much taller than the woman. His hair was brown, with thick waves near the ends, appearing as though he had slight curls. His face was spotless, his cheeks rosy. Kai noticed his brown eyes and watched as he looked her over. A stare Kai would describe as - suspicious, taking over his features. His clothing was similar in colour to the woman he was guiding. It reminded Kai of a butler's suit.

"My daughter and I found Lady Redsi just outside the wall, where she had hit her head. I've done my best to clean it, miss." Margaret curtsied to the individuals next to her.

"Thank you, miss. My colleague here will return later to pay you for your troubles."

As the woman spoke, the man extended his large hand to Kai, bowing his head respectively.

Kai peeped at Margaret next. *I don't know these people.* Trying to speak telepathically.

Margaret didn't seem to understand Kai's desperation.

"Come, Lady Redsi, we have been waiting for you."

Kai was escorted by those two individuals to the glamorous castle and taken through golden gates, heavily guarded. The man with them showed the guards a pinkish glass tag he had pulled out from inside his buttoned shirt. The guards nodded and allowed them entry with that presentation.

Kai was then guided to a side door, away from the forever-stretching green terrace with multiple luscious, dark green bushes. These tall bushes were each shaped into something, one of a rose, a bunny, a deer, and even a knight. She ogled at the fancy paths; every stone was symmetrically aligned. The grass to its sides was perfectly cut, giving the air of a pristine front garden. Her eyes continued up the endless green to many climbing stairs and huge arched doors framed in gold as well. Kai presumed that those doors entered the main building.

The 'servant door', she was told, was where people like them were allowed to enter from. That was where they were currently approaching. A little tower that seemed attached to that captivating palace.

Those escorting Kai were quiet, saying bits and pieces when necessary. Kai noted that only the woman spoke to her. The man they both clung to had stayed silent.

Many eyes surveyed the trio; some widened at the sight of the new girl. Whispers and murmurs followed those stares wherever Kai was currently being led.

Strangers one and two brought Kai to a private room after walking forever up spiralling stairs in that separate wing. The room itself was bare compared to the outside terrace. No pictures brightened up the stone walls, and cobwebs consumed a corner between the wooden ceiling brackets. Only a bed, a dresser, a desk, a wardrobe and a small circular table were inside it. All seemed to be made from the same dark wooden material.

Kai lingered by the closed door as the woman settled on the bed with the man's aid.

"I'm told you hit your head. You also have no clue where you are, and for some odd reason, you cannot speak. Is that correct?" the woman straightened her back, addressing Kai.

Kai nods her head, unable to answer back vocally.

That man watched this, tapping the woman twice on her puffy black shoulders, signalling her in his silent language.

The blindfolded one spoke again, her tone flat, "I see... I'll get straight to it, then. Have you ever heard of the Rosethorne Kingdom, miss?"

A head began to shake, Kai stopping mid-motion. *Rosethorne?* She wondered why that sounded familiar.

That man tapped the woman three times now.

The woman spat out three simple words, hatred seething into every syllable, "The Cursed Rose."

Kai's memory slammed into her, and that veil of fog lifted. She laughed, only air coming from her lungs, head shaking in denial.

"You made a wish, did you not, Miss Redsi? On the advice and counsel of Vanessa. Or, dare I say, author, E. R. Sula."

Kai's blood ran cold; her memories before waking up here were revealed. Vanessa's face transformed, that mark on her hand, her insane rambles about wishes coming true. The scenes played out in reverse, rewinding to the moment she ran into the older woman.

That man tapped the blindfolded one twice as Kai took everything in. Her face paling deathly white as she realised something to herself.

"You see, Miss Redsi, we, too, made that same mistake. Thus, we understand what you may be experiencing at this time. Allow me to introduce ourselves. My name is Ava Sebastian. I, like you, come from the real world. This here is Charlie Flounder. We were both mere college students before all this." Her hands gestured blindly to the room.

The brown-eyed man, Charlie, waved at Kai after Ava's words.

Kai swallowed; *how do I know that name?* Her eyes enlarged at Charlie; her shaking finger pointed. *Coma kid!?*

Charlie's face fell, confusion stared at her pointed finger.

"Charles, grab Miss Redsi something to write with. Would make things for us a lot easier," Ava suggested. Sitting still as stone, her hands clutched a handful of her white apron.

Charlie opened a drawer near the bed Ava was sitting at, fetching the items asked for from within it.

A sheet of paper and a quill were set on a small table, and then Charlie gestured his hands to the trembling girl to sit.

Kai hesitantly stepped for the table, a cold sweat running down her back. *This is just some lucid dream.* She stared at Ava and Charlie, sceptical of them. Her quivering hands picked up the quill and dipped it into the long ink tub atop the sheet's corner.

> Do you attend The Imperial College?

She held her breath as she slid the paper around, anxious about his answer.

Charlie's face lit up; his head nodded, showing more emotion than he had since meeting at the bench. He opened his mouth to speak — or rather, projecting out noises. Loud, drawled-out sounds responded.

Kai had no idea what he was saying as she tried to watch his lips form words.

"Settle down, Charles. She won't understand otherwise. Miss Redsi, Charles said, 'Yes, I do. Do we know each other?'" Ava was gripping her apron, her knuckles gone pale.

Kai scribbled more.

> You'd been missing for weeks, as well as a girl from another school, from speculation generating.

Charles started to explain to Ava, but Kai couldn't understand clearly. She could only make out vague words through his noises, not overly confident if they were words at all.

"I see..." Ava whispered, seemingly speaking to herself, "Then, we have no choice but to progress with the storyline. In hopes of figuring out how to get out of here..."

Kai wrote again, wondering what she had said.

What?

Charlie spoke very slowly, trying to respond as if he couldn't hear his voice. Kai vaguely made out two words from what he was saying, 'the' and 'we'.

"Charles was trying to say, 'As long as we proceed with the storyline and meet the conditions that appear, we should be able to return'. That is what we guess, anyway. That bitch was vague and cunning in explaining anything further to us."

Charlie attempted again after Ava. Still, Kai needed help to grasp a few things, utterly clueless about the noises he made.

Ava sighed, "You'll have to forgive him for his outbursts. But Charles is partially deaf, and as I'm sure you can tell, I am blind. These were our payments, and I will go out on a limb here and say yours was your voice."

Kai blinked at Ava and then at Charlie in disbelief. It was scientifically impossible; this was definitely a bad dream.

How could she be inside a book? Her voice taken from her?

There was no way any of this was possible. Vanessa was a weird woman, true, but that would make her some witch?... Witches weren't real.

Kai's stomach clenched, and her head spun as she tried to organise her thoughts.

"You're probably thinking, *this cannot be, this can't be true.* You probably think we are two looney strangers inside a dream, messing with your head even further. Quite frankly, I cannot blame you, Miss Redsi. Charles and I thought the same when we fell into this world." Ava's hands came up, removing her blindfold and unveiling what was concealed beneath it.

As the cover came away, eyeballs showed. There were no pupils or irises, just red blood vessels at the sides of the organs, adding colour to them behind thick black lashes.

Kai swallowed the pooling of saliva, bile rising in her throat as her tongue rolled back.

Ava continued, unable to see Kai's whey face, "And like you, we were blessed to have someone explain things to us. Someone who showed up knowing we would appear. Other's just like us that got conned into Vanessa's impossible, voodoo bullshit."

Kai gaped at Charlie, who was sympathetically nodding his head. Before she could reach and write another question, the woman said something to Kai that halted all intentions.

"They failed to complete their conditions, Miss Redsi. We have no idea where they have gone or what has happened to them in our reality…"

Chapter Eight

Kai turned away just in time, puking. She had collapsed onto all fours, throwing herself off the chair, a sweat now collecting on her brows and top lip. The contents of stomach acid burned her throat worse than when she attempted to speak.

Please, please! She prayed, hoping to wake up from this fever dream.

"Charles, get her some water, please."

Charlie carefully approached Kai's leant over form, offering her the wooden mug. "I no-ya sarrrd. Werr rrrr doooo."

Kai's gaze shook, tears rushing forth as she accepted the water given. A silent understanding was in his stare as Charlie backed away, giving her space.

"We're scared too, Miss Redsi... I didn't think what Vanessa said was possible. We just tried it out of curiosity. I mean, who wouldn't try if it meant having your desires fulfilled?" Ava huffed, putting that blindfold back on. "We thought it was some manifesting gimmick, like the videos we always came across on our Tik-Tok feeds... We didn't believe anything would happen, and I sure didn't ask to be forced inside a book. I just wanted to get my dream job. Now here I am, working as a dish bitch inside a bloody fictional novel."

Kai had shifted, sitting against a wall as Ava spoke. The smell of stomach acids was still evident in her senses. She looked at Charlie, mouthing 'And you' to him, smelling the sickness on her breath.

The young man mumbled. Thankfully, Ava translated, "He wanted a job with me..." A blush took over her cheeks with those quiet words.

Charlie smiled at Ava as he stood, grabbing the quill and paper off the table. Returning to Kai's side, he mouthed 'And you' back before he passed the items over.

Kai wrote as a sneaky lone tear escaped, gliding down her left cheek.

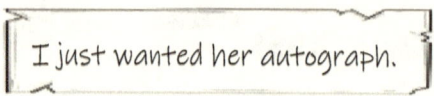

I just wanted her autograph.

Charlie responded with a grunt, patting Kai on her shoulder. He then explained to Ava, who understood him by some gifted hearing.

"I think what Tristan told us may have been true... It doesn't matter what we wished for or our intentions."

Kai studied Ava, her fists clenching her apron. She didn't even want to begin imagining how terrifying it must be to not only be here but not to be able to see where *here* was.

Ava's voice proceeded as Kai dazed out, "My wish take me? May the flesh never rot and fall away putrid before my very eyes. May thy mother's blessing rest on my weary soul and keep me." She derisively repeated a handful of the words Kai had also said, "*May thy mother's blessing rest on my weary soul and keep me... Keep. Me!?* That bitch made us say those stupid lines. That was our undoing, her real intentions!"

A shadow flashed over the room, causing Kai to flinch, her attention shooting to the tiny window for the cause.

Loud steps approached the door, heels clicking roughly. Then, harping shook the door as those steps halted. "Ava, Charles?! Why are you two not in the kitchen?!" a cranky old voice screeched on the other side.

Ava and Kai's attention hurried to the door in alert, Charlie hopping to his feet, signalled by them. He quickly shuffled for the entry, Ava standing and straightening her skirting.

Kai had no idea who was on the other side but thought it best to rise to her feet and mentally prepare herself.

The door opens before Charlie gets to it; the solid material nearly slapping away his outstretched hand. Colliding with the stoned wall with a disturbing bang.

A stern-looking woman barged in, dressed in the same manner Ava was. "You two will be docked for..." her words stop, her stare falling onto Kai. "You must be the one causing all this fuss?!" Her green eyes went hard, and the wrinkles around her eyebrows deepened.

Kai wobbled in her spot, not knowing if she would be sick again. Thankfully, Ava spoke up for her, "It's my fault, Madam Stark. My cousin Kai dropped into the kingdom a day earlier than expected and got injured on her travels. I was tending to her injuries... Well, Charles tended to her injuries, ma'am."

Stark's eyes narrowed at Ava and Charlie, who both had their heads down. "I'm aware you are visually impaired, but I did not think you were intellectually impaired as well, Ava."

That mean gaze cut to Charlie, scoffing at him. She dragged his chin up with a firm grasp on it. Using hand motions, the woman pointed at his head and then shrugged exaggeratedly. Kai couldn't see that scowl on her face.

Charlie mouthed an apology to her, his head submissively going back down.

The mean woman regarded Kai last, "Outsiders are supposed to report to the head help. Get moving!" She pointed out the door. "And you two – GET TO WORK!"

Kai trembled, standing in some random office, fidgeting with her fingers. After being chased from that room, Madam Stark practically dragged her to another part of the castle, questioning her.

Unfortunately for either of them, Kai couldn't answer, further frustrating the woman. She huffed and grumbled as she pulled Kai down the long hallways, bringing her to the head help.

The leading butler peeked up at Kai from his seat at an extensive desk stacked with four tall piles of paper. "She's mute?" He fixed the thin silver glasses that kept sliding down his pointy nose.

Stark nodded, her attitude doing a complete one-eighty. The mean mugging maid was nowhere to be seen, just another obedient servant. "Yes, sir. The child has something wrong with her voice, but her eyes and ears work fine."

The older man focused on Kai, or more so, her face. "She isn't half bad... not being able to speak could be a good thing... She won't accidentally set off the princess..." he mumbled. The man rose from his chair, hands coming together. "Miss Kai, welcome to Rosethorne. I am Pennel, the head servant for the Rosethorne family." Smiling wide at her, he removed his glasses and placed them inside his coat pocket.

Kai stiffly bowed, and Stark's eyes widened at the side.

"Madam Stark, does the girl have no etiquette training?" Pennel hummed.

Kai straightened like a board with his words, recalling that women in the book curtsied. They only firmly bowed their heads in some situations when it was appropriate. She immediately mimicked a curtsy the best she could, holding out the skirt of her tan dress.

A low laugh rumbled from Pennel, "Ah, I see, you're nervous... That is expected when starting your first day with the royal family. I'm glad we don't have to jam in some last-minute training before your start."

Stark shook her head; a look of relief crossed her stern features, lifting the hard edges.

"Madam Stark, take her to her quarters and show her where the girls clean themselves. I believe she is starting tomorrow?" He flicked through a notepad, slightly leaning over the desk. "I will fetch one of the ladies-in-waiting to have Miss Kai run up to speed with duties."

Before Kai knew it, Madam Stark was escorting her back to the wing she came from, explaining where *this* and *that* were. She knew they had come from this area as Kai spotted her sweaty palm print still imprinted on the dusty stone wall from earlier — when she stopped, nearly sick with anxiety as the woman drilled her with questions.

The sudden spikes and drops in Kai's emotions shattered her mind and body, hardly registering what the maid was directing her hands towards. She tried to listen to Stark explain where they were permitted and where they were not, stiffly nodding her head.

All the information went into one of Kai's ears and directly exited the other. Her brain refused to retain any of it.

"This is the maid's shared bathroom. You will serve close to Her Royal Highness. Please keep your hygiene tip-top." Stark abruptly stopped, twisting. Her stern gaze went from Kai's throbbing head to nervously flexing toes. "Her Highness may not appreciate your hair colour. It may be best to cover that," she spat out.

Kai vigorously nodded, and her hands reached, tying her long hair into itself.

Stark scrutinised Kai's face, noticing the washed-out girl paling further. "Your eyes are also strikingly offensive... Let's pray for the fact that you cannot speak, may appease, Her Highness." She turned, marching onwards without another word.

If it weren't for Kai shaking in the worn-out slippers, she probably would have been seriously irked by that comment. She loved her eyes. They were the very same eyes she inherited from her father and grandfather.

CHAPTER NINE

The sun had passed its highest peak, slowly descending into the sky. Shadows grew inside the bare room from the few pieces of furniture; the only sound within was from Kai's steady breaths.

After Madam Stark had left her alone, her mind spiralled into madness. She found some stationary on the miniature work desk inside the prison cell-sized room and sliced her hand open. To confirm whether this truly was a dream or not.

The pain and rush of warm blood from her impulsive action solidified her current and biggest fear.

She didn't know how she should feel. Kai blankly stared at the brown circular rug that disappeared partially under the single bed. Going over everything that had happened, she applied pressure on the new wound on her hand, hoping to slow the bleeding.

Part of her was confused, scared, and even terrified, trapped inside a novel, not knowing how to get out or if she could. She thought about the many responsibilities in the real world she needed to take care of and the people she couldn't reach at the click of a button.

The other, excited, anxious, and ecstatic, emotionally torn in two.

She had always wished to be physically present during some of her favourite scenes, but now that she *was* here, she felt conflicted.

Kai could practically recite the pages, so progressing through the story should be a piece of cake. The only thing was that the novel didn't elaborate too much on the side characters.

It hardly mentioned the names of the background personas, like the servants. Not unless they had a massive influence on the story's plot, supporting the more written roles.

A line Kai could recall about the help was that Princess Scarlett Rosethorne 'went through maids faster than she did her allowance' — which didn't help her current state of mind.

Kai wouldn't be just some maid serving inside the fairy tale, but a servant working close quarters to the spoiled princess.

As she thought more about it, a scene of the heiress demanding one of the butler's heads to be severed surfaced. An attempt was made against Scarlett, and her lover, Prince Warrick, was inevitably injured in her place, saving the day.

Kai swallowed. *If I die here, can I return to the real world?* She contemplated the results of death, wondering if the story would restart or if she would disappear — forever.

That Tristan fellow Ava had mentioned just vanished. She tried to recall if there had been speculation on similar cases of folks admitted to the hospital in the last few months with the same indicators as Charlie's.

Kai mentally kicked herself for not listening to Stace's crazy talk.

This author - or witch? – Kai didn't know what to make of that.

Vanessa was committing serious crimes; this whole situation was right up Stace's alley. She would have had a field day and probably had a closet full of theories to solve it were she in her shoes now.

Kai's introspect stalled, sadly smiling; she missed her best friend's comfort. Stace would have had the right words to keep her morale from plummeting were she here.

"Miss Kai?"

A sweet tone carried from the other side of the door, pausing her depressing thoughts.

"Are you in there?" Proceeded by a few gentle knocks.

Kai scooted off the wooden stool and opened the door for the stranger.

A black-haired maid with big brown eyes appeared, a soft smile on her freckled face. That smile quickly fell, the girl's skin going green. "Your hand?!" She clutched her chest, staring.

Kai could only mouth words to the girl, helpless to explain the situation.

"Oh, dear mother above, I'm so sorry! Madam Stark did mention you were mute!" She quickly reached for Kai and dragged her towards the bed. "Hurry, sit down. I will fetch the doctor below. Keep pressure on that!" As quickly as she spoke, the maid dashed out, leaving Kai to the room's silence and the mayhem inside her mind.

Kai's attention drew down to her hand, noticing something strange.

She could have sworn the cut she gave herself was much longer and more profound. The start and end of her gash that once stretched Kai's entire palm was already sealed shut; the middle section of the wound was the only bit still open. Like a mouth, the skin pulled away when she flexed her fingers outwards.

She sat there bending her fingers, even as the cut oozed, a steady river of red trailed down her palm and continued over her forearm.

Not long after, as Kai dizzily stared at the magically healing wound, the maid returned, trailed closely by another individual.

Words were muffled inside the room, but Kai didn't want to care. All she wanted right now was to lie down and close her eyes for a few hours... and she did just that.

The room slid to the side as her head hit something firm.

Kai had the strangest of dreams.

She stood alone in a vast, gloomy plain of greys. The sound of flapping wings pounded around the depressing skies as black feathers descended around the emptiness.

There was an indescribable feeling as she watched each feather gracefully fall, none ever touching.

Kai's lips parted, trying to call out for whoever was above her, when pain gripped her throat, robbing her of her words.

An awful cackle followed the pain, booming into her skull next with each of those thunderous flaps, and the feathers around blew into a frenzy.

They scattered, getting further away from Kai, fleeing from the insane laughter.

The area quieted as the last feathers disappeared, and a ticking clock sounded off. Kai could see nothing, an infinite void of desolation as she walked searching for something — or someone.

Those ticks grew with each of her steps, getting louder and louder, and that cackle returned.

Kai stumbled forward blindly, hands on her head, trying to block out the sounds that rattled her skull, making her close those eyes from the ache. Staggering, she tripped over herself and slammed into a rock-hard ground.

Kai grumbled, wishing to escape that disturbing laugh like those feathers did.

"Ah, you're awake."

Frosty blue eyes opened, groggily squinting at blue hair against a green shoulder. The ticking and laughing faded away to silence with the stranger's voice.

A man sat beside Kai's tiny bed, examining a book. Strange, coloured eyes paused as the individual noticed the patient moving, peering up from the content within.

Kai noticed the familiar prison cell-sized room and confirmed she was still inside the book. *At least the laughing is gone*, she assured herself, taking a moment to regain her bearings.

Momentarily forgetting she couldn't speak, Kai tried to open her mouth, wondering who the strange man was. Awful sounds project out — no coherent words could be said.

"Laryngitis," the blue-haired man stated, his voice like silk. "You have symptoms of it. While you were out, I examined your throat to see if you were truly mute."

Kai sat up, a glare offered to the man. His face remained neutral, showing nor telling any reaction to her scowl.

Though his face was void of emotion, Kai appreciated the beauty of it. His lashes were long and sapphire, like the hair upon his head, tied back in a loose hanging ponytail pulled over his shoulder. His attire was the same as those she had seen inside the inner wall: old-fashioned and bright. His immaculate suit had complimenting dark tones of yellows and greens on his overcoat, enhancing the violet irises behind those long lashes. His nose was straight, going down to thin lips. Not a single sprout of facial hair sprang from his bronzed-coloured skin.

His features jarred her memory — she knew this character.

"Good evening, Miss Kai. I am Dexter Ubar. One of the stationed doctors employed here for the royal family."

Kai nodded her head at his pleasant introduction. Of course, how could she have forgotten Dexter, Princess Scarlett's first and longest-standing crush.

His features alone were so vastly different to any other character written, the author giving him an absurd hair colour and unnaturally coloured eyes, not to mention her constant emphasis at the beginning of the book on how Scarlett was beyond fascinated by the man's unique features. Her fascination — borderline obsessive.

That was before she met Warrick, the Crown Prince she would be wed to.

Her head angled, staring intensely at the doctor. If she recalled correctly, sometime in chapter nine, it was revealed to the reader that Dexter was secretly a wizard hiding within the palace walls.

She couldn't quite remember why, however.

"I fetched a few tonics and have placed them on your workstation. Please take one every morning and every evening before you head to bed." Dexter began to rise from the wooden stool. "Should help clear up that raw throat. I'll have to examine it once again after treatment to see if you have any permanent damage. As for your hand, keep it wrapped, keep it clean."

Kai hardly listened to the man, reviewing every scene in the book that depicted the doctor.

A quill and notebook were offered to Kai during her zone out. "Is there something you wish to add before I leave?"

She didn't realise what she was writing before it was too late, her mind far from where she should have been. Kai passed over the notebook, the feather's tip going into her mouth, just as the tip of her pen usually did in class.

Kai quickly regretted doing that. She spat it out, trying to pull out the stringy bits on her tongue.

Dexter read the note aloud as she made spitting sounds.

"I see why the princess likes you so much." His face exploded with colour; his eyes cut to Kai.

Kai suddenly fell back into the present moment, and her face warmed with heat.

It never said in the book that anyone other than the royal family spoke of Scarlett's obsession. No one else was *allowed* to speak of it.

After the princess tried to drug the doctor, the family kept him in the servant's wing and never permitted him to treat the princess personally. Those who knew of the incident were sworn and threatened to stay silent. Some were even killed off to ensure the accusations never came to light for his safety and the princess's reputation.

"H-How...." he muttered, gawking at Kai in shock. His nostrils flared as he inhaled and exhaled deeply.

Booming drums echoed; all Kai could hear was the blistered beating of her heart. Her chest palpitated remarkably. *What have I done?!* She screamed at herself.

Dexter ripped the note out of the book, and his hand ignited with blue flames, burning it. He was further troubled by the woman's lack of surprise at his sorcery reveal. Her eyes barely acknowledged the flame in horror like most would have.

"How did you know?" his silky voice tried again; every one of those words was laced with suspicion.

Kai trembled; a shaky finger raised, pointing to her throat.

Violet eyes squinted, aggressively passing the notebook back.

Fingers twitched as Kai carefully accepted the book. She wrote down the first excuse that came to mind. Claiming she had heard people's whispers concerning the princess and the doctor when she arrived.

Dexter scanned the note's contents, his eyes slicing back to the muted lady.

Kai could see he wasn't buying it; she only prayed that her slip-up wouldn't get Ava and Charlie into trouble.

"Speak not a word of it," he spat out as if Kai was the one who tried to assault him.

Pointing again at her throat, Kai trembled still. This caused Dexter to flush red even darker than before.

He twisted swiftly, his coat's tail spinning out with him, and fled from her quarters.

As the door slammed shut, rattling the hinges, Kai let out a shaky breath.

She needed to be more careful. Her knowledge of the book and what was to come could be used against her. The last thing she needed was to be branded as a witch.

The kingdom had forbidden magic after a witch had cursed the first Rosethorne Queen many eras ago.

Kai tiptoed down long halls, slowly retracing the areas Stark had shown her, trying to find this shared bathroom that was mentioned. The flickering torches lit the extended corridors as she peeked around quiet corners.

She thanked whoever for this small victory, glad no one could witness her creeping around suspiciously. Nobody walked or lingered in the hallways. Not even guards were stationed at the floor's entries, like during the day.

Kai believed the bathroom was the floor below, or that's what she thought Stark said. After spending what felt like ages wandering, Kai began to believe it was the floor above the one she was assigned.

She was so preoccupied with her thoughts that she didn't hear the silent steps approaching from behind; something touched her shoulder gently, making her jolt forward. A silent scream erupted from her throat as she pivoted in panic, arms raised, ready to fight.

Discovering a familiar smiling face standing behind.

Charlie waved, mouthing a few words, 'What are you looking for?' Utterly oblivious that he had frightened the life out of the new arrival.

Those fists flattened over her heart as she caught her breath. *If I don't get myself killed, I'm starting to think I'll die of a heart attack sooner or later.* Today, she was teetering to detonate with all these surprises.

'Bathroom,' Kai mouthed bashfully, letting her heart settle.

A head shook as Charlie chuckled; his long finger pointed upwards with a firm nod.

Kai huffed. *So, it was upstairs!* Mentally berating herself.

Bowing her head in thanks to Charlie, she stepped aside, aiming for the stairwell at the end of the hall.

"What are you two doing at this hour?"

A silky voice terminated her planned departure, making her spin back. She noticed Charlie had his head lowered, and that doctor was exiting a room not far up the hallway from her peripheral view.

Dexter carefully closed the door to the room, approaching the two suspicious servants with hurried strides. "I asked you two a question."

Both the servants shared a look, but it was the boy who attempted to speak on their behalf.

Dexter squinted at him, watching his lips. "You must be the impaired young man, working with the kitchen staff... my apologies." The doctor's head barely inclined, his hard stare cut to Kai next, that formal tone back to being fierce, "And why are you on this floor?"

Kai could only offer an awkward smile, mouthing her reason to him.

Hissing at her like a cat, those violet eyes narrowed considerably, "The lady's shared lavatory is two floors up."

Kai gestured to Charlie, mouthing more, 'I know now, thanks to him.'

She spun again, hoping to find it soon — before she wet herself.

She could hear the doctor make a sound, but she thought getting as far away from him as possible was best... and to keep out of his sight moving forward.

It was clear he didn't like Kai too much after her little slip-up.

CHAPTER TEN

K ai sighed, feeling exhaustion sweep in while she relaxed.

After using the toilets and taking another wrong turn, she stumbled upon a room where most of the floor was steaming water. Kai didn't even think twice, stripping down and entering the pool.

Pillars surrounded the ancient-looking lavatory, and shimmering translucent curtains were strung along some walls, gently swaying from the draft, wisping across the floors. Torches and dozens of white candles lit it up, making those curtains glimmer like stars. The other stone walls, bare of those curtains, had hanging shelves and wicker baskets of flowers.

As Kai admired the shimmering, swaying material, she momentarily forgot about her injured hand as it drifted under. A strange sensation began in her palm as the bandage soaked in the warm water.

She whipped it out, hastily removing the fabric wrap so bacteria didn't seep into the cut further. Only to find no wound inside her hand, just a fine line across her right palm.

Her attention slid to the reflection on the water's surface, moving the hair that covered the other injured spot.

The bump on her forehead was also gone— there was hardly even a bruise, a slight discolouration darkened the area.

Kai stared at herself in question, trying to recall if the story mentioned anything about healing aspects for the characters.

She spent a good while in thought, brainstorming a game plan on how to proceed before she decided to trek back.

With careful steps, Kai snooped around the spacious bathroom, messing the stone floors with wet footprints, trying to see if clean clothes were stashed on one of those hanging shelves.

Ensuring the thin woven piece of fabric was wrapped securely, she gathered her dirtied dress and slippers and planned to return. Finding nothing here other than hygiene products from what she could tell, she hoped that small wardrobe had a spare change of clothes.

She had just stepped out of the shared lavatory, walking with haste, so quickly that she didn't notice the figure leaning against the wall, waiting on her.

"Mother above!"

Kai stopped, turning in annoyance at that startled voice – the doctor.

Hands covered his face, and the tips of his ears were red. "It is shameless to walk around an indecent woman! I can see much more than just ankles!" that usual dreamy tone was muffled against his palms.

Ankles? Kai's eyebrow rose as her stare dragged down. The oversized towel stopped just under her knees, showing off how pale her calves were.

She shrugged, unbothered, and continued to return to that room.

To her delight, the castle was extremely warm, even during the evenings. By the time she reached the room below, her body was pretty much dry; only her hair continued to drip. Kai closed her door, securing the latch as she dropped the cloth covering her body.

It was the beginning of spring in the book... Going over the facts, she tried to pinpoint where the story was progressing exactly.

Kai opened the creaky doors to the wardrobe, finding a couple of plain gowns and many uniforms. Some, even with trousers. She opted for one of the darker gowns crammed towards the back, throwing it on. The only thing she liked about this place so far was that they didn't have bras.

She proceeded to pick up the towel, leant over, her wet hair brushed against the floors. Kai was already missing the convenience of having a blow dryer.

It was going to take ages for her hair to dry naturally, which meant tomorrow, she was going to have a nest of knots.

A knock shook her door, pausing her.

Kai side-eyed the entry, wondering if she should pretend to be asleep. Her stare confirmed the key was still in its place, locked, so there was no chance whoever was out there could come in. Not unless they had another big key to go in that see-able hole.

Another two knocks followed, as well as a tight cough.

Kai rolled her eyes, choosing to answer out of curiosity. Wondering why this man continued to pursue her.

The person on the other side double-takes, ensuring she is dressed.

"Can I have a word with you?" Those firm cheeks were still dusted with pink as he looked down at her.

Dexter must have been over six feet tall as he towered over Kai's frame, even from outside the threshold. Kai had to raise her chin to look up at him.

An airy noise responded to him as she shifted her weight. Leaning against the door's frame, Kai's other hand firmly held the door in place, taking her stand.

She tried to avoid this one, but he kept appearing before or behind her.

Dexter asked again, nicer this time, "Can I come in, please?" Shifting his weight from heel to heel.

Kai's head flopped back, glancing into the room. *Whatever he has to say, it's probably best inside the room…* She pushed the door, letting it slowly creak open wider. Her hand gestured to enter dramatically.

The doctor inclined his head, muttering, "Thanks…" As he hesitantly entered the quarters.

Using her foot to close the door, Kai headed to the little bottles on the side.

Dexter cleared his throat, brushing off his lap as he settled into a stool at Kai's small table. He watched the strange, muted lady down the potion like the drunks in the pubs. Her face unflinching as she swallowed down the bitter taste of medicine. Her full lips smacked together, slamming the bottle down. Those blue eyes were like two blocks of ice sliding towards him.

His hands involuntarily clenched against the fabric of his trousers. He once thought the king had a pressuring stare —until today.

This woman's eyes were on their own level, as if she could see right through him. Even as she scowled or trembled like earlier, those eyes were piercing, like she carried the world's weight within them.

Dexter observed Kai when another alarming thought came to the forefront: the absence of his reason. He had forgotten why he had marched after her once she left the lavatory.

Arms folded, waiting for him to speak. There was an edge of exhaustion on the woman's face and a gleam of temper flaring beneath the surface if he didn't get straight to the point.

The doctor was looking for anything to talk about to avoid the embarrassment if he admitted he had forgotten why he was there. Initially, he followed her to see if she was looking for the bathroom as claimed or having a secret rendezvous with that deaf servant.

His mind raced, thinking perhaps he was the one who told her, but then he wondered, how would the boy know if he was deaf?

So, he followed the little lady, who eventually found the bathroom. Her face lit up; a stunning smile grew as she scampered quickly inside it.

Dexter leaned against the wall just at the entrance and waited.

Seconds turned into minutes; minutes turned into an hour. By the time she waltzed out scandalously, he had been standing by for nearly two hours against that cold wall.

She was unbothered by the place's temperature, sauntering off with nothing but a brown piece of fabric wrapped tightly around her petite curvy frame.

He shook his head, ridding the thoughts that nearly conjured after that. A slight noise had his head come up; his eyes clashed with icy blues. Her thin red eyebrows came forward, and the corners of those lips tilted downwards.

Dexter suddenly stammered out, "Y-Your hand!" His stare shot for the bandage, which was no longer wrapped around her right.

Kai concealed that hand, forgetting she had left the cloth in the bathroom, discarded on the floor.

She shook her head, trying to shrug it off.

Internally, she was shitting bricks.

The doctor peered up at her face. An emotion he couldn't place fleeted across her feminine features and gone before he could identify it. "You went into that shared bathroom with an open wound. I need to clean it," he claimed — relieved he quickly came up with a valid reason.

The woman shook her head again, her lips mouthing a 'No need'.

Kai's behaviour was again suspicious to him. He stood, and the little lady stepped back with a jittery hop.

Confirming she was hiding something indeed.

"Miss Redsi, I am a doctor. It is my job to take care of *all* the king's subjects. Your hand, please?" Dexter extended his own, waiting for her small, injured one.

Shit, shit, shit —Kai's mind was racing, trying to think of how to get out of this. She couldn't help the shake that followed as she quickly slammed her right fist into his waiting palm.

It all happened in slow-motion for Kai, as the doctor's face twisted with her strangeness, and then he flipped the hand over to inspect. His eyes enlarged, staring at the healed palm.

The small sandwich the maid had left Kai earlier on her table was about to come back up her throat. All that sweat she scrubbed off was reaccumulating on her back.

Dexter blinked. *I'm sure it was this hand.* He unquestioningly offered his other, waiting for Kai's left limb, to study both.

The now trembling woman slowly brought it up, and he looked on unsettled.

Two perfectly intact palms. There was not even a single scar to indicate there was ever a wound present on either of them.

Dexter surveyed the woman's face, going green around the gills. "Are you a witch?" he quietly asked.

The woman's head shook side to side with insane speed. Dexter was sure she had given herself whiplash with that intensity.

Her icy eyes stared at him with anxiety as he gently dropped those hands and stepped back to give her some personal space.

It didn't matter what he asked. Dexter had an inclination that she wouldn't disclose anything further with him. He debated whether he should bring this matter up to the king.

Dexter nodded; his lips pushed forward. At that moment, he decided to dig into this Kai woman to have all the facts before presenting them to King Tyrell.

"Well... goodnight then, miss." He wasted no time, leaving the lady frozen in her spot, alone in her room.

He would take her down if she proved to be a threat to the kingdom. For now, he would watch Kai and gather what he could on the pretty little woman.

He stopped halfway down the hall, his attention pivoting back towards her door with that thought.

CHAPTER ELEVEN

O range and pink radiant rays streamed through the dirtied window of Kai's new living space. They were casting shadows from the tall and lanky columnar oak tree just outside it, over the bare walls. Light and darkness danced on the stone enclosure. Kai's eyes followed as they continued to push each other back and forth.

She didn't know how much sleep she had gotten, passing out when she was unable to keep her eyelids open any longer.

She watched her door for ages at night, waiting for that doctor to return. Deciding then, too, that if he did return and had her dragged away, she would then snitch on his ass. Fuck the story's plot.

Kai raised her wrapped-up hand and rubbed the gunk accumulated in the corners of her eyes. After encountering the doctor, she ripped up one of the lighter gowns in the wardrobe, using the shredded fabric as a medical wrap. She wouldn't make the same mistake twice, not with people suspicious of her now.

An excited tone continued to blabber inside the room, but Kai was too tired to understand what it was saying.

"Rise and shine!"

The little maid from yesterday pestered her to get out of bed, her cheery voice too much at the moment.

Kai rose as the maid flitted to that free-standing closet, pulling out uniforms and inspecting them. "Today, you will be shadowing me. See what it is we do for Her Highness. Tomorrow, we'll…"

Kai's head throbbed as she massaged her temples. The maid continued to prattle about duties, unaware of muted one's miserable state.

"Change into this quickly, and we'll get started!"

Grumbling with complaints, Kai dragged her tired body up to her feet. *Why couldn't I fall into this novel as the princess?*

Even her cheap spring mattress in the apartment was better than that wood slab.

Kai got straight to it, putting on the cosplay-looking uniform. She huffed, jumping up and down, trying to get the white tights on. The maid assisted Kai, her voice continuing to chirp, explaining how the skirt and aprons should be worn properly. As Kai was tying the thick, white strap around her back, the brown-eyed maid handed over a white cap, waiting for the final added touch.

As instructed, she was forced to wear a bonnet, concealing most of her hair.

When they finished, Kai followed the maid, Mary—finally learning the girl's name between her long explanations of chores.

They were currently headed over to the Princess' Palace. A detached building north of the main one to strip and remake the bed. From there, they would follow with laundry and then wait on the princess in the afternoon. Whatever that entailed.

They stepped off the spiralling staircase, and rather than exiting out of the door immediately to their right; they pivoted left down a narrowing corridor with many alcoves of mysterious exits. They walked through the bigger doors adjacent to the entrance of the servant's wing, entering another wing that proceeded to the main building. As they continued, the walls and structures became progressively more cultivated. Kai observed the surroundings closely during their trek, pinpointing the settings from the tale.

The walls further inwards beheld massive paintings, some even strung up huge tapestries of battlefields. The stone walls suddenly morphed into white polished rocks, so different from the wing Kai was residing in.

They passed by many more articulate doors and white stone corridors, where servants dressed like them dusted down the unused furniture decorating the sides.

Kai was so absorbed in their surroundings that she stumbled out yet another exit, this time outside. She nearly squealed with glee as they strolled around a specific garden, keeping to the near-white, rocky paths.

It was even better than how she imagined it from the printed pages.

A white iron gazebo similar to a birdcage was positioned at its centre. The air was heavy with flowery fragrances from the purples, yellows, and orange bundles of inviting flowers in bloom all around it. Separate clean stone blocks in the shape of Lily Pads lead to that gazebo from around the green courtyard. Inside that iron cage was a white table with two white chairs matching the frame overhead. There was something whimsical about this area, the rising sun giving the space a beautiful glow.

This is where Prince Warrick kisses Princess Scarlett's hand. The sun was setting in that chapter, and both parties stared deeply into each other's eyes. Where both the protagonist and male lead realise — they are madly in love with each other, never admitting it out loud.

It was after one of the grand balls that Eros - the antagonist, attacked…

Kai still had no idea where she fell into the storyline, hoping she didn't miss this mushy scene. Some of her favourite bits were the cheesy dialogues with the beloved characters.

Her mind drifted away, wondering what the characters looked like. Would they appear just as her brain imagined them to be?

Kai eventually saw the job site they were requested to be at while pondering. The sky was slowly going from pink to blue, and a smaller white palace surrounded by flowers in the distance grew closer.

Whites, pinks, and red roses engulfed the place, growing wild and untreated. The bushes claimed the smaller palace, swallowing it deep within its thorny fortress.

She baulked back, recalling the lines from the book which described the separate building as glamorous and pristine, inside AND out.

Mary glimpsed back and caught the look on Kai's face, slowing her steps to match. She explained the situation before them, "It doesn't matter how much the gardener prunes it... It grows back three times more furiously."

Kai nodded, wondering why this was so different from what she read.

Mary pulled out a tag similar to Charlie's and gained access to the building, showing the two guards stationed at the grand entrance. Kai stayed close to Mary's heels; her anticipation faltered, considering how glamorous the inside was.

Or rather, ridiculous, it was.

The front foyer of the estate was a gilded monstrosity. The furniture lining the walls was gold, the grand piano near the broad staircase, and even the white pedestals held up gold figurines. The floors were white marble, specks of twinkling gold mixed into the solid material. The walls were accessorised with a rose-gold wallpaper. The only other colours adding to the place were from the portraits, framed in even more thick gold.

Her stare focused on the images, each varying in different poses, each of the same person.

The woman was beautiful, as it was written. Thick, wavy, deep mahogany hair, full lips, and deep blue eyes. The Princess, Scarlett Rosethorne.

One of the portraits was of the royal heir lying down in a flourished grass field, her long, mahogany strands splayed around. Another, her running through a similar meadow, that hair trailed behind like a veil. Again, dancing, her hair flowered out mid-spin.

Her dress wasn't painted nearly as eye-catching as her locks in the image, as if the painter applied a blurred filter.

All the portraits focused on Scarlett and showcased her features. No one else, or any other item within the images, to steal attention away from it.

Kai physically cringed, the number of self-portraits giving her the ick. She saw her reflection ping off each gilded item as they passed, heading for the huge staircase. She couldn't stand photos of herself, let alone ginormous paintings. You had to be really in love with your image to enjoy looking at these every day.

A narcissist, Kai thought.

Her eyes spied more of those paintings of the princess on the next floor. Those portraits were close-ups, showing off Scarlett's face from different angles.

The book never mentioned anything like this.

Mary stopped Kai; a hand gently touched her forearm as she leaned in. "Control your expressions... if the princess saw the look on your face while observing her portraits, she'd have your eyes out... Don't even trust the others with your truest thoughts. They'll find any dirt to throw to gain Her Highness's favour."

Kai swallowed, nervously nodding her head. Mary offered her a tight smile and a squeeze before continuing.

Guards were still as stone, stationed and watching them pass. Unlike the other guards around the main palace, the guards here were each fully suited in gold, helm and all. Kai would have assumed they were just part of the interior decor if not for their bright eyes.

They round to the right on the second floor, and another wide stairwell appeared, leading to a third floor. They trekked up to the last floor of the palace, this area having no doors but one at the very end of the corridor. The same wallpaper from the first covered the stretching walls up here.

"Her Highness is still in bed. We enter, open her curtains and curtsy. Hold your curtsy until she has risen and our colleagues have escorted her out."

Kai's breaths came in quick shots the closer they approached; anticipation brimmed. Two other women were already waiting. One, the older of the two, had a hand hovering over the gilded door handle.

They all entered the dark room together; Kai followed Mary's motions, heading toward a dark wall to their right. As Mary took one of the large curtains, Kai took the opposite, opening them up wide simultaneously.

The room only had two windows and massive glass panels stretching one wall. As the sun exploded into the room, Kai shuffled for the next curtain to the second window.

Unlike any other floor, this room was void of any real colour. All white and light shades, from walls to furniture. Except for the unruly, untamed locks, which were currently spilt over the side of the circular bed.

Kai ran into the window - where the curtain was - momentarily spaced out. She hastily grabbed the drowning material and yanked it open. Mary already had done her side, waiting.

"Apologies, Your Highness, but it is time to rise."

Hearing the others begin their duties, Kai was down, curtsying as Mary had instructed. An unladylike groan boomed throughout the space, making Kai tempted to peek.

"Five more minutes!" a voice hollered. The princess thrashed, trying to hold the heavy duvet from the two maids trying to remove it.

"Your Highness, you must start preparing. You have appointments!"

Kai could hear the battle between the servants and the princess, her head still low, staring at her shoes.

"Whom on earth could be so important to disturb my beauty slumber!?" Scarlett's voice echoed again.

"The Crown Prince of Crestblood! You must get ready; the king demands it!"

Kai held in the laugh; her shoulders shook as she focused. Her thighs trembled slightly from holding the awkward position.

"And why must I? It is, Father, who likes that air-headed prince!? That imbecile called off our engagement, humiliating me in front of the ladies of court!"

Oh? Kai's cast-down face twisted — another thing was different from the story she knew.

Princess Scarlett loved Prince Warrick; she only ever praised the prince privately, moving on from her crush on the doctor. Nothing was written about her dislike for him or that they cancelled the engagement.

"Let him come and wait!" A crash followed after Scarlett's screech, the girls serving — gasped. "If I am not worthy of that entitled moron, then he is not worthy of me!" Small feet rushed by Kai with a sudden shove.

That person pushed Kai out of the way, yanking the curtain closed behind her.

Kai fell hard, her hands not quick enough to break her fall, her hip taking most of the impact. She scowled, glancing up, met by a figure with floor-length, red hair.

"I don't have time for princes who are not grovelling at my feet, for my hand!" Eyes glinted back towards the maids, lashes like the thick curtains protecting those eyes. "And you!" Those glinting blues were gleaming down at Kai, a painted fingernail pointed. "Sort that face out, or my father will have your head. Do you know who I am?!"

Kai twisted her neck, her scowl tossed to her left. That excitement she felt before entering diminished. All those years of gushing over its characters were in vain.

This wasn't anything like the book she had come to love.

Chapter Twelve

Kai stayed down on the marble floor, head cocked to the side. The princess continued to shout, barking like a mad dog at the maids rushing to her. Shoes scuttled by, and mahogany hair swept the floor towards the exit.

"Are you okay?" Mary shuffled to her when the doors closed, and a gentle hand reached out in comfort.

Kai's cold blues were met with teary browns; it was clear Mary was upset. Nodding her head, she plastered on a fake smile. There were no words to express her disappointment, even if she could speak.

Mary sighed, her hand now waiting. "Her Highness isn't a morning person..." she softly consoled, pulling her colleague up.

Kai fought the eye roll as her eyelashes fluttered. The story mentions the princess had personality flaws, acting spoiled at best. Why she went through maids so quickly made sense to Kai now.

Who in their right mind would work for someone so nasty, so self-entitled?

The girls began their duties and stripped the humongous bed. Kai had never seen one so big before— it took up a generous amount of the room next to the plain furniture. Stringy red threads littered the sheets, so bright against the cream linen. The girls rolled up the overflowing fabrics, bundling them together in their arms.

"We'll take these to the laundry and bring the new bedding..." Mary started going off with how they would then wash the princess's things and the smells Her Royal Highness disliked on them.

Kai's head thumped, a growing sensation at the base of her temples, which spider-webbed behind her forehead. She watched Mary softly grin as she spoke about the chores, wondering how she could enjoy this.

They strolled down to the first floor, heading further into the ridiculous estate. Kai appreciated her modern-day life more, even if, at times, things seemed hopeless, and she was beyond stressed with bills and grades. Things could be much worse.

Her life could be this: serving someone like the princess. Living in a tiny, dull room, worse than her old dorm.

Mary dumped her bundle into a big wooden barrel, and Kai followed her actions, so lost in thought that she had no idea where they were now.

"I'll quickly run back up and make the bed. The others should have Her Highness's dirtied garments. So, I'll bring those down and start that as well. You can start filling the tub. The soaps are there. Please, be careful of your hand."

Kai stood there for a moment, studying the substantial wooden tub. Two iron rods were attached to it, wrapped around the barrel. One higher than the other. Those rods eventually straightened out and connected to a fire pit built into the floor, coiling around the unlit contrapment.

How on earth do I fill this? She pondered.

After searching for something, Kai found a wooden bucket stationed by an exit, using it to bring water to the excessively bigger barrel.

She was sweating by the fourth trip, filling a bucket from the water pump outside the back door.

A *utility room*, she presumed. It was out of the way from the main room she was working in, similar to her grandfather's house. The 'laundry room' had three doors. One was where Mary left, one was towards the utility room, and another connected to a kitchen.

Grumbling, Kai dumped the heavy bucket into the tub. She groaned when she observed how little the tub was being filled with each ineffectual trip.

Kai stomped over to the soaps, giving herself a small break. Sniffing the different liquids, she chose the one that smelt the cleanest. It reminded her of her grandfather's laundry detergents, a clean scent with a hint of sweetness, and some Lily. She poured a cup of it into the barrel and watched the pinkish liquid dissipate. Not anticipating what was coming next, Kai took a deep breath and went for more water.

When Mary returned, Kai had already dumped eleven buckets into it. The material inside was not even close to being submerged.

Mary paused at the white door, clutching the clothing she had gathered tightly to her chest. She fought a smile, a protruded tongue in cheek.

Kai gave her a questioning look, wiping the warm sweat from her forehead with her thick, long sleeve.

The brown-eyed maid said nothing as she placed the clothing onto the countertops that covered an entire area between two of the three doors and opened a cupboard directly under.

A coiled-up hose was revealed.

Mary unravelled it, placing it inside the wooden tub. She shuffled back to the cupboard and proceeded to crank the circular pump within. Water gushed out with each spin, faster and quicker than all those daunting trips.

Kai's jaw dropped, watching.

"Sorry... I thought I had mentioned this," a giggle slipped out with Mary's words.

Kai braced her bucket, throwing the little water left at the bottom at the giggling maid.

Who, in turn, erupted with gleeful laughter, shielding herself.

After hanging the washed laundry to dry, the girls returned to the main palace. Kai cursed the entire time, wishing they had laundry machines. Mary had done the extensive scrubbing as Kai couldn't wet her hand. She felt guilty for having to play pretend with an injury—but she was left in charge of stirring the massive barrel. It went round and round until Mary deemed the load finished soaking.

Kai wished she could rip the stupid hat off her head and let some air into her heated top. Her back ached profusely, and her scalp itched from the buckets of sweat she produced. The hairs on her neck were soaked, sweat trickled down her spine, and her uniform back was damp.

She couldn't believe the servants worked in these kinds of conditions; the horrible uniforms were too thick for the amount of labour that was required. She felt awful, longing for a skin-melting, hot shower.

Another thing Kai missed about home. Baths were excellent for a soak every so often, but having water run down your body - removing all the grime with it - was more appealing.

"The kitchen staff should have already prepped the table; all we need to do is stand by. If Her Highness asks for something, then we move. You'll know."

Kai inclined her head to Mary's brief — glad they had nothing to do but stand around. She only hoped it was somewhere shady as the sun relentlessly beamed down today.

"Can you not do anything right?!"

Her small celebration was ruined, as the princess was already squawking orders when they arrived. A finger waved around, her bewildered face - red.

The dolled-up princess wore light makeup that enhanced her already beautiful features. A long pink dress gathered behind her long legs as she stood before her seat. Her hair was up in complicated braids, circling her head. Some material hung at her pale shoulders, exposing her slender neck. Around her throat was a glinting blue jewel, the size of an apple, which lay at the centre of her collarbone. The sparkling blue stone matched Scarlett's flaring eyes.

"I don't ask for much; all I ask for is things to be done right the first time!" She picked up one of the porcelain teacups and smashed it into the stone ground beneath the pavilion. "Is this what you call refreshing?!"

Mary sighed through her nose, even though her face was deadpan. Kai prayed they were sent away so she didn't have to work near that princess.

Servants, men and women alike, were on their knees, begging for forgiveness. One maid soaked in tinted liquid, the side of her face red and welted.

Kai didn't recognise any of their faces, glad Ava and Charlie weren't among them.

Scarlett continued to shout, "Take this away, and bring me something else!" She plopped down in a huff, arms crossed. One laced-pink glove snapped fingers.

"That would be us..." Mary whispered as she obediently stepped forward. Kai followed hesitantly, curtsying behind Mary, who stopped near the table.

"You two will serve. The rest of you are dismissed. Clean this mess up!"

Those on their knees shot up, immediately doing as they were told. Kai barely registered the black and white fabrics whiz by, clearing the mess before disappearing.

"You." Scarlett's stern gaze was on Mary, a thick bottom lip stuck out. "Go. Bring something refreshing. Do not disappoint me."

Mary curtsied deeper. "Yes, Your Highness." Disappearing next towards cherry blossom trees, pursuing the crowd that took off.

Kai was alone, still respectfully low in the garden, holding the uniform's heavy skirt.

"And you." Scarlett spoke to her, "Fix this; it offends me." The princess's gloved hand brushed the air towards the table.

Kai nervously approached, assuming she didn't have to curtsy any longer. Her eyes surveyed the setting, wondering what it was that offended her.

The servants had already removed the placed drinks and cleaned the smashed debris nearby. All there was on the table were plates and a stacked tray of colourful cakes, such as cupcakes and macaroons. Silverware was placed upon creamy, bright napkins by the cakes, and at the centre were flowers strategically placed to compliment the table's setting. Generously large roses of reds, oranges and yellows were placed in a glass vase — Kai even noticed some baby breaths were mixed in.

She picked up the silverware and wrapped the napkins around them. Just as she did when setting up the tavern cutlery for customers who decide to dine in with their alcohol. Kai neatly placed the wrapped bundles beside the white plates, bringing the dishes two inches closer to the edges of the circular table. She side-stepped around, fussing about with this and that. Picking out baby-breaths from the flowers, she tucks them into the folds of the napkins.

"What are you doing?" a bone-chilling tone asked.

Kai's eyes gradually met Scarlett's, whose thin right eyebrow was sky high. Kai gestured at her throat.

Scarlett's face twisted further, and red rose into her puffed-out cheeks. "I asked you a question, and you dare ignore your master?"

Kai shook her head and, this time, attempted to speak. Disturbing sounds came out.

The princess made a face of disgust, but someone rushed back to the scene before anything else could be said.

Luckily, Mary stepped over with quick strides and a silver tray in her hands. "My apologies, Your Highness." Her words came with haste, "Miss Kai is mute. She cannot speak, Your Grace." Somehow curtsying gracefully with that tray.

Kai nodded and backed away from the table, curtsying as well. Her back ached more from how much these people had to bend to their superiors.

The wind cooled the heat radiating on the back of Kai's neck; she closed her eyes briefly, enjoying the sensation. Open-toed heels appeared before her line of sight when her eyes opened, then a folded red fan.

That fan touched Kai's chin, forcing it up.

Scarlett was looking down on her. "How unfortunate," she whispered amusingly. She stared intensely at Kai's face; her other free hand reached, pulling the bonnet back.

Damp hair fell forward, some still stuck to Kai's sides.

"Did my father bring you in? Is he trying to remind me what could become of me if I don't start doing as he commands?"

Kai shook her head, not even realising she was holding her breath.

The protagonist was inches away from her sweaty face, and rather than being ecstatic, she was terrified.

"Are you lying to me?"

Kai shook once more, feeling lightheaded.

Deep blue eyes squinted, and that fan removed itself from Kai's chin. Scarlett twirled; her dress brushed against Kai's own, the scent of roses wafted with the heiress's action. "Go stand over there, somewhere I cannot see you. You look particularly filthy." Scarlett sauntered away, hips swinging side to side.

She claimed her seat, picking up the silverware wrapped in the napkins and examined the little added touches of flowers.

Releasing that breath, Kai did as she was ordered. Curtsying one last time, much more profound, before she fled behind the princess to a stone wall shaded over —wanting to vomit.

Scarlett was a scorned tyrant queen, not a spoiled princess!

CHAPTER THIRTEEN

Scarlett tossed the bundle onto the table, clattering the dishes set on it with the impact. Her eyes briskly glanced at Mary, setting out new refreshments. "What do you call that servant?" she asked.

Mary placed the glass jug of pink lemonade down. "Miss Kai, Your Grace." Her head inclined, eyes closing briefly before she carried on working.

Scarlett fanned herself, the shades of red on the roses of the folding fan reminding her of the wet, soggy girl. The maid's hair wasn't nearly as impressive as hers but radiant as if it were dipped into the brightest of paints by the goddess.

And those eyes...

"If the mere sight of her offends, Your Highness... I will have someone else tend to you in her stead."

Scarlett drifted back to Mary, now curtsied at the side, waiting. "No... have her tend in place of Bethany. That girl is beginning to become a bore. I need more entertainment." Her deep blues studied the table.

The maid didn't change much, but how she shuffled things around pleased Scarlett strangely. So little effort made the table appear cleaner. More space was opened, and the set-up gave the impression of it being less forced. She even slid the plates closer to the two chairs, giving the centrepiece more space to show off. More influence. Not to mention, she actually set up the silverware by the plates the first time. Rather than leaving them piled together for her, the princess, to fetch.

Mary cleared her throat and gained Scarlett's attention. "Today is her first day, Your Grace. I'm afraid she doesn't quite have a handle on her duties yet. I can send one of the other ladies who have more experience with serving for someone of your stature."

Scarlett flicked her fan closed against a palm, head cocked to a side. "I said she is to tend to me instead. Are you denying me, your master, of what I want?"

Mary's eyes shot open wide, her voice laced with remorse, "Of course not, Your Highness!" She was on her knees the next second. "How dare I, a mere maid, deny you, our beloved Rose!"

"Then, see to it that, *Kai...*" Scarlett found the servant's name bizarre but liked how it was short and quick to spit out. "... is ready to begin working for me first thing tomorrow morning. If she stumbles, she stumbles. I could use the laugh."

Not far back, Kai shivered.

Enjoying her brief reprieve away from the two people at the centre of the courtyard, she tugged at the high collar of the uniform. The wind gently blew, carrying cherry blossom petals across the yard. A few of those petals stuck in those damp hair strands as Kai leaned against the stone wall covered in moss patches. Hiding in the shade of one of the many cherry blossom trees.

Her mind was a shattered mess.

She needed to meet with Ava and Charlie so they could start brainstorming what the conditions were. She wouldn't survive long in this world; things were nothing like she had initially anticipated.

She wanted to get the hell out of there as quickly as possible.

Kai wasn't even sure if the storyline was the same, either. The only thing she was sure of was—that nothing here was the same as what had been read a million times. At least, not the two characters she had the unfortunate pleasure of meeting so far.

She didn't even want to entertain the thought of what the *other* characters could be like.

Mary strolled her way over to Kai. "Are you okay?" Noticing how her new colleague clutched her chest, panting hard.

Kai glanced, shaking her head. *No!* She wanted to scream; this uniform was killing her. This whole place was going to be the death of her!

A sympathetic look fleeted across Mary's features as she turned and positioned herself towards the princess. "You're not going to like this... but as of tomorrow morning, you will officially be tending to Her Highness. Replacing Bethany, her handmaiden. Congratulations on your promotion."

Kai's ears began ringing.

"I'm unaware of your prior experience serving peculiar lords and ladies, so I suggest you visit the library and brush up on protocol. She's excused you this afternoon... to prepare."

Kai walked with haste, almost jogging, fleeing to the sanction of her private quarters.

'*As of tomorrow morning, you will officially be tending to Her Highness. Replacing Bethany, her handmaiden. Congratulations on your promotion.*' Mary's words echoed inside her skull, adding more tension to the building pressure.

Scarlett's intimidating stare flashed before her like a strobe light of images. Kai turned a corner unthinkingly, slamming into something hard, and staggered back. Someone scoffed as she tried to shake Mary's words away, her vision blurred.

"Excuse you." Violet irises peered down on Kai, looking on from the tip of his nose.

Kai mouthed a 'Sorry' and fled from another face. The ones she needed most now didn't exist in this make-believe world.

"Hey, wait?!" that voice started shouting.

Kai picked up the pace, sprinting back to her room, skirt clenched tightly in fists. People all over gasped and shouted as she raced by, but she would care about etiquette later.

She knew if she slowed down or stopped, she'd collapse. Anxiety bubbled to explode; her chest ached with that building agony inside her head. She tasted the salty tears that ran down her face, flying up stairwells.

Kai repeated, *not yet, not yet.* She told herself not to give in till she was in her room, away from prying eyes.

Once she busted through the threshold, her knees buckled, and her head slammed onto the firm bed. The tears wouldn't stop flowing as her breaths became harder and harder to draw.

I want to go home! She cried, clutching that ache.

Kai was delirious as she wailed and shook. Unaware of Dexter, who had stepped in through her wide-opened door.

The doctor coughed at the entry, watching the petite lady weep. A concealed head was pressed into the side of the mattress, and a wrapped-up hand clutched her fast-constricting chest.

He knocked on the door without luck, trying to gain her attention. Those shoulders continued to shake, her head still down. He heard Kai gasp, struggling to breathe, and that's when his feet moved on their own. Hands reaching out.

His doctor instincts took over, taking full control of himself.

Dexter yanked her away from the mattress with a force he knew he shouldn't have used with a lady. Noticing her pale skin was blotchy red, and shades of purple bloomed up her throat when her face was finally revealed. "BREATHE!" he demanded. A hand firmly tapped her damp back, wondering what she inhaled, what she might have been choking on.

A gruff cough responded as Kai squirmed away from the doctor's touch. Her hands gripped the sides of her head.

Dexter watched Kai settle against the wardrobe, trying to wrap his head around what had happened. He observed how her breaths were still laboured, but she was breathing. Clearly, nothing was lodged in her windpipe. He also noted how she was not reacting in the slightest to her own condition.

He pondered, *was she not choking?*

Kai's breaths evened out as he sat there observing her for some time, studying the weird phenomenon that was a woman. Curious if the suspicious, quiet maid had discovered a new way to choke on air.

Kai's features came into view again, and a hand swiped away the liquids running down her face. She was flushed, her eyes red. Those cheeks were nearly as bright as the hair on her head.

"What's wrong?" Dexter asked, his considering stare darting between her strained eyes.

Icy blues wobbled to meet his own, hands exasperatedly gesturing at her throat.

Dexter felt the heat in his own face and rose for stationary. Usually, he carried some with him while he worked. But today was an exception. He spent the day reading in the library, not needing it.

The information he was searching for couldn't be written down. So, there was no chance of others discovering it.

He snatched the paper and quill from the small desk and passed it over. Watching as Kai wrote, her small hands twitched slightly. Dexter hung onto every letter she placed on the page.

> I'm fine. Can you leave?

Dexter felt insulted, and not just by the lack of manners she offered. "You're fine? You do not look fine!" his octave raised. "I came in, and you were choking for air! Tell me how that is fine?!"

This girl barely had to do anything to rattle him; her few written words offended his intelligence.

Kai wrote again, hardly bothered by his ungentlemanly outburst.

> It was a panic attack. I'm fine.

He stared at the paper, then at her. Violet eyes blinked rapidly. "Panic... attack?"

Those icy blues dared to roll as she continued to scribble on the page. Her handwriting was unique to him. Dexter watched on stupidly until Kai offered him the sheet.

> My doctor said it is an anxiety disorder linked to trauma. It's a natural response to stress or danger.

The doctor sat in front of Kai, legs crossing as he settled. He extended his arm, gently grabbing the paper as he read it repeatedly. His face was as if he was trying to decipher some foreign language. "Is it life-threatening?" he mumbled.

Kai's head shook softly, sniffing the nasties that threatened to drop out of her nose. She lifted her sleeve, attempting to wipe it away.

A violet handkerchief was offered. Dexter still watched her, his tone barely above a whisper, "It's improper etiquette… using your sleeve."

Dexter told himself he only cared because he needed to keep an eye on the woman, careful as she accepted his offer.

The room was silent; birds chirped outside the window perched on the tree directly opposite it, filling the awkward stillness. Kai mouthed her thanks; her thumb rubbed the velvety material between her fingers.

There was an unexplainable sadness deep within her light blue eyes, which rattled Dexter somewhere within. His mind recalled his investigation on the girl, and his conscience bled with guilt surveying her.

After a roundabout conversation with Pennel, he discovered the maid's full name, Kai Redsi. Related to the blind woman from the kitchen, Ava Sebastian, he was told.

He spent his day off digging for the Redsi family name and the Sebastian one to see where they hailed from—hoping to uncover something about the suspicious woman. While he spent time with the dusty books and scrolls, he decided to find an explanation for those insane healing abilities.

Nothing in the royal archives was able to explain it from a non-magical perspective. Not unless the said individual was of unnatural birth from higher beings and entities.

Yet, sitting before him, dripping in heaven-knows-what kind of liquids, wasn't a suspicious person at all. But instead, someone very broken.

Lost. A feeling he knew all too well.

"Is there anything I can do to assist?" he finally broke the silence, observing the strange way Kai wiped her nose.

She swiped upwards, pushing the cloth, unlike the ladies here who pinched beneath their noses.

There was nothing to prove to him that she was brought up with the education their kingdom provided as if she was half-savage-like, born and raised far away from civilisation.

When Kai was confident nothing would leak from her nostrils, she took back the paper.

It's okay. I've dealt with it for years.

Dexter studied her small, callused hands. He noticed the rough bumps were in specific areas, one on her thumb and another on the side of her middle finger, as if she was accustomed to having something far more expensive between them.

"I can make you a tonic to help keep you calm should you feel those symptoms arise?" he offered, unsure why he wanted to help further.

Kai shook her head again, placing the items to a side. She stood carefully, brushing off her skirting, and inhaled deeply.

Dexter rose, too, unable to take his eyes off her. Observing how she suddenly pulled herself together. That sadness was gone from those eyes when those frosty blues opened with clarity.

CHAPTER FOURTEEN

Dexter paused by a semicircular archway, the whole stone wall lined with that same structural design, staring out to the garden in the distance. He retrieved the crinkled paper he tucked away in his pocket like a thief before excusing himself from the woman's quarters and began examining it.

He had never heard of a panic disorder or an anxiety attack in his field—a new medical discovery on people's brain functions and how they affect individuals. Clearly, the doctors of her origins were better educated and more knowledgeable on people's physical and mental well-being.

His drive to discover where Kai hailed from was more intense, like a person with a substance use disorder wanting their next hit.

Dexter's thoughts strayed as he admired the clean handwriting, smoothing out the wrinkles on the sheet with his thumbs, studying how each of her letters had their own characteristics. It was as if they had their own personality with each stroke; how strange it was to him that none of the letters actually touched.

Like she was allowing each of them their own space, to be... to exist, another thing she did that was different from the people in his kingdom.

Even lower-class citizens wrote similarly to the higher class if they could write at all.

"Your Grace, Your Grace! Please, slow down!"

Dexter side-eyed to that man's shouting voice. A well-dressed soldier draped in a purple cape and a sword sheathed at his side was marching well ahead of the yelling.

The clipped golden crest on the gentleman's pectoral warned Dexter of foreign royalty. Charging his way.

He tucked the note swiftly back into his pocket, bowing as that individual rushed past with large strides.

The tall man stopped abruptly by a large fluted stone vase and twirled to Dexter; his glossy cape swung with him, flicking the overhanging leaves.

"Have you seen a little woman with bright red hair come this way?" the stranger suddenly asked, that accent of Raevegon. A gloved finger rose, pointing in the direction he had intended.

The man chasing him quickly caught up. "Your Grace, you are supposed to be meeting with Princess Scarlett! You must go before we offend them further!"

Dexter straightened his spine. His stare clashed with golden eyes.

He knew those insane irises and heard many stories of the victories they had won.

"I greet the defending sword of the South. We welcome you, Prince Warrick Crestblood, Crown Prince of the Raevegon Empire. I am Doctor Dexter Ubar, physician to-"

The doctor doesn't get to finish his proper greeting as the man cuts him off, "Forget the formalities. Yes, or no?"

"Your Highness!?" the other man shouted in disbelief.

Warrick ignored his aide and repeated, "Have you seen a woman with bright red hair run this way?" Those golds urged for an answer.

Kai's teary face rose in Dexter's conscience as he stupidly lied to the foreign royalty. "I apologise, Your Highness, but I have not." Then, he bowed once more after his words.

Pivoting, Prince Warrick continued on his chase, not offering anything else. His aide was hot on his tail, still yelling after him.

Dexter rose, his eyebrows turned downwards. His thoughts festered with curiosity. Was this visiting Crown Prince the reason for the muted lady's state of being?

Kai pulled herself together and chased off that pestering doctor, making her way to the library. She aimlessly wandered before stopping three other servants dressed in a similar manner and asking for directions. This place was huge, every hallway strikingly similar to all others, disorientating her.

Finally, she stood before the giant, opened doors, and gawked at the four floors' worth of books. Seating areas and desks were placed inside the colossal room, giving the appeal to come and stay awhile. She had no idea where she was meant to start, feeling overwhelmed by what beheld her. She searched for someone within to guide her further.

Kai found the ancient man, chains around his vein-ridden neck with smaller books dangling from it. His green robes shimmer from the high above chandeliers, making him easier to spot. Her notebook was at the ready, and Kai asked where she would find the reading material needed.

The brown-eyed man smiles, several remaining teeth greeted. Kai could spy between those remaining yellow stubs, half a tongue. She tried not to show the unsettling feeling that began in her gut, on her face—wondering why half his tongue was missing, as if it had been cut out.

The man raised an old, wrinkled hand and grabbed one of the many books dangled from the chains. He wrote, 'second floor' and then directed Kai to the back section, a trembling limb pointed beyond.

Kai climbed the stairs, eyeing the bookshelves and reading each section. They had everything, from fiction to nonfiction, archives to scrolls of history. There were even glassed boxes and bookcases, which showcased and preserved relics. Swords, daggers, teeth, skulls, one even had a stretched-out leathery wing...

Kai felt like she was visiting a museum rather than a library.

As the man directed, she turned down the last set of shelves towards that back corner. Spotting two familiar faces at the rear.

Charlie was skimming through the titles, a finger hovering in the air. While Ava sat on a decorative chair behind him, hands feeling a book in her lap—a cosy, quiet moment.

Kai dashed forward excitedly, alarming Charlie as he flinched away from her.

"What's wrong?" Ava's worried tone raised, pausing from her reading.

Charlie sighed with relief; his eyebrows furrowed. He wobbled his finger in Kai's smiling face, fighting a smile of his own.

The three sat on the floor, and Ava chattered away with the written developments. Kai had whipped out her book, running them up to speed on her events. Her little grey notebook became her new friend around here, conveying all the words needed.

Ava ran her fingers along the written content, deciphering the sentences from Kai's deep, engraved letters. "Troubling indeed..." Ava muttered, "She's a real bitch from what we've heard."

Charlie nodded along, making a face.

Kai sat there, dejected, with her protocol textbook, which Charlie was kind enough to fetch. She was going over the basics of what was expected of handmaidens while the pair examined her findings.

Ava reached, trying to feel for Kai's arm, tapping her crossed legs.

Kai silently engulfed her limb and gave it a squeeze for reassurance.

"I agree. We should start meeting every evening and brainstorm. I know it isn't ideal for you... I hear she hasn't kept her handmaidens for over a few months, except for that old crone. But you'll see and hear different aspects of this place. It could be our lucky break. So, let's put our heads and senses together and get the hell out of here."

Kai squeezed Ava's hand harder, nodding in agreement. She was glad they were on board with her plan and beyond grateful she didn't have to figure it out alone. She didn't even think of a back of strategy if they weren't.

The three silently conspired, stopping if Kai or Ava heard something suspicious nearby. They had been in that quiet little corner for well over a few hours, deciding to move once their bellies began to ache.

Kai helped Charlie escort Ava back down the never-ending steps, each checking out books for the evening. Learning from Ava's developments, these two were punished to brush up on their protocols as well after they skipped and helped Kai yesterday.

She was glad to run into them, thanking whomever she needed for this grounding moment. Even if they weren't friends outside this horrible, sick voodoo magic, Kai told herself she would be — after. She would forever be indebted to them for simply being here, even if none of them *wanted* to be.

That anxiety in Kai's chest lessened the more she spent with them, deciding to tag along with the couple to fetch something to eat. Too embarrassed to admit out loud that she had forgotten where this staff hall was or that she wasn't quite ready to depart from the only things that reminded her of home.

That reminded her of the real world beyond this.

Kai paused as they strolled out of the eastern wing, returning toward the direction of the servants' tower. Something glossy had caught her attention from the corner of her peripheral view.

She squinted at purple material that moved like waves. A silver sword was placed within a hollowed-out shield of golden threads stitched into the fabric.

"YOU UNGRATEFUL SWINE!" a familiar scream chased after that flapping cape.

Kai yanked Ava and Charlie behind a wall, covering Ava's mouth with a hand when she started to protest. She mouthed 'Princess' to Charlie when he gave her a puzzling stare, flicking her head to the other side of the wall.

Another servant rushed by the stashed-away trio, fleeing from the voice in the yard. Kai and Charlie poked their heads around the corner, ensuring only parts of their faces were visible, spying on the scene about to unfold.

That cape had stopped in its tracks, and knee-high black boots spun around. Kai and Charlie could now see the individual's furious face.

"How dare you address an honoured guest in such a manner," the man said with a bite to his tone.

Scarlett came into view, her pink dress dragged behind. That beautiful face morphed into a hideous glare, her once neat hair dishevelled. Even the mascara on her lashes was smeared, adding to the crazed look. "HOW DARE I!? HOW DARE I!?" still shouting. She stomped her heels like a spoiled brat. "HOW DARE YOU KEEP A LADY WAITING!?"

Many onlookers were peeking around hidden areas. Some even stopped out in the open.

The man raised his chin, and golden eyes glowed unnaturally. "I am the future emperor of the Raevegon Empire. Lower your voice when you address me, Princess."

Charlie gave Kai a questioning glance as he noticed her perk up. She smiled, mouthing 'Prince Warrick' a slight blush took over her high cheekbones.

He was handsome, better than the face Kai imagined when she read the book or dreamed about the scenes.

His thick, chocolate-coloured hair was pushed back. Some of those strands defied the style and hung over his face near those thick eyebrows as if reflecting his personality. His skin was sun-kissed like the man lived outside and didn't know what shelter was. A faint shadow of facial hair was on his jaw and under his nose. Perfectly portioned lips lined up under a straight masculine nose. The man's crease-free uniform screamed - I am a man of power. The suit's whites, silvers and blacks added to his charming appearance.

That purple cape was attached to his left shoulder, the right — covered in black animal fur. As Kai's eyes skimmed him over, she noticed a black and silver sheath stationed at his hip.

But what screamed - I demand respect - were those golden irises, which were currently blazing back at the princess.

"I apologised to you for my tardiness. As I explained, something arose and needed my immediate attention. However..." He stepped closer, his boot crunched stones. "Since then, you have dumped a cup of liquid upon me, insulted my empire..." His leather-gloved hand pointed at a man dressed similarly, rushing towards them. "And insulted my people." His dignified tone hardly raised as he continued speaking, "You expect me to sit there and deal with your childish tantrums and ugly table manners after all that?" That blazing glare gave Scarlett a look over. "Absolutely not." Pivoting briskly, away from the spying eyes, his back straightened. "Come, Roger. Let us go speak with someone with actual etiquette."

Roger flew past the fuming princess, not even bothering with a bow, as he caught up with the prince.

Scarlett clutched her dress, screaming in fury at her departing visitor's back. "YOU ARROGANT FOOL!"

Charlie grabbed Kai, yanking them away before she blew their cover. He gripped Ava's hand, dragging both women away from the princess bellowing in the stone yard. Her high-pitched squeals chased away even the pigeons perched above.

CHAPTER FIFTEEN

C harlie escorted Ava back to her quarters, and the two said their goodbyes to Kai after finally getting some grub.

They laughed during dinner earlier at what they had witnessed. Even though Ava couldn't see, she was in stitches over the fit the princess threw. Hearing her voice undignifiedly screech, just like a pig's squeal. Kai nearly choked on her sandwich as Charlie tried to explain what her face looked like. Not realising in the moment, he was mimicking it.

The whole servant canteen whispered or gossiped about the hilarious scene until Madam Stark arrived, and the hall fell deadly silent. That was the trio's cue to leave, as she eyed up the three of them with a nasty scowl.

Kai felt more confident with a game plan set in place and a full belly. She just needed to survive during her shifts, tending to the princess and gathering what she could so they could find a way home.

She was approaching her quarters, a book clutched under her armpit, when she noticed Mary knocking on the door. Kai slid next to her and playfully knocked on the door as well.

Mary giggled at her sudden appearance. "Ah, sorry. I forgot you were probably trying to find the library. Did it go alright?"

Kai showed her the book, wiggling it.

"I'm glad," Mary sighed, "You didn't look too good when you left...
I just wanted to check on you and offer a little run down of what is expected in the morning."

Settling at the small table while Mary talked, Kai pulled out half a sandwich and biscuits she stuffed into her pockets for later. She glanced at the woman and noticed Mary's eyes gleam towards the items being laid out.

Kai was all too familiar with that hungry stare. The days of scrounging up all her pennies for a pot noodle surfaced. She decided to offer them to Mary instead.

The brown-eyed woman hesitated; her eyes widened. "No, no, that's yours! I'll swing by the food hall on my way back!" Her hands waved in front, protesting.

Kai wouldn't take no for an answer; she had seen first-hand how hard Mary worked. She never complained to Kai about her duties or labour stress. She guessed the poor girl hadn't eaten anything and came rushing here when she could.

She pushed the food further away from herself and rubbed her abdomen. Trying to show Mary she was full.

Mary's browns shook as her head hung low, and a blush dusted her cheekbones. "If you insist," she whispered, carefully taking the brown paper wrap off the items.

Kai beamed. To ensure Mary didn't feel uncomfortable with her watching, she flipped the textbook open and tried to study.

Nibbling on the ham sandwich that was offered, Mary shyly peaked. She braved a bigger bite, noticing her colleague focused on her notes, savouring her first meal of the day.

The room was silent as Mary filled her aching belly, and Kai wrote notes of things to remember. Mary would cover her full mouth of food, explaining in detail what Kai was making notes on. The ambience between the two was comfortable. The candlelight on the table flickered, which emitted dancing shadows around the room.

After Mary finished the last biscuit, she sighed patting her stomach. Her gaze accidentally locked with Kai's, who, in turn, was smiling wide at her.

"Thank you..." Mary said, feeling grateful.

Kai scribbled, turning the notebook around.

> Teamwork makes the dream work.

Mary blinked, reading over the note, and a smile twitched. She glanced up, nodding in agreement. Having a female companion looking out for you was a rare and refreshing thing to her.

The girls went over a few sections. Mary then explained that Kai needed to meet Madam Barnsley at dawn. The two of them would then wait for herself and Bethany so they could usher the princess out, and each would begin their respective duties for the day ahead.

Kai continued to write, noting the new routine she would have to adopt. She couldn't accurately time everything into a tidy schedule, usually relying on her mobile phone. Without her calendars or even the simple digital clock on a screen, Kai was at a loss for what to do.

Mary's hand stopped Kai, her face falling. "I like you, Kai.... which is why I think it's best to warn you..."

Kai waited, her quill frozen on the page. Watching as Mary pulled away and immediately began to pick at her fingernails.

"Bethany is... not too happy about being demoted. She worked really well with the princess... Well, because their personalities were similar." Mary glanced at the door, her voice quieter. As if she was afraid, Bethany, herself, was listening in. "She might start some drama for you. Please be careful. Whatever you do, whatever you must do... stay on the princess's good side. It can be a vicious position. Many will be preying on you to slip up."

Kai tossed and turned all night, not from Mary's warning but from the lack of technology to wake her when she needed to be up.

Mary's words of caution weren't a surprise; having read something inside the novel about the maids gunning for each other's downfall, Kai knew people wanted to be closer to the spoiled Rose.

Kai was beginning to miss her shifts at the tavern. She even missed working with Zachary and dealing with his antics over this ill-tempered princess. Her brief dreams between her jolts awake were filled with faces she wished to see.

The sky cracked with oranges, pushing out the dark blues and purples. The stars were diminished from the incoming light as birds began to sing their morning songs.

Kai sat up, deciding to make her way to the shared lavatory to get ready herself before meeting with Madam Barnsley. She thought she might be off to the right start if she was earlier than the senior handmaiden.

After sorting herself out and ensuring she wore a clean uniform, Kai went down the quiet corridors. She headed towards the Princess's Palace, where she would wait for Madam Barnsley in front of the building.

Kai pulled out the notes she drafted, reviewing them one last time. To say she was nervous would be an understatement; she hoped she didn't forget one vital thing that could potentially upset Scarlett.

She didn't fancy being in the frying pan with that scary princess.

Even Stace's dad wasn't nearly as frightening when she would occasionally slip up at work. His Italian accent made her hold her breath when he would tell her off on his rare visit. Scarlett made his temper seem like child's play.

A white palace being devoured by roses steadily got closer. Kai's steps slowed as she noticed someone already waiting. She tucked her notebook into a pocket, hoping the individual wouldn't comment.

Madam Barnsley stood at the bottom of the first step, tapping a heel on the stones. Unlike the other maids, she was dressed more sophisticatedly.

She wore a dark, buttoned-up top tucked into an ankle-length flowing skirt. A bow tied at the back of it. Her hair was in a tight bun, pulling her face tighter. But even that didn't help hide the deep lines upon the woman's forehead and around her flat, tight-lipped mouth.

"Here I was thinking you'd be late. Perhaps Her Highness's impulse, for once, may pay off." The woman eyed Kai head to toe, followed by a clicking sound with her tongue. "Tomorrow, dress better. You're not just a maid anymore, Miss Redsi, but a handmaiden to our beloved Rose. Look the part."

She spoke no more, eyes narrowed as she lifted her feet and ascended the stairs.

Kai respectfully bowed her head, kicking herself. No one, nor the book, mentioned the attire.

The women entered the ridiculous palace and headed straight to the second floor. Kai kept her stare off the portraits, keeping Mary's warning in mind. She couldn't trust herself not to slip up.

Madam Barnsley guided Kai to the royal suite, where they would prepare everything before escorting the princess.

Kai didn't have time to examine the glamorous surroundings. She was handed things the moment they entered and was careful not to drop them. They filled a lavish gold bathtub with flower petals. Roses, to be exact, and then with boiling water. Then, she was given oils to add and told she needed to memorise the scents, as they were Her Highness' favourites.

Surprisingly, Barnsley carefully explained to Kai what they were doing and what they would be doing that morning and every morning after.

After readying the bathroom suite, Kai followed the briefing woman into the side room. The separate area had three red couches that squared off the centre of the space and a bunch of wooden mannequins around it. The head handmaiden continued to chatter, pointing around to the dressing table at the far side, with mountains of cosmetics, and then to a huge walk-in closet attached to the spacious side room.

Once they had selected a modest gown for today's meetings and placed it on one of the many mannequins, they finally headed up to the third floor. Kai pursued Madam Barnsley, following her actions right down to the swing in her hips. She swung around to wait by the door for the other two to join, and right on the beat, Mary and Bethany marched down.

Mary was the only one who offered Kai a small smile, while the blonde woman sneered.

Kai assumed that she was Bethany, as she recalled her in this exact spot yesterday morning, chin held high.

With her face kept neutral, Kai listened to Madam Barnsley's cue and opened both the wide doors for the girls.

As the light poured into the bedroom, no one had to speak. Scarlett was already up and sat against her white cushioned headboard.

Her pale arms were crossed, watching Kai stop dead in her tracks. A smirk crept up her rounded cheeks. "Shame... Here, I was thinking, what sort of punishment would I have to give you for your delay." She got out of bed, her hair falling to the floor. "Ley dear, did you bring what I asked for?"

Madam Barnsley shuffled forward, offering something concealed to the princess, her head down. "Yes, Your Grace, and good morning to you."

Scarlett ignored the greeting, removing the black ringing from the wrapped-up cloth. Her blue eyes cut to Kai; a pale finger gestured for her to approach.

Kai hesitantly padded forth and curtsied deep.

"Such lovely manners... I see you're wearing that ridiculous uniform and stupid hat again." Scarlett was in front of Kai, guiding her up to stand. A hand removed the bonnet and threw it to the bare floors.

Scarlett then attached that black ringing thing around Kai's throat.

A collar with a silver bell.

Kai did her best to keep her features schooled. She didn't know if she wanted to laugh, cry or cuss at the woman currently inches away from her face.

Scarlett put a finger to her chin, her head cocking to the side. A smile grew on her mug as the princess took in the new addition. "From now on, when you serve me, you are to wear your bell, pet."

Kai's breath hitched; that word her grandfather sometimes said triggered her. No one was allowed to call her that unless they wanted a nasty chewing. Her grandfather was the only one who got away with using it.

"Also, Ley, give the poor girl her weekly wage. Tomorrow, I will not take any excuses if you appear before me in those rags." Her blues not once left

Kai's.

Barnsley curtsied. "Yes, Your Grace. Now, let us be on our way. You have much to do this morning. The seamstress and designer will come later to choose your dress for the ball."

Scarlett's intense stare finally released Kai's stoned body, and she groaned as she stomped away.

The silent maid stiffly rotated on her feet, catching the sneering grin on Bethany's face. Bethany's shoulders shook with silent laughter as the bell around Kai's neck jingled with each of her heavy steps.

CHAPTER SIXTEEN

As humiliated as Kai felt with every noise made around her neck, she did what was asked of her. She helped Barnsley wash the princess down, massaged her body after her bath with gorgeous smelling oils, gave her a second bath, and helped the princess finally get dressed.

Kai had a newfound appreciation for carers back home.

Having to bathe someone who could clean themselves was weird and exhausting. Let alone someone who genuinely needed the help. With every new and strange task Kai was experiencing, she found herself appreciating the little things she took for granted—more and more.

Luckily, Madam Barnsley took the lead in the roles. Kai only held things or offered a helping hand when the older woman didn't have enough limbs.

The princess was quiet; occasionally, she smiled at Kai as she did her job. Or rather, smiled at the noisy thing around her throat.

Besides the humiliating moment in the bedroom, the morning went by calmly. They were now in the overly excessive dressing room, surrounded by the golds of the interior design, the mountains of dreamy, shimmering fabrics which littered the red furniture and accessories readily available for the princess.

Barnsley and Scarlett were currently going head-to-head over the day's makeup.

Kai couldn't believe the galls of the woman who argued back with Scarlett. Even when the princess threatened to have her beheaded, the handmaiden merely nodded, saying 'Yes, yes', and brushed it off.

"I will look like a clown," Scarlett huffed, throwing the green eyeshadow - she was handed to approve - away. "Are you trying to piss me off, Ley?"

Madam Barnsley fixed her sleeves as if ready to throw down with the stubborn princess. "Obviously not, Your Grace. You are beautiful, no matter." Her arms crossed, staring the princess down. "But the designer will be judging you on your appearance. She hails from the Raevegon Empire, after all. Do you want your prospective subjects gossiping behind your back?"

The bickering continued to go back and forth, even as Kai finished clearing the mess of fabrics on the side. She hung them up and put them away completely, her head splitting, listening to them squawk. She wanted to get this over with and get the stupid collar off. Having something tight around her throat, rubbing whenever she moved her head - was just as annoying as the jiggling.

"Do you honestly believe I care what they think?"

The little patience Kai had left jumped out the window as she physically rolled her eyes. Kai spun with a stamp of her heels and stepped forth.

The women quieted for a brief moment and eyed up Kai. Who, in turn, offered a sloppy curtsy.

The princess spoke up, "What is it, pet?"

Kai whipped out that notebook from her pocket, prepared to write today rather than trying to gesture like a mime. She flipped the book over, holding it up. So those in company could read it.

> I'd like to show you a clean but glamorous face of makeup.

Barnsley was the one to scoff, a glare with her words, "You've only just started, and you dare suggest-"

"Silence." Scarlett raised her hand and stopped the Madam from finishing her lecture. "Brave... or stupid... I guess we'll find out," she giggled, leaning back in the chair. "Go ahead, pet. But if I'm displeased... you *will* be punished. Mark my words."

Kai silently thanked the gods and tucked the notebook back into her pocket. She was careful as she approached Scarlett, mouthing, 'Please excuse me' before she touched the princess.

Starting with a light cream base from the numerous mountains of other creams on the vanity, Kai colour swathed against Scarlett's clean cheek. When she was satisfied with the colour match, Kai spread it evenly across her face and down her neck. She played with the greys and browns, giving shadows and a bronzed effect like Stace usually did her makeup on a night out. Since she couldn't see a contour palette, Kai used plain eyeshadows. She avoided anything with sparkles or sheens to the formulas.

Scarlett had enough cosmetics littering the dressing table to create anything.

Then, picking up a red eyeshadow, Kai lightly filled the princess's eyebrows. As she did this, she could hear Barnsley fuss even more behind. Scarlett's hand was frozen in the air again.

The princess was excited, trying not to wiggle with emotion. She was curious to see what her new handmaiden was up to—already plotting what she would do to her afterwards. Scarlett kept her eyes closed so as not to spoil the fun.

She could feel Kai touch every inch of her face. Drawing on the outside of her lips, next.

She thought, *this stupid maid had just signed her resignation letter.*

The girl then patted her lips, eyes, and cheeks. Scarlett felt the setting powder being brushed off, knowing from routine the girl was close to being done.

Barnsley gasped softly to her side. "I think you can open your eyes, Your Grace..."

The princess' eyes shot open. The person in the reflection of the mirror made her blink rapidly.

Her thick lips looked juicer; Scarlett barely noticed the outline she felt her handmaiden draw on. Whatever Kai had done gave her lips more depth, which she didn't know was possible. Her eyes were done with shimmering gold and darker brown at the corners, elegantly winged up and out. A sharp line was somehow achieved, making it appear clean and lifted. A darker brown eyeliner, with hues of red, was tightly lined along her eyelids. Going with the eye-shadowed wing. Her already long lashes seemed fuller, longer even, as she turned her chin back and forth, peering. Scarlett noted the same colour pattern was buffed out under her eyes, making her irises pop. The faffing about of her eyebrows - made them seem fuller. Giving them a groomed shape to match the well-done eye makeup.

Somehow, the maid even made her round face seem lean, like she had prominent cheekbones hiding under all that flesh. Her whole face was slimmed down, and her features enhanced.

Her stare cuts to Kai, curtsied at the side, obediently waiting. Then, they shot to Barnsley, who stared at her widely.

"Well?" she anxiously asked.

Scarlett couldn't tell what Ley thought, her reaction making her want clarification. Usually, the older woman was easy to read.

Barnsley's lip twitched; her hazels dragged to the other handmaiden. "Marvellous..." The woman's gaze was back on Scarlett, squinting. "It's like some kind of witchcraft... she even changed the shape of your face." A hand hesitantly reached and hovered over the contour.

Scarlett clapped her hands. "Rise." Watching as Kai listened to her command. "Though, I am slightly disappointed..." The girl's right eyebrow tweaked with her words, making Scarlett smile wider. "I was looking forward to punishing you..."

The three women made their way from the dressing room. Barnsley changed the dress to match the makeup. Scarlett was gliding around in a Champaign-coloured gown, her hair and eyes the main highlight of her appearance. Kai loosely braided the princess's hair, and Barnsley added small gold clips throughout it.

Even Kai had to admit she was stunning. Scarlett was pretty without makeup, but the modern-day touches gave her a movie star appeal.

And the way she carried herself added to it, so as long as she didn't open her mouth.

They finally got to the drawing room, where the guests inside rose for the princess. They curtsied and bowed, respectively, just like everyone else was expected to.

Kai and Madam Barnsley stationed themselves at the doors. Kai was told to listen to the conversation and wait for their summons.

The pleasantries were simple as more people pulled out more fabrics from various boxes. Kai couldn't believe the perks and extravagance of being a royal.

The designer stood, going over the options and how they were crafted. Getting to one in particular that jarred Kai's memory of the book. The overly powdered woman gestured to an orange dress with thousands of tassels hanging off the bodice, sleeves, and skirt. She told Scarlett that she would appear as the light of the party.

The flame that carried the kingdom, if she chose it.

In the novel, the reader had the perspective of hearing her inner monologue — hoping to make a fool of the princess. It was Scarlett's closest maid who had objected and ultimately helped avoid humiliation.

Kai waited and side-eyed her senior supervisor to the left.

Madam Barnsley stood poised, not doing a damn thing. Those hazels barely flicked over to the options before they were immediately back on her mistress, dismissing them.

Scarlett seemed easily appeased when people showered her with false notions of attention-grabbing or fame. She nodded, enjoying the sugar-coated words the designer fed her.

That fake customer service smile Kai was all too familiar with was plastered on the designer's face.

Kai debated for a fraction of a second before jumping in. Her hands crossed before her as the bell around her throat went wild.

Scarlett's face dropped into a scowl, and Barnsley muttered under her breath behind. But Kai had done it now — she couldn't back down. All glaring eyes were on her; even the designer cussed at the 'mere maid' for daring to interrupt.

Kai retrieved the notebook with shaking hands, ignoring everyone's death-implying stares.

> It will take away from our beloved Rose's eye-catching features. She must wear the dress; the dress must NOT wear her.

Falling to her knees, Kai held the notebook up, her head down submissively. Mimicking the servants she had seen in the courtyard just yesterday.

Nasty remarks were thrown; the notebook was eventually taken from those trembling fingers.

"Ley… thoughts?"

Kai remained on the floor. Her stomach was in knots, hoping she had done the right thing.

Madam Barnsley hummed, "She makes a valid point, Your Grace… Do you have nothing else to offer, Her Highness? Something that isn't… so much?"

A firm hand is placed on Kai's bicep, pulling her to her feet. Deep sea blues sparkled down.

By some gifted grace, Kai survived her first day serving the princess directly; Barnsley excused her just after lunch. A bag of coins passed over.

"You did exceptionally well today, Miss Redsi." Something cleared inside those hazels, and they regarded Kai more positively. "Go. Get yourself situated for tomorrow. We have another busy schedule ahead of us."

She patted Kai twice on the shoulder, leaving her outside the palace, spaced out.

If it hadn't been for Madam Barnsley backing her in that appointment, Kai was sure she would have been placed on the chopping block.

However, as a fan of the story, Kai couldn't just let the designer make a fool of Scarlett. Although she was intimidating and had a downright awful attitude, Kai couldn't risk the story going astray.

Not if progressing was her only possible ticket out of here.

The story was already so vastly different from what she knew. She swore to herself she would do her best to stay true to what the story was about when it came to the main characters.

Kai swayed during her trek, hardly registering the jingling of the bell. Her soul had left her body after that intense showdown. The designer kept insisting on the dress, and the princess finally showed her true colours. Losing her mind on the 'lowly worker' for trying to sway her with 'rags'. She screamed at that designer that she was a princess, not a 'circus act'.

Kai could still hear her screeching words as she stumbled across the courtyard. Boots kicking stones approached her, and that silky voice came, "Miss Redsi."

Kai's head flopped to Dexter, her body lagging a moment after, hips twisted.

His expressionless face dropped into disgust, those surreal eyes at the thing around her throat. She could practically see the cogs turning in his skull, mouthing 'The princess' to him before his mouth could open.

His violet eyes widened as his boot slid back, and pity washed over his features.

Kai shrugged, continuing on her way. She needed to put the money away and sit down for five minutes. She also needed to go into the town and get clothing suitable for tomorrow.

Her list of things to do increasingly grew.

She barely registered the footsteps that followed over the noise of the bell, but then again, Kai really couldn't care less. She just wanted to sit down at this point.

Dexter followed Kai, studying the sway in her steps, her complexion ghostly white. That atrocious animal collar around her neck infuriated him.

Collars were an old relic, outlawed after slavery was abolished.

Seeing one around the muted woman's fragile throat while she stumbled weakly, jiggling, and gaining onlookers' attention, didn't sit right with him.

CHAPTER SEVENTEEN

Kai's door opened for her, and a big hand with well-kept, clean nails held it. She stumbled in and dropped the sack of heavy coins on the table, with sagging shoulders, her butt plopped down onto the wooden chair.

Dexter entered after, closing the door behind himself.

Joining Kai at her table, he settled into his seat across from her. He couldn't help but notice the pitiful girl had bags under those striking eyes. Blankly, she stared at the pouch she had put down.

Something was unsettling about that dull stare; a face flashed in his conscience.

"I'll go get you some water, perhaps a tonic to help boost your energy..." he offered.

Tired frosty blues gradually rose, and Dexter noticed the ring of darker blue that seemed to outline the outer rim of her irises. His attention flicked downwards as those plump lips moved.

'Thank you.'

He gave her a tight smile before he excused himself.

Kai waited till the door closed, letting her head hit the table hard; the coins shifted in the bag, making a cringle sound.

The pain from her forehead was hardly as sore as her feet were. She guessed she felt run down from the lack of sleep. The exhaustion finally kicked in as that adrenaline plummeted. The aching feet were probably from the lack of support — this world was in serious need of comfort for labouring workers.

The ticking of a clock started to sound off inside her room, steadily getting louder. Kai rolled her still laid head, wondering if she was hearing things. No clocks were on the surfaces, and her dirtied window was closed.

A random breeze wafted around, and the essence of a voice whispered into it, "Tick tock, tick tock. Finish the conditions before the chiming of the clock."

Kai's head whipped up; her eyes darted around the empty space. No one stood inside the room with her.

Slow movements caught Kai's attention, dragging her attention back. Words appeared on the wall. Kai's breaths came in fast, watching every letter etched into the dusty stones as if fingernails had inscribed them.

Break.

The.

Curse.

Her mouth goes dry as the ticking continues to echo. The words got bigger as the wall closed in on her.

"... Redsi?"

The ticking got louder and louder in her ears, and the room shook.

"Miss Redsi?!" Dexter's concerned voice broke Kai out of her trance.

Her dry eyes blinked at the doctor at her side, still shaking her shoulder. She snapped back to the wall in panic, the writing no longer there.

"Are you alright?" His attention dragged to her line of sight, squinting at the area. "I brought you that tonic..." he mumbled. "Drink up. You should feel its effects within minutes." Dexter picked up her unwrapped, clammy hand and placed the vial within it.

Kai hadn't even noticed when he entered or when the jug of water and the biscuits ended on the table. She tried to swallow, her wrapped-up hand running through her scalp, messing her hair up.

Dexter studied the fear drain from her eyes, returning to the moment. As she stared at this and that, he paced the room, trying to sense the source of that weird smell.

When he entered, Kai was staring at the space above her bed. Her eyes slowly moved as if something was there. Moving across it. He smelt the presence of magic, a darker magic. It had a decaying aroma mixed in with metals, but he couldn't see anything.

At least not whatever she had witnessed.

His suspicion of Kai possibly being of unnatural descent was confirmed. That strange reaction and that murky shadow that moved within her dilated pupils swayed his unsure mind.

He whispered to her, waiting until she had finally calmed down, "What did you see?"

Many emotions fleeted across her face as her head shook in denial. She opened the bottle, no bigger than her thumb, quickly downing the nutrients and slamming it to the tabletop.

"I can't help you..." he tried again, keeping his voice low. "If you don't tell me."

Whatever it was, it terrified her. He was sure of that.

Kai gave Dexter a weird smile, pretending to be distracted by the snacks on the table. The doctor decided to leave her be, his scrutinising stare returning to that wall.

Something was definitely in here, and whatever it was, Kai Redsi had the ability to see it.

Kai escaped from the doctor, who was progressively more irritating with each passing day. She wished he would stop appearing, or at least avoid her —like she did him.

Her paranoia followed her as she walked through the bright town, constantly checking over a shoulder. With every tick-sounding noise or slight breeze, Kai would freeze.

She waited to hear if that clock began or if that familiar voice would start whispering, wondering when this romance novel became a thriller.

She would wait until evening to run to Charlie and Ava and see if they saw or experienced something. She didn't want to get them into further trouble if she busted into the kitchen to tell them during work hours.

Kai chewed on her lip. *Break the curse...* repeating the words that appeared on the wall.

The novel did mention a curse, an old queen from the kingdom's history befell one, that was passed down through the generations. The details of that curse were conveniently left out, or she didn't pay close enough attention. The story's main focus elaborated on the romance with the main characters.

Her mind drifted to the Princess's Palace, to the roses that engulfed it.

Could that be it?

She pondered every detail as she found the shops to purchase smart attire. Building up her own theories to present to the others.

The sooner they broke the curse, the sooner they got to go home. This lead gave her an extra push, and feeling more confident, she was getting closer to escaping.

A bell rang as Kai opened the glass entry to the cute little boutique. She frowned at the thing above the door, knowing she would have to listen to that noise first thing tomorrow morning.

"Welcome, welcome!" The shopkeeper rushed over with arms out wide. The woman wore a dark green playsuit, a skirt exploded at the back in various colours, similarly dressed to a peacock.

Kai pulled out her notebook, shaking her head at the strange style. Writing her order up, her size and the number of things she needed, she kept Madam Barnsley's outfit in mind and chose to go with something related.

The strangely dressed shopkeeper dragged Kai around to the different clothing racks, showing her other tops to bring out her eyes and hair. Kai denied anything bright, writing she needed darker clothes for the job. She pointed at a darker rack closer to the counter full of accessories.

The less she stood out, the better.

She left after taking some ready-made items, the rest tailored and delivered. The shopkeeper's eyes nearly launched from their sockets when Kai wrote the castle as the delivery dropped. She paid the gobsmacked lady and waved a silent goodbye out the jingling door.

She was glad that was one thing sorted. Hopefully, Scarlett would leave her alone, too. Once, she looked the part.

Kai paused outside the shop, taking in the bustling town. The sky was clear, a never-ending blue sea above. The sun floodlighting down on the bright, buzzing area.

There were so many different sizes and shapes of folks strolling the streets. People bounced from stall to stall, dressed in Gilded Age fashion.

Many of the women wore such vibrant colours on top of darker ones. Their corsets tightly hugged their bodies before their skirts exploded around them after their hips. Some had long sleeves and high necklines, and others had droopy shoulders with no sleeves.

The men escorting some of these women wore long topcoats, matching the colour scheme of the ladies on their arms. On top of their heads were tall standing hats, top hats. Some with feathers, others with sparkling brooches. Many of these men were smoking pipes or some cane on their other side for show.

Kai wondered if this was what history looked like and felt as if she was witnessing what Great Britain was in its growing prime.

The stalls lining the streets sold different things. Some selling knick-knacks, others hair accessories, veggies, bags... It reminded Kai of the farmers markets her grandfather used to take her to.

The noise from the chattering folk and laughing children running with food had Kai missing home. Her gaze surveyed the fantasy world around her as fried meat and different types of pastries wafted into her senses, making her mouth water.

Kai decided to snoop around the stalls with the few coins she had left in her pockets and get some food along the way.

She stopped at a stall, chewing on a chicken skewer she bought, examining hair clips. The clips looked like something Stace would like. Catching the beaming sun, the crystals embedded within the gold and silver reflected different light colours. They appeared expensive, even if the price tag said otherwise.

Her mood soured as she missed her best friend. She wondered what Stace would make of all of this or if she would write it off as Kai officially losing her mind due to stress.

"You?"

Kai glanced at a tall, hooded man facing her direction on the other side of another grazing customer. She dismissed the moment and stepped from the stall to head for another.

"Wait, excuse me, miss?"

Kai started to weave in and around bigger groups of people, beginning to wonder if he was originally speaking to her. As she peeked back, she noticed that a hooded individual was following, attempting to push through the crowds.

His voice sounded familiar, but she couldn't pinpoint it to anyone she knew. Something muffled the man's tone.

Kai just wanted to enjoy the rest of the afternoon unbothered until she had to meet up with the others. Her day had already been eventful, to say the least. She wouldn't waste any more energy on anything else.

The man was relentless; she saw his hooded head nearby every turn she made, scanning the crowds. So, Kai pulled one of the shirts out of the brown paper carriers and wrapped her head up. Assuming her hair was probably giving away where her location was.

Many people stopped and stared at the hair. It seemed an unusual colour to these folks of browns, blacks, and blondes.

After a little game of cat and mouse, Kai successfully evaded the stranger. She decided it was a good time to return, just in case she was swindled or robbed next.

Why else could he be following me? Her inner monologue rationalised. Kai beelined for the castle walls, showing the temporary tag Barnsley had given her inside her pay. A note explained to return it tomorrow, or else.

The guards hardly glanced at it, flicking their heads to allow Kai entry.

"Hey, wait!" that voice shouted.

Kai's neck twisted, almost giving herself whiplash. That hooded man picked up the pace — catching up. His cloak swayed behind him from the speedy strides.

Kai did the first thing that came to mind and ran.

"WAIT!?"

Kai ran like her life depended on it, sprinting as fast as she could to those servant doors. She clutched the bag to her chest, her eyes pinpointing the door in the distance. Straight across the terrace, she jumped over the bushes she could, disregarding the stoned paths. Even as the man continued to yelp behind, she focused on making it to that door.

The wooden entry was meters away now, and Kai's lungs burned from the intense exercise. Someone was stepping through as Kai flew by, immediately hanging left and ascending those stairs.

Her legs hiked up, skipping a step or two.

Kai knew the moment she busted through the door; she would bring up the snacks she ate in the market.

CHAPTER EIGHTEEN

"Slow down, Charles, I don't quite understand. You're speaking too fast!" The trio was sitting on Ava's floor, the sun saying goodbye to the warm and humid day.

Kai rushed over when she could — once she was confident the hooded stranger wasn't following her anymore. Running them up to speed with her first clue, her notebook scribbled with so much information. Lines and arrows of black ink pointed around to her diagram of theories.

Charlie's face lit up, like an afterglow at dawn, reading over the notes.

Kai's head went back and forth between Charlie's hardly recognisable words and Ava's short responses of acknowledgement.

Ava gasped all of a sudden, and her rough hand shot out. She gripped Kai's forearm, a tremble in her words, "You... You got a clue?!"

Kai nodded as Charlie tapped Ava's shoulder twice.

A thick bottom lip shook, and Ava drew in a small, shaky breath. Charlie continued to explain, and with that, the grip on Kai's arm became firmer.

"It makes sense..." After calming herself down, Ava began to explain her theory. "We've been here awhile now, but unlike us, you've been projected into the midst of the plot. I'm speculating from what we were told previously and from what you've provided. But I think, with you being in the front lines, the clues will be revealed as long as we keep to the original storyline."

Kai and Charlie listened to Ava's analysis. The trio sat close in a circle, each one of their legs crossed, protecting the snacks Kai brought over from her trip to town. A candle flickered on the table, providing them light from behind Charlie. The shabby room was dimly lit but enough for the three conspirators.

"From my recollection, I'm assuming we must be somewhere between chapters thirteen and eighteen. From what the kitchen is preparing for, the ball coming up is to celebrate the engagement... So, Charles, you will look into this curse and continue what you're doing, Kai. The protagonist and male lead must fall in love. Neither can die. As much of a pain as it is, you need to stay close to Scarlett and bring her and the prince together. They are the endgame. I will ask around with the senior staff, in a roundabout way, to see if they know anything about a curse."

Kai watched Ava intensely, her head nodding in absolute to Ava's well-thought-out plan.

It made sense, considering things weren't as she knew them. The one time she fixed something from going astray, a clue was revealed from her knowledge of the book.

Charlie spoke, and Kai looked to Ava to translate.

"Fuck... I forgot about that..."

Kai's eyes went between them; anxiety bubbled in her gut at the tone Ava used. Inaudibly, she asked 'What' over and over.

Ava shook Kai's forearm. "The antagonist makes his first appearance at the ball, going after the princess, doesn't he?"

Racking her skull, Kai tried to recall the villain appearing mid-way through the novel. Warrick is injured protecting the princess but luckily fends off the antagonist.

Kai slumped her shoulders, and a hand ruffled through her hair.

The relationship between Warrick and Scarlett didn't seem very promising. With a week till the ball, Kai wondered how she would bring them together. The way Warrick stared at Scarlett came to mind, and her thoughts spiralled.

She had a feeling he would rather her demise than her hand. There was definitely no love between those two... yet.

Morning came far too quickly for Kai's liking, she grumbled, brushing her teeth with some gritty, unscented paste. Using a pathetic stick these people called a toothbrush, readying for the day. Kai missed the minty scent of Colgate and the reassurance it gave her.

There was something unpleasant about walking around smelling your own bad breath. The hygiene care in this world seriously lacked the innovation their toothpaste provided.

She decided not to put a bonnet on, considering Scarlett continued to rip it off her head. So, she plaited her hair back, with wet hands — she slicked away any strays. Kai trekked back to her room and reminded herself to wear that collar when she was closer to the princess' separate residence.

She wasn't in the mood to listen to it jingle.

Kai tucked in her dark green, long-sleeved blouse and secured it with a chunky, plain belt around the hips. Keeping everything in place. Her skirt was like Barnsley's yesterday, ankle long, double-layered, flowing around. Careful not to constrict her movements, but still gave a sophisticated air.

While she was in that boutique, Kai paid a little extra for the leather loafers at the window, asking if the shopkeeper could replace the gold chain over it with a silver one. She decided to have it match the god-awful thing dangling at her throat. If she had to wear it, she'd at least make sure it matched something with her outfit.

Let's do this!

Kai mentally cheered herself on, satisfied that she looked the part even if she was dressed years beyond her age.

The journey to the palace was quiet, the oranges of the sky spreading, the guards on shift swapping outs. She nodded her head respectfully to any of the eyes she clashed with. Kai could still feel their stares following as she proceeded on.

Holding the collar in one hidden pocket and tapping her trusty notebook in the other, she reviewed her game plan. Figuring out how she was going to bring the main characters together.

She slipped the collar on once she passed the last arched doorway, leaving the main palace, adjusting it so it wasn't as tight as Scarlett had it, giving herself room to breathe. Kai told herself to tune out the jingling or use it as a reminder that she had a plan to execute.

A reminder of her goal to get home.

She advanced towards the white palace; her pace gradually lessened as she noticed something odd. Every rose was turned, each facing her direction. The petals were wide open, flowering out from its centre. The yellow pistils watched, standing by.

"Good morning, Miss Kai."

Her stare broke from the strange occurrence regarding Madam Barnsley with a respectful and firm head nod.

The woman gave Kai a once over, and her head nodded. She seemed pleased with Kai's effort; no criticism was offered.

Unravelling the tag she had slipped into her notebook like a bookmark, Kai passed it over with two extended hands.

A grey eyebrow rose, accepting the pinkish glass tag. "I had forgotten about this…" Barnsley examined it before she stuffed it into her own skirt's pocket. "I will speak bluntly with you, girl. So far, you're doing well. Better than I anticipated and from what Bethany had to offer. However, do not let these small achievements cloud your judgement or boost your ego. Everything we do, everything we are, is for Her Highness's sake and, most importantly, for *her* future. Please continue with your ethics of obedience and loyalty. Maybe, just maybe, someday, you'll even replace me." The woman turned; her skirting spun out as she stepped toward the massive doors.

Kai fought the urge to laugh. *Fuck that, someday, my ass is gone!* Following three paces behind her senior chaperone, Kai held her chin up dignifiedly.

She knew Madam Barnsley was coming from a genuine place when it concerned the princess. Last night, before falling asleep, she recalled the woman's name from the original story.

Madam Jade Barnsley was initially Scarlett's mother's lady-in-waiting.

Jade was the only daughter of a duke, sent to the queen's side, where she stayed even after her death. Upon the queen's death, coincidently the same day as Scarlett's birth, Madam Barnsley swore to her dying companion to raise the lonely princess.

Madam Barnsley was Scarlett's biggest supporter. Kai knew it wasn't just the princess she had to be careful with, but Jade.

Kai stared at the back of Jade's head, focusing on the older woman's neatly twisted bun. The grey hairs swirled like a whirlpool to the centre, not a single hair out of place. Madam Barnsley's perfume gently cascaded off her, smelling of clean soaps and disinfectants. Kai thought about the character's role in the story and how she might use that to her advantage.

She was so absorbed in strategising that she didn't even notice the portraits on the second floor. Missing the many stares that followed, deep blue irises dragged from one corner of those painted eyes to the other.

Scarlett needed coaxing out of bed that morning; thankfully, Madam Barnsley took that job. Kai idly stood by, watching the older woman's face change when she regarded the sleepy individual. Beyond that hard exterior was a woman who unconditionally loved this princess as if she were her own child.

The women did almost everything they did yesterday; Scarlett even snapped her fingers for Kai to do her makeup once again.

"Less glam on the eyes, but do that with my cheeks." Scarlett examined her fair skin in the reflection and pointed at her face. "I want to see father's reaction."

Kai did as she was told and contoured while Madam Barnsley

straightened Scarlett's purple gown that she was to wear, trusting Kai to do her job without micromanaging.

The morning flew by. Kai kept five paces behind the gliding princess, next to Madam Barnsley. They were now on their way to the main palace's dining hall, where she was told they would be waiting elsewhere until the princess was finished.

Two guards carefully followed behind the handmaidens, who followed their mistress. They entered the main section of one of the many gardens: the queen's garden. Many Lillies were in bloom on each side of paths from a side entrance before entering the grandest of buildings. The air carried the faintest of fragrances. The yard was the quietest of any other gardens.

Person after person bowed and curtsied as they passed by, but the servants here were all stone-faced as they lowered their heads to the young heiress.

After the grand entrance opened, a white hall with red Egyptian-styled carpets stretched the polished floors, leading to another set of wall-length doors.

Barnsley signalled Kai with swift eyes and a sneaky finger point. Breaking off from following the princess, who marched towards those big stained oak doors.

Beyond that was the king. Kai was amazed and equally confused by how many more guards lined the corridor towards that entry compared to Scarlett's private residence.

The two maids entered a side sitting room, where they would have tea and a light snack, waiting for the appointment to end.

The room was spacious, and high ceilings of complicated white swirls decorated the ceiling above. A crystal chandelier hung low inside the waiting room, lighting up the space. Not a single window along any of the tall, decorated walls. The surroundings hung paintings of old royals, some on horseback amid battle, others posing as they do for self-portraits. Two extended sofas and two red and gold chairs similar to the long couches, boxed in a small table.

The table was full of snacks and steaming cups of tea.

Kai immediately dug into a moist vanilla cake and savoured the raspberry jam with custard cream at its centre. She found this part of the castle rather generic, much like its rest. It seemed to her that the glamour and luxury were mainly from Scarlett's palace. Kai wouldn't have thought this was where a king primarily resided if not for the size.

There wasn't nearly as much gold here as there was over there.

"Where did you learn to do makeup?" Jade asked while Kai was in thought.

The cake gradually slid down Kai's throat as she placed the last bite back onto the small white plate. Wiping her hands, she then pulled out her notebook.

My best friend taught me. She's even better at contouring than I am.

Barnsley's eyebrow rose, sipping the tea. Her pinkie finger found the coaster and guided the cup back to its spot in her hands. She sounded out the new word, breaking it down into three sections, "What is con-tour-ing?"

Kai explained the method she used and how enhancing facial structures or completely changing them together with a few tweaks in routine was quite a popular trend back home. She sat back and examined Jade's face, which barely reacted as she read over the notes offered.

Her voice whispered, "Interesting…"

A loud crash alerted the waiting women, followed by a frustrated scream. Barnsley shot up first, dropping the book from her lap, and hurried towards the dining room. Kai shuffled after her.

When they busted into the room, Scarlett was holding a broken glass. Her fingers were around the thin base as she pointed its sharp, broken edges at a guest sitting across from her.

The king, who looked exactly like the princess, was shouting at his daughter's animalistic behaviour at the head of the long table. Guards had surrounded the princess, their swords drawn. Who each eyed up the guards on the opposite side. Those soldiers, too, had their swords drawn and ready.

Prince Warrick was the only indifferent one, still sitting elegantly cutting his breakfast. Two hands held the polished utensils, his knife cutting into a thick piece of gammon. The chaos - or the fact the woman across from him - had a weapon, didn't seem to faze. Warrick seemed more interested in the juicy piece of ham on his plate.

Kai mimicked Barnsley's lead, who rushed for the princess to calm her down. She took it upon herself to remove the broken flute shaking in Scarlett's hand while Barnsley got the princess's attention.

"YOU DISGRACE ME, YOU UNGRATEFUL CHILD!"

Warrick set down his silverware, beginning to address King Tyrell, "Your Majesty, it's quite all..." his voice trailed off as bright red hair bobbed about across.

That individual was trying to snatch that broken glass away from the crazed princess; her straight spine faced him.

Scarlett was now shouting back at her father, "IF YOU LIKE HIM SO MUCH, THEN YOU MARRY THE FOOL!"

Kai grabbed the glass in the nick of time before Scarlett could turn it on the king. She used her wrapped-up hand so she didn't get sliced up; her heart was in her throat.

Usually, when drunks in the tavern pulled stunts like this, Zac would handle it while she called the police. She began to appreciate Zachary's bravery now that she was experiencing it first-hand in such a close encounter.

Madam Barnsley was still attempting to quell the enraged woman, a hand on her back. Another firmly on Scarlett's shoulder, which kept her from breaking away.

"GET HER OUT OF HERE!" the king bellowed as his hands frantically waved dismissively in front of him. Guards stepped forth with his command, herding the three women out.

Kai swiftly dropped the broken flute on the table, her hands showing the guards she wasn't armed as she swiftly curtsied to the huffing king. She spun on her heels and followed Barnsley.

The Crown Prince was paralysed in his seat, gawking at their guarded exit.

CHAPTER NINETEEN

After a guarded escort back to the separate palace, Jade guided Scarlett to a luxurious sitting room on the first floor. She snapped at the hovering servants to scram while Kai promptly scampered away to fetch some refreshments.

When Kai returned, she thought Barnsley had successfully calmed the princess down. Scarlett even had something to drink from what she offered.

Curtsying, Kai backed away from the coffee table. It was evident that Scarlett still seethed with silent anger as her right eye twitched staring at her drink.

"What happened, flower," Jade rubbed Scarlett's back, cooing to her.

Kai bit the inside of her cheek, feeling like she had imposed on a private moment. She turned, choosing to close the wide doors, not knowing if she may have been allowed to leave.

"That imbecile suggested I was to be a queen..." Scarlett's aggrieved tone started. "Not empress, QUEEN!" The sound of a table flipping over followed, and its contents crashed to the floor.

Jade gasped in surprise, a mix of grief in her sharp breath.

Kai spun around in alarm and slammed her spine against the solid material.

"WHO DOES HE THINK HE IS!?"

Like lightning, Kai stepped over, immediately clearing up the mess and

Jade shot up from her seat. Following around the pacing, the enraged princess.

"HE IS INSULTING ME!" Scarlett stopped abruptly, shoving off Barnsley's motherly touch. Her glare pinned to the red-haired maid on her knees, trying to pick up the scattered items. "He is, isn't he?" she whispered.

Without notice, Kai was yanked up from the ground, a crazy face suddenly in hers.

"HE'S INSULTING ME, ISN'T HE?!"

Jade flew towards them, trying to stop Scarlett from shaking the wide-eyed girl. "SHE IS MUTE, PRINCESS!"

Scarlett let go of Kai, her hands diving into her scalp and pulling at the hair. The light makeup was already smudged under Scarlett's crazy eyes, black smeared downwards as if fingers clawed from them.

Kai staggered, her breathing coming in quick. She knew she needed to calm Scarlett down and reverse the distance between the characters.

Her hands patted down her pockets, alerted by the fact she had left her notebook behind. Kai searched for the drawers at the gilded side tables along the walls.

Jade still coaxed the crazed protagonist, "Shhh, don't pull at your beautiful hair... It's alright... It's alright."

Kai found some stationary items and wrote faster than a time crunch for her exams. She continued to talk to herself, a firm reminder to steady her breaths. Kai presented an answer with a hesitant head incline, hoping this did the trick.

Scarlett swiped the paper, drifting back. Her face scanned the page as if it held the meaning of life upon it. She read Kai's words in a questionable tone, "Perhaps he is considering... the stress of running an empire? Slowly easing you in as his empress?" Her psychotic face looked at Kai.

Kai nodded sharply, gaze finding Barnsley for support.

"Yes, reasonable and thoughtful..." Jade took that silent cue. Shuffling to the side, she was again within reaching distance of the princess. "Perhaps you should calm down. This isn't good for your health. We'll arrange to discuss this further with His Highness another day."

Scarlett stared at Kai, her eyes going from the paper to hers. "Do you really think so?"

For a brief second, Kai wasn't looking at a crazy, ill-tempered princess but a scared little girl. Kai couldn't help but feel the person before her was desperate for something… much like she was.

All she could offer the small, trembling child was a tight smile.

Barnsley closed the door carefully to Scarlett's bedroom as Kai waited patiently just outside. She could see the exhaustion on the woman's features and wished she could offer comforting words. It wouldn't have been nearly as sincere if she tried to write everything out. Instead, she reached and rubbed Jade's arm. Surprising the woman as a result.

'Are you okay?' she asked.

Jade's stare shook as she gestured silently. They walked away from the door, heading to the first floor.

Madam Barnsley walked with Kai to the kitchen, where Jade slumped into a chair. Kai quietly, too, save for the jiggling at her throat.

"I'm sorry about that…" Barnsley's voice wavered, her wrinkled, spotted hand toyed with the other. "She's not a bad child… she's… she's…"

Kai reached again; a gentle hand laid on Jade's. 'Scared,' she mouthed, surveying the emotions that seeped into Barnsley's face.

Jade watched Kai's lips and nodded her head. "I'm all she's ever had… She doesn't react well to sudden changes; she needs to feel involved. She's… She's easily frightened, masking her fear with anger… She's not a bad child." Jade repeated, a thumb pressed to Kai's resting hand.

Even as the tired face dropped, staring at her lap, she continued whispering those exact words.

Kai got up and decided to make the woman a warm camomile tea. Letting her have a moment to gather herself.

The two sat in the quiet kitchen as servants popped in and out doing their jobs. Fleeing away the moment they noticed Jade sitting there. The sun poured in from the surrounding windows, the bright walls making the room even more brilliant. Kai set two cups at the small wooden table and reclaimed her seat, sliding one to the silent handmaiden.

"Her Highness never had the queen at her side..." Madam Barnsley began telling Kai a tale.

How Jade raised Scarlett herself, how the king hardly visited. And when he did, it was only ever nasty remarks spat at the princess. Wishing it had been a prince born. Jade told Kai everything she already knew, but Kai nodded along anyway. Listening to the poor woman bleed her heart out.

"It's that damned curse..." Jade said, catching Kai's undivided attention. Her hazels were lined with silver. "If only it didn't exist... If only it went away... maybe my Scarlett wouldn't be so afraid."

Kai touched Jade's still fidgeting hands, pausing her. 'What curse?' Her eyes darted between those teary ones.

Madam Barnsley sobered up with that slip-up. "I'm sorry... I shouldn't have said that." She stood quickly and straightened out her skirting. Her eyes hardened as if she could suck those tears straight back in. "Swear to me, you won't repeat any of this elsewhere?"

Kai observed the lightning-speed change, tucking away the slip of information. Her hands gestured to her throat, shrugging in response.

Madam Barnsley excused Kai for the rest of the afternoon since Scarlett had chosen to spend it behind her sealed doors.

Kai used the opportunity given to her and raced back towards the main palace. Hoping her notebook was still in that waiting room. She hastily turned a corner, nearly colliding with a solid chest.

Violet eyes stared down at her, an eyebrow cocked. "Have you learned nothing?"

Kai bowed swiftly and then stepped around him. She needed that notebook; she didn't have time for this guy's crap.

That silk voice spoke up and stopped Kai, "If you're going back for this, I wouldn't bother."

She turned promptly; Dexter held up a familiar grey book. Doodles were drawn on the corners of it, confirming to her it was the one she was currently searching for as her stomach dropped.

"I think you and I need to have a little chat."

All sounds drained away as Kai stared at her notebook. *He didn't read it, did he?* She couldn't remember if she ripped out all the contents of her game plan from the book. Usually, she stashed the sheets between her mattresses. But the days were always hectic, and her luck was so poor.

She felt as though she had missed something.

Dexter twisted, speaking over a shoulder, "Come." He walked off in significant strides without glancing back.

All Kai could do was pray as she followed along nervously.

Dexter walked through corridors, past two different kinds of gardens, and swerved towards cleverly hidden stairs near a draining outlet. Kai kept a healthy distance; her heart pounded in her ears, and her hands were clammy. Down those stairs, she found Dexter opened a rusted iron gate, which popped out from the side of the castle's walls.

He offered his hand to Kai. "The path is narrow and steep. Allow me."

Kai tried not to tremble, placing her hand into his as he guided her down it. Wild bushes and shrubs closed in the path; bugs of all sorts whizzed by.

She wondered if he could feel her heartbeat thumping in her sweaty palms as she did.

They walked for a few minutes, steadily descending, and eventually appeared before a small lake. A hill clipped off, enclosing it, a high cliff and a waterfall dropped into the lake directly across from where they stood.

"I've come here for years," Dexter's words were low, next to Kai's ear, sending a shiver throughout her. "It's a good place to chat without someone accidentally eavesdropping." He released her hand and jumped down a small ledge. Waiting below, Dexter offered support to Kai.

A head shook as Kai landed next to him with a small leap.

The doctor offered nothing more as he walked over to a decent-sized boulder and sat.

Kai stood there, waiting for him to begin.

Dexter stared out at that waterfall, continuously pouring down. His eyes dragged to Kai's anxiously waiting ones. He noticed the little lady was dressed smartly, not that he was entirely surprised. Considering who she was representing now.

He found this suited her better, except for that horrible thing around her throat.

Dexter retrieved the notebook from the coat's inner pocket, holding it up. He extended his empty hand out. "A trade. You give me that ridiculous collar, and I give you the book."

A curious expression crossed her features as she hesitantly removed the item. Inching over, Kai passed over her collar, careful the book was given over into her palm simultaneously.

Dexter accepted; his fingers coiled around just as Kai gripped the book. The doctor tossed the horrible ringing thing into the lake the next second.

Kai scrambled towards the lakeside in an attempt to rush after it. The notebook clutched closely to her.

The jingling bell hit the surface with a splash and was forever silenced and swallowed by the dark water. Her nasty scowl twisted for the man sat calmly behind, watching still.

"You are not a slave, Kai Redsi. Or a pet, or someone's plaything... Surely, I needn't remind you of this?" The wind picked up, bringing in a warm breeze as the doctor continued, "She's a tyrant, Kai, much worse than her father. Do not be fooled for a second by her false sincerity."

The muted lady prevailed to stare at him with those curious eyes, that scowl softening, and for a moment, he wished time would stand still.

The late afternoon sun beamed off the top of her head as an orange glow of light hovered. The wind ruffled her long dark skirt and the loose fabrics of her blouse's sleeves, which caused them to sway in the same rhythm as the long grass surrounding the lakeside. The waterfall beside her in the distance added to the unreal image as she hugged that book.

It gave him a strange sense of déjà vu.

His gaze darted away, knowing he was staring far too long. Clearing his throat, he decided to be forthright, "I won't lie to you... but I had a flick through that book." He caught the way her fingers clenched from the side as if she were protecting something precious within it. "You're trying to break the curse," he stated, staring at the ripples in the lake.

Cursing at herself for her carelessness, Kai swallowed. She didn't see a reason to lie about that as she hesitantly nodded.

"I've been trying to break it, too." Dexter stood, brushing himself off. "Is that why you're here?" His surreal irises were back on Kai. There were undertones of different blues within his eyes, which sparkled as the peaked sun hit them.

Kai inclined her head again, mentally debating.

He couldn't know any more than that. Kai was glad for once; she didn't have a voice so that she couldn't slip up with words at any pressing moment. She didn't think the people here would believe her if she admitted this was just a story.

A fictitious novel she read growing up.

"I suspected you," the man suddenly said. "The way your hand healed, it was... unnatural."

Kai stiffened.

"The way you hardly reacted when I did this." Dexter lifted his hand, a violet flame brighter than his irises conjured at the palm. "Even now..." The shades within his eyes glowed brighter, flickering like the flame, watching her. "Any normal person would have freaked out... but you... it's like you're used to it. As if you knew all along that I was a wizard."

Kai slowly moved her head, aware now of how he had been observing her the last couple of days.

She was giving away vital details with her body language, regardless of being unable to speak.

"And yesterday..." Dexter's hand went down, and the flame flickered to nothing, brushing against the side of his trousers. "I smelt strange magic in your room as you stared off, petrified. Something dark moved within your eyes. I couldn't see it with us... but you did."

Kai felt her eyes widen; it sounded like he was describing what she had witnessed when she saw something dark move within Vanessa's eyes.

"I want to offer a partnership." That hand Dexter used to conjure flames raised, waiting. "Work with me... and we'll break this curse together."

Eyes blinked at that waiting offer; Kai was slightly confused. She was pretty confident that those were the lines meant for Prince Warrick.

CHAPTER TWENTY

The last bit of the day's light was being chased away by dark clouds rolling in. Kai quietly strolled with Dexter, who was escorting her back to her room, silent too.

Her mind was racing. She needed to tell the others and get their approval before she told Dexter of their involvement. They all needed to be on the same page on what to feed this character.

No one could know this was just a book.

She didn't even want to begin thinking about the calamity that would follow by doing so. She sighed deeply, kicking a stone in her path. Things were getting more and more complicated, all due to her negligence.

"There you are!"

Regarding Dexter at the side, Kai stopped as they both turned to that voice.

Prince Warrick smiled wide, quickly jogging over from the stoned walkway. His eyes were unable to stay on one spot, surveying the woman.

His aide threw his papers into the air behind the prince in the distance—over his shenanigans at this point.

Dexter and Kai both paid their respects. She wondered if she had passed the part where these two became friends or was about to witness it blossom first-hand. She drew a deep breath, trying not to seem too eager to watch this play out.

Dexter thankfully spoke on both their behalf, "We greet the defending sword of the South. We welcome you, Prince Warrick Crestblood, Crown Prince of the Raevegon Empire. I am Dexter Ubar, physician to the Rosethorne Palace."

Warrick's blazing golds never left the curtsied lady. "You may both rise." Waiting to hear the girl speak next, introducing herself.

When Kai rose, she was met with a bright, expecting ogle. She tried not to baulk back as her hand slapped Dexter to the side in reflex.

"Oh, yes… my apologies." Dexter gave Kai a side look, and his lips twitched with her contact. "Your Grace. This maid is mute. Please excuse her manners."

Warrick finally broke his stare regarding the doctor, "She's mute? And what is her name?"

There was a long pause as Kai side-eyed the doctor, straining her eyes. His face was neutral, but his eyes screamed in some strange defiance, roaring to life like the flames he could conjure in his hands.

Her breath hitched when the doctor finally spoke.

"I'm not sure, Your Grace." Lying through his perfectly straight teeth, "I was trying to find that out as well…" He glanced at Kai and then back to Warrick. "I was just on my way to pay a visit to her superior."

The prince began patting himself down, his attention dashed to his aide, who was exasperated, leant against a wall.

"Hold on, I will go retrieve some paper. Please, excuse me for a moment." His long legs quickly worked to where that man stood across the courtyard.

Dexter gripped Kai's hand when his back was turned, pulling her away. The doctor ran away from the scene and dragged Kai along, too, in silent protest.

"Roger, Roger! Give me paper and something to write with quickly!" Warrick jogged up to his aide and puffed with excitement.

The middle-aged man squinted at the prince. "What for, Your Grace?"

The prince's words rushed out as he impatiently waited for the items, "I found her, that red-haired lady. She's mute, though, so I need paper!"

Roger raised a thick brow, gazing over the prince's tall shoulder. "You mean, the one that keeps running away?"

Warrick smiled. "Yes, her. She's just over-"

He turned and found the area empty.

"She ran away, or rather, she was dragged away, Your Grace." Roger huffed, "Now, since that's over, can we please review these reports? I want to go to bed at a decent time tonight."

Warrick's head bobbed, wondering where she was taken. He was sure he had told them to wait, but then again, the little lady also seemed to have an issue with her hearing.

He smiled to himself, twisting back to Roger. A mischievous glint began in his eyes. "What was the head butler's name? I wish to speak to him."

Kai finally yanked her hand free from Dexter's clenched one, breathing hard. His legs were much longer than hers and could cover more ground — making his jogging — her running. Her legs ached from being dragged up the stairs, and her lungs burned for trying to keep up.

Dexter let out a deep sigh, turning to the miserable-looking woman leaning against the wall in the stairwell.

Kai gave him eyes and gestured her hands behind, back down the steps.

A smile cracked out of the doctor, taking in the angry, miming woman. "I'm sorry, you just looked... worried... I acted on impulse."

Kai's jaw dropped. She put her hands up in defeat, done with today.

It was the first time she broke out in an actual sweat, and now she desperately needed a relaxing bath. She mouthed a 'Thank you' to the doctor and bowed her head before passing him on the steps.

His hand gently grabbed her wrist, subtly tugging her to stay.

There was a look Kai had never seen before on his face as she glimpsed down.

"Don't worry... I'll think of something if this comes back to bite us."

Kai's brow raised, mouthing more manners. She left the doctor standing there, alone, wondering what that was about.

She stomped up the remaining steps, her legs shaking with each lift. She thought it best to visit Ava first, above the floor the bathroom was on, and then bathe. So, she just needed to walk down the stairs after all that running.

Kai knocked on the familiar door, Charlie opening it with a big smile.

She drove straight into today's events, throwing ripped-out sheets to Charlie as she continued writing.

The boy's face went greenish as he read the notes over out loud.

Ava placed snacks around; her hands paused from feeling the empty spaces. "Makes sense... the princess is a descendent of the historically cursed queen."

When Charlie got to the part about the wizard doctor knowing, Ava flinched, drawing her hands back in defence.

Kai looked at her in concern and then at Charlie. She didn't like that reaction or how Ava then reached and squeezed Charlie's hand as if they were telepathically debating something without her.

"Do you recall why the wizard was hiding in the novel?"

Kai mused over it for a moment before shaking her head.

Charlie tapped Ava once with his thumb on her hand, signalling her of Kai's answer.

Ava continued with that confirmation, "Well, we wanted to know... So, we searched the archives for the Ubar last name. Only, it doesn't exist. This led us to start looking into sorcerers who were executed and found archives that went all the way back to the first witch's name. The one who cursed the first Rosethorne queen, known as Elphaba Ravena Alus. She was practically a goddess of her kind."

Kai listened intently, Charlie nodding in thought.

"I'm not sure how reliable the material is, but we should be cautious." Ava swallowed, leaning in, her voice barely above a whisper, "What if Dexter Ubar is here to do damage to the royal family... they condemned his kind, did they not?"

Kai made a strange noise as the air evaporated from her lungs.

"Maybe…" Ava put a short finger up, her hand riddled with minor cuts. "He's trying to break the curse to redeem his kins honour, or he's trying to ensure it does *not* get broken…"

Charlie rubbed the back of Ava's hand as he spoke, "Weir shund sherr da burndon."

Ava was nodding now, too, as she reached for Kai's hand. "You can tell him about us. We'll share this burden with you. However, we should proceed cautiously with how much we divulge to him… I don't like the vibes he gives off…"

Kai left after silent snacks, the trio each in deep thought. She went down the stairwell, finally for a bath, surprised by the visitor inside.

Mary was neck deep in the water, her head back and eyes closed.

Kai started to drag her feet, hoping to alert her of her presence. Not wishing to spook the girl with a silent approach.

Mary's head angled; a smile offered as her eyes opened. "Hey Kai, you're just in time. The water is perfect tonight."

Kai joined Mary as Mary ran Kai up to speed with the gossip spreading since the explosive reaction at the morning dinner. Apparently, the servants were speaking ill of the princess, many saying that her temper would start a war between the kingdom and the southern empire.

"I just don't understand… the princess used to be so lovely and soft-spoken." Mary shook her head, adding, "The moment she hit puberty, it's like she became another person."

Kai played with the water, causing ripples to flow away from her, listening as Mary rambled about politics. Something that didn't interest Kai.

"Our kingdom would prosper joining the empire… as a princess, you'd think she'd have better training to control herself."

Kai stopped and observed Mary now. It was the first time she'd ever heard her complain about something.

"I'm sorry, I shouldn't say such blasphemy... I'm just worried." Mary's browns met blues. "Off topic, but they speak of you, you know?"

Kai's head tilted, wondering what she was talking about.

"The king has now inquired about the bright-haired girl at his daughter's side, wearing a bell. An investigation was opened after hearing one of the doctor's complaints. It appears it was Bethany who offered the collar, suggesting it to the princess. She has been booted from the palace just this afternoon." Mary nodded at the wide, frosty eyes staring at her in bewilderment. "His Majesty flew into a fit when he heard the handmaiden influenced the princess to do something so disgusting... She'll never be able to get another serving position in this kingdom," Mary added.

Kai's facial expressions constantly change, like the coming of the seasons making Mary wish she could speak. She wondered what kind of things the girl would say if she could or if her voice was nearly as appealing as her cute expressions.

"Rather than countering with schemes of your own and promotion of power, you just went along with it complacently..." Mary smiled softly, admiring that fact. "Keep doing what you're doing, Kai. If no one has told you, you're doing a splendid job. I think you're exactly where you need to be... You're loved by your fellow people."

Mary left shortly after her speech, which was meant to encourage Kai. Instead, it left her stranded down a rabbit hole. She was repeating her words over and over.

'You're loved by your fellow people...'

Those were the exact words that Vanessa had told her to say. She couldn't shake the ominous feeling after Mary left, recalling how different this world was from the written one she knew on paper.

Vanessa's words echoed inside her mind, overlapping the haunting replay already swirling.

'That old thing? I wrote that when I was just starting...'

Kai quickly jumped from the water, scrambling to return to her room. The walk was a blur as her mind dissected every microscopic thing.

She locked the door, going over all her notes under her mattress.

Cursing, Kai threw the sheets around, wishing she had her phone so she could google when the book was published. She could briefly recall seeing '19' on the title versa page, skipping over the bits that didn't add anything to the story.

She wondered if Vanessa was *actually the author's name...*

The flame from the candle on the table ignited higher, and Kai flinched back from the notes as a strange shadow expanded on the floor.

Just as she caught her breath from the strange moment, a knock at the door had her fumbling to hide the pages.

CHAPTER TWENTY-ONE

K   ai stepped for the door as the knocking started again, realising she was
         still wrapped in her towel. She hurried for her wardrobe heaving out
         a thick robe and throwing it on.

Pennel's voice began on the other side of the solid wood, "She may be asleep, sir. Our employees work long days. Can this not wait until morning?"

A deep, gruffly voice responded to him, but Kai couldn't quite catch what was said.

She unlocked the door and jarred it open, peaking as she hid behind it, greeted by Pennel and another individual dressed in a military-style uniform.

The emblem of a sword within a shield, at his shoulders.

"My apologies, miss, if we woke you." Pennel gave a strange look to Kai's peeking face, his shaking. The older man looked worried about the individual next to him. Deep lines were evident under the head help's eyes and forehead.

Kai also shook her head, mouthing, 'It's fine.'

"My sincere apologies, my lady, for disturbing you." The gentleman neatly dressed next to Pennel spoke, "His Highness had a message to pass along. To the little lady who continues to evade him."

Both Pennel and Kai moved back in surprise. Pennel's gawk turned to Kai—a questioning gaze on his ageing face.

A letter was presented, and a silver seal secured it shut.

Kai looked at it and then at Pennel, shrugging. When the old man went to reach for the letter, the soldier pulled it away.

"His Highness has requested that I see the lady receiving it in her *own* hands." Those dark eyes squinted at Pennel.

The letter held out once more for the hiding woman.

Kai defiantly narrowed her eyes at the man, and a hand snatched the paper. Only then to shove it over to Pennel with such sass.

This caused the man to make a noise as Pennel respectfully inclined his chin to Kai.

"My orders are-"

A finger raised, and then Kai scurried further inside, swiping the notebook off her table. She returned to her cracked open door and finished her scribble, showing her explanation.

> Your objective was completed. I received the letter with my own hands. Excuse my rudeness, as I do find it odd I'm even receiving one. I will not be dragged into some ploy; my loyalty is to the Rosethorne Kingdom.
>
> I apologise in advance if this offends you.

The gentleman next to Pennel frowned as Pennel himself nodded. "Thank you, Miss Redsi. It seems you're doing better than expected." He smiled at her, his attention next to the gentleman. "Miss Redsi, as I have explained, personally tends to Her Highness. She must be extra careful when receiving things from foreign guests. She does not mean to offend you or your superiors. The girl is just following our protocols."

The man's thick eyebrows bunched forward, that frown still on the woman. "Are you suggesting scheming intent? That the Crown Prince would be trying to get information off you?"

Kai shrugged nonchalantly, eyes back down on the pages in her hand. The tip of the grey feather flopped back and forth as she continued to write. Her little pink tongue poked out from between her lips.

> Pennel will open the letter, and if it isn't anything suspicious, I'll take it.

The man scowled further. "This is disgraceful. You dare insult-"

Kai raised her hand and rudely stopped the man from ranting again. She could have sworn she had seen steam emitting off his head as she peered down to write.

> I am insulted you think so little of my health to wake me. It's disgraceful and shameless to show up at a woman's door in the middle of the night. Someone might assume this was suspicious.

Pennel's corners twitched. Whether he was upset or not was uncertain. "Rightly so," he began. "I suggested this was to wait till morning to avoid any misunderstandings."

Kai had no idea if anger or shame caused red to explode up the foreign man's thick neck, but she was glad there was a door between them. This way, he couldn't see her knees clack together from her pretend front.

His chin went up as he spun on his heels and marched away, back straight as a board.

When he disappeared, Pennel faced Kai with a crooked smile. "I commend you. We can't have these Imperial brutes bullying us around like that. Just because we are the smaller kingdom." He offered her the letter.

Kai shook and gestured the hand holding the quill to look at it, himself.

Pennel was glad the girl continued to stick to her principles, passing a test he secretly took on her.

Suspicious himself if she was in cohorts with the empire.

He peeled open the seal and scanned the words with confusion. "You keep running away from His Highness?" His ageing eyes glanced up at the quiet woman.

Kai shrugged, having no idea what he was referencing. Today was the first time she came face to face with the male lead.

Pennel pointed at the neat handwriting. "He states on numerous occasions?"

A page was flipped, and Kai wrote what she thought he may have been implying for the butler.

I may have misunderstood his actions earlier. When he walked away, the doctor and I left, too. You can check with Doctor Ubar to confirm.

Pennel closed the letter, returning it. "I see… Well, there isn't anything alarming as far as I am concerned. But I suggest you burn it after reading it yourself." His voice lowered slightly, "I will have the servants near to keep an eye on him. If the prince is harassing you, please report it. I do not need to remind you that he is to be engaged to Her Highness… stay vigilant."

Kai idly nodded, wondering where this was coming from.

"Anyways, keep up the good work. Please, excuse me." Pennel inclined his head, leaving Kai standing there with the letter.

She waved at his disappearing back and then locked the door. Tossing the notebook mindlessly on the bed, she opened the letter with a thumb.

Beautiful handwriting filled most of the page, and many of the letters swirled with long elegant tails. Her cheeks burned as she investigated further than the lines Pennel had referenced. She didn't bother reading the rest, or rather couldn't.

Kai rushed to the candle, igniting the letter. The parchment paper flared with light, being devoured from the flame.

As she watched the paper burn, she understood Pennel's warning. Vowing to keep out of sight from this just-as-crazy prince with the last cinders flickering to nothing on the table.

The captain marched towards a private royal suite in the guest wing of the central palace. His march was more of a stomp, headed over to report to the Crown Prince and his childhood friend.

He found Warrick sitting on the edge of a stone patio wall outside the private suite, staring at the stars peeking from the gaps in the clouds. With paper and pencils in his lap, there was a faint smile playing on the prince's lips.

Something he found Warrick doing a lot, privately, as of late.

"Your Grace." The captain bowed.

Warrick stood, and all the pencils in his lap fell to the ground and scattered. "You delivered it, then?" His golden eyes waited.

The captain thought about his words before carefully speaking, and his thumbs tapped his thighs. "Please, excuse me if I am overstepping… What exactly was within that letter?"

The prince smiled again, obvious this time, stunning the captain.

"She has a lovely name, doesn't she?" Warrick peered down to the paper in his large hands, led from the pencils smeared on the sides of his palms. "It suits her beautiful features…" he mumbled, staring at the sketch.

"That's what you wrote?" the captain asked.

Warrick chuckled, "No. I asked the lady for a moment of her time and pointed out she continued running away from me before I could do so."

Puzzled brown eyes stared at the prince; the captain's voice was full of suspicion, "That's it?"

"No…" Warrick showed his friend the sketch he drew. "Darren, I think I'm in love with her."

Darren glanced at the sheet, acknowledged the attempt to draw the maid, and then back to the prince. "You are joking, right?"

Warrick shook, a hand running through his thick hair, forcing it back. Led from his palms smeared on the flesh between his forehead and hairline. "I am not."

"WHEN THE HELL DID THIS HAPPEN!?"

Warrick sat as his eyes locked on the sketch. He began to explain to the captain the first time he saw the girl.

First, running down the halls, tears brimmed in her sparkling eyes. Something deep within him ached, and he was chasing after the quick fox without even realising it.

Disappointment festered when he couldn't find her as she disappeared into thin air.

Then, he ran into her in town. Her bright red hair was a beacon, calling to him. She was grinning sadly at the hair clips displayed. And again, he never got a moment to speak with her as she evaded a second time, swerving into the crowds like a trained assassin.

"I got sidetracked chasing her; that's why it took me so long to return yesterday."

He admitted he was distracted during his investigation, but once the prince finished, he hastily returned. Only he saw bright red hair poking out from under a wrapped-up head and tried to catch the girl once more.

It frustrated him how this woman continued to flee and successfully got away.

Of all his twenty-six years, whatever he set his mind to, whatever his goals or aims had been, he obtained them.

Yet somehow, this petite, quiet woman was always a step ahead.

"Honestly, I don't know if she was ever trained, but our soldiers could use a lesson or two." Warrick laughed. "Then, this morning, when I was having breakfast with that rudely mannered woman and the king... I thought about her, and that bright red hair appeared before me. Bravely removing that glass from the princess, I noticed she already had a wound on her hand..."

A frown took over his handsome face, wondering if Scarlett was the cause.

"Did you know she wore a slave collar?" He glanced at Darren, spacing out on him. Observing through the man, as if Kai stood there. "It had a dangling silver bell attached to it... how humiliating that must have been. Then I found out the poor woman can't even speak, isn't even able to stand up for herself." His hands clenched, crimpling the edges of the paper.

In panic, he loosened his grip, smoothing out the sides.

"I think she can stand up for herself just fine. Voice or no voice."

Warrick paused his fretting. "What do you mean?"

Darren crossed his muscular arms, briefing him on his mission, "She was insulted that I thought so little of her health. Called me shameless for appearing at her door so late."

A huge smile erupted on the prince's face, and all his white teeth showed. That smile reached his eyes as they, too, began to glow with the same intensity as the sun.

The captain continued, not finding this amusing, "That head butler would have read the note. She insisted he read it to ensure nothing suspicious was written within…"

"She's loyal to her kingdom. That's a good thing, Darren."

The captain shook his head. "This could become a problem… maybe not so much for you, but for her."

That smile was wiped clean from Warrick's face.

"If your betrothed found out you fancied her handmaiden over her… That slave collar around the girl's throat should be the least of your worries."

Chapter Twenty-Two

K ai waddled out from the last corridor, heading toward the Princess's Palace. Note tightly clenched in her hands. She needed to present it to Madam Barnsley, hoping the princess didn't blame her for not having the collar.

She didn't care if Dexter got in trouble for it. She never gave him consent to throw that thing away, to begin with.

Leisure steps paused, catching small movements around the estate. The roses turned towards Kai, this time noticeably. Even the ones under the balconies twisted away from the building and angled down towards her.

"You may head on in."

Her head snapped to the guard stationed a few feet to the side.

His eyes stared at Kai, even though his head was still forward. "Lady Barnsley ordered us to allow you entry as she's rather busy this morning. You are to head on in, miss."

Kai bowed her head to the armoured gentleman and climbed the white stone steps.

Her attention was lured to the flowers as theirs was to her.

The palace was bustling with servants; some dusted things down, and others carried long curtains to and from rooms. The place was much noisier than what she was used to these last few days.

Kai headed for the stairs towards the second floor to begin her routine, curiosity brewing.

"Ah, you're here, good." Jade was smoothing out a dark green sparkling gown in Scarlett's dressing room. "We have a guest coming today. Our Rose will be a tad bit thornier. Keep your wits."

Kai silently approached Madam Barnsley with the note offered.

The older maiden took it carefully and read it over. "Ah... she will most likely be displeased by this... Luckily, we have someone to blame it on. I'll speak to her. Just be aware she may try to find more things to critique you for. So, in the meantime, do your best, and no matter what happens today, do *not* intervene in conversations. Even if you have her best interest at heart."

A sigh of relief slipped past Kai's lips as she mouthed a 'Thank you' to the woman.

She immediately dived into her tasks, filling the gold tub next door with boiling water and flower petals and adding subtle fresh scents of oils into the mix.

Surprisingly, the princess was not as upset as Kai imagined she would be. She scowled as Barnsley explained and snapped at Kai for not protecting it better. But overall, the princess's remarks were saved for Dexter as they got her ready for the day.

"That man is forgetting his place," she hissed as Kai washed her long hair. The strands went a deeper shade with the water poured on it. Scarlett leaned into Kai's touch as she massaged the shampoos into her scalp with one hand. "He dared to bring this up with father. Did you know this?" Those deep blue eyes were open, eyeballing the woman above.

Kai frowned, shaking a head in response.

Mary *had* told her, but the last thing she wanted to do was potentially set the princess off for gossiping with others.

"He's a sly, handsome bastard... I can't believe I thought something of him once." Scarlett's hand came down, hitting the murky water. "If there is one thing I have learned, love is for the weak."

Madam Barnsley and Kai listened to Scarlett moan all morning, neither interrupting.

Silently, they both carried on with meticulously tending to her.

Kai had just finished doing her makeup and placed the brushes in a tub to be cleaned later.

"I quite liked the collar around your neck..." Scarlett teased, "What did you think of it, pet?" She surveyed Kai, collecting the used tools.

The maid paused, shrugging. Her focus never broke away from her task.

Scarlett smiled a sinister grin at the plain answer. "You don't care about much, do you? Most women would have run away by now." She lifted her arms as Madam Barnsley tightened the corset. "Or they would have been thrown away for pissing me off... I didn't mind Bethany, but she only flattered me because she liked the benefits, that much I know..." She mindlessly talked, letting the older woman work at her hips. "Why don't you run away, pet? What benefits are you in for?"

Kai shrugged again, causing Scarlett to laugh a snort.

"You can tell me. You have my highly valued word that I won't get angry. Though, if you choose not to tell me, and I figure it out... then not even the king can save you." Her blues squinted, observing for any subtle reaction to her words.

The maid glanced up, blinking those big eyes as she slightly frowned. As if she had no idea why.

Kai knew she couldn't tell the princess she was trying to break the curse. Or the fact, she was trying to bring her and Warrick together - so she could get the hell out of here. Kai shook her head and pulled out the notebook, her quill tucked inside.

Scarlett felt anxious, watching on as the muted maid wrote.

The tip of her pink tongue slipped out between her lips, focused on her answer.

When the book was shown, Scarlett immediately read the words turned over to her, "I just wanted to live a different life. A change to my stressful and sad existence."

Jade faltered, tying the corset, and her eyes widened. It appeared to Kai that those were not a good choice of words.

Scarlett took the book, rereading it. Slower to herself as if she was trying to digest Kai's words, her deep-sea blues crashed with icy ones.

"What was so sad about it?"

The princess noticed that glaze over with her question, realising that the look she often caught on the muted girl's face... was one of sorrow.

The same look her father had on his face when he would stand before her mother's massive paintings in the corridors.

Kai swallowed, mouthing three words that Scarlett made out straight away. She closed the notebook, returning it to her new handmaiden. "How did they die?"

The muted maid turned those eyes down, and Scarlett noticed her chest falter as it rose with her breaths. A trembling hand wrote another three words, slower this time, before offering the page.

The words had deeper indents into the flimsy material as if the pain was still heavy upon her hands.

The handmaiden kept her face concealed. Vibrant hair covered Scarlett's view, but the girl's weird breathing was telling enough.

Scarlett stared at the three words, burning them into her mind.

They were killed.

"What a shame." The princess left Kai alone after that, with only a few words offered.

Madam Barnsley was even throwing her pitiful stares afterwards. Kai did her best not to acknowledge the looks.

She knew she could have lied when she was asked... But, since falling into this world, she felt she was slipping further away from who she was. Losing herself to the lies this place offered her to escape her actual reality.

She didn't want to play this façade anymore. She didn't want to live with keeping up with the lies.

She wanted to leave.

Kai wanted to go home to her stupidly expensive apartment, watch dumb cat videos with Stace, and hear her grandfather's voice. She even wanted to go to work, argue with Zac, laugh with Stephen, and serve her friendly regulars. She wanted to return to her everyday life, where the only person she was responsible for tending to was herself.

And even then, she did the bare minimum.

The breath was knocked from Kai again as she paused, trying to breathe, mixing the infused fruits in the kitchen. She slapped her cheeks, telling herself to get it together. The last thing she needed was to trigger a panic attack before she finished all her tasks.

"Is the punch ready?" Madam Barnsley slipped in at some point, heels clicking.

Kai shook the thoughts away, nodding as she strained the liquid into a glass pitcher.

Jade grabbed one of the silver trays piled with breakfast-appropriate snacks. "Good, the Crown Prince should be here soon. Let's get that table sorted before he does."

The jug in Kai's hand nearly slipped. That anxiety she tried to shove away at the forefront.

"Your Grace, slow down!" Roger - Warrick's aide, tried reprimanding the charging young prince. "You won't live a very long life always rushing!"

Warrick glanced over a shoulder, flashing him a friendly smile. "You're beginning to sound more and more like my father, Rog."

The prince walked well ahead of his aide, his mind screaming for the man behind to pick up his pace.

The thought of seeing Scarlett so early had Warrick's waking mood ruined, soured that he had to listen to her screeching tone and watch her pick at her nails.

Acting uninterested in any real conversation that didn't involve her looks.

When he first met Scarlett years ago, she appeared as if she couldn't be any more bored—rudely yawning or staring off dazed when anyone tried to converse with her. Only when they flattered her with compliments did she perk up.

Scarlett huffed out, 'Why did she have to marry someone so boring looking.' Those were her words when her father forced him to dance with the young princess he would be wed to.

Since that day, he couldn't get along with the judgemental, self-obsessed cow for the life of him.

But today, seeing Scarlett meant seeing Kai, as she would serve the princess personally. It was a sacrifice he was willing to make.

Roger flew off with a lecture behind the daydreaming prince, but Warrick had long since tuned it out, marching down the long corridors. His attention and goal fuelled his heart and pumped all that blood he needed to the necessary limbs.

"Your Grace!"

Warrick paused after Roger's strange tone of voice, further away than it was previously. He twisted, discovering Roger had stopped at a sharp turn.

His finger pointed away. "It's this way... You're heading towards the servant's wing, sire."

Chapter Twenty-Three

arrick delayed at the big red doors and fixed the high collar of his suit. His palms, within his dark leather gloves, were suddenly clammy.

Roger stared at him stupidly. "Your Grace?" He noticed that faraway gaze in those golden eyes - thin lashes fluttered. Never actually closing, as if whatever was in front of him might disappear.

Roger wondered what had gotten into Warrick this morning; he was usually well put together. Lately, it seemed his prince was seriously distracted.

"She's right there," Warrick whispered.

Roger followed the man's line of sight, realising it wasn't the princess he was staring at. Two handmaidens stood off to the side, poised and waiting, both clad in dark formal attire.

One, in particular, glowed.

Standing out in the middle of the stretching green terrace, even the unruly roses around the yard seemed dull in comparison. Lucent red hair reflected the sun's early light, giving the woman a glowing halo. Strands of the woman's hair flicked with the early morning's gentle breeze, resembling a dancing flame.

Roger glanced back at his prince. "The one who continues to evade you?"

Warrick hummed, attention locked in place. He had no idea a person could hold so much power over him. Warrick couldn't help but wonder what she thought or felt after reading his letter. She didn't seem nearly as eager as other young ladies had been when he would throw attentiveness their way.

No, Kai Redsi acted as if his title was nothing more than some writing on paper. As if she couldn't care less that he was what he was. Even with their brief encounter, her eyes perceived him equally as she did the doctor next to her.

"Your Grace, you are here to discuss the wedding. With the *princess*, mind you..."

That did the trick, yanking Warrick back from his stare. He frowned at Roger, his tone dropped seriously, "I'm aware."

A dark boot moved, and the prince finally marched across the wildly kept stone patio. To join Scarlett at that little table.

Warrick tried to keep his gaze on his expecting seat but failed. His eyes swept over to the maid zoned off into space.

Today, she had her hair in some strange updo, a hairstyle he had never seen any other woman in high or low birth wear before. Half her hair was in a messy bun, the other half down. The free strands swayed slightly by her face, fanning her.

He particularly liked the wavy strands hanging at her sideburns.

Gloves clenched as he imagined tucking them behind those tiny, rounded ears. Heat rose to his face as a thought fleeted through his mind, pondering if her skin was as soft as it looked.

Deep mahogany hair forced his obedience swiftly to the front.

Princess Scarlett was rising from her seat. "Greetings, Your Highness," her tone flat, unlike her loud appearance. The sequence in her dark green dress sparkled like a sun catcher, assaulting him.

Warrick stopped, his hands tucked behind him. "Princess." He firmly bowed his head, keeping his back straight.

"Please, have a seat." Scarlett gestured a dark-laced glove towards the chair across the table.

Mumbling his thanks, Warrick claimed the spot she gestured to. As he peeked up to Scarlett settling, he noticed directing behind her, just left of her temple — Kai stood in the distance.

He silently prayed to the mother above with thanks for this blessed position.

Kai spaced out, trying to recall which scene this was in the story.

She couldn't think of anything until later in the novel after the villain attacks, when Warrick and Scarlett silently had tea, enjoying each other's company. Their scenes together always involved the main palace and the gardens over there, so the timeline seemed a bit jumbled.

There were only five more days till the celebration, which meant five more days till Eros made his dramatic entrance.

Kai made a face in thought. *I can't wait to see that.*

Vanessa didn't cover Eros's personality in-depth, giving him a very complicated point of view for many readers. Some argued on online forums that he was morally grey. Others said he was despicable.

Besides the scenes with the mains, she was curt with his background, only bringing him in to add chaos to the story—the typical bad guy trying to steal away the princess without any real explanation.

She recalled the author saying, '*He resembled a fallen angel.*'

Kai was curious: would he resemble the biblical description of an angel? All Vanessa wrote in the book for the reader's imagination, besides that a hood usually concealed his head, was 'red eyes glinted from the darkness within'.

Oh, and his black wings! Kai's eyebrows rose thinking about it. *He entered with the flapping of black wings!*

Someone cleared their throat, catching Kai's attention. Jade was giving her side eyes, her mouth moved, 'Stop that.'

Jade occasionally caught the Crown Prince looking their way during his serious discussion with Scarlett. She just so happened to dart away so as not to clash eyes with the prince. That's when she noticed Kai making faces, deep in thought about whatever was going through her mind.

When Kai's breathing hitched, realising something to herself, Jade caught her attention to snap her out of embarrassing the princess. The senior handmaiden mentally shook her head, keeping a watchful eye on the young one.

"Who is that over there?"

Scarlett huffed after the prince's question, "My new handmaiden."

"You seem to go through maids faster than your allowance," Warrick stated, sipping from his cup.

A frown nearly formed as Madam Barnsley kept silent beside Kai. Controlling her facial expressions, she pulled her attention over.

She didn't like the prince's attitude and was further irritated as he continued.

The prince's words went flat, "Is she the one that wore a slave collar His Majesty was talking about?"

This time, Scarlett laughed under her breath, telling those standing by she would freak out soon. "You and my father must be ever so close to discussing my personal affairs... It was an innocent little joke..." Her words dropped to a grumble, "Mind your own business."

Warrick's grip on the delicate handle of the teacup tightened, and the leather groaned against the solid, sleek material. "Slavery is a joke to you, is it?"

The princess flicked her braid over a shoulder, eyes narrowed on her unwanted guest. "I don't quite understand why everyone is so pressed with what I do with my servants. It's their job to serve me. Is that any different to a slave?"

Warrick placed the cup back on the saucer, steadily releasing the air from his lungs. Insulted on Kai's behalf.

"On the contrary, Princess," he spat out her title like poison upon his tongue. "A monarch must always consider their people's rights and welfare. Your innocent little joke had me questioning what position you were truly suited for."

The leg Scarlett had crossed over peeked out from the slit in her dresseyeliner, beginning to move. Rocking up and down. "Ah yes, I meant to ask this."

Jade's eyes cut over to the two talking. Kai's also crept. The wind paused, too, as if it held its breath for what was to come.

"Ask away."

Scarlett crossed her arms, her head tilted back as she regarded the prince. She looked at him from her nose. "I am to be queen until you deem me ready to fill the role of empress, yes?"

Both women stood behind, sucked in a breath. Jade shifted on her heels, ready to launch.

Kai locked eyes with golden ones, her head ever so slightly nodding—yes. Hoping he wouldn't scold her for trying to influence his decision.

There was a long silence. Birds chirped, singing to each other, filling the atmosphere. Many other faceless people were on standby, tapping anxious fingers to their sides. Many broke a sweat as they waited for the detonating response.

Warrick raised an eyebrow, an amusing smile twitched at his corners. His sour mood lifted, locking eyes with those anxious ones behind the princess. "Yes?"

Scarlett rose to her feet, brushing off her sleeves. "Fine. That's all I wanted to discuss with you. The butlers will escort you out." She turned, snapping her fingers at the women waiting.

Warrick shot up. "That's it?!" His hands are out on the table.

Everyone paused, eyes on the excited Crown Prince. Even the butlers stopped their approach.

A hand reached and rubbed the back of his neck. "I mean..." Warrick covered his mouth with his other hand and cleared his throat. "There is more to discuss. I've not even been here an hour yet."

Colour rose to the man's face, deepening his undertones.

Scarlett pulled her hair over a shoulder, caressing the thick, tight braid. Her eyes suspiciously narrowed on Warrick. "I have things to do, Your Grace. So, let's save ourselves the troubles from any potential upsets and stop here for today. Excuse me."

She stepped away from the dumbfounded prince standing alone in her yard.

Scarlett strutted with clicking low pumps, heading to her dressing room. Her handmaidens followed five paces at the rear with shuffling feet.

Scarlett squealed once they got to the room on the second floor, "I'm going to be an empress!" Jumping towards Jade, her face flushed with pure excitement.

Kai was carefully closing the double doors.

When Madam Barnsley frowned at the princess, she turned that joy towards Kai. Her deep blue eyes resembled the ocean's tide reflecting the sun's rays when her climbing smile reached them.

Kai didn't know what else to do, so she offered her two thumbs up and a genuine smile.

Crisis averted! She let out a sneaky sigh, relieved things went as they did. She couldn't imagine if things hadn't or how Scarlett might have lashed out.

The women had a relatively easy morning after that, as Scarlett was motivated to do paperwork. The handmaidens stood on each side of the royal's neatly organised desk. All they had to do was pass files over or take them away.

After a light snack, Scarlett excused her maidens, deciding on an afternoon nap.

She waved a hand over her shoulder, bidding farewell to the women, "Barnsley, you are excused for the day. Excuse some of the staff as well. Pet, fetch me in a couple of hours. We can discuss my makeup for the ball this evening over dinner."

Kai stood at the desk, ensuring the stacked files were evenly aligned. She blinked at Jade. *What?* Wondering if she had heard that correctly.

A hand found Kai's shoulder, giving her a not-so-reassuring tap. "Best of luck. Have lunch in the kitchen, and then bring in the dry laundry. We usually…" Madam Barnsley listed chores she normally did while the princess napped.

Kai wiped out her notebook, scribbling down all the tasks she needed to complete. Nervous, she was tending to the princess alone.

The older woman ceased at the door, peeping at Kai. The muted maid's well-shaped brows were turned down, focused on her planning. She decided she wouldn't reprimand Kai for her slip-up earlier. Today turned out to be a good day, and she wanted to leave it.

Jade smiled as she stepped away to enjoy the warm, free day.

After her carefully thought-out schedule, Kai waltzed down to the kitchen, deciding to eat before she dived straight into it.

She found some peanut butter in one of the high cupboards, and a strange thought emerged as she retrieved it. *Do they have peanut butter in this world?* She carefully opened the jar, smelling to confirm. The aroma of peanuts filled her senses, making her stomach growl.

She then shuffled for some jam, opting for a PBJ sandwich, cushioning her roaring stomach before she tried to fill in Jade's punctual shoes.

Kai was at that little table against the wall as people walked to and from. Many smiled and whispered about the princess being in a good mood. Many of those faces smiled at Kai, waving a hand. She covered her mouth as she waved back. The atmosphere, for once, was peaceful. She could feel the vibes from every person coming and going.

The sun was beating down relentlessly, not a single cloud in the blue sky, while Kai reached up again and removed the clips from the laundry field.

She walked up and down, feeling the materials for anything damp.

Kai constantly pulled out a violet handkerchief, wiping her brows. Pausing when she realised whose it was.

Shit... I'm supposed to return this! She made a mental note to clean it tonight, pondering how it was in her pocket.

After the laundry, Kai tidied up the dressing room and Scarlett's office, making her way to the third floor. She guessed it was about time to fetch the princess.

She opened the double-arched doors, heading for the floor-to-ceiling windows.

Scarlett muttered in her sleep, "It's not my fault..." Time and time again, in a small and broken tone.

Kai opened the first long curtain, and the sun poured into the room like a wave. She went to the other three and listened to the sleep talker.

"Save... please... I didn't... this."

Kai hesitantly approached the bed, trying to figure out how to proceed. Usually, Madam Barnsley spoke to the woman, as Kai could not do so. She started with a shake at the corner of the pillow as Scarlett's head thrashed back and forth—a sweat collected on her palling round features.

Her method wasn't working, and Scarlett continued to thrash.

She prayed she wouldn't be scolded or arrested for touching the sleeping princess as she decided to shake the princess's shoulder, opting for a good firm push.

As Kai reached, Scarlett's eyelids flew open on contact. Her blue eyes — black.

Kai stumbled in alarm, hitting the floor as the princess slowly sat up.

The heiress spoke to Kai with a voice that was not her own, "How are you enjoying things so far, pet?" Followed by a low cackle.

That laugh was unforgettable, chasing Kai awake in the night. That voice was the same one responsible for tricking her into this world.

Scarlett grinned, looking down at her cowering on the floor.

Vanessa's voice replaced the princess's, "Break the curse, Kai Redsi, or your existence will cease to be. Do you wish to wither away to this conjured reality?" That horrible, haunting laugh echoed as the woman convulsed before falling back limp and hitting the pillow.

Kai stayed on the floor, her breathing coming in harsh rasps. She surveyed around the room, spying for anything to prove to herself that this was a dream. That maybe none of this was happening, and she was still inside her little room.

The body in the bed squirmed, and a groan slipped past the person's lips.

Kai rose onto shaking limbs, peering over the edge of the mattress at the princess.

Deep blues locked on. "What's... What's wrong with your face?"

The muted maid's face was pale, green around the gills as her head shook in denial.

Her handmaiden appeared to be on the verge of tears.

Scarlett rose, rubbing the sleep from her eyes. "It's creepy, you know…" Her head tilted as she peeked at the woman, trying to compose herself. "Watching someone sleep…" Scarlett grumbled, "Even if I am the most beautiful woman in the kingdom, it's rude."

Those blues glanced towards her open windows. Glad Kai could follow commands without Jade here.

Awful gurgling sounds pulled Scarlett away from thought, and she snapped her attention to the side of the bed.

Kai was clawing at her throat, going purple in the face.

"What's wrong with you?" She scowled.

Crumbling to her backside, Kai slammed onto the cold floors, unable to gasp for air. Her vision blurred as someone began shouting in her face. Hands were on her at some point, but Kai couldn't see. Her vision went black as her head flopped, and that darkness swept through.

CHAPTER TWENTY-FOUR

K ai woke with a dry mouth and an ache in her skull, those eyes opening to plain white ceilings. She sat up painstakingly slow and noticed she was in some strange hall.

The walls are white, and even the many empty beds around the room are bare. The whiff of medicine lurked heavily in the air; she could almost feel the muggy atmosphere as if it clung to her flesh.

"You're awake! Alert the doctor!" a voice shouted as Kai's attention swayed to it.

A young man, who didn't look a day over sixteen, jogged over.

His large hand immediately reached for Kai's forehead. "You've broken your fever, thank the mother," the blonde man said. Touching more of Kai's face, he attempted an examination of her eyes.

Kai weakly swatted those large hands away. Her lips moved with no sounds. *'Who the hell are you?'*

The man kept trying, no matter how often she pushed them off. With quick thinking, Kai reached behind, pulled the pillow up and hit him with it, trying to get him away from her.

"I think the patient is delirious!" he shouted in surprise, blocking her assault.

A silky voice chimed in, entering behind the unknown individual, "Or maybe you didn't explain to her where she is or who you are!"

173

Untied blue hair appeared in Kai's vision, she followed those free-dancing strands to the person they belonged to, noticing hard violet eyes were on the young man.

A firm hand stopped the pillow. "Really, Josh, when will you learn?" Those violets slid to Kai, softening. Pupils ever so subtly expanded. "How are you feeling?" Dexter asked.

Kai stared blankly, and then her head drifted, observing the unknown room.

"You're in the medical wards... you've been unconscious forty-eight hours."

Her face twisted, and she glanced at the doctor.

"You ingested poison," he added. A worried expression was plastered on his honey-toned face.

"Yeah, I heard the princess was shaking from shock when the blood started spewing from your nose!"

"Joshua!" Dexter shouted at the man, pushing him away from the bed next. "Out, out! Get out, you useless boy!"

Kai barely acknowledged their interaction.

Poisoned?

Her memory came to her in glimpses, first folding cream sheets, then waking the princess. The young heiress's face went crazy, and Vanessa's voice came from her lips.

She reached and touched her throbbing head, trying to recall it all.

I was having a panic attack, wasn't I?

"Hey, why don't you lay back down."

After chasing the man away, Dexter was back at her side, ushering the patient to rest. He fluffed the pillow, placing it at the head of the bed. "It usually takes a week to detoxify large amounts of poison from the bloodstream." His hand gently laid on her shoulder as his words went quiet — but loud enough for her to hear, "Even if you have insane healing abilities, it's best not to push your luck."

Kai was guided back down, her stomach in knots from the pain inside her skull.

She couldn't understand how she could have been poisoned.

"The palace is on lockdown... an investigation is still open." Dexter pulled the quilt up, ensuring the blanket was securely crammed to her sides. "They found traces of toxic jellies from a poisonous plant in the jam you used for your sandwich." His hand found her shoulder again, faintly squeezing it as those icy irises fought to stay open. "That jam you used... was one of Scarlett's favourites... Your cheeky dip in may have saved her life."

He had no idea if Kai had heard him, as those eyes shut entirely. Her breathing became steady as those fluttering lids stilled.

Shouting echoed from the entrance as boots came barrelling into the ward like a galloping horse. A man huffed for air, skidding to a stop by the end of the bed.

Dexter stood up, straightening his uniform's coat. His tone was stern with the unwelcome visitor, "The patient is resting. Visiting hours are not permitted while the investigation remains active."

Warrick gobbled down the air, watching the woman's chest rise and fall. "How is she?" those worried words questioned the doctor.

Violet eyes hardened as fingers curled into fists at his sides. "Even if you are a Crown Prince, you are not above our king's orders. Leave at once."

Warrick's features morphed — that princely glow gone to cinders. "You will watch how you address me, sir."

Dexter offered a ridiculed smile, arms crossed stiffly. Disregarding all respect and etiquette towards the foreign heir, he continued mockingly, "Strange, isn't it... The day you visit the detached palace, an incident occurs?"

A hand slid to the hilt of a sword, and the Crown Prince's fingers tightened around the handle one by one. His voice was a threatening growl as he spoke through clenched teeth, "I could have your tongue for that."

"Go ahead, but we both know it'll add more suspicion to your case." The doctor smiled wider, a challenging defence.

Whimpers stopped both men's intentions, their stand-off of dominance broken.

Kai's face had paled further, skin ashen. Her head flopped back and forth as awful sounds escaped her lips.

"GUARDS!?"

The Crown Prince's chin angled towards the shouting man.

"By the king's orders, no one is to enter!"

Two armoured men wearing the golden rose symbol on their chest plates marched in. They stopped in unison on each side of Warrick.

Those violets hardened into steel, only on him. "No one." The doctor dismissed the prince now that the guards had arrived. Reaching over, he immediately began to check on the twitching girl.

Warrick puffed out his chest, standing taller as he assessed the doctor.

He glared at the offensive man, recalling his defensive attitude during their previous encounters. All the while, he was escorted out of the medical ward with two armoured men watching him keenly.

Kai slept for another ten hours, waking in a faintly lit room with an overbearing desire for food gnawing at her gut. There were candles all along the walls, brightening the space with an orange glow. She sat up, swinging her legs off the side of the bed, only to pause.

A figure was asleep on the bed next to hers.

"She's been here since dinner..." a voice whispered.

Kai blinked with confusion; Dexter was leaning against the semicircular archway. The room's shadows concealed most of the upper half of his body.

"Her Highness's senior handmaiden has come as often as possible, demanding an update on your condition. She had heard today you woke briefly and has stayed since..." The doctor pushed off the wall and approached the two beds silently, finally revealed to the light. "It's uncharacteristic of her."

Kai watched Madam Barnsley as Dexter watched Kai.

Jade had a knitted shawl around her shoulders, her hair down for once. Her brunette strands were wavy and scattered across her face. Worry lines were more profound on the woman's forehead and around her mouth, most likely from frowning.

"Thanks to you, the guards found someone had tampered with our kitchen's goods... Even if you didn't know it then, you saved the princess from being here instead." Dexter's gaze broke away, going over to the older maid, resting peacefully. "They've detained five members of the palace's staff. Hopefully, we will have answers and the criminals behind it by morning."

Kai nodded, offering a thumbs up. *That's good*, she thought to herself.

A grumble roared and Kai's hand quickly clenched her aching belly, refusing to look at Dexter. Heat rose to her cheeks as the roaring continued like a lion wanting to be released.

The corners of the doctor's lips twitched upwards. "I will go get you some soup... you must be starving," he added quietly.

Kai nodded shyly, mouthing a 'Thank you', still refusing to look at him.

Dexter left through that entrance with a spring in his steps as Kai's attention was on the evenly breathing woman.

Her shut eyes reminded Kai of Scarlett's. They even had the same shape, if not for the years that began to pull at Jade's.

Kai recalled the incident in Scarlett's room and how darkness greeted her when those blue eyes were consumed. It was similar to possession, something straight out of that exorcist movie Stace forced her to watch one night.

Horror stuff made Kai's skin crawl.

She tried to recollect information from within the book, what the curse was precisely and how it led to the story's plot. Her mind drifted back to the doctor.

I should ask him.

They had agreed to work together; he was her best option in knowing what it was, and then, she could figure out how to break it. She also needed to check with Ava and Charlie.

One thing that bothered her was she couldn't remember a poisoning scene in any of the chapters.

No — there was definitely no arc of an attempted poisoning.

Scarlett usually avoided all the severe events by some lucky grace, Warrick injured in place, saving her.

"It's not proper to watch someone sleep."

Kai blinked, Jade's frowning mug coming into view from her zone out. She closed her eyes and bowed her head in apology to the older woman.

Clicking noises came from the woman's joints as Jade pushed herself up. She watched the silent maid, the glowing of the hall giving her a strange outline. Even in her patient gown, there was something alien about her.

Something not of this world.

"How do you feel?"

Kai glanced up, heat rising to her high cheekbones, rubbing her belly.

"You nearly died because of food, and that's what you want the moment you wake?" Madam Barnsley glared at the weird child and then scoffed, "You're..."

She just couldn't fathom her way of thinking.

Kai offered a sheepish grin.

She didn't care if she had just been poisoned or not. That soup the doctor offered sounded good to her right about then. She just wanted to stop the ache in her stomach.

A silence fell between them as they both stared off at nothing. Kai waited impatiently.

It felt as though he had been gone for hours, and the silence made seconds feel like minutes.

"If I had been there..." Madam Barnsley slowly started. "I would have made her scones for when she woke... and that jam would have been inside her food." A weird noise slipped past the woman's lips. A wrinkled hand laid upon them.

Kai understood where she was going with this. Madam Barnsley felt guilty, potentially poisoning the princess in her stead—someone she loved like a daughter.

She frowned, mouthing as slow and readable as she could to the head maiden.

'It's – Not – Your – Fault.'

Jade stared at Kai's lips, twisting away after. She rose from the side of the bed, straightening out the sheets. "They won't get away with this..." she said, words barely a whisper.

Barnsley made her way towards the exit, her face never showing to Kai. "Rest up. I'm told you should be discharged tomorrow if you keep improving. Our Rose has excused you for another day but expects you to be right by her side straight after." With a clicking of heels, the madam vanished into the darkness of that exit.

Kai sat there for a while watching that exit until the warm soup arrived. Someone else brought the food as Dexter was called away for another patient.

She attacked that hot bowl of soup like a rabid animal, nearly choking on the chunky bits within it the moment her hands made contact. She didn't care what the wide-eyed butler thought as she scoffed down the food. All Kai cared about was how delicious those chunks of potatoes were and how the ache in her tummy subsided to a comforting warmth.

CHAPTER TWENTY-FIVE

There was a shift while Kai was out, and she felt it on the trek back to her room the following day. People of all sorts stopped to gawk, not because of her hair or the rumours of being mute like they usually did.

They stopped, and some inclined their heads. Others turned to whisper to one another, and a hand covered their mouths. There were even a few suspicious stares and judging, calculated eyes.

"That's her!"

"That's the one who saved the princess."

"What loyalty. She's already up and about."

"She's probably keen to return to our Rose's side."

Kai kept her stare low, not enjoying the attention one bit. She preferred when they hardly took notice, or if they did, it was because of how bright her top was—dismissing it quickly, like seeing an exotic animal and moving on to the next.

She didn't know the jam was poisoned; she wouldn't have eaten it if she had done so.

The fact she 'saved the princess' bothered Kai.

The rescuing acts within the story belonged to Warrick. They were exponential to their growing romance, to Scarlett and Warrick's happy-ever-after.

Her god damned ticket home!

"It's been like this since the investigation began," Ava whispered to Kai.

Charlie and Ava popped in just as she was given her discharge papers, bringing the news that the investigations had wrapped up.

Two servants are to be hung tomorrow morning for their crime against the royal family.

Unfortunately, one had offed himself — a toxic pill under the help's tongue. Silencing any potential leads he could have offered. The rest of the findings were kept under tight-lipped officials by order of the king.

Ava whispered again, leaning close to Kai, "Gossip spreads like wildfire." Her grip tightened.

Charlie kept silent on the other side of Ava. Occasionally, he glanced around and offered smiles to those scrutinising stares that watched the trio.

Kai was sweating buckets by the time they reached her room, but the awkward walk faded to the rear of her mind with the surprise that waited on her table as the door opened.

Charlie and Kai shared a look helping Ava settle on the bed.

"I can smell flowers..." she mumbled.

Like Kai's hair, a pot of bright red carnations sat on the circular wooden table. Kai tapped Ava on her shoulder twice, signalling she was correct.

Charlie snooped around the fancy pot wrapped prettily in a purple silk ribbon. A decent-sized bow was front and centre, clashing with the dark pot the plant sat inside. He mumbled to Ava and Kai behind him, trying to find something around the plant.

Kai was beginning to pick up more and more words but still relied on Ava for a straightforward translation.

Ava pondered, "Strange... you would think an admirer would leave a name."

Kai wrote a note for Charlie to read, not concerned about the flowers. She prioritised running them up to speed on what had happened before her collapse.

The trio sat together on the edge of Kai's single bed, leg against leg, deep in their thoughts.

Charlie still spooled over the notes, Ava's hands flexed against her skirting. Kai kept thinking about Vanessa's voice that poured out of Scarlett's mouth.

Each was deeply perturbed by Vanessa's ability to reach them while they were here. Able to pop up in a character's body and taunt them.

A knock pulled them out of thought as Kai rose for the door.

Charlie signalled her to sit down, shoving the notes to her to hide as he opted to answer.

When he opened the door, he found Dexter Ubar standing on the other side, a bouquet of blue flowers in his hands.

"You're that boy…" Dexter said, only to stop as Kai joined Charlie. She ushered him to come in with a waving hand.

He hesitantly slid inside the small room, seemingly smaller, with three others inside it. His eyes paused on the blind woman briefly and then on the flowers that were already on the table.

Dexter had seen similar ones being carried through the halls yesterday by one of Warrick's foot soldiers.

The muted lady scribbled on a note, passing it to Dexter as he stared daggers at those flowers.

> This is Ava and Charlie. They, too, have been trying to break the curse.

The doctor peered up at the three strange folks. One mute, one blind and another partially deaf, from what his supervisor had explained.

He had started digging in on *Ava* and *Charlie* when Kai arrived. Getting sidetracked as the days progressed, his focus was solely on her.

His voice was full of scepticism, "Did you tell them?" Those eyes were locked on Kai.

"She didn't have to, sir."

Dexter's stare dragged to the girl, whose skin was like a welcoming cup of dark-roasted coffee. That blindfold was so bright against the warmth of her tones.

"You see, we were the ones that told her about you."

Dexter twitched; his balance staggered.

Kai could tell that unsettled him; considering her knowledge, no one — not even the royal family knew — that he was a wizard.

"We would like to go home, Mr Ubar, and are unable to. Not until this curse is broken," Ava explained precisely what the trio had planned.

Agreeing to give him half-truths.

Kai amply nodded as she listened to the orchestrated information being handed over.

Dexter snapped, "And how did you know? Who told you?"

Feeling Charlie's gaze narrow, Dexter watched him from his side view.

Those doe eyes the kid had couldn't conceal the flick of aggression, reading Dexter's body language.

"I understand your suspicion of us, but believe me, as we too are suspicious of you. So, until we can all trust each other, let us drop the useless questions and assumptions. We just want to break this curse and go home. That's it."

"Why?" the doctor asked, disregarding her words. His fingers clenched the stems of the flowers still in his hands.

Kai was glad that the composed one of the three had the gift to speak. There was something reliable about Ava, even if they couldn't rely on her sight.

Watching the doctor's strange behaviour had her knees wobble. Images of him roasting them all alive came to her mind, making Kai nervous. He could do so and would be foolish not to if he wanted absolute silence for his secret.

"We cannot tell you that. Please understand that we are already taking a dangerous risk by telling you this."

Dexter observed Charlie next, meeting those brown eyes.

Charlie, in turn, waved at him. A small smile offered, eyes still narrowed.

A smile that told him, 'Touch her and you're dead'.

His violet's dragged to the quietest one, fidgeting with her fingers. Dexter slowly extended the bundle of blue Lillies and offered them to Kai. The handwritten note swung from a sapphire ribbon, keeping the flowers together.

A blush crept over Kai's cheek as she mouthed a 'Thank you' for the flowers, refusing to meet his stare.

He could see the guilt plastered on her rosy face. Those slim white fingers rubbed the petals between them, distracting herself.

"I do not quite understand..." Dexter's stare was still on the girl, waiting for those pale blues with whisks of colour subtly within to meet him. Wishing she could open her mouth and explain things to him, herself.

His beating heart threatened to combust, and a growing feeling of betrayal nipped at the corners of it.

Ava pulled her blindfold off and turned in the direction of the doctor. "We had things taken from us... and in order for us to have them back, we have to break this curse."

Dexter's chin angled towards Ava's voice, his eyes slowly breaking away from Kai with his actions. Bile rose in his throat, and his beating heart stilled.

The door flew open and slammed shut before anyone could register what had happened. Charlie approached the door, turning the key with a tongue click.

Silence filled the room once more, the gust of wind from the door slamming shut, blowing away the tension within it seconds ago.

"Well, that went well," Ava exclaimed, placing the blindfold back on her face. She shifted herself off the bed and lowered herself carefully to the floor.

Kai placed the flowers on the table, following Charlie's actions as he joined Ava on the ground.

The trio sat in silence, waiting to see if he would return and who he might return with.

"Do you think he's going to be a problem?"

Kai zoned out on the stone's patterns; her head gradually rose. Charlie was watching her, waiting for an answer, his hand hovered over Ava's shoulder.

She shrugged, not knowing the answer to that.

She wanted to trust the doctor, as she trusted the character portrayed in the story—Warrick's reliable sidekick. However, everything was screwed. The story she knew was not the story she was experiencing one bit.

For all she knew, Ava's suspicion and funny feelings about the doctor could very well be true.

Dexter Ubar was probably here to ensure the curse did not get broken for whatever ancient reason —that wasn't her business. It all sounded like politics to her.

Kai's head throbbed. This was supposed to be a romance novel, not some political - or magical - agenda.

Charlie tapped Ava three times as Kai's head went back down, deeply contemplating.

Kai truly wanted to believe that the Dexter who helped Warrick in the novel was a good guy and would help them like any good guy would. She wanted to believe the guy looking out for her since removing the collar was genuine.

She may not have cared initially much for him, but he could very well be the make-it-or-break-it to them going home.

"Well, if push comes to shove, there are three of us against him. Let's focus on finishing the conditions that appear and getting the hell out of this place."

Kai started to nod, listening to Ava's reassuring voice.

Ava's pitch raised suddenly, arms crossed in a huff, "To be honest, I'm sick to death of the food here. Why is everything so bland? I thought fantasy books made food seem unreal. This was nothing like I expected."

Kai and Charlie shared a look at Ava's complaints, huffing out with airy giggles.

Dexter Ubar tapped a finger against his desk, revisiting this morning's shock. He pondered how to proceed forward, kicking himself for not finishing his investigation on those two.

He didn't appreciate surprises.

He had been so engrossed in his work over the past few days that he failed to realize how many people were observing him.

The girl's face surfaced in his mind, recalling how the light in Kai's vivid eyes faded with Miss Sebastian's words. Her fingers caressed the petals with slow and steady strokes. Slowing further when the blind one confessed that something had been taken from them.

They stopped entirely. Kai's eyes flicked to movement to her side, and that icy edge dulled to a barren wasteland.

He found it strange how Kai Redsi's condition hadn't improved, given her speedy ability to heal and his potions to aid. With Ava's carefully chosen words, it made sense that there was more to it.

He was convinced those three were cursed themselves. His confirmation as he followed Kai's line of sight, to empty eyes watching.

Paranoia whipped his calves to flee, so he left, not giving them any more room for talk.

What he didn't understand was why.

What had they done to bring upon a curse, and why did they have to break the Rosethorne one as retribution?

Who had done it, and what was the connection between it all?

Even though that woman couldn't see, he felt those empty eyes peering into his soul. As if she already had the answers and wanted confirmation from his lips.

Then there was the boy, Charlie Flounder. Keenly observing as if he could hear his innermost fears. For a young man, he was indeed heedful. He marked everything that moved within the room. Every movement, every breath, even the shadows, those dark browns swiftly flicked towards it. Not missing a thing.

And then there was Kai... Dexter's mind was still torn in two when it came to her.

His thoughts constantly drifted throughout the last few days, wondering how she was doing while he worked away. Or how he would see something that reminded him of her. He tried to keep the bright-haired girl at arm's length but found himself drawn...

Like a siren, without her voice.

His drumming finger ceased as all his rambling thoughts led him to the same conclusion.

Those violet eyes shot to his locked door. "See no evil, hear no evil, speak no evil..." he mumbled.

Dexter pushed away from the desk with such force it rocked it into the wall, racing for the library.

Chapter Twenty-Six

Kai didn't know what she had quite expected returning to her position, but currently being buried alive in heavily stacked fabrics, wasn't it... She only had herself to blame, interrupting that appointment with the designer when she first started to serve.

An ecstatic Mary busted into her room at the crack of dawn, scaring the living bejesus out of Kai with squeals of joy as she was dragged back to work the other day.

It had been days since the attempted poisoning, and everyone acted as if it didn't quite happen, making Kai feel better facing that ridiculous palace.

New faces scurried everywhere within Scarlett's place, people rushing about with panic for the ball fast approaching.

Treason was a thing of the past.

Kai was trying to sort through the thirty-six dresses gifted or bought for Scarlett for tomorrow's ball. Each dress was sent over by the king himself, each a half of a whole.

Prince Warrick's people were waiting for confirmation of Scarlett's choice.

It was customary for high-ranking nobles to match their outfits, especially couples. Kai opened her big damn mouth – or big damn notebook – and volunteered to pick only the most flattering dresses for Scarlett. They had agreed to narrow it to two, and Scarlett would choose between them.

But the dress described in the story wasn't among the jaw-dropping works of art.

Throwing the glamorous dresses worthy of a deity around, Kai sifted through, repeating the details mentally.

Purple glimmering sleeves hanging loosely at the biceps.

She picked up every purple gown and brought the gathered materials to a lounge chair.

Shimmering lace at the throat.

Examining the isolated gowns, she breathed deeply with frustration.

"Is something the matter?"

Kai was so consumed glaring at the colour matches that she hadn't heard Jade's approach.

Madam Barnsley stopped beside the frowning young girl, who hugged herself and observed the nine dresses she had pulled from the lot. A wrinkled finger pointed to the fourth one, laid over the backrest. "The silver and purples would fit nicely with the prince's traditional suits, commemorating the empire's colours."

Kai gave the dress a once over, shaking her head. It was a low cut.

Scarlett had the chest to pull it off - sure, but Warrick appreciated the modesty of covering one's flesh.

The attire Scarlett should be wearing at the too-quick-approaching ball was a high lace collar covering all of her fair skin. Her skirt flowed around her, moving like wheat grass in an open meadow with every step or twist. As the light hit the gown, it was supposed to shimmer an indigo, the dress dazzling all who looked upon it.

The perfect dress to complete the image of a fair and lovely princess as she danced with her fiancé in front and centre. All eyes would be on the couple, or more so, Scarlett and her fairy-tale dress.

The dress Jade pointed towards was far more mature than Vanessa had written in the pages.

Jade pointed to another, this one, less fabric than the others. A fitted silhouette, which exploded out just at the thighs, a flat-toned gown. No frills or tassels to decorate the plain thing. What made it stand out, what made it worthy of being a ball-clamouring get-up, was the under-fabric and exposed back. With every step, the high slit of the skirting should flick open, the dress revealing a sparkling red inner-skirting sewn inside the inner walls. That same red outlined the open spine, and the red ribbon tightened the lower abdomen and crisscrossed.

Kai grumbled; a hand rubbed her chin.

It screamed to Kai like a dress out of its timeline. It was far too modern from the rest of the Victorian-era fashion sense.

She was running out of time.

Scarlett wanted the dresses chosen and was waiting for her after her midday nap. But the dress depicted wasn't here! She had checked the list thrice, ensuring the numbers matched the mountains of fabrics before her. Thirty-six different codes, thirty-six anticlimactic gowns, and the tags matched each digit recorded.

A hand found Kai's shoulder, giving three gentle taps, each more of a rub to soothe. "I'll leave it to you, then." Jade offered Kai a tight smile and gathered the items she had dismissed or ignored.

Kai raked her skull, brooding over the book. Trying to remember how she had received the monumental dress. A dress that was gifted to Scarlett by her admirer...

The prince.

Scratching the back of her neck, Kai considered how big of an impact this would have on progressing. While unconscious, she learned that Warrick and Scarlett had come head-to-head again. Ruining that step of peace between the two.

Scarlett had believed some of the spreading theories that the empire was behind the attempt. Jabs and insinuations were thrown at the Crown Prince during a dinner with the king.

Warrick and his people were naturally insulted by this.

Even though they had made arrests, they hadn't gotten any real answers. So said Madam Barnsley, who informed Kai of their updates. The old woman didn't believe he was responsible but claimed 'she wouldn't put it past the Crown Prince's people. Eliminating an unwanted Crown Princess.'

But opinions like that could easily have your tongue. It was warranted enough to begin a war.

It was ludicrous, a minor kingdom going to war with an empire of eight kingdoms. Rosethorne would last the first few days. It increased the possibility of the united empire's involvement since they couldn't exactly retaliate.

Kai had two more meetings with Charlie and Ava since Jade's political information, with no appearance or input from the doctor.

The trio believed in two things as of standing: One, the doctor was currently shitting his pants and avoiding them, which made them inclined to think he was a common enemy. And two, the curse had to be related to love in some sense. It was the only way to explain why everything was different.

Something needed to change between the prince and princess, or else...

Kai's hands found her temples as she walked over to sit on one of the only empty seats not covered in exotic gowns. Another headache crept, and she felt the sensation building behind her skull, spreading at a slow and steady pace like a burglar attempting to steal her sanity.

She had no choice but to opt with Madam Barnsley's input, as she knew the princess best, choosing the low-cut dress.

She didn't dare suggest the other... Kai double took, looking at the dress one more time.

It may have been a test.

She picked the third safest option. A light purple gown with champagne-coloured sleeves. That same champagne colour hinted at bits and pieces around the massive skirting. It was the closest to what the real deal should have been, still offering that air of fantasy, grace, and beauty.

Kai carefully displayed the options on two wooden mannequins for Scarlett to pick between. Deeply sighing out in defeat, Kai carried on with her chores.

All she could do was pray this did not affect her objective.

Scarlett sat on a chair before the dresses and examined every square inch of the fabrics. Jade stood between them, informing the princess about each of the picks, who the designers were, and how she could wear her hair with them.

The princess did not once mention the poisoning or utter any words of good wishes to Kai in the last few days. If anything, she averted her eyes whenever Kai met her stare.

"I don't care for that one..." Scarlett mumbled.

She was leaning to a side in the chair, her pale pink silk robe in disarray. One bare leg crossed over another, slightly swinging. That insane sea of wine-coloured hair cascaded around her, swallowing the back of the chair.

Her finger drifted to the second dress. "If we go with this one, you can do a makeup look to match the sleeves." Her blues, like the ocean, briskly glanced. "I want my eyelids to sparkle just as bright."

Kai, stationed next to her, had her notebook at the ready, recording her preferences.

"Then I shall inform the others of your choice, Your Highness." Jade curtsied to the leisurely rising princess.

Scarlett waved a lazy hand, making her way towards the bathroom. "You're dismissed. I'm sure you also have things to prepare for, pet."

Kai stopped her jottings, peeking towards Jade, her round eyes widened in silent question.

The princess stopped in the doorway and spoke over a shoulder. That hair covered her deadpan expression. "All citizens are to be in attendance... It's a celebration, after all."

Kai's stare flew to where the princess disappeared from, blinking at the now-emptied doorway.

Madam Barnsley followed Scarlett through that exit, and a finger pointed to a side table. "Compensation pay is just there. Our Rose was benevolent and threw in enough to cover a gown for your heroism. Keep it graceful but simple, should she call upon you in the crowd to serve."

Dexter Ubar was leaving the chemists with a brown luggage in tow, filled with all the restocked supplies for the infirmary. The late afternoon sun rained down pleasantly; the smells of freshly baked bread carried on the wind.

He pulled his gloves off; his occupied hand blocked the rays agitating his vision. Turning back, he bid a final farewell to the old man running the shop as he stepped down the wooden steps.

"I see a bright future for Rosethorne, Dex!" The toothy, grinned fellow waved insistently to him.

The doctor shook his head, admiring the man's enthusiasm and positive thinking.

He prayed the man was right and the kingdom was heading for new heights only if that princess matured enough not to sentence them all to death, offending the great empire first.

Going over what he needed to prepare and the orders for medications for the week, he made mindless steps towards the palace.

"Charlie says that a hairpin will elevate your appearance, even if the dress is boring."

Dexter's head wiped around for that voice, seemingly getting closer. He slowed his pace, beholding the three individuals he had deliberately avoided.

They stood in front of one of the stalls selling shiny hair accessories. The man pointed and mumbled to the woman. The blindfolded one, Ava, was still as stone, translating from what he could tell.

Kai nodded as her fingers toyed with a sparkling gold clip twinkling from the sun.

He had no idea why, but he slid behind a building's corner—staying within the shadows, trying to get as close as possible without being noticed.

"She can't wear that, Charles!" Ava pulled the arm attached to her, jarring it once in protest. "You said her hair is bright red. If the clip is also red, what's the point of wearing it?"

His head peeked around a shaded pole, spying on them.

It appeared as though they were shopping for the ball tomorrow evening. He had no idea what Kai was writing as she showed the boy, who mumbled some more. Then the tight unit moved on, multiple bags carried between Kai and Charlie on each side of Ava.

Dexter stepped forth and advanced to the spot where the three had stood previously.

His gaze lingered on the stand full of diverse, shining items. A particular clip was displayed with brilliance, slightly unaligned from the potential customer who was touching it.

CHAPTER TWENTY-SEVEN

K ai collapsed onto the bed. Bags of shopping congested her once neat and clear floor. An unsavoury burp gurgled up her throat as she patted her content stomach, full of street stall dishes. A soft smile played on her lips, musing over Charlie and Ava this afternoon, admiring their relationship.

Admittedly, mildly envious.

She finally understood Stace's need to be with someone.

She wanted someone to look at her like Charlie looked at Ava. It reminded her of how her father watched her mother in the kitchen. A memory of them came forth, which felt like a lifetime ago.

Kai rolled over and pulled a pillow down. She clutched it to her chest, hugging it for comfort. Her stinging eyes settled on the bags nearest the table, though her mind was elsewhere.

She could barely remember what her mam's voice sounded like but could still faintly imagine the soft humming she did whenever her mother zoned off.

A vague memory of sunlight poured in from their kitchen window as her mother worked around the separated kitchen island. The smell of coffee and baked goods carried throughout the small cottage.

Kai envisioned her father leant over the granite island in his fluffy black robe, his dark brown hair dishevelled as it always was, first thing in the morning.

He had a big white mug of coffee in his hands, eyes unable to look away from the woman baking.

He always stared with such love and satisfaction towards his darling wife.

Bright red hair glowed like a red light bulb as her head came into view, straightening up with a sheet full of goodies in her mitt-covered hands. Her mother had a lover's twinkle in her green eyes as they clashed with her husband's blues. A smile exploded on the woman's beautiful face as she winked at the man.

Completely unaware of the little person who watched them from the kitchen's entry point, tightly holding a teddy bear.

Kai twirled a strand of red hair around a finger, bringing it into view — the same bright shine she tried to hide.

Something warm slid across the bridge of Kai's nose, which travelled under the other eye. She sat up quickly and wiped away the sneaky tear with a sleeve. Remembering such things wouldn't bring her closer to leaving this fictional prison. She needed to prepare herself for tomorrow's events.

Kai tucked away the cosy memory into the deepest part of her heart and scooted off the bed, heading for the biggest bag.

Charlie and Ava helped Kai select a modest dress for the occasion, a dark navy ball gown that cut across the collar bone, its sleeves starting mid-bicep. The sleeves were of dark lace, quarter cut-offs. The gown was tightly fitted to the hips, where the navy-blue material flowed naturally.

It was plain but still elegant.

The gown reminded Kai of a prom dress, something she might have seen in her reality. It was relatable, which is why she opted for the ready-made thing.

She wasn't entirely a fan of wearing dresses, to begin with. Kai even skipped her prom night because she couldn't bring herself to wear a gown or spend all that unnecessary money.

The dress slid out of the bag; the skirting pooled around on the floor. Kai examined the pretty laced sleeves that stopped just after the elbows. It was a skin-coloured tulle fabric, making the dark lace patches appear floating around the upper arms.

She had to admit, dressing up appeared fun—magical even, but remembering how much she paid even for this modest thing had her stomach churned.

Doesn't matter what period you live in. Everything is stupidly expensive.

Kai shook her head with silent complaints as she straightened out the dress and hung it in the wardrobe. She then began placing all the other items cluttering the floors inside the closet when a knock at the door discontinued her plans.

She waited for the knock to begin again and was met with silence. Tiptoeing to the door, Kai peeked out the keyhole. Only to find no one was there.

She cautiously opened the door to an empty hallway. Her dismissing attention caught sight of a small, lonely, wrapped-up box on the floor just before the threshold.

She squinted at it before she picked it up and brought it inside. The velvet box was no bigger than her hand, fitting perfectly inside her palm. As she stepped towards the table, wondering who had left it, Kai jumped in surprise as more harping began.

This time, a voice with it.

"Miss?" a familiar grumpy voice asked, banging another round.

Kai placed the box on her table next to the flowers she continued to ignore. Its petals wilted and brown. She headed back to the entry, releasing a sigh.

Upon opening it, she found that man behind it, the same one who had appeared with Pennel the other day. A giant purple box, tied with gold and silver ribbon, was in his hands.

Her icy stare narrowed at the box and then to the soldier.

He cleared his throat and presented the oversized item, "A gift from His Highness. He hopes you will accept it as nothing more than that."

Accepting the box with sceptical hands, Kai nodded, mouthing a 'Thank you.' The man offered her a curt nod as he spun on his heels, leaving her alone in pondering thought.

An ominous feeling once again rose inside her as she slowly closed the door with a foot. Kai stared at the flimsy bows that wobbled with her every step. She slid the box onto the table, next to the collected items occupying the top.

With twitching fingers, she pulled the largest silver bow, and the fabric flopped to the sides, gathering on the tabletop. She carefully lifted the cover off and revealed what was inside, only to slam the cover back on immediately.

The force was so quick and abrupt that she damaged the sides of the box as the material caved in around certain sides.

Kai backed away from the gift, staring on in horror.

The purple shimmering material that changed to indigo when the lighting hit it had her heart in her throat. She didn't need to see the rest to know what it was. Her backside landed on the bed as she continued to space out. Mary's words echoed inside her mind, overlapping with the words Kai was made to say.

'And loved by my fellow people...'

Kai swallowed, mentally talking to an envisioned version of Warrick as the words from his letter swam around her mind's eye.

'You don't truly feel that way. It's that wish!'

Her mind continued to spiral, trying to make sense of all this nonsense. She pleaded with her delusional imagination, *'You don't truly feel that way... It's that cursed wish... nothing more.'*

Darren knocked on the open door, watching as Warrick's face raised. A slight flick of the Crown Prince's head signalled him to enter.

He quietly closed the door and approached the solid desk illuminated with lit candles. With every stride across the room, Darren braced himself. This was either going to go one or two ways.

"You delivered it, then?"

The captain paused, arms and back straightened. "Yes, Your Grace."

"Did she say or write anything?" A chuckle escaped from the prince's lips, following his words.

Darren shook his head. "No. I delivered the box as commanded and left."

Warrick hummed in response, attention still immersed in the work laid out on the desk.

Brown eyes flicked to the map where the prince's forearm rested, noticing the notes and new markings inked into the parchment. "Your Grace, please excuse me if I am once again overstepping… However, as the future emp-"

Warrick's golden eyes snapped up to the waiting captain, halting him. "You are indeed overstepping, Captain." He flicked the paper onto the desk and leaned back in the seat. The leather from the backrest groaned. "As I have told Roger, I will tell you just the same. My decision remains unchanged; none of your reasons can sway my heart and mind. I will go forth with this agreement as planned, but that's all. I cannot - will not, love Scarlett. She will be what she will be, only in name."

The captain inhaled steadily. Those blazing golds kept him from stepping out of line. "I apologise if I have offended you, Your Grace." Swiftly, he bowed, his stare now on the foreign red carpet that covered most of the marble floors.

A frustrated sigh escaped from the prince. "I understand all of your concerns. I do. Your words come from a genuine place for myself and the empire. But I implore that you respect and support my decisions as your future emperor and friend."

Darren straightened. "Yes, Your Grace." Completely surrendering to his prince's resolve.

There was no point in arguing with the man.

Chapter Twenty-Eight

The day of the ball was pandemonium. Servants rushed around every square inch of the ginormous white and gold palace, readying for the evening's celebration. Streamers were strung along archways and down long corridors, white ribbons attached to short golden polls—lining many of the stoned walkways. To guide the filing guests into the permitted areas. Show-stopping roses of deep reds, purples and blues were placed around every entry and exit, and floral archways were made up at every doorway. Smells of roasted pork, beef, and chicken cascaded from the bustling kitchens, mingling with the strong flower fragrances the drafts pushed around the occupied spaces.

The sun was high in the sky, not a cloud in the bright blue oasis overhead to ruin the highly anticipated day. The citizens outside the palace and the outer-wall residents decorated the town with handcrafted streamers of their own.

The entire kingdom was in celebration mode.

"One would think this was the actual wedding," Warrick grumbled, glaring down disdainfully at the servants who smiled below.

They were putting up more floral arrangements on his ward's entry, many shades of deeper reds from where he observed out a window.

Behind Warrick, his aide - Roger, circled a suit, which was carefully displayed on a mannequin at the centre of the suite.

He fixed the long-trailed cape from any wrinkles threatening to ruin the sleek material, mindlessly replying, "Your future citizens are celebrating a milestone, as they should."

The prince pushed off the wall and swaggered over to where Roger was rounding like a bird, pecking at the suit.

Warrick grabbed one of the golden tassels that hung from the epaulettes. His mind drifted elsewhere. "Quite the heavy burden, to wear such a crown..." he mumbled.

Roger paused his fretting regarding the solemn-sounding prince, "You should see it as quite the honour. Representing the citizens of all the kingdoms with one dignified voice." His gaze lowered. "The sun's duties for others must always be the top priority, making their wants second nature or non-existent. For the good and prosperity of all, presently and hereafter."

Warrick let the tassel drop from his fingertips, his attention back out the window. "By uniting all the kingdoms under one glorious banner, we'll stand a better chance of weathering the storms to come. I know... I know."

Kai was exhausted when she was finally dismissed, swerving her way through the busy corridors, careful she didn't pump into the other servants who carried boxes or flowers.

The princess was now on her way to join the king and her fiancé for dinner before the ball. Where she would later enter the grand hall with her betrothed, and the official announcement would be made.

This meant that Kai had time to get herself ready for the celebration and mentally prepare for the villain's appearance. She hoped all went accordingly and the trio would receive another clue to bring them closer to leaving the pages.

Kai had just stepped out of the stairwell, her movements delayed to a snail's pace, as a figure stood frozen at her door.

A hand was raised in an attempt to knock, only to shake their head and turn away. Nearly smashing into her for a change.

"My apologies," Dexter started, baulking back in surprise.

Kai offered nothing as she went around the doctor.

She had been so busy tending to Scarlett this morning that she had utterly forgotten Dexter's existence. Considering how he had been avoiding her the last few days, she thought maybe, just maybe, their roads would no longer cross.

That would have been one less thing for the trio to worry about.

Her hand had just gripped the doorknob and began to twist.

"Do you have a moment?" Dexter turned, hands stuffed into pockets. His eyes not meeting her questioning ones, the floor appeared more attractive. "I believe I owe you an explanation."

Kai nodded amply as she opened the door and gestured for him to follow with a flick of her chin.

The least she could do was listen to what he had to say, get a feel if he was indeed someone they needed to keep far away from. Or rid, completely.

Upon entering, the doctor lingered by the shut door. Kai advanced towards the wardrobe and began pulling out the things needed for the event.

"I thought m-my existence was a secret... I left in a panic because of the that...."

Kai placed the dress on the bed and regarded the stammering man with a twist of the neck. His eyes were locked on a stone tile just at his dark loafers, those hands inside his pockets – clenching.

"I was alarmed..." His voice dropped to almost a whisper, "Not even the-the king is aware... of my truest nature... My... My kind doesn't fare well here."

Kai let his words sink in before she dug out her notebook from the skirting's massive pockets.

> Your secret is safe with us as long as ours is safe with you.

She passed over the book and allowed the doctor to digest her words. She would have to burn that page after.

Kai made sure to destroy all pages the trio had been plotting on, never to make the same mistake twice. With the uncertainty of the doctor's compliance, they couldn't have evidence against them should he betray them.

Kai didn't care what excuse he may or may not have orchestrated at the time since the trio had already agreed to proceed regardless of his involvement. But also prepare, just in case he had schemed against them.

It was no loss to them if he didn't want to cooperate. He was just a side character. This world was his home. How could he understand their disposition?

"Do you have an escort?"

Kai straightened out the sleeves, hardly glancing at Dexter.

His eyes skittishly crept up from the notebook, briefly meeting hers.

She shook her head and went back to pretending to be busy.

"Neither do I... Would..." Dexter inhaled a shaky breath. "Would you allow me the honour of escorting you... and we can start planning on how I can help you all."

Kai stopped, tucking her hands behind her back.

A blush had taken over the doctor's honey-toned flesh. It exploded around his cheeks and even as far as his ears.

She took a deep breath of her own and considered his words and actions as of late. Kai couldn't tell if this was all an act or if he was genuine with her.

Dexter exhaled a long breath, hesitant outside Kai's door once more. Her demeanour towards him had changed, and rightly so. That once twinkling gleam of curiosity in her icy blues had been replaced by a cautious, almost indifferent dullness.

Her very actions alone screamed – I don't trust you.

He nearly collapsed onto his knees with relief when she agreed to attend the ball with him, allowing him the chance to make things right.

He straightened out his topcoat, ensuring the clip at his coat's pocket was secured, before firmly knocking three times.

The door opened in slow motion, or so it felt like. A vaguely unfamiliar woman stood before him, holding the door.

He knew it was Kai by that spectacular radiant hair colour and those icy irises that popped out even more with the smoked-out, dark eyeshadow. Her lashes were longer and darker as well. It was the first time he had ever seen her wear makeup.

Her hair was guided to a side, a braid going over the top like a headband, disappearing behind an ear where all that hair was gathered. The strands were secured behind that ear with that clip he had left in front of her door, which matched the sparkling clip attached to his coat's outer pocket. The rest of her red hair was freed, pulled over a shoulder, so very bright against her dark-coloured attire.

That dress swayed with her slow movements. It was an elegant, navy-blue gown with laced quarter sleeves. The mid of the gown synched her waist even more, making her covered-up chest appear bustier.

But what had his gaze constantly coaxed was that deep-rouge lipstick painted on her plumped lips, demanding full attention to the face with those bold eyes.

Dexter quickly averted his stare, covering his mouth with a feigned cough. "Uh... You look m-marvellous," warmth rose to his cheeks as the words fumbled out of his mouth.

Movement plucked his attention as Kai curtsied, a soft smile on those gloriously painted lips. He gawked at them as she mouthed a 'Thank you'.

Dexter couldn't help the nervous tremble as he offered her his arm. Laced, gloved hands gently grabbed hold, following tightly next to him as he escorted the beautiful maiden through the halls.

Occasionally, he would catch Kai's frosty irises, glancing at the gold gleaming clip on his chest. He fought the smile that twitched at his lips with her frowns.

He realised he hadn't explained exactly who gave the matching clip in her hair.

The clip was a slightly curved golden feather with diamond-like gems going up the base, surrounded by tiny gemstone-like stars.

The same one he had seen her toying with in the town's market.

A content feeling spread throughout his chest, leaving him satisfied and warm as he strolled with her in a blissful silence.

Dexter occasionally pointed, explaining to his stunning partner who the people surrounding them were as they neared the hall's entrance. He clarified who she needed to keep a healthy distance from and who was important to watch for.

People who would lie and cheat her to get closer to the princess.

He watched Kai's attention scan the captivating, spacious room, hardly acknowledging his words. A wary glisten took over her sparkling eyes as if she was anticipating something.

Waiting.

People of all sorts of backgrounds approached the two, and many of Dexter's acquaintances inquired about who the lucky lady was on his arm.

Lord Ballio held out a waiting hand as he greeted Kai, "Good evening, my lady."

Dexter fought the choking laugh frothed in his throat as Kai scanned that expecting palm before smiling and waving her little fingers.

He found it adorable how quickly she could turn on her oblivious charm and play innocent.

"This is Lady Redsi, my lord. You'll have to excuse her-"

Before the doctor could explain, Ballio exclaimed loudly, "Our little hero!?"

Dexter noticed Kai flinch at his side.

"Brave as she is stunning!" the loud man continued. His eyes practically undressed her there on the spot.

CHAPTER TWENTY-NINE

Kai felt strange in her own skin dressed up, but having people constantly approach and make ridiculous statements had her wanting to flee altogether. This was a different experience than working behind a bar, where she was protected by a large counter and had many options she could use as a weapon in self-defence cases.

Lord Ballio, a short and scrawny man, seemed to enjoy hearing himself talk. He yapped and yapped to Dexter, constantly throwing praise towards her. The stench of strong alcohol wafted into her face with each of his directed words.

But the man's lingering stare on Kai's chest had her slyly tug at Dexter's elbow, throwing in some brisk, pleading glances to leave.

Wanting to linger away from the dance floor, closest to an exit.

She slid her fingers down his arm when she couldn't successfully catch his attention, pretending to hold his hand.

He tensed with her deliberate action.

Kai curled her index finger and traced letters into his smooth palm.

His back straightened as he seemed to focus on her manoeuvres. She kept the movements slow, hoping he could decipher what she was trying to spell.

"Are you alright?"

Dexter snapped out of his tenseness, his free hand rose, fanning himself. "My apologies, my lord. It is rather warm here, don't you find?" He turned his chin towards Kai, blinking profusely. "Do you mind if we get some fresh air before the evening begins?"

Kai offered him her classic customer service smile, a gentle nod to her head, playing along.

"Please excuse us."

Dexter guided her through the crowds, careful not to speak much more than a 'hello' to anyone in their paths.

As much as Kai wanted to admire the beautiful hall that was marvellous and fairy-tale-like, with flowers placed around it and massive paintings hung on some walls — a feeling of uneasiness swept through her. On one side of the hall was a wall of windows that looked out to the most extensive garden of the palace. The trims were arched and circular, allowing as much space to view. Even the ceiling was glass panels curved upwards, making the roof appear even higher past the chandeliers.

That ginormous, stretching glass was going to come crashing down at any moment, and the story's true villain would finally make his grand entrance.

She wanted not to be under it when it did.

Kai inhaled a deep breath when she pushed past the threshold, heading onto the stone patio. So many flowery aromas filled her nostrils as she allowed the hand she was holding to drop.

Her eyes focused on the changing sky as the stars slowly appeared like a glitter of sparkles high above. The sun was setting, the sky a range of purples and pinks, making the hall behind her glow in an after light. Small stones of red and gold lights flicked to life along the paths outside, making the garden appear even more whimsical.

For a fictional world, it felt so real. All of this felt too natural, making her wonder which parts of her were reality.

Dexter coughs, pulling her attention back. "Is everything okay?" His eyes scanned her face.

Kai held her hand out, waiting for his. When the doctor complied, she began tracing letters into his palm once more.

The doctor watched; her actions left behind white lines, which faded quickly into his flesh colour. He nodded his head to her bland excuse. "I wasn't entirely sure what you were trying to convey... I'm sorry you couldn't bring your book. I just thought it might have drawn more unwanted attention to yourself."

Kai waved her hands in front of her, not bothered about that. She was thankful for once she couldn't speak, in whatever form.

There was a pause between them; the chatter and music reverberated onto the balcony.

Dexter still observed Kai, his stare squinting. "Are you sure you're alright? You seem... edgy."

She nodded and gestured at the hall, making exasperated faces along with it. Kai couldn't explain, even if she could, that something would happen.

She had hoped she was doing a better job at hiding it.

The doctor ran a hand through his neatly tied back hair, pushing away the strands that fell into his face.

He seemed to have been contemplating something when suddenly, an announcement bounced off the inside walls.

"HER ROYAL HIGHNESS, PRINCESS SCARLETT ROSETHORNE, AND HIS IMPERIAL HIGHNESS, PRINCE WARRICK CRESTBLOOD OF RAEVEGON!"

The sounds of horns and trumpets followed, booming in a rhythm.

The two on the stone patio shuffled for the open balcony doors. The prince and princess were on the massive climbing stairs, entering the hall through wide open red doors.

Warrick's attire was exactly as Vanessa had written it within the story, at least to Kai's imagination.

He wore a dignified white, gold, and silver suit trailed by a long, sleek purple cape. That cape looked to be tinted blue when the lighting found it. Yet, he still carried the mien of a high-ranking royal who knew how to use the bulky sword latched to his hip. A white-gloved hand rested on the hilt of it, the other hand down at his side. His tanned skin seemed to glow with all the white he wore. His hair was styled to the side, not a strand out of place. But the face he wore was not one of pleasantries or lovesickness, which was depicted within the romance.

Kai placed a finger on her chin, reflecting. She wondered if perhaps they had words before entering the hall. Her eyes shifted over to Warrick's partner with that thought.

Scarlett wore a purple shimmering dress that changed to an indigo, similar to Warrick's cape. Purple glimmering sleeves hung loosely at her sides; her hands free of gloves waved to the guests. Her hair was up in a bun, and strategically pulled curls surrounded the lining of her face. A decent-sized purple flower was placed behind an ear with chunky, sparkling blue earrings reflecting the hall's glow just under them. Her makeup matched the colour design of the dress Kai had given her this morning, which she chose to wear at the last minute.

Scarlett was shocked when Kai appeared before her this morning, offering the stunning dress. Kai withheld nothing as she wrote that the dress was a gift from His Highness.

She just didn't elaborate on who she believed the dress was for. All she cared about was that the main character had her gown, and the trio would get another clue once the story was set straight.

"Merlin's beard," Dexter mumbled beside her.

Kai peeped, noticing the look of sheer surprise on his face. All the characters within this plot would — should be star-struck by the main character this evening. It was all going according to plan.

"That dress is made from the underbelly of a dragon... The double-coloured shimmering material." Dexter leant towards Kai and pointed a hidden finger to Scarlett poised on the landing, above all the people. His breath tickled the side of Kai's face. "It was rumoured that Prince Warrick took down a dragon a few months ago... To think he'd prepare the hide of it as a gift for her, perhaps the rumour about them is false."

Kai stood straighter, happy with her quick decision at dawn. As she twisted to look back at Scarlett, she felt a piercing stare blaze upon her.

Prince Warrick glowered in Kai's and Dexter's direction, a brewing storm on his face.

"Smile, *my Love*." Scarlett glanced, almost growling at Warrick with smiling teeth.

Warrick's stare was locked in. Disappointment and annoyance gripped his chest as he watched the two figures so close to each other.

It wasn't hard for him to spot the beautiful maiden dressed elegantly dark this evening. Not with her hair being the only pop of colour among the sea of creams and browns of people down below.

It was quite a shock to him to see Scarlett enter the dining hall earlier in the dress he had sent over for Kai to wear. Unable to hide his rage, he accused the selfish cow of stealing it.

Only to be told it was *re-gifted* to Scarlett.

A hand found Warrick's arm, nails digging into his bicep. "Let's have this dance and get this over with this already."

He couldn't break away. His eyes narrowed in on the man leaning into Kai.

Even her companion for the evening had colourful hair, making them both equally different yet perfectly matched, side by side.

He realised then *who* that man was.

Warrick caught the soft smile that tugged on those painted lips as the man spoke closely to her cheek. His eyes finally met those far-away icy ones. That smile she wore was gone. Instantaneously.

Scarlett teased again, "*My Love?*"

Warrick spat out, "Do not. Call. Me. That." Every syllable was harshly thrown.

Amusement flashed in the princess's face; her eyes followed his line of sight. A natural smile graced her lips as she waved to her well-cleaned-up handmaiden in the back. Her impulsive wave slowed as she noticed the man next to Kai.

"Why is *he* with her?" she seethed.

"Your Highnesses..." a wary voice spoke up behind the two stoned royals, "The guests are waiting for you to start."

Scarlett swiftly schooled her features and marched right down the stairs without the prince.

Warrick robotically pursued.

The royals eventually positioned themselves at the centre of the room, violins and cellos beginning the dance. Protocol formalities were offered before the prince and princess stood face to face. Shimmering materials swayed around the floor moments later.

"You seem to have a problem with your doctor," Warrick stated, his eyes flicking to the side, coincidently towards the patio area.

Scarlett, too, was guilty of peeking, wanting to see if they had moved.

Storming down those stairs, she noticed her pet wearing a clip in a similar design to the clip at the doctor's chest pocket. Fury found her feet as she practically guided the prince around the dance floor. Enraged that the doctor dared to remove her gift to Kai, only to replace it with one of his own.

Claiming *her* person.

A thought stopped her dead, and the prince halted with Scarlett's cease.

"Was the dress an actual gift to me or *my* servant?" The princess squinted up at the handsome face, shoulders squared.

Warrick finally looked upon her thoroughly for the first time since dinner. An eyebrow rose. "Does it matter? You're wearing it now," he said all too plainly.

The music stopped as whispers and murmurs hushed around the hall.

A psychotic smile crept up Scarlett's face. "It was for *her*, wasn't it?" Her eyes widened with those intentionally loud words.

Warrick stood taller and glared at the crazed woman.

Before either could say anything to spoil the moment further, the glass above the hall shattered, doing them both a favour.

Shards of glass, bits of the brackets that held the panels in place, and black feathers rained upon those in attendance. Screams, crashing debris, and enormous fluttering wings echoed inside the spacious hall. Several ropes also dropped from that newly acquired hole in the ceiling, and people dressed in dark uniforms descended.

The people inside the event scurried for exits or pushed towards the corners and walls, attempting to escape the showering onslaught.

Many of the millions of candles were snuffed out by the strong gust of wind that came with that pivotal arrival. The largest chandelier came crashing down, and some of the dangling jewels were blown off and became bullets within. The massive paintings on one of the walls were destroyed, and the glass structural design towards the patios was also blown out.

Guards had rushed in, signalled by the screams, and surrounded the people to protect them. All able bodies were immobilised, and all alarmed stares were on the dropped-in visitors.

Those huge flapping wings had ceased, posed up and stretched above a figure crutched dramatically on top of the circular unit of the candelabrum. Right at the centre of the dance floor, that figure slowly raised his hooded head amid the chaos. The upper half of his face was concealed, but a sinister smile was offered to everyone quieting down and watching on in terror.

Red eyes glinted, and a voice carried above them all, "Good evening."

CHAPTER THIRTY

D exter gently linked arms with Kai, grumbling under his breath. She didn't know if she had heard him quite right, but it sounded like he said something about Warrick. She finally broke away from the prince's demanding stare-down, realising he probably figured out Kai's treacherous scheme.

Clearly, he was not amused that Scarlett ended up wearing the dress she was given.

Kai told herself to worry about it later. Her eyes slid over to the princess, catching the subtle wave Scarlett offered as her face turned nasty.

With no idea what was happening, Kai guessed things were about to take a terrible turn for the worst with Scarlett's stomps down the broad steps. The princess looked mere words away from exploding.

"We should ready ourselves," Dexter began to her side. "Once their dance finishes, it'll be time for ours. It's customary for…"

Kai nodded silently. His words faded away as she watched two figures descend, then disappear into the crowd of folk surrounding the hall.

The music surged and flowed around the massive chamber; two heads bobbed about the dance floor from what Kai could see.

She stood on her tippy toes, trying to gain more of a look, spotting two familiar individuals dressed up nicely. Ava and Charlie, hand in hand, nearer the front of the crowd. They both looked marvellous, except for Charlie's face.

Charlie's attention was fastened above, not on the two swaying royals claiming the dancefloor.

His face was of pure terror.

Kai's stare drew up, and red beady eyes glinted, peering into the hall through the glass. Her nails dug in as her hand shot to the side, shaking Dexter.

The music seized, people murmured, and then the roof came down.

Kai let out a silent scream as she dropped low. Dexter grabbed and shielded her from the raining debris.

The hall was filled with thunderous shouts from guards to attendees. Glass shattered and echoed around, women wept, and bodies of fabric dashed from the tumbling disaster.

As the dust settled and people quieted down, a deep, broad, accented voice greeted, "Good evening."

Kai peeked up, spying between Dexter's arms that caged her protectively. A man with ginormous black wings was at the centre of the dance floor, surrounded by figures either cowering away or sprawled out on the ground still. There were also people dressed in all-black in a defensive stance near him, ready for a fight. Their faces were covered entirely by cloth as shining daggers reflected in their hands.

The man at the centre had his face obstructed, too. White teeth gleamed nearly as bright as his ruby red irises, scanning the surroundings.

Kai sucked in a sharp breath as if all the air had been evaporated from the room.

He carried the same sort of energy Vanessa did. That same strange feeling gripped her guts. It screamed at her to get far, far away from him.

She didn't need to confirm who he was—Eros had finally made his dramatic appearance.

They had officially reached the pinnacle point of the novel's storyline.

A guard shouted, "IN THE NAME OF THE KING!" Many others encircled the not-invited guests.

But their commands were cut off as the story's villain spoke, line for line,

"I thought all citizens were welcomed to this tiddly gathering?"

The hall became shambolic as soldiers advanced at the party crashers, swords drawn.

Those black wings stretched out and flapped forward once without notice, pushing the men away with their weapons. Those ruby reds found Scarlett among the crowd. "Get her," he demanded with a point of a finger.

His men rushed, but Warrick and his guards broke the line of men. None of them were stationed before the princess, none of them protecting her. Only a handful of Rosethorne's knights stood before Scarlett and the aggressors.

Kai's thoughts scrambled, drawing a blank. This wasn't part of the story.

Warrick should have been the only one standing before Scarlett, protecting her in this moment.

The people who could walk fled from the battle commencing at the heart of the hall. Steel on steel clashed, blood sprayed, painting more of the dirtied floor. The fleeing guests made it hard for the knights from outside to get in from the entries.

Warrick was clashing with an assailant at the side as Eros stalked unchallenged towards the terror-frozen target.

The princess had crumbled to the ground since their arrival without anyone to guard her now. Her people had their hands full, unaware of that being prowling closer.

Kai had no idea what was happening before it was too late. Bodies were pushed away as Scarlett's small figure in the distance got closer. Dexter's shout was getting farther behind as her feet raced forward. She whirled around, shaking hands out, shielding the princess with her body.

Coming face to face with the villain of the novel.

Eros terminated his advancement, a hand raised and planted on his hip to her efforts. His head cocked to a side; those wings stretched out again. Before he could do anything, a dark figure flew at Kai.

Something gleamed in the figure's hand.

Warrick turned when he noticed Eros paused, noticing Kai had somehow appeared before Scarlett. He was shouting, shooting for her next.

A blade came down, and Kai stumbled back, unable to dodge the full extent of it. The tip of the weapon caught her arm as she brought them up before her, blocking that gleaming object.

Another silent scream ripped out of Kai's throat as the steel tore into flesh. She barely had a moment to gain her footing when the attacker swung again, upwards this time.

Fear and pain blocked out all rationality within Kai, as she believed this was it. She was about to find out whether she could return to reality or meet her parents.

A figure materialised before her — taking the blow, something crashed with that blade as steel on steel rang out. Blue hair began shoving the attacker aside.

Hot liquid oozed out of Kai's forearm, the pain unlike anything she had experienced before. She clutched her injured arm to herself, staggering more. Her chest began to tighten as her breaths came in fast.

"What bravery."

That voice had Kai's swaying sight on it.

A head was still cocked to a side, observing. "So, it's you," he added mysteriously. A smile climbed his cheeks, reaching those scary eyes.

That was the last thing she saw as the strength in her legs gave out, and Kai's knees buckled when the world went dark.

"Kai? ... C'mon darling, it's time to get up. You're going to be late for the bus."

Kai's eyes slowly opened, blinking away the sleep from them.

A face similar to hers came into view from the darkness.

"Let's go, up, up, up." Her father was sitting on the edge of the bed, smiling down.

Her bottom lip quivered, "Daddy?" her voice so small and foreign.

Blue eyes, like winter melting into spring, sparkled. "Yes, Princess?" His voice warmed like a holiday aboard under bright summer skies.

Her little hand grabbed a handful of the cashmere cardigan he was wearing, squeezing the soft material a few times. She felt the soft fabric between her fingers, and relief bloomed in her heart. "I... I missed you," she cried.

Her father's face morphed into pity; his arms scooped her petite body up. "What on earth has gotten into you..." A hand rubbed the side of Kai's head the moment it was laid flat against his chest. "Bad dreams?"

Kai's head nodded gently; her eyes closed. Her father's clean, crisp scent surrounded her, just as the warmth of his body did.

"They're just dreams, Princess. They're not real. They cannot hurt you."

Kai rubbed the side of her face against the soft warmth of the fabric.

Her father's strong beating heart got quieter, eventually stilling into silence. A cold draft nipped at her exposed toes, causing her to bring her knees up more. She went to open her mouth to relay how cold she was when nothing projected from her throat.

Her eyes opened again as she found she was no longer cradled in her father's arms but lying in an unfamiliar bed.

She hazily sat up and noticed dark sheets over and under her. A thick quilt covered everything but her toes.

The surroundings were three walls of pure ice, one dark wall, some blocks of frozen furniture, and an ice floor.

Her breaths came out in puffs of clouds observing the new scenery.

Kai rubbed the sleep and tears that had collected in her caruncles, arm stinging slightly. She blinked in confusion at the bandage that covered her left forearm, going past her elbow.

As rationality came tumbling back to her, panic had Kai rising from the bed. The last thing she remembered was Eros standing a few metres from where she stood, and a man had sliced her arm open.

Bare feet touched the ground, and Kai immediately jumped back onto the bed. The floor was so cold it burned the pads of her toes.

Kai sat on the bed, defeated, staring at the ground of ice.

That dream of seeing her father again and returning to her old home's bed had shaken her resolve. Completely fooling her into thinking that maybe she had returned to the past. When everything was right and bright with the world.

A hot tear slid down her cheek as Kai covered her face and cried into those hands.

She wanted to go home.

Not that little room in the palace or her small, stupidly expensive apartment, but home. Back to Ireland, in that small, cosy cottage her father bought to raise his family in, back to a time when her only worries were the nightmares that chased her awake.

Kai sat there awhile — eventually, the tears stopped falling, and her sad thoughts stopped slamming into her, wave after wave. She used the bandage to wipe away all the liquids that leaked from her face when glinting reds caught her attention.

Something was standing within that dark wall.

Chapter Thirty-One

S tillness and silence, Kai held her breath and ceased all movements. She realised that the wall was the exit. There was no door, just a massive crater-sized hole in the ice-boxed room — leading out somewhere. The man's enormous wings caused the darkness. His frame swallowed the entire area.

The being had to have been well over six feet tall, his wings even bigger to have absorbed the entry.

Eros had a hand on his chin, staring without a single blink, frozen as the blueish glowing ice around them. The only movement he revealed was the occasional rising and falling of his chest. No clouds puffed out from his breaths as hers did.

Kai dared to swallow; her body temperature plummeted further as he finally entered the room.

Those mammoth-sized wings tucked inwards and delicately pulled down over his shoulders to pass, rippling out once they cleared it. His steps were silent, stealth-like, as he made enormous strides across the space, closer to the bed.

Those ruby reds locked Kai in place from fleeing.

His head cocked to a side; those pupils dilated as he scanned her over.

Kai finally got a clear look at his face, gobsmacked by the picture-perfect silhouette of his features.

Dark lashes protected ruby red eyes, so thick it appeared like he had a thin coat of eyeliner on the edges of his waterlines. Accompanying those deep crimsons were thick dark eyebrows that slightly protruded from his spotless forehead. Slight waves riddled his dark hair that naturally fell around his head, framing his heart-shaped face. Kai paused on the slight-pointed ears that peeked out from that thick hair. Her attention did not linger too long as it drifted to the five o'clock shadow along his strong jawline, going down to a pointed chin. His top and bottom lips portioned perfectly to each other, adorned with a strong masculine nose above. His skin was impeccably flawless, marked only by strange sorts of markings. Curve-like red lines dragged down his firm cheeks, continuing to his neck and showcasing chest.

A strange symbol resembling a clock connects with the red lines above at the centre.

He wore a sleeveless, black, boob window top, showing off that symbol and his impressive arms. Muscles upon muscles, not a shred of fat anywhere to be seen. One noticeable vein went over each bicep. More of those raised-up veins upon his forearms, going down onto the backs of his hands. Her gaze lingered as more of those lines decorated his hands, the red swirls almost like a rose.

Kai's stare dragged over.

That skin-tight top outlined every muscle and groove along his chest and further down the abdomen. Deep indents disappeared into his pants as if guiding her attention elsewhere.

She found herself pondering, *if evil, why hot?* Completely taken back by the sinful specimen before her. Her thoughts flowed to another question: why did Vanessa leave out such significant details about the story's antagonist?

He was evidently written to be the most breath-taking male in this world. Without his disposition and her knowledge of the story, she would have assumed *he* was the main character.

She didn't understand why Vanessa wrote such a glorified persona if she wouldn't have them as the lead.

A corner of the being's lips cocked upwards. His markings moved, slipping into the folds of his cheeks. An illusion like red dimples. "If evil, why hot?" his strong accent was so loud in the cold space between them.

Kai blinked several times and wondered if she had heard him correctly. *I couldn't have said that out loud,* she mused. Her hand rose to her throat, rubbing it in circles.

"I couldn't have said that out loud." Eros's white teeth flashed at her with a predator-like gleam.

She carefully started to shuffle until her spine hit the frozen wall on the other side of the very wide bed. Black feathers fell off the edge, floating away from the mattress with her movements.

The man cautiously moved, too, crouching. His back arched up; those wings caved around him. "What an interesting inner monologue you have... Tell me, does your physical voice sound like that?"

All thoughts evaded Kai as she stared bewildered at him. Her body began to tremble as the blood drained from her face.

Eros shuffled, still crouched. His movements resembled a vulture zoning in on its meal. He spoke again with amusement in his tone, "I have ways to make you talk, you know?"

Kai's hands shot to her throat, screaming internally, *I can't speak!*

Both of his eyebrows raised. "Is there something wrong with your voice?" his own was low now, almost a grumble in that chest.

Her head nodded quickly, images of her losing her voice and Vanessa's wicked grin flashed looking down on her. Thoughts of how Kai relied on paper now to convey her words to those in this world mixed into the frame-by-frame playback in her mind.

"What a fascinating imagination you have." He reached the bed, still creeping forward, and climbed onto it.

Kai couldn't go any further back unless she were magically absorbed into the wall behind.

Eros stopped his advancement, kneeling on the bed. "Who is that woman to you?" he asked suddenly.

Kai shook her head, not understanding the meaning of his question.

Perhaps he referred to the princess and why Kai was adamant about protecting her in the hall.

A scary presumption rushed into her mind. *He can't see my thoughts, can he?*

His large hand raised along with her inner monologue, pointing to his temple. He was answering her private thoughts yet again, "I can see the images clearly, as though they are my own. I just have to reach..." His hand extended, then mimicked a pull in the air between them. "And can see the things you have seen... a world unlike this one." His wings flexed, twitching. "That witch's face is familiar, yet it is not... So, I'll ask again." His tone dropped into a lethal warning, "Who. Is. That. Woman?"

Kai could only answer honestly, knowing now what kind of power he held. *She is an author... Someone responsible for putting me here.*

Wings flexed again; Eros's head cocked to the other side. He watched every single subtle action Kai offered. From the trembles to how her lips mimicked her inner voice. Never missing anything.

"A book? Are you saying that imagination of yours... is your world? That you are trapped inside a book from it?"

With every flicker of those wings, his crisp scent wafted into Kai's face, slowly disarming her. The fragrance reminded her of evergreen, similar to the Scot's Pine and Shrubby Junipers that grew wild in the back of her childhood garden.

"Show me," he demanded, and with his words, a sensation crawled over Kai's flesh.

Invisible feathers traced over her body, circling her nape.

Every thought was seduced out of her, flashing like a frame-by-frame clip, leading her up to her fall into this world. The winged man was in her face, his nose nearly touching hers when the thoughts ended—ending right to this moment.

Her whole life had flashed before her eyes in a matter of moments. Kai let out a breath she didn't realise she had been holding, eyes watered from the assault of memories.

Eros whispered, "Kai... Redsi." His warm breath fanned her cheeks.

She knew she should have been afraid, yet her body warmed with his closeness, his scent like a spell over her. Heat and goosebumps spread over the surface of her arms like wildfire. The way he said her name had her toes involuntarily curled.

She closed her eyes and swallowed, trying to pull herself together.

The man crossed his legs steadily, and his eyes darted between Kai's closed ones. He was observing her as if she were the exotic one there.

Two men sat across from each other by a roaring waterfall. Both were equally as exhausted and sore from the attacks four days ago.

The engagement announcement was never made following the events.

The kingdom had been on lockdown since the attack, the hall cleaned up, and the surviving suspects were being interrogated. Everything was being combed through thoroughly to discover who and what had crashed the joyous day. Many families mourned the loss of lives that had been taken that night.

Dexter tossed a stone into the rippling water, watching the rock drop and sink—a physical representation of his current feelings.

He rushed after Kai that night when she had thrown him off her with desperate strength. His stomach plummeted as he witnessed that long, reflecting blade descend on her. Even though she was pale as death, Kai stood her ground and defended a woman who would replace her like a broken quill.

He clenched the remaining stones in his hand and recalled how her face twisted in anguish. How Kai's lips parted, and what he imagined would have been a scream coming from them.

For the first time in fifteen years, he had used his magic out-right, right in front of so many witnesses. Appearing before her as that assailant went to slash a second time.

Dexter wasn't a soldier. He didn't even know how to hold a sword, let alone a dagger. He did his best to deflect, dodge and counter afterwards. But by the time he took down his opponent, Kai Redsi was gone.

One black feather in a small pool of blood replaced where her planted feet had been previously.

Her cautious scans of anticipating concerns resurfaced in his mind, causing him to conjure many more questions.

Did she know this was going to transpire? Is that why she was so on edge? Did she know the ice demon?

These questions continued to haunt him ever since her disappearance.

Across from Dexter sat Warrick. A decent-sized cut decorated the prince's right cheek, now scabbed over. His uniform was in disarray, very different from his neatly put-together image. He sat on the edge of a massive boulder half submerged in the earth floor. His glowering stare zoned out on his scuffed boots.

One minute, he was clashing swords with two goons. The next, he was rushing for the girl.

The little woman was bleeding and staggering backwards, defending the undeserving princess. He cut and slashed anyone in his path to get to her, yelling as he watched her eyes close and her body collapse to the ground. But even before she hit it, a massive blur of feathers scooped her up and took off to the skies.

Warrick had paused, watching helplessly, when one of the goons nearly removed his face from his brief distraction.

After the Rosethorne knights had detained the few surviving, he took off with personally selected guards and searched the kingdom, to no avail.

The muted little lady was gone, taken by the winged monster of the Frozen Wastelands. Someone Warrick and his father were all too familiar with.

It was no surprise when he saw the wicked creature crash his engagement. He might have thanked him if it were Scarlett he had taken, forgiven everything he had done previously to him…

But of course, that beast was the Bain to the Crestblood's existence.

The lines began to blur, wondering why the creature was so vexed about causing mayhem for him particularly.

Before his anger suffocated him, Dexter shot up to his feet.

Throwing the remaining stones in his hands, the strange doctor shouted,

"Damn it!" His face was red from the force of his scream.

Warrick watched the man huff and puff, beginning to pace at the lake's shore. His violet eyes glowed unnaturally, similar to that creature's.

After hearing the king would not lend help the following morning, to search for the mere servant - who was willing to throw her life away, not once, but twice for his daughter. The man, Dexter Ubar, was frantic. He stormed out of the throne room and had been searching ever since. He stepped away from his duties as the doctor until he could find her.

Warrick came face to face with him in one of the out-skirted taverns. There was a silent agreement and many stale ales between the two men to do anything they could to bring her back.

Since then, they had been meeting at this strange, quiet lake outside the castle. Sharing any intel between the two of them gathered separately.

"I'm going to assume you found no leads either?" Warrick asked, his attention dejected on his boots.

Dexter leant over, catching his breath. "The frozen lands span across a vast valley. Mountains of nothing but ice with interconnected tunnels and corridors leading to mother-knows-what!" His messy hair swayed around his head, concealing the look of utter defeat on his face.

"Don't you wizards have tracking magic or some kind of spell that could be useful in these situations?" Warrick sat upright, an eyebrow raised towards the man.

He had heard of a few wizards and witches in these lands, most dead now, all thanks to the king.

Dexter threw him a glare. "Careful of your words," he hissed.

The imperial prince shrugged off his offensive behaviour. "My people have dared to venture those treacherous lands before... and none have come back alive. We need something or someone that can point us in the right directions in and out."

"You cannot use magic in those parts," Dexter's words spilt out more and more depleted, "That creature... has absolute control over it." His eyes simmered to nothing and then flared as something seemed to strike him.

Dexter was straight as a board, his attention wiped towards the castle.

Warrick stood, too. "What is it?" Drawing his sword.

"I think I know someone... or two... that may be able to help," the doctor mumbled, his attention dragging to the prince. "Miss Redsi was working with two other people within the castle. They may know where and how to get her back."

Warrick re-sheathed his sword, giving the man a firm nod. "Lead the way." His morale steadily returned with those promising words for the first time in days.

Chapter Thirty-Two

An airy sigh released from Kai's mouth, and she smacked her lips together, feeling somewhat more stable now that her stomach was full of warm soup. A chicken soup that her damsel-snatching host graciously served her.

Eros was still sitting inside the room, perched on a backwards-turned ice chair, watching. She tried her best to ignore his dominating presence and the smell of him every time those glorious wings flexed and pushed the cold air throughout the space.

She was bundled in new clothes, which were far too big but enough to cover and keep her from freezing. Her host reached for her face earlier and pulled away quickly when he felt how cold she had become.

With a flash of darkness, Eros threw heaps of fabrics at Kai from the chest of drawers near the corner, commanding her to change quickly.

He perched back down on a conjured seat, surveying her. The barbaric being didn't try to avert his eyes when she asked him to do so.

"Why? So, I can give you a chance to run for it? I don't think so," he claimed. His deep chuckles exploded when she dove under the thick quilt to give herself some privacy to change from her dirtied, tattered dress.

Since then, he had been silent, somehow sending people to bring food without opening his mouth.

The old woman who brought the bowl bowed deeply, leaving the steaming tray on the ground outside.

Is this your kingdom, then? Kai asked, glancing secretly to the exit where that woman was. She briefly recalled Eros dwelling in some wasteland. His scenes were non-informant, just packed with action.

A beast with no ownership of anything or himself.

Eros chuckled again, "You tell me, Princess."

Kai couldn't help the frown that took over her features, glaring at the man.

A smile greeted her as if he genuinely enjoyed sitting there, observing.

Scarlett is the princess, Kai pointed out.

Eros cocked his head, black hair shifted to a side. "But not the princess that arrogant worm wanted. His face was marvellous when he realised you stood between me and that wilting rose. I should thank you for that."

Why are you so angry with Warrick?

That was never mentioned to give a reason for the readers. The more and more Kai thought about it, the deeper the rabbit hole dropped.

Her suspicions flowed to another question: why was Eros – Warrick's adversary? What kind of backstory did those two have? There were so many plot holes and dead ends that made no sense in her once-loved book, things she had never ever questioned before.

She watched the winged man contemplate the question as she spiralled with her own.

"I suspected my life was stuck on some magical loop for a while..." Those eyes finally broke away as Eros examined his hands.

A breeze of a thought whistled into Kai's mind. *Do these characters restart their parts right where the story began? Are they able to be aware of this?*

She strung together her theories as his voice continued, "Do you know what it's like to wake up every day and feel like you've done this a million times?"

Kai shook her head in response.

"Do you know what it's like to build yourself up, fight the powers against you constantly, only to lose? The same feeling of defeat, over and over again, the same outcome..." Eros flipped his hands over, glaring at his palms. "That same impulse every damn day to just crush someone, and you don't even know why anymore?" His hands clenched into fists. "As if it was implemented into your skull for no apparent reason."

Kai's eyebrows furrowed, listening to the man's low words, talking to himself.

Trying to figure it all out.

"But then..." His eyes shot back to Kai, twinkling. "For the first time, something happened. That all-knowing feeling morphed into uncertainty... Things weren't going the way they had been. Those moments of déjà vu stopped, and it was all confirmed to me when *you* appeared." Eros's teeth were on display, grinning. "I'm trapped inside a book."

He crept to his feet, still straddling the chair.

Kai sunk back, spine pressed against the wall.

"Those dreams... that woman - that *witch*," he growled. "This is all her doing, and you'll help me get out of this. Then, I'll strangle her scheming little throat for daring to jest with me."

Kai's head shook, her cheeks wobbled. *N-No... you're... you're just a character within a book!*

Eros pulled away from the seat, his wings tucked back. "Good cess on me. My wish take me... may I only prosper?"

Chills ran up Kai's spine with Eros's advancement.

"The first drop of happiness quenches my heart — may it boil into my bones. May the flesh never rot and fall away putrid before my very eyes." He ran a hand down one of his arms, the air filled with whispers.

A clock ticked away, mingling in with those hushed words.

"May I fade into nothing, like snow in summer..." He stopped at the edge of the bed, gazing deeply, repeating those exact words she had done.

Images not of Kai's memory swirled into existence, his fading voice swallowed by that ticking clock.

With every tick, images flourished. A stone-aged civilisation, a village of happy folk, then children running down well-walked paths. Flags familiar to Kai waved on a cool breeze, stationed on watch towers near a glorious temple.

Wagons pulled vegetation, a roaring bonfire and those same folk danced around it in circles. A book now appeared, with handwritten ink. A publishing marker snagged Kai's full attention.

Argos, Peloponnese, Greece. The date was ruined from something touching the ink, smearing it. Unable to show what year it was.

A face materialised before she could even register what was happening. Or below her — as the image blinked, appearing to look down.

A younger version of Vanessa smiled up, batting her eyelashes. A wreath of red roses intertwined around her head, and some veil was linked to it. A large, tattooed hand flipped that veil and cupped her cheek.

"... and keep me. This, I wish," Eros's words ended, and so did the images.

Kai's vision and hearing returned; the room vibrated in strange waves. Her breathing came in harsh rasps, and a cold sweat broke over her body from that unnatural sensation.

"I'm starting to remember." Eros smiled, somehow, before Kai again.

She was so transfixed in those memories she didn't notice when he crawled onto the bed. A hand was cupping her face, a thumb caressed her cheek, brushing under an eye.

"I'd like to go home now, please, and you're going to help me."

Kai didn't even want to entertain the thought before — that maybe these characters weren't characters after all. But if what she saw was true, then Eros, too, was once another person who got trapped inside the book.

Kai's mind was so overstimulated that she felt her brain was on a skillet, currently being scrambled.

That feather-like touch turned fierce. Eros gripped her firmly, forcing her to look at him. "You will help me, won't you, Kai?... Let's go home."

Charlie guided Ava back to her quarters after their shift, equally distant, which was not a norm between them.

Ava had fallen terrifyingly still after hearing Kai was gone, with the villain no less. Her attitude and enthusiasm to escape plummeted.

The trio had believed the arrangement between them was their best bet in getting them out of there and back to the real world. However, the one thrust to the plot's front lines was now absent.

Ava trashed her room in blind terror, weeping for hours until the sun had risen and disappeared, hurting herself in the process. Even when the head kitchen staff shouted at her, Ava stayed mute as if she no longer had a voice.

Any hope she had – diminished, silently accepting that they were trapped. Accepting that they would disappear within the lines and neither would ever see their loved ones again.

No matter what he did, Charlie could not pull Ava out of the depression she was declining into. Even his morale threatened to descend into madness without Ava's reassuring attitude.

They had just rounded the stairwell, stepping off onto Ava's floor. Charlie stopped, yanking her back and closer to him.

She mumbled, sounding like she couldn't care less, "What's wrong?"

Charlie's stare hardened at the two individuals marching away from Ava's door, right to them.

Dexter's hands gestured. "This is Mister Charlie Flounder and Miss Ava Sebastian. The two that had been working with Miss Redsi."

A ridiculed laugh escaped Ava's mouth, showing more emotion than she had lately. "Oh, I see... You got rid of Kai, and now it's our turn!" Her hold on Charlie dropped, trying to move forward blindly.

Warrick turned to the doctor, Dexter's face one of disbelief.

"Here to have us discarded so your secret doesn't get out?!"

Charlie grabbed Ava with both hands, pulling her jerking body backwards. His eyes were on the Crown Prince.

If they got beheaded, they certainly weren't going back to their reality.

Confusion deepened on Dexter's features. "You think I was the one responsible for Miss Redsi's disappearance?"

A hand covered Ava's mouth as she drew in a deep inhale. Charlie acted fast before she shouted out what she truly believed.

He knew she could be sassy and downright aggressive regarding the people she cared about. He had listened to her sputter theories the first few hours after the news. Ava swore on her grandma's grave that the wizard had something to do with it or was involved somehow.

The prince had angled his body, facing the doctor. "Why would she have reason to suspect you, I wonder?" his tone full of suspicion.

Dexter didn't engage with the Crown Prince's insinuation. His eyes dulled as they darted between the two servants' closeness. "I care about her..." he said in a small voice. A blush flushed his cheeks with that confession.

Charlie's eyebrows nearly hit his hairline, but Ava wasn't buying it.

"Bullshit," she spat out at him between Charlie's fingers. A wince proceeded as Charlie's grip tightened, keeping her from saying anything more.

A frown formed on Warrick's mug, but he quietly listened, watching the interaction.

Dexter's hands had clenched at his sides, staring at the woman's blindfold. "I have spent every waking minute since her disappearance to find her. What have you done to help bring her back?"

His words hit Ava like a bucket of cold water. Whatever nasty remark she thought about saying was gone as the truth washed over her.

"I did not come here to waste precious moments arguing with you. I've come to ask for your help... because my gut tells me you know *exactly* where she is."

The corridor fell silent. The flames down the long hall flickered and danced. The sun outside descended, and even the birds quieted down for the evening.

Warrick now focused on the servants, observing the quick surprise that fleeted across the young man's face.

It seemed the doctor's assumptions were correct.

"So, are you going to help us or not?" He decided to get straight to the point and not give them a moment to think about it. "I will not ask any questions until all is said and done. However, if anything happens to her... Our agreement is void, and so too are your lives."

Charlie stiffened like a stone, but it was Ava who spoke in response, "Our lives were void the moment she was taken."

Warrick wondered what she meant by that but could not ask as Dexter cut back in.

"Help us, and maybe we can also help you." The doctor's hand reached out, earnestly waiting.

"Your Highness... you must eat." Jade sat on the edge of the mattress, worried for the bedridden princess.

Scarlett hadn't left her palace since the incident; paranoia had taken hold. She was petrified to leave the confines of her room.

The poisoning had rattled her, but this had struck true.

The king had not even bothered to check on his daughter, scrambling to reinforce security around the palace for his own life.

"That creature..." Scarlett had been muttering madness since that night, thinking he'd return for her. "He's come for me..."

Jade placed the tray on the side table. Yet another meal would go cold and wasted. "Our Rose must eat."

Scarlett's face was dreadful, lacklustre, and gaunt. The roundness in her face began to diminish, sinking into her skull. Her lips had started drying, splitting from where she had sucked them in and chewed.

"He's come to kill me." She was rocking in place on the bed.

Madam Barnsley pulled the vial from her pocket and popped the cork off it. "Please, drink this." She placed it on the princess's lips, successfully getting her to take the sedative.

It seemed to be the only thing to keep her sane, just like her mother long ago.

Once Scarlett fell asleep, Jade went to the servant's wing to find the doctor. She didn't care if this would come back to bite her; she knew in her heart that he was the only one who would be able to help her, Scarlett.

Regardless of their history, Doctor Ubar had magic fingers.

Everything and everyone he helped – healed. Jade believed only he could save Scarlett at this point.

The sun had disappeared from the sky when she reached his door. Her raised hand halted, pausing as she heard multiple voices within.

The Crown Prince and two others were already inside, discussing something that sounded serious.

Jade placed her ear carefully to the door, wondering why the royal guest was within and who the others were. Her eyebrows pinched together, listening to the voices.

"Then we trade her for the princess..."

CHAPTER THIRTY-THREE

Kai was stiff like the frozen walls, not knowing what to do with herself. She was currently being carried bridal style down the cold tunnels in the arms of Eros. She tried to keep her attention trained on her folded hands, bunched together on her stomach. Her gaze briskly glanced to the wings that would appear over his shoulder—a temptation to reach out and stroke them.

"Here," his voice startled her, making her flinch.

Kai's eyes shut, hoping he didn't notice.

Eros frowned at that, carefully setting the girl down on a carpet.

Mouthing a 'Thank you', Kai immediately scanned the new room. A small library with many shelves packed with books.

The winged man entered the room further; his wings brushed against her shoulder, teasing her. She kept a firm hold on her fingers, practically shaking with restraint.

A book was pulled off the first reachable shelf. Eros flicked it open and showed what was inside. "I've been logging everything for some time... Testing out different routes." He offered out the book, and those eyes patiently waited.

Kai carefully took it from his incredibly large hands, noticing the well-kept almond-shaped fingernails. His fingers were long, and some of those markings swirled around them.

God... Even his fingers are nice to look at, she thought.

She was absent-minded, going over the notes immediately, unaware of the smirk plastered on his face. Going through the lengthy journal, she wandered up to one of the many bookshelves and grabbed another. That one, too, explained similar events, waking up to a snowy morning weeks before the engagement party.

Her frosty blues examined etched grooves in the ice. The shelf was labelled – the night of celebration. Every ice wall was crammed with books, every shelf labelled.

She began reading the other shelf directly above, noticing more of those cravings – the kidnapping. Kai decided to pick up a book from there and scanned the contents. It also started within the story's timeline, well before the happily ever after.

"I started writing journals some time ago when I began to suspect I was stuck on a loop."

Eros's voice suddenly sounded off in her ear. His warm breath made her jerk forward as it grazed her Helix.

He grabbed another book, the first one his fingers graced, a tassel marked a place in it.

Kai stopped herself from nearly colliding with the unit, fumbling to keep a hold of what was in her hands. Her fingers stumbled as she put the journals back in their places, trying to calm the erratic beat of her heart – which was currently thumping in her gut.

Are all of these journals? She asked, attempting to defuse the situation going on inside her.

"Yes."

Her eyes eventually landed on Eros, leaning against a frozen pillar. One of his ginormous wings went around it as he flicked through another book. The strange luminescent stone wedged into the iced pillar gave his wings a soft glow. His shadowed-over face was inclined, that nose in the book.

"I always referred to the last journal to see if anything had changed, to my dismay. Other than my actions, everyone around me appeared to be a puppet. Set to perform the same tasks, day after day, year after year. Same names, same faces." He closed the book in one hand, and his stare cut upwards. Looking at Kai from his eyelashes, those reds aglow from within the shadows. "The run-up to the engagement party this time around is where the noticeable breakaways became concrete." Eros pushed off the pillar as he approached, never breaking their eye contact.

The book was out waiting between them.

Kai slowly took it from him, daring to break off their intense stare down. Heat again rushed to her face, and this time in her lower belly.

She opened the journal, trying not to think about it, and noticed many of his neat writings had circles around them. Side notes and question marks riddled the pages, too.

"Each journal is a brief to some grand event, many in which I took part. Other's where I would watch from afar." Eros explained to Kai how he even spied on situations and observed them. "I was there only last week... checking on progress."

He put some distance between them, fingers dragged across the spines on the shelves.

"Every time I killed that beloved prince, the loop happened. The princess was my target this time. I was sure the prince would magically be in her place. Only, neither were poisoned... someone else... intervened."

Kai ceased mid-turn of the page. The side notes blurred as she stared past the paper.

"No one else has ever been added to the mix. It's always been the worm, that wench, and..." He pivoted and finished, "Me."

Kai stared wide-eyed at the open book; those irises were the same colour as the walls around. Her thoughts were so very colourful to Eros. They gave him an inside perspective of the events and how they all transpired.

"I had people reporting that worm's whereabouts. I knew to strike that day once I was sure he had left the scene...Only, my plan to kill the princess was foiled by someone else." His finger pointed to a bookshelf. "Even when their relationship started getting rocky, he was always there for her. The dynamic between them started to fall apart years ago. Progressively getting worse with each new loop." That hand ran through his silky hair, similar in shine to his dark wings. "I thought I was going insane... No one else seemed to believe we were replaying a section of our lives, missing a grander picture."

You spoke to others about this!? Kai asked with worry in her tone.

He nodded his head. "I tried to inform that worm... my words were written off as crazy talk." Those eyes dulled as his voice continued, "I've tried to pursue peace, tried to disregard my involvement in these loops completely, and that same day would just repeat... The days carried on only when I played my role to be the bad guy. And, once they get their happily ever after, it all restarted, anyway. I wake up here in this shit hole with no memory of who I was before this place," he growled, fists clenching.

His eyes ignited; the reds gleamed as if a fire had been lit within.

Kai's gaze dragged down to the symbol on his chest. The red swirls that oddly resembled a clock. The same clock on Vanessa's palm, similar to the one she had also drawn. The big hand was stationed at eleven, the smaller one at twelve.

Are you the only one aware of this?

"Apparently." The man's stare was locked on something in a far corner.

What happens if you die?

A thick eyebrow rose, and Eros side-eyed Kai. "Never tried. Don't plan on it, either," he said curtly.

Kai swallowed with that harsh tone, wondering if she was pushing it too far.

Eros angled fully to her, watching as her neck bobbed. "I lost my memories as payment, and slowly but surely, it's all tumbling back. Just with you. Strange, isn't it that?"

She never answered. Her head swam with more theories.

Eros watched the emotions fleet across her feminine features, waiting for those icy blues to look at him.

Whoever – or whatever Kai Redsi was, she was his salvation. And for the first time in forever, she felt like home to him. Something he hadn't been able to feel in what felt like an eternity.

Kai's attention finally met his, and Eros bristled with it. Sadness met his gaze, and then he felt it.

Pity.

If... Her mind began to speak to him; her lips trembled as she mouthed silent words. *If you are indeed from my reality...*

Her thoughts flashed to him, again showing the strange world of metals and flashing lights, those weird gadgets that seemed to glow like magic.

You've been here too long... and your body... Her words stopped as the imagery went dark, graves and tombstones revealed.

Eros understood, even if she couldn't muster the courage to finish. "You don't believe I *can* return."

Warrick glared at the doctor. "Then we trade her for the princess, simple."

Dexter frowned from his notes, wondering if the prince was listening when the two servants talked. "Her Highness isn't going to agree to play bait for a servant girl. Especially if she was the actual target." He removed his glasses and shifted over to the servants. "Is this Eros, really after the princess only?"

"Yes," Ava replied, and Charlie nodded in agreement.

"That spoiled woman doesn't need to know the full extent of it. Let's lure him so I can end this, once and for all."

There was a loud scuffle at the door, which paused the four within.

The prince and the doctor shared a look. Dexter rose from his chair when his door swung open on its own.

"I apologise for intruding, Your Grace." Darren stood tall, holding an older woman by the scruff of her dress. "I found this one eavesdropping outside the door." The captain shoved Madam Barnsley into the room, and the woman stumbled over her heels.

The handmaiden's eyes went between the people inside as she stabled. The Crown Prince, the doctor, and two servants.

"Is that so?" Warrick said, moving closer to the woman. His hand inched to the hilt of his sword.

Dexter glared. A hand snuck behind, sliding his notes entirely out of sight.

Jade stood taller and brushed off her sleeves—a stoic look plastered on that aged face. "I've done nothing of the sort. I was just about to knock when this hooligan-" Her hazel eyes cut to the captain. "Grabbed me and shoved me forward." Her face twisted back calmly as she looked at the servants dressed in Rosethorne uniforms.

The odd couple from the kitchen, she noted. Suspicious of the group of people even more.

The prince offered a charming smile. His irises glowed with irritation. "Lying to a royal is enough to lose your head."

Jade snapped to him as her eyes narrowed considerably. "Conspiring against our princess is enough to start a war."

Warrick's mouth opened, arguing, "Conspiring? I am the hero of this empire, the one saving your sorry states!"

The bickering began back and forth. Even the captain jumped in, threatening the older woman.

It was all too much for Ava. Her ears began to ring, well and done with all of this. She tried to breathe deeply, releasing an annoyed sound from deep inside her gut.

"Oh, for the love of god, I am so sick of you fucking people!" she suddenly raised her voice.

All eyes cut to the vulgar shout.

Charlie tried to grab her as Ava swatted at his hands. Her blinded face twisted to the direction of his movements. "They're fucken characters inside a story, Charles! We don't have to tiptoe around these morons! And why should we?!"

"What..." Dexter blinked at her in bewilderment, his words failing him as he witnessed the sheer horror in Charlie's face.

The boy's head shook slightly; his lips moved as if to say...'*What have you done?*'

Ava threw her hands in the air and screamed out her grievances, "You're all just made-up people written on some pages! This place-" Her arms theatrically swung around her. "Isn't even real! You're all living in a simulation! The longer you fight it and prolong the inevitable, the longer *we* have to go home!" She stomped her feet, bellowing more. The ringing finally subsided as she just let go. "That's how we know things, okay!? Because we've read this stupid story and listened to some psychopath that trapped us within it!" she huffed and wheezed with the last of her words.

No one spoke.

A hand slapped over her mouth as she realised what she had done.

Charlie's skin was white, greening around the gills as he blinked in disbelief at Ava. His thoughts halted, wondering what reaction the others had on their faces, but he was too scared to look. A sweat collected on his top lip as chills ran down his spine.

The captain eyed up his prince, curious who the crazy maid was.

Warrick gaped at Ava as scenes flashed inside his conscience. Summoned by her choice of words.

'We're not enemies, Prince. We are puppets, none of this is real.' That creature had repeated something similar.

His head suddenly felt light with the weird memory. His knees wobbled as he raised a hand to his forehead. A growing pain began at the base of Warrick's skull with the strange visions.

The candles started to snuff out.

The room shook next, and dust fell from the ceiling brackets. For a brief moment, a shadow grew inside the room and devoured all the light within.

As a clock ticked, Charlie pulled Ava to him, protecting her against his chest.

The captain had rushed to the prince, grabbing him, too. Shoving him behind, his eyes darted around the room for the invisible enemy.

Madam Barnsley yelped and collapsed to the floor on all fours.

The rumbling stopped as the darkness weaselled away. Only one candle remained. All eyes surveyed each present, and each had the same collective thought.

What the hell was that?

Paranoid that his words may incite whatever *that* was to return, Dexter whispered, "That's why Kai was edgy, wasn't she?" His violets dragged to the servants. "She knew... knew that monster would come?" The words came out shakier than he had intended, unable to calm his racing mind.

The room reeked of dark and ancient magic.

Charlie met the wizard's stare. The light cast an ominous dark shadow over the boy's features as he nodded his head firmly once.

Dexter stumbled back into the desk. The scene of Kai being terrified in her room replayed in his mind. Recalling the shadow within her eyes, her quick healing abilities, and Ava's mysterious words.

"W-Who was... was the witch that c-cursed you?" he asked, tone cracking with the stammer.

There was an all-knowing sensation that crept into him. His instincts screamed. That feeling gripped his guts like claws as he anxiously awaited the answer.

Ava sucked in a sharp breath, gripping Charlie with dear life.

Darren, Jade, and Warrick hung on every word they exchanged.

"She... She called herself Vanessa... Her pen name was E. R. Sula, that... that was the name she used for this book."

Bile rose in Dexter's throat as he recalled a dream. A strange dream that came to him often, as of late. "Sula... Or Alus?"

Charlie's eyes widened further, so wide it was a wonder how his eyeballs didn't fall out from their sockets.

Chapter Thirty-Four

Kai was back inside that frigid bedroom, toying with a feather she had found between the sheets.

Earlier, as she and Eros stood debating her realisation, the area trembled with an earthquake's force. A shadow devoured the light, and her blood ran cold as she heard that clock.

The ticking echoed louder and faster than ever before.

Books jumped off the shelves and crashed to the cold floors. The sound of ice cracking like thunder ensued, and visible splits appeared on the walls.

Arms engulfed her, tucking her under wings as Eros snarled around the space. Those glorious forelimbs shielded the two individuals from the force of nature, provoking chaos.

It all happened so abruptly, then stopped. The colours around the room were duller as the darkness disappeared, taking some with it.

Eros scooped Kai up and returned her to that room before leaving her alone. She wrapped herself in the quilt, trying to make herself smaller, non-existent.

An ominous sensation hung in the air. Kai could taste it on her tongue.

Eros had been gone awhile, and Kai couldn't exactly wander, even as restlessness settled in.

The ground was far too cold for her heels, and her host supplied her with everything but protection for those exposed feet.

She sat up, finding a black feather larger than her forearm. Kai ran her fingers along it, watching as the strands of the hairs bent back and then neatly straightened. Eyes spied the exit, listening and watching for its owner to return. When she was sure he wasn't, Kai ran the feather down a cheek, enjoying the feel of it.

Her eyes closed, absorbing the sensation of it against her flesh, igniting the receptacles in her cheek and brain. That fragrance of home stronger, calming her frantic mind.

Kai imagined her father's garden and her mother's baked goods again. Cosy memory after cosy memory brought a smile to her face. She inhaled deeply, letting those images ground her when a noise inside the room interrupted her moment. Her eyes peeked open towards it.

Eros stood at the exit.

She stashed the feather with lightning speed, hiding it under the quilt as a slight warmth rose to her face. Quickly trying to change the weird atmosphere, she sparked a conversation. *Where did you go?*

A smirk grew on his lips, teeth peeking. "Missed me?" his tone was gravelly.

Kai's face radiated; that warmth turned into an inferno. She averted her gaze, unable to look at him any longer.

Her inner monologue continued, hoping she didn't sound as bothered as her body was. *Did you see what the cause of that weird shake was?*

Glad her mental voice was easier to control than her physical one. Kai didn't think she could rely on her voice box to convey her steer away if she could speak properly.

Advancing towards the bed, Eros didn't respond immediately. He twisted and sat on the edge of it. His wings lifted and spread out, brushing against Kai's legs.

She watched as they rippled from the corner of her eyes, the man's head going into his hands.

"Somethings happening… I can feel it," his voice wore out, sounding almost pitifully.

Kai didn't know how to help him or why she suddenly needed to with that tonality.

She understood the feeling of exhaustion, living a life constantly pulled at the seams of your stability. But she could hardly help herself, let alone someone else.

His shoulders dropped further as she sat in contemplation, sympathising with him. The thoughts spilt out before she could stop herself from that subtle action. *What do you need of me?*

Dark hair raised, the side of Eros's cheek showed, speaking over a broad shoulder, "We have to break the curse."

Kai leant forward, chest flat against her raised-up knees. *Do you know what the curse is?* Intrigued by the fact that this was the first time anyone inside this place had spoken freely of it.

Eros hummed in response. That head rotated forward, his muscular back rising and falling with steady breaths.

Kai ogled as the hardened flesh beneath his tight shirt constricted and expanded.

She tried again, *what was it?* Gripping the quilt tighter.

"I loved her once…"

Kai's head went silent, and her stomach dropped.

Those wings tucked in closer as if soothing the man. "We were to be wed… ha…" a sad laugh turned into a low grumble. "I wanted to love and wished to be loved in return. Elphaba… promised me that."

That name rang alarm bells in Kai's skull.

Elphaba Alus? She asked in disbelief.

A head nodded. Still, he did not turn. "Elphaba Ravena Alus was a beautiful woman full of life. Full of wonder… or so I thought."

Scenes began to play in her mind, that same village with happy residents rushing about. The sky was an open sea of blue as laughter carried through the air. A man and woman sat together on a thin blanket, shielded by the shade from a nearby apple tree.

Eros and Vanessa.

Elphaba, Eros's correction whispered into Kai's vision and the image zoomed in on the woman.

Her dark brown eyes glinted with delight, sensually eating a strawberry. A bashful smile was offered to the person sitting with her. Long brunette hair cascaded around, pooling at her backside like Scarlett's did. Her skin was kissed by the sun, her nails long and white. Vanessa wore bright red robes, resembling Roman, maybe Greek culture.

A style from an old civilisation in Kai's history books.

The scene drifted to another; a ring slid onto the woman's fourth finger. A metal loop in the shape of a feather. One lone ruby at the centre of it.

Vanessa's face lit up with joy as she pounced onto the watcher, kissing them all over their face.

Kai's heart wobbled.

"Eros," the woman said, "*I think we should do personalised vows!*" Vanessa pulled away; her hand immediately stretched out as she admired her ring.

Lips moved as no sounds projected; the scene changing.

The creature, Eros, stood inside a temple. Pillars reached up high all around the hall, holding the ceiling up. Smoking bundles of strange plants burned on hanging gold plates around the space, alongside pedestals with statues.

There were no wings on the man's back, but still, he was marked with all those strange designs. No clock riddled his chest, but swirls of red decorated his bare arms down to the back of his hands. His face was clear of those patterning reds, and his body glowed a bronze.

A more civilised version of the villain Kai met.

He was clad in robes, too, and people circled him, preparing him for something. A wreath of gold leaves was placed on his head, encircling the back of his skull.

"She never loved me... she loved what I had," his voice echoed outside the scenes.

Eros, inside the memories, opened his hands. Red-tinted streams of lights – resembling arrows shot out from his palms, decorating the space – the room filled with flowers. Rose petals appeared in a path leading out from where he was.

The scene swirled. Vanessa and Eros stood together at a rose archway outside a temple. Many of those petals decorated the area, scattered down the numerous stairs to the monumental building. The sky was a dark sanctuary with twinkling stars, more stars than Kai had ever seen at one time. Many torches lit a path towards the couple at the altar, and people stood below, smiling at the pair.

A romantic celebration.

The wingless man began reciting the words Kai and many others had done. His hand laid on Vanessa's cheek, rubbing it softly.

With the end of his vows, Vanessa's lovesick grin turned hideous. Her eyes illuminated an unnatural light. "Got you," she said in a sardonic tone.

That handsome face dropped as Eros searched her crazy one. He clutched his chest moments after, knees buckled from under him.

As he fell, he grabbed Vanessa's robes, confused eyes still locked on her face.

The sky above darkened further than just night. An endless void of black swallowed the stars. Lightning flashed the skies further in the distance, getting closer.

People began to flee, screaming in horror as the woman started to cackle insanely. Her body smouldered with an ominously dark aura itself.

Vanessa mocked, "You poor unfortunate soul, sound familiar?" Finally cupping his face, she leant down towards Eros.

Kai's gut filled with terror, watching the scene unfold.

Tears streamed down Eros's sculpted cheeks; his breathing laboured.

"You wanted love so badly," she sneered, dropping her hands. "Fool." Straightening, she looked down disdainfully. "Now it's time for you to feel what it's like when someone else plays god." Her hands raised above her head, shouting up at the flashing skies in a language Kai could not recognise.

The scenes ended abruptly as lightning crashed onto the spot.

Kai jolted and slammed against the wall behind her. She gasped hungrily, inhaling air, a cold sweat consumed every square of her skin.

Eros still had his hands in his hair, head dejectedly inclined. "She fooled me… as she did many others after."

Kai surveyed around the space, wondering what was real. Her mind was a mess from her consciousness being thrown around through someone else's memories.

"She sent me here, transformed me into this…" His fingers stretched out. "Receive true love's kiss to break the curse, or be bound to her forever." He laughed, a small one, "I was once a being loved by many… I answered many prayers and wishes of my own, heartbroken when the few who asked me couldn't receive their blessings… What they wanted… needed." He stood from the bed and swayed to the exit. "She had a son, who she loved very much."

Those wings tensed as he fled from the memory, Kai unable to do anything but watch him leave. Her muscles tingled as a strange shake began.

"I could do many magical things, Kai… but I was forbidden to save those from a fated departure. To break the laws of life for one individual… That would have caused an impending doom, an unstoppable calamity for all. I remembered her too late, as she got her vengeance on me."

He finally peered at Kai, his eyes sombre with regret. Nothing more was offered as he left the room with drooping shoulders.

Tears flowed uncontrollably down Kai's face, her heart shattering as she came to understand. Eros wasn't the typical archnemesis for the male lead…

Eros, in Vanessa's mind, was her enemy – for not saving her son.

'We're *not enemies, Prince. We are puppets, none of this is real.*'

Warrick paced his suite, back and forth, repeatedly. His boots scoffed the marble floors as that creature's words repeated in his mind.

Scenes of many lives came to life inside his imagination.

That servant girl's screams mingled into the mix, "*You're all just made-*

up people written on some pages! This place isn't even real!"

Her last words of home echoed somewhere far away within his conscience—a face sneered at him, a face that was somehow familiar before twisting into an old angry hag.

Warrick grabbed handfuls of his hair and shouted, "What is wrong with me!?" Then grabbing the closest thing – a desk, and flipped it over.

His aide and the captain rushed in with the loud crashing sounds.

Dexter Ubar sat with his chin in his palms, staring at the dark lake alone. He recalled a dream that came to him lately, as the waterfall was a whisper in the background compared to his roaring mind.

He hated this particular dream and disliked the way it made him feel. It provoked all these foreign feelings that were his, yet they weren't—made him question his identity.

A woman sat at the side of a bed, weeping into the sheets, a hand holding his weak one. "I'll find a way to save you, my son. My beautiful baby boy…"

The woman wept as he laid still, eyes closed. The dream offered him an eagle's eye view, watching from above countless times.

She continued to call herself 'mother' and called the slumbering body 'Dexter.'

Though his hair was not the colour it was now. It was black with a sapphire sheen, only when the light streaming in from the window above hit it.

He felt the woman's desperation and the feeling of defeat, not being able to reach back and comfort her. So, alone she cried, next to a stilled body that wore his face.

A massive shadowy figure entered the room. "Alus?" followed by muted words given to the woman.

She jumped up, anger and grief evident on her ageing features, screaming at the figure. The dream ends there, offering nothing more than the mysterious moments of those maternal bonds.

Dexter tried to envision his birth mother's face; a fog muddled it up. Her name was gone just as quickly as he thought he had remembered it.

Instead, that woman's face surfaced every time.

Dexter ruffled his hair and observed the moon's reflection on the water's surface. Bugs tread the top, causing ripples in the reflection to fight against the others from the waterfall. Ava's words came in waves, along with those clashing motions, *"She… She called herself Vanessa… Her pen name was… E. R. Sula."*

A cold chill ran down Dexter's spine, wondering if the acronym was a coincidence. But his instincts argued with his mind.

Elphaba Ravena Alus. His seventeenth great-grandmother. The first witch who was responsible for the Rosethorne curse. He found it incredibly hard to fathom that she was alive and, in another world, at that. His head throbbed with all the revelations.

This was a book? This world wasn't real?

Streams of information poured in one direction, pooling inside. His train of thought continued to flow like that waterfall in the distance. An ominous sensation of the all-knowing drowning him.

Chapter Thirty-Five

Eros plodded down the desolate corridors, finally rid of the pathetic feelings of his past failures. Carefully, he carried a tray in his hands, containing warm sustenance for the feeble body that now needed his care.

The scene inside his room delayed his advancement, and his boot hovered over the threshold.

Kai Redsi had fallen asleep at some point. Tear stains glistened down those rosy cheeks, with her head angled. In one hand clutched tight was the quilt she secured around herself, the other, one of his feathers.

He wondered if that was the same one she had tried to stealthily hide under the quilt – when he interrupted that private little moment.

Creeping forward, Eros placed the food tray on the dresser, attention locked on the bundled-up lady. He reached into his trouser pocket with free hands and retrieved the clip he had removed from her hair.

Which was, coincidently, a feather, also.

He searched deep within, feeling that thread that connected her to him. He tugged at it, observing how the slumbering woman's eyebrows tweaked.

A smile twitched on his lips. He pulled again with more force, and her eyebrows turned downwards.

Eros bit back the chuckle brewing in his gut at how her little nose scrunched up.

Elphaba's icy words echoed in his skull as his attention continued to travel down from Kai's nose... to her lips.

The dark lipstick she had painted on was long gone. Those plump lips were still stained from its intensity. Eros's thoughts reached further, progressing down the string that banded their minds together.

Kai was dreaming of that strange world.

The accent of her mental monologue fascinated him. A merry tone carried her words, weaving a magical spell around his very being. Even from the memories he was glimpsing as she slept, the voice from her dream-stated lips sounded cheerful, briefly lifting higher at the end of her words like a tune. That tone was more emphasised and deliberate when those funny-dressed folk in that strange tavern visited. A beautiful smile graced her face as she threw a wink at them, serving them glasses of liquor.

He wished to hear more from this peculiar bar maiden, who was currently fast asleep in his bed, wearing *his* clothing.

That thought and the sight before him made those wings tense, and his ego hummed with satisfaction.

Eros carefully sat on the bed, rolling his shoulders back so his wings stayed put. Even they seemed bewitched by her, noticeably trying to reach out with every opportunity.

Kai's lips were parted slightly, and a tiny breathy sound slipped between them—a soft snore.

His own lips twitched once more. A warmth spread inside his chest. He dared to reach, a feather-like touch to a lip. His finger faintly pushed the juicy thing down.

Kai did not stir, her neck still crammed to one side. Those eyelashes fluttered with her cosy dreams of home.

Eros could see another little room manifest in a dark sky within a tall building. This building had hundreds of windows, some illuminating from a light source within. A strange man manoeuvred a white-wheeled carriage with no horse, dropping Kai off at that tall inhabitant.

With the way that man looked at Kai, a possessive snarl built inside Eros' throat, his lips spasmed to curl.

He wanted to gouge the man's eyes out.

That finger withdrew as he delicately grabbed those thin arms, laying Kai down properly. Eros gently bundled all her hair together before setting her head back, stroking all those radiant strands away from her face. His attention was still lured to those lips.

He positioned himself on the bed, wings now able to relax. Kicking his boots off, Eros settled down onto the mattress.

He paused, watching to see if his movements woke her. When he was sure he could continue, Eros pulled Kai into his arms, savouring the moment.

Intoxicatiting pheromones cascaded off her with every one of those soft snores, and Eros drank them in, sneering at the man in Kai's mind as he covered her further with his scent.

Kai dreamt of her usual days back home, going to school during the day and serving at night. She dreamt of Zachary driving her home and Stace calling, screaming into her ear. The dreams tugged her into a soothing warmth, a security that guarded her from being consumed with hiraeth.

Her family's cottage began forming, and a green yard unravelled like a rug. She stood in the garden, studying the homely thing.

Her father's carefully tended flowerbeds, filled with lavenders, roses, and hydrangeas, bloomed all around the house.

Each plant was her mother's favourite.

She could briefly see phantom figures of her parents pruning them.

The trees in the distance swayed some peaking over the house. Most of the windows were open, carrying the scents of baked goods to her spot. The grass was freshly cut, lines from her father's ride-on lawn mower still upon them.

It was a peaceful place far away from the noise and pollution of the big cities.

Kai stood basking in it, allowing her head to fall back. Rain spat from the partially clouded skies, and a dark item carried on the breeze, seizing her attention. She lifted a hand and caught the soft object carefully with her fingers.

Kai squinted at it in her palms and then looked high above, wondering where the feather came from.

Agapi Mou.

The whisper of a voice rained strange words around her family's home.

Kai closed her eyes, breathing in the strong scents of the cakes and evergreens, letting the cold rain droplets run down her face.

She was met with darkness when she opened her eyes again, and something was tightly fastened around her sides. She blinked, recognising fabrics pushed into her face, the sound of heavy breathing and movement on the other side.

Inclining her head the best she could, Kai studied red markings on a throat– a strong jawline above it.

Her breath hitched in surprise; her heart thumped loudly. Embarrassment rose to her cheeks, realising she was in Eros's arms.

The man stirred, either from disturbance or coincidence. Rolling onto Kai, a wing stretched over.

Eros mumbled in his sleep, still caging the girl, who was now under him.

Kai let out a breath as his weight settled on top of her, wondering to herself when this transpired. She tried to shove him off with no luck. Her movements only caused the man to stir more, nuzzling his face into her hair.

She frowned, trying to call out to him mentally, *hey! Hello? You're crushing me, dammit!*

When all else failed, Kai began to pinch the fast-asleep man on top. Her nails grabbed bits of flesh between the cloth of his attire.

A soft snarl sounded off at her side, vibrating into her chest with every pinch. But still, he did not wake.

One wing was bunched together, crammed against the wall, the other spread out off the bed. One of Eros's legs intertwined with hers, the other up. His propped-up knee pushed into her inner thigh.

Kai's one limb was pushed out unrestricted, but she couldn't move it much with the giant wing bunched together above. She was trapped awkwardly, aware of the arm wrapped around her, resting on her hip. The other gripped the material at the back of her shoulder.

Kai huffed as insecurities crept into her self-conscience.

She had only cuddled with Stace on her couch when watching movies together under a thick quilt. Never actually glued to her so intimately, and never with someone of the opposite sex.

Even when she and Stace shared a bed, neither woke to the other cuddling them. The most being back-to-back. The fact she was lying with this man – who she hardly knew, had her grandfather's voice roar inside her ears.

"You can date once you're married!" His kind face scowled, and an imagined finger violently shook.

Her mouth drew into a tight line, trying not to laugh at the memory. How upset would he be if he knew about this? Kai didn't dare answer that.

Her thoughts drifted, dwelling on how long it had been since she'd been here to the outside world.

Was her grandfather worried about her? What had happened to her body?

The arms imprisoning Kai tightened more as Eros twisted his head and nuzzled into the nape of her neck. His lips brushed against her skin.

With the weight still on her, Kai's thoughts vanished as she drew in a sharp breath, the best she could anyway. She was alerted by the skin-on-skin contact at the side of her throat. With his heat above and her rising temperature, Kai believed she was about to combust at any moment.

Back in Rosethorne, Charlie scurried around Ava's room, packing bags.

"I'm sorry, Charles," Ava mumbled, head down. Fingers picked at unevenly broken nails.

Charlie grumbled, unable to hear her; he hastily shoved the clothing into a fabric sack.

After they had all departed from the doctor's quarters and that strange shake occurred, Charlie regained his composure. Opting to flee from the kingdom and head to the wastelands for Kai. He didn't believe the kingdom was safe for them anymore after Ava's terrible blunder.

She revealed too much.

He dashed back to Ava's wardrobe and yanked off the outfits hanging within.

"Charles... Please... Talk to me."

His actions were halted by that quiet voice that seemed to penetrate through Vanessa's curse. He peered over to Ava and noticed her shoulders trembled.

A long sigh released from his throat as he took two large steps towards her. A hand laid on her shoulder, another on the back of her head, guiding her to him. Charlie nuzzled the top of her head with his cheek and smelt the fragrance of clean soap from her scalp.

Another thing he missed about home.

He didn't like the cheap soaps they were made to use while bathing here. He missed Ava's collection of shampoos and how it made her smell of an assortment of fruits—his fruity goddess.

Ava clenched a handful of Charlie's buttoned-up shirt. "I... didn't mean to... I just... I just snapped," she cried.

Neither of them heard the footsteps approaching the cracked-open entry. A leather-gloved hand pushed it open wider, spying on the two within.

Charlie double-took to the movement in his peripheral view, his hold on Ava tightened protectively.

Prince Warrick stepped inside; his golds eyeballed the packed bags. That usual confident bravado was low and unreadable, "Going somewhere?"

Ava's crying ceased, realising someone was in the room with them.

"If you're going after Miss Redsi, I'm coming with you," the prince stated with a weird expression on his face.

"He'll try and... and kill you," Ava offered, sniffling up the dripping mess she could feel in her nose.

Warrick strolled in further, dropping into one of the chairs ungracefully.

A hand ran through his messed-up hair as he let his head fall back. "No, he won't..."

Charlie loosened his hold on the girl; head cocked, scrutinising the character.

"I'm having these... illusions... Images of many lives... my life, playing on repeat." There was a tiredness upon Warrick's face, an ageing presence as if the male lead himself was defeated for the first time. "We have a lot to talk about, me and him."

CHAPTER THIRTY-SIX

Madam Barnsley stumbled into a room; her pace terminated with a wobble at the end of the circular bed. Tears had welled up and fallen during the trek, her top even darker in patches, just at the chest. She watched Scarlett slumber, trying to recall the moments of her childhood.

Scenes of a child played out; an open meadow came to mind. However, it was not the Scarlett before her who laughed and ran freely.

A little girl with big, round hazel eyes that twinkled with delight chased a white butterfly. The deep blue dress she wore trailed behind her little kicking legs. The girl looked in Jade's direction and waved her small chubby hand. A smile blossomed on that plump baby face, and curls of mahogany hair wisped around the carefree child.

An old hand raised, covering Jade's quivering bottom lip. This little version replaced all the memories of Scarlett fabricated in her brain.

"Mommy! Come play with me!" the child's happy voice echoed across the endless green pastor, filling her with longing and regret.

Her child. *Her little Rosie.*

Memory after memory assaulted Madam Barnsley like violent tides against a high cliff.

The girl's father, her husband, with his deep blue irises and copper locks. His death left them without anything in a cold world of despair. How hard the years were after, on her and her growing Rosie.

She remembered the day she met that stranger, the one who offered her a deal to give the child a better life. A better world where she could blossom and live freely without the dreary sorrows their village had to offer.

Where Rosie lived in luxury, not worrying about stretching the last of their coppers.

Jade dropped to her knees, fisting a handful of the bedding. Her sobs ripped out of her uncontrollably as reality and fiction clashed together.

The cold, hard truth stole the air from her lungs. Realising her wish had become their curse.

Kai could finally wiggle her way out from under Eros, who was still fast asleep, sprawled out on the bed. She slapped her cheeks a few times to rid herself of the impure thoughts that aroused her.

Eros responded with a throaty groan every time she moved, sending a fluttering sensation to her nether regions.

She took a deep breath, hand over her heart, and calmed herself.

Kai couldn't understand for the life of her why her body reacted the way it did around him or why her mind was a gibbering mess, either. She chalked it up as an effect of his persona, rationalising it the best she could.

She crawled to the end of the bed, noticing the man had no shoes on. Thick socks covered his feet, and her attention next searched the floors.

Discovering two leather boots were discarded.

Kai tucked a tress of hair behind an ear, peeking back. She reached down next and plucked one of the boots up. When she was sure the man wouldn't spring up, she sprang into action.

Slipping the oversized things on, she wiggled her toes, which stopped three-quarters well before the tips. She had to quietly shuffle towards the exit, holding the boots up so they didn't bang against the floors with each step.

Kai successfully got out, checking back once before she continued on her way.

The tunnelled corridors glowed a soft blue from the ice enclosing the spaces. Kai could feel the chill solidify around her nostrils with each intake.

She moseyed her way leant over awkwardly, coming to a fork in the path. Kai recalled Eros taking the immediate left, so she, too, took that route.

The last thing she wanted was to freeze to death inside this frozen labyrinth. The halls were much cooler than the small rooms; the frigid air bit down right to the bone.

She knew from the map in the novel that Eros's fortress was at the heart of the wasteland. She wasn't reckless enough to venture into unknown waters, even if her curiosity nagged her to go right and see what she could uncover.

A room amply got closer; strange rocks glowed upon the walls.

Kai slipped the boots off when her limbs reached that dark furry rug. She straightened her aching back from uncomfortably walking here, a hand pushed at her hips, leaning back slightly and stretching the other way.

Kai's unhurried stare examined the bookshelves, searching for one in particular.

That strange shake knocked many of the books off those cold ledges. Massive dark cracks now decorated many of the glowing walls. Books littered the floor in this once cold and organised room.

Kai sifted through some of the items nearest, finding the one she wanted. She sat down and got comfortable, surrounded by books she had begun stacking. She had looked at this one earlier, the journal with all the notes. Considering everything being said, she couldn't focus before the room violently shook.

As Eros stated, the notes were each of his check-ins at the palace. Watching from high above, the same faces scurried below.

One had a circle around it, saying, 'Check journal number three-zero-eight, new faces?' Kai searched her two sides, grabbing that numbered journal she had stacked previously. Flicking it open, she found the noted page.

Same day, same weather, same news of an approaching engagement. However, the notes varied further on.

One servant walked across the stone yard, carrying items to and from.

The other, a red-haired girl, stumbled across the yard with a bell ringing at her throat.

He described her as 'a red-haired fairy stumbled across the stone yard, wearing some strange ringing bell at her thin throat.' An eyebrow raised at the miniature doodle of herself.

A stick figure with bright blue eyes and crayon-red hair was under the account. The arms of the stick figure were not proportioned properly — one hand had extremely long fingers compared to the other. The *dress* she was wearing was basically a triangle.

Tongue in cheek, Kai fought a laugh, snickering at the drawing— something she would have mistaken for a child's attempt. The image of a big, evil villain slumped over with crayons came to mind. Kai couldn't stop the giggles at her imagination, shaking a head.

After pulling herself together, Kai continued reading another excerpt, which went on in detail about Ava and Charlie. Only their names weren't there. Kai knew it was them by how Eros described her friend's skin tone and how she clung to the man who led the way.

Her eyes lifted from the journal, surveying the hundreds of books inside. Eros's words whispered in her ears, "*Receive true love's kiss to break the curse or be bound to her forever.*"

Her nose scrunched in thought. *What is this, a Disney rip-off?*

The words baffled her. If breaking the curse required Eros to kiss someone, were the conditions the same for everyone?

Vanessa had also told her to break a curse, and she presumed it was due to Scarlett's heritage. Her assumptions proceeded to spin their webs, her eyes back down on the notes.

Her heart sank. A hunch she tried so desperately to avoid declined further — fermenting.

Maybe these weren't characters at all… but once people from her world, each cursed with their own conditions. Vanessa had preyed upon so many naive people. Feeding on their moments of weakness, to feed into her sick game. This stupid book.

Did she have to break all their curses or just one?

"Agapi, what are you doing?"

Kai's head whipped to the entrance, startled by that voice.

Eros stood frowning, rubbing the sleep from his eyes. His wings lazily dragged on the cold floors. "Were you not comfortable?" His bottom lip stuck out, slightly pouting.

Her eyes drawled down. His shirt had risen up, those sculptured lines showing between the breakaway. Dark hair trailed down from his belly button and disappeared into the waist of his trousers.

Kai averted her eyes as swiftly as she whipped her head, and heat rushed to her face. *Something is definitely wrong with me!*

"What is?" Eros asked, moving closer. His eyes were clear now, alert and scanning her over. He crouched near Kai, a hand extended, feeling her forehead. "You're warm," he stated.

Kai momentarily forgot about his quirk. *Excuse me,* she mentally said, still not looking him in the eyes, as she gently removed that hand. *Could you not do that mind thing and ask before you start touching me? We need to set some boundaries between us.*

A low chuckle responded; Kai scowled towards it.

"My apologies, but how else are we to communicate?" Eros withdrew his hand and rubbed the spot in circles where Kai had made contact. "So, care to explain what you're doing in here?" His tone took a dip, "I thought..." There was an underlying sadness in it as those words trailed off.

Raising the book, Kai gestured she was reading, keeping her mind silent. Eyes narrowed at him.

Eros nodded, a slight grin offered. A finger pointed to a note in her hands. "That was the first time I noticed you. The first of many things that began to convince me I wasn't crazy." His fingers dragged off the page, slyly touching Kai's tips at the side.

That smirk grew wider as he noticed Kai's back straighten with the contact.

Rising, he flexed his wings and lifted those heavy extensions off the ground. His shoulders rolled, waking up properly. He peered down to the quiet lady, catching the dilated pupils, gawking at his mid-section.

Her mind was quite colourful to him again, envisioning things she shouldn't. That smirk was seemingly permanent on his lips as he pivoted towards the shelves, and a hand rubbed the back of his warming neck.

"I think, perhaps, this route is the correct one. Considering how things were beginning to change." Eros stopped, inspecting all the ruined books.

Kai shook her head behind him. *I don't understand one thing... How are they still here, with every loop, I mean? These books should have been reset, like everything else, right?* Her voice projected at him with valid questions.

He leant into it, eyes lazily shut, and enjoyed how her voice itched all the right spots in his skull. "I have no idea... Never really thought about it, either," his words came out huskier as he succumbed to the sensation in his mind.

Kai blinked rapidly, confusion again on the surface. *Okay, then, are all the characters given terms to break a curse?*

Eros's shoulders raised and dropped; those wings followed with his action. "Doesn't really matter. They're not our problem."

Her thin eyebrow raised as her head shook, returning to the notes. Kai wanted to argue back with his statement. However, when she first came to this world, she had only thought about herself. Eventually, Ava and Charlie, too. So, she couldn't precisely preach like she was some saint sent here to help them all.

What about Tristan? She thought to herself, marvelling over what had happened to him.

Eros twisted with insane speed, his thick eyebrows together at his t-section. "Who's that?" he asked with a snarl.

Kai frowned at the beastly man. *Someone who had also been conned into here, and apparently, he just vanished.*

Those red eyes narrowed on Kai. "Why are you concerned about him?" Those muscular arms crossed, making those biceps appear bulgier.

Aren't you curious about what happened? Where do we go if we don't break our curses before the clock's chiming?

Eros shook his head. "Bound to her forever, obviously."

A fingernail tapped the page, and Kai's attention drew back.

Bound to this book forever? She reflected. *May the flesh never rot and fall away putrid before my very eyes...* Dissecting the words, she wondered if the answers were within them, like a clever little riddle.

So, failing to break the curse, we become part of this world forever? Sadness swept over her as faces surfaced in her mind's eye. Brown eyes sparkled, spilling juicy gossip. Pale blue eyes twinkled, rattling on about his gardens. The thought of never seeing Stace or her grandfather again rattled her to the very core.

The chiming of a clock... Kai's sad stare dragged up to the frowning man, who observed her still. *What does the clock represent?*

Eros noticed her attention on his chest, and her voice echoed into him. A hand raised to touch the marking. "Is that what this is..." He slowly sounded the word out, "A cl-o-ck?"

Her stare focused, studying. *What time did you two marry?*

That scowl on his face hardened, recalling the memory. "We never finished the ceremony... but the full moon was nearly at its peak."

Full moon? The memory of stumbling home after work resurfaced. *Is that when she pulls people in?* Kai couldn't recall what moon was in the sky that night, as she never really took notice. Not when it was raining ninety-nine percent of the time.

"Would make sense... moon phases are powerful elements to witches." Eros tried to follow along with her mind. Curiosity festered as she speculated to herself. He found her thoughts so peculiar, analysing everything she knew. Watching as she stumbled down stone streets, many of those roads had horseless carriages of different colours stationed up and down the sides.

Kai suddenly shot to her feet, the book slamming shut in hand. *What moon phase is approaching?!*

CHAPTER THIRTY-SEVEN

The castle was shambolic; plaintive cries echoed into the dark skies. Many people wandered aimlessly, confusion on their faces. Some cowered in dark corners, rocking with insanity away from the flashing storm overheard.

Dexter Ubar searched every person with pity as he marched the grounds, guilt striking his conscience. Face after face, crazy mumbles after another added to the accumulating storm within him.

His steps slowed as he eyed up the separate palace in the distance. The rain continued to pelter down, soaking him through.

It had been years since he'd come this way, this being the first time—coming willingly. Dexter took a deep breath and stepped out of the last stone archway.

The wild, thorny roses turned one by one facing the approaching visitor. That same ominous sensation swept over Dexter's arms, making the hairs stand on ends. Lightning flashed, and the opened flowers appeared like gaping mouths, ready to strike.

He never liked the feeling these grounds gave him or its mistress. Or, the day-long headaches that chased him to bed and the dreams that chased him awake.

The skies rumbled with thunder; no guards were stationed at the front.

With every flash that continued to illuminate the scenery, the wild bushes surrounding the estate cast monstrous shadows over the building.

Dexter lifted his heavy feet and climbed the drenched stairs to the main entrance. A part of him screamed to turn back and run. The other was calm and quiet, certain this was where he needed to be.

He hated this indecisiveness.

The doors were jarred open as he pushed in, the ridiculous front foyer eerily quiet. Many would be asleep or cowering somewhere, like the rest of the castle.

Patient after patient visited him tonight, each rambling about strange visions coming to them. Every person recalled strange memories, an insanity of delusions.

Each lost without rationality, as they could no longer distinguish what was real—one by one, person by person, all the same symptoms.

All reeked of dark and ancient magic.

Dexter placed a hand on the railing, staring up the wide staircase. "Hello?" he called out.

'Hello?'

'Hello?'

'Hello?'

His voice echoed, bouncing off the walls and answered him in return. Dexter had an inclination to check over his shoulder once before he hiked up the steps.

He forced his attention ahead, uncomfortable with the eyes from the paintings perceived to follow. Watching his every move, smiling down with delight as he returned here after so long.

Still, no guards watched the halls, and some servants tucked themselves away, unaware of him passing by.

They collectively mumbled, "I want to go home." Just like many others had done this evening.

Dexter reached the second stairwell, flinching back in alarm.

Floating feet hung from the railing above, the individual's face blue. A neck visibly snapped in two.

He swallowed the sickness rising in his throat as his eyes locked with those aged, lifeless hazels, still wide open.

"I'm sorry..." he whispered to those eyes. Even though he knew she could no longer hear him, he believed he owed her that apology.

Regaining his composure, Dexter forced his feet to move on, to keep going.

The doctor stepped off the last flight of stairs, and the dark hallway stretched out, narrowing further. That part of him screamed painfully to get out of there while he still could. He shoved that cowardly voice down.

Madam Barnsley's lifeless eyes surfaced in his mind; Dexter used it as a reminder to that voice – that they owed this to her and many others.

No guards or servants stood at the open door. More lightning flashed inside the room on the other end. Dexter's knees clacked together as he made it to the threshold. A hand gripped the doorframe to refrain from fleeing.

The room within was destroyed as the wind blew through a broken glass panel, pushing the curtain to and from. A table was wholly turned over, its contents scattered to the floors. Sheets were dragged from the ginormous bed, and blood stains blotted the off-kilter mattress. Dexter continued to scan the room as the smallest of cries alerted him, coming from the furthest corner.

Mahogany hair peeked out from the shadows that trailed into the darkness.

He treaded into the room, and a steady headache crept into his skull, threatening to steal his sanity. "Your Highness?" he called out, watching as glinting eyes flashed.

"Leave me," an enervated voice commanded.

That headache slammed into him in full force. That weak, faraway tone cried to him, *"Please don't leave me... Don't leave me alone in this hell, Dexter!"* A memory came with that ache, staggering him back like a blow to the gut.

Mahogany hair and hazel eyes looked upon him, tears spilt over the girl's face. The young girl wept onto his chest as he was unable to reach and console her.

Dexter clutched his throbbing head, forcing himself to remain inside the room to see this through until the very end.

Eros glanced up to the ceiling and then back to Kai. "No idea. Can never really see the sky here. It's always snowing."

Kai pivoted, and Eros appeared before the exit with a flash of feathers.

"Where are you going?" he asked, blocking the way.

Kai's intentions terminated, pulling the journal to herself. Her chest puffed out in defiance. *I'm going to see what moon phase is outside,* she declared.

A thick eyebrow cocked up to her response. "And you know how to get out, do you?"

The little woman's face scrunched and slowly relaxed as she considered his question. Her head shook next. *No, I don't.* Kai's stare dragged over his body, freezing Eros to the spot. Her gaze lazily returned to his face, meeting eye to eye.

If you want my help to break this curse and get out of here, I need to know what moon is in the sky.

An idea crossed Eros's mind, and the words tumbled out just as swiftly, "We could stay here... Just you and I."

Kai blinked those vivid blues.

Eros stepped towards her, continuing, "It wouldn't be so bad... being stuck here with you." Hunger seeped into his stare, and the pupils within those ruby reds exploded.

This isn't my world. I have a life beyond this, responsibilities and people who love me. Her foot slid back, and that confident tone wavered. *Y-You wanted to leave also, did you not?*

Step after step, he stalked Kai. "Maybe I don't anymore. Maybe all I needed was you," Eros claimed. Still creeping as she inched away.

Fear and excitement rippled through Kai, with him amply trying to close the gap between them. Her body warmed with expectations, but her mind screamed with rational thoughts. *If this loop begins again, we won't know each other!*

This pulled the being out of his trance, stopping his advancement.

Kai proceeded as her heart was ready to explode. *You said so yourself that when the loops begin again, you have no memories... If that happens, neither of us will remember the other.*

Anger and something like anxiety swept across Eros's features. Kai pushed further, hoping to get through to him.

Returning to reality would be the only way to end the cycle once and for all. To take back what is constantly robbed from you... So please, help me.

His lips parted, but before words came out, his attention snapped to the exit. Kai couldn't get an answer from Eros because he was gone in a flash.

Three black feathers floated to the ground where he previously stood.

She was dumbfounded, asking herself what the hell that was about. Did the man change his mind suddenly? Kai couldn't understand why. On top of that, she believed that the time referred to each full moon, as they tended to be at their highest peaks at midnight. Which meant the trio had a week, maybe only mere days, to break this curse.

She bit her nails, attention scurrying around the floors as if they carried the needed answers.

True love's kiss?

Was Eros meant to be the one to have the happily ever after with Scarlett? Her mind raced for some logical answer, some direction to hold her nerves from plummeting into a depression of defeat.

Ava mumbled in surprise, "I can see..." As she gripped the hands that held her waist.

Warrick pulled the horse's reins, directing his steed closer to Charlie's. "What do you mean?" A head turned to them.

Shaking hands rose, taking off that blindfold. Ava's white eyeballs scanned the valley of mountains before them. "I..." She sucked in a sob as that faint glow brightened. "I can see things... an illuminating path, leading somewhere," she managed to say at last.

"Then, perhaps this was fate," the prince stated, straightening in his saddle. "Lead the way, Lady Sebastian."

Charlie offered the prince a curt nod as he kicked his horse forward in the direction Ava pointed. The three raced across the last of the foothills, entering the snowy domain.

They had ridden hard through the night. A storm flashed upon the kingdom far in the distance. Here, the temperatures dropped, and clumps of snowflakes spilt from the skies. The air howled as the winds pushed the snow drifts higher. The trees were barren, unlike the flourished ones they galloped by. There was only one clear path that led into the mountains, more bare trees and ruins of stones next to it. A roaring river flowed not far off, which echoed in the open space with the howling.

They continued on horseback, entering the blizzardy domain with no other signs of life.

Ava's finger drifted and pointed further inwards. "The path goes, and then..." Her finger shifted to a mountainside. "It shoots up, there."

Warrick dismounted his white steed, dropping into knee-high snow. His golden eyes investigated their whereabouts with caution. "I see..." He noticed something along the side of a summit. "I think there are stairs. Let's find out where they start. That should lead us to some entry."

Bundled up in furs and layers of clothing, Charlie helped Ava dismount. They both trailed closely behind the prince as he made his way near the steep slope, generously trampling snow, creating a path.

As predicted, they found snowy steps that led up, circling the side.

"The path reappears, flowing before us." Ava's finger wavered as if tracing what she saw to the gentleman.

They carefully ascended those stairs, Warrick leading the way.

"Be warned, some areas narrow greatly! Just a yard from us now," he turned, shouting back so Ava could hear over the howling gusts pushing them against cold rocks.

They scathed the side of the mountain, cautiously ascending.

After walking and shuffling sideways and a couple of near misses, they got to that entrance, Ava pointed out.

Warrick unsheathed his sword, taking in the crater-sized hole of an entrance. "Stay behind me, steady your breaths. We do not know what else dwells in there… We communicate with signals. Just point if we verge off the path."

Entering the mountain was even colder than being outside it. Ice walls covered the sides and ceiling, glowing a faintish blue deeper within.

Ava's finger would drift as Charlie tugged on the prince's sleeve to redirect.

They snuck through the tunnels, eventually reaching one ample open space. Long, thick icicles came down into the margin, four tunnels on the other side. Clouds of air puffed out from each of them, the snow undisturbed on the ground, and even the footprints they left behind magically disappeared.

Warrick glanced; Ava's finger was directed at the third tunnel. He signalled Charlie to creep along the sides and not walk directly into the open area.

There were many dark holes above them, many possible things that could have been watching. Warrick would not take any chances of being out so open.

They crept forward for ages until they came to another open space with even higher ceilings and ledges.

Warrick's eyes glimpsed, checking back to his companions when the howling wind echoed inside. His eyes shot towards the numerous tunnels that appeared again across the snowy margin—then scanned the ledges above.

No snow stirred off the ledges. He couldn't even see shadows on the icy walls to alert him of another presence.

"Which way," Warrick whispered, his stare secured at those possible directions.

Before Ava could answer him, another voice did, "That depends on where you're planning to go, worm." That voice shook the sword, sharp icicles high up.

The frozen material rattled as the room filled with the sounds of chimes.

Warrick shot to a fighter's stance, sword up and ready. "I come in peace!"

"Is that so?" it answered.

An oversized silhouette appeared on one of the ledges, and feathers tumbled down.

Alerting, both men down below. Their necks twisted to their host.

The shadow was wings caved around an individual. Red eyes reflected light between feathers, watching the three trespassers. "Your sword would suggest otherwise."

A gloved hand raised in surrender as Warrick carefully sheathed his sword back into its respected place. "It's habit… I repeat, I come in peace."

Those wings opened like thick black curtains, revealing a strange-looking man with red markings. His face looked down disdainfully at the prince.

"Where is Lady Redsi? What have you done with her?" Warrick asked the being.

Eros smiled a predator's grin and growled, "I ground her bones to make my bread."

His taunt triggered the prince. "DO NOT TOY WITH ME!" shouting back at the man high up.

The icicles above shook, and a couple fell and crashed to the ground. White exploded upwards, creating a cloud and minimising visuals. The ice shattering sounded similar to glass breaking on impact.

Ava yelped, clinging onto Charlie beside her, alarmed by the noise. His eyes were frozen on those red ones, the same ones he had seen the night of the ball. Fear was too light to describe how Charlie felt looking at them.

Eros chuckled, "Temper, temper, worm."

He then leapt from the ledge, landing gracefully within moments as his wings spread. The force stirred the snow to move around the space, whisking it around. Creating a mini blizzard inside.

"Don't you have your own princess to tend to?" He smiled, his powerful extensions tucking back.

"Where is she?"

Eros pushed his lips out. "Who?" Wanting to toy with the prince more.

Warrick's handsome features took on a new look, perceiving him as the story's true villain.

Eros rolled his eyes, turning his back. "She's safe…" He waltzed over to one of the tunnels, gesturing at it. "You can check for yourself if you don't believe me." That smug smile offered as he pivoted to face him again.

Warrick inhaled deeply in an attempt to calm himself. "I'm sorry…" he said, causing Eros's coy grin to falter. "I didn't believe you, then… When you told me we were just puppets… but I do, now. Return the Lady to us, and let us talk. Just you and I."

Those wings tensed, letting the prince's words sink in.

Warrick repeated, unsatisfied with the being's silence, "Return Kai to us, and we can settle our accounts. Let's help each other."

Eros snarled at the prince using the girl's name. "Watch your manners, boy. Your father would have raised you better than that to address a lady informally."

Warrick returned a look, ready with his retort. His face shifted as something dawned on him. "You… care for her?" he mumbled out in disbelief.

Those wings rippled out, making himself bigger as Eros's stare hardened. "She's mine," growling even louder.

The room rumbled with fury, echoing back that growl.

Dexter sat against a wall, metres from where Scarlett hid in a dark corner. Memories hammered into him, one after another. Of the girl next to him and his life before all this.

Rosie.

The girl from the village that he had courted before he had fallen ill with sickness. That sickness which left him practically paralysed and would have eventually killed him. That's when he woke up here, under some implemented script, that he was a doctor.

He was a doctor of all things when doctors then couldn't even save him. None of the tonics and potions he and his mother had conjured could aid his sorry state either.

His head flopped over; Scarlett had fallen asleep against the wall. Lightning flashed, showing her for brief seconds.

No, his Rosie had fallen asleep. Though she was slightly different from how she used to be, some of her features remained.

The roundness in her chubby cheeks was now sunken in, in desperate need of a meal. The lush hair that wisped around her, the beautiful hands that used to kneed bread and sell them in the village square. His heart splintered, seeing what she had become.

He blamed himself for all of this, for all the people trapped inside this world because of his mother's selfishness.

His mother... His heart nearly split into two, from either guilt or hopelessness.

The memories offered him all the truths, one that was a bitter pill to swallow.

His mother was Elphaba Ravena Alus.

CHAPTER THIRTY-EIGHT

Warrick felt his aggression cleave to the forefront. "She is not an item for keeping. Release her!" he shouted while unsheathing his sword.

Eros barred his teeth at the prince like a wolf readying to launch. A hand whipped to a side, materialising a frozen sword—a claymore of ice. "Grand coming from you. Do you believe I cannot see for myself your intentions!"

The prince's sight blurred with anger from the creature's blatant show of disrespect.

Kai dashed through tunnels, trying to ignore the burning sensation of her feet. She took lefts and rights randomly when she heard the first snarl. It reverberated in waves through the empty halls, awakening a weird tug inside her and forcing her to go back.

She followed that strange urge when she heard the second one.

"She's mine!"

That feeling yanked harder, commanding her to sprint unquestioningly in no actual direction. Kai hiked her knees up, lungs burning for a reprieve. Her toes had gone completely numb from the cold.

She was running down a long hallway when the space shot opened. Kai slid to a stop, nearly falling off the sudden drop.

Down below, two men fought. Warrick and Eros were in utter fury, slashing and dodging each other. Their eyes shadowed over with some strange abnormality.

Cowering against the ice walls, Ava covered her ears as Charlie used his arms to shield her.

Kai panicked, remembering Eros claiming the loops began again with Warrick's death.

She was unsure whether she would remember herself if the loop restarted. Or if she'd become another character in the lines of the paper.

Kai knew she needed to stop them somehow.

She was so close, yet so far.

Frantically, Kai waved her hands, trying to catch someone's attention. She even attempted to shout to Eros's mind when some strange wall bounced her words out.

Kai searched around in panic, and then she tried to pick up snow. She attempted to make snowballs, but the snow was too soft to stick together as it slipped between her fingers or crumbled with no actual shape. She cursed at the runaway flakes, trying to think of something else.

The fabric wrapped around her forearm sprang an idea. Kai ripped off the makeshift bandage in a hurry and bunched it into a ball.

She drew back her arm and threw the flimsy thing towards the battling characters, ready to kill the other.

The cloth unravelled itself, barely going a few feet as it floated to the floors.

Kai threw up her hands, grabbing handfuls of hair. Her attention went over the drop as a crazy thought leapt into her. She noticed broken ice at the centre of the space and debated just how crazy this might be...

Charlie, down below, caught movement, noticing a dirtied fabric gracefully fall.

His brown eyes surveyed to see where it came from when the red hair above had his eyes widen. He shook Ava and mumbled to her in excitement.

"KAI!?" Ava shouted in question. She couldn't see her, but Charlie explained it looked like she would jump.

This stalled the clashing of iron and ice as two heads twisted, and those eyes cleared.

Kai was so focused on pushing herself to leap she hadn't noticed the figures pause. Before anxiety could cripple her, she closed those eyes and leapt from the edge. Arms waved chaotically as she fell, and a silent yelp jumped from her lungs.

Voices screamed as feathers swept her plunging body up, crashing to the ground with a twist. More debris rained down, and feathers and icicles crashed into the snow.

Kai peeked and opened one of her eyes, noticing she was on top of a snowy man with black hair.

His eyelashes were covered with snowflakes, which narrowed considerably at her. "What the hell were you thinking?!"

Her attention scanned the other three. Two were wide-eyed. Ava was shaking Charlie, asking if she was alright with quivering lips.

"You could have died!" Eros tried again, gaining the attention of those icy blues.

Kai offered a smile that had his frown waver, then arms wrapped around his neck. *Thank you,* words whispered into his mind as her warmth kissed his flesh.

He was frozen there as Kai gently removed herself. A hand was out waiting to assist him. Eros spaced out on the face beyond those slim fingers; that grin just like the one he witnessed in her memories still played on her lips.

No mask was upon her face as that smile reached those vivid eyes. The dark blue rims of her irises were more emphasised. The intense, lighter shade within sparkled like melting snow in spring. A tinge of green peeked out from around those pupils like grass shooting up from the snow.

"Lady Redsi." The prince staggered towards them. "Are you alright?"

Eros snapped out of his trance and shot up without that hand – quickly forcing Kai under his wings. An arm was out, shielding her.

Warrick paused, sword raised once more. "Release her this instant."

That frozen sword, inch by inch, appeared in Eros's hand. His grip tightened around the frigid handle. "I don't take orders from you, worm."

"Watch your tongue!"

"Go to hell!"

"Very well, but I'm taking you with me!"

Kai was revealed as Eros dashed forward. Swords in fits of passion across the margin.

"Kai, Kai, come over here!"

Her attention slid to Ava's voice as Charlie waved his hands in their direction.

She didn't have a moment to consider anything as the area began to tremble, and those icicles above wobbled, chiming loudly. That shadow Kai had seen before grew inside the spacious room, and Vanessa's words whispered to her.

"Tick tock, tick tock, finish the condition before the chiming from the clock!" her words got louder as those icicles continued to ring out.

"This time, it's you who dies!"

Kai's attention snapped back to the raging characters. Eros was staggering about, holding his face, with Warrick rushing at him. The prince's sword was positioned to his side, both hands on the hilt, ready to drive it up.

She did the first thing that came to mind and sprang forward.

Kai felt it seconds after like an iron cast poker sitting in the fireplace for hours was shoved into her gut. The sword drove well and true through her. Dirtied golds were in her line of sight, pushing the weapon one last time, ensuring it had made its mark.

A burning cough choked out of her, and something warm spat up with it. She tasted the iron on her tongue as that warmth leaked from her lips.

Those golds cleared to a bright sparkle and then froze over as Warrick's pupils pinpointed.

Someone roared, "NO!!"

Whether inside Kai's ears or outside her body, she did not know.

Tears welled in those gold eyes as her knees buckled. A high ceiling greeted her, and her head barely registered hitting something soft.

Kai's sense of feeling fled from her as a coldness began to creep up from her toes over the rest of her flesh.

Another face appeared in hers, something red running down the man's cheek. "No, no, no, no," he kept repeating; silver-lined this one's dark waterlines.

Kai's eyelids felt heavy, threatening to close. Or perhaps that strange sensation in her heart was the cause of the weight.

Dexter Alus was his true name.

The son of the witch who was responsible for putting innocent, suffering people inside this place. Turning their lives inside out and robbing them of their most authentic realities. He understood now how she was still alive after all this time...

The headaches were nowhere near as painful as his chest. He stood with a wobble and staggered over to Scarlett, clutching the agony.

"I'm so sorry, Rosie..." He gently grabbed the princess. "For all of this." Picking her up from the floor, Dexter carefully carried her to the bed. So delicate and slow, as if she would wither to dust with one wrong move.

The princess was gaunt, her lips cracked and bleeding. Dark circles had devoured the space under her big eyes, her cheeks sunk inwards, a grey colour. Many of her nails were broken, many scratch marks up the woman's arms. She weighed next to nothing. Dexter could even see her rib cage through the creamy nightgown she wore.

"I never intended for any of this," he began, placing her delicate frame on the bed. His hand brushed the matted hair back, away from her sick profile. "I love you... so... so much," he whispered against her forehead. "I'm sorry for all of this," he repeated and planted a lingering kiss as a tear dropped onto her face.

"No, no, no, no…" Eros's eyes darted between the sword shoved into Kai's gut and her stuttering lashes.

Her plump lips moved, trembling. *It's okay.* Even her mental voice was getting quieter, pulling away as if she was leaving him.

"Charles, Charles, what's going on?!" That girl asked behind.

Kai was growing colder, her skin taking on the colour surrounding them.

"It's okay, you're okay. We're going to be okay," Eros lied to himself and Kai. Wiping the tears that were also cooling on her fading cheeks with his thumbs.

Kai offered him a weak smile, and that voice reached out with hushed words, *I wish… everyone had the love my parents had… I think… The world would be a better place… if they did.* Then her voice faded to silence, and those icy blues dulled to nothing.

That twinkle of a coming spring was gone as the light within them was snuffed out.

The area started to shake with it. The walls around them began to shake and illuminate as a light devoured everything.

There was screaming and things falling, but Eros didn't mind. His blurry vision was locked on the bleak, opened eyes that no longer focused on him.

CHAPTER THIRTY-NINE

K ai watched as those reds became obscured. Memories of her mother and father violently flashed in their stead.

They smiled at each other and stole kisses when they didn't think she was watching. The pretend fights in the kitchen, when father would throw food at her and spark a food war.

Kai smiled weakly at the memories, wishing everyone got to experience that. To experience the unconditional love of a warm home.

She didn't know what was happening or what would happen. Fear did not come to her as she watched her parent's love story play out. Then came the warm flash of light. She lifted her arm to block it out, as it burned much more than the pain in her stomach.

"Kai?!" a familiar voice suddenly cried out as if it sat there with her.

Kai's head flopped to the side. Something like a cushion was under her skull. She peeled open her glued eyelids to brown, teary ones on an olive-toned face.

"Stace?" her voice came out grumbled. She wasn't even sure if it was her voice.

It had felt like years since she heard it.

"Oh my god!" Tears spilt out of those eyes as Stace launched herself.

She was shaking and convulsing from weeping so hard that Kai couldn't understand a single coherent sentence Stace said between those sobs.

"Pet?" an older voice chimed in from the other side.

Dropping the paper cups of coffee in his hands, he hurriedly hobbled over to the bed.

"Oh, thank the lord!" Shaking hands touched his greying hair as he leaned over and embraced the girls on the bed. "You're awake… you're finally awake!" his fragile tone was laced with so many emotions.

After listening to them cry and a doctor coming in to assess her, Kai sat up in the hospital bed. Her attention scanned everything, from the monitor screen blinking with her heart rate to the blankets on the two chairs by the window. Her eyes followed the tube that was connected to her arm. The liquid was being induced into her, giving her body slight chills.

Her heart was not ready to believe it quite yet. She didn't want that false hope only to wake up in that book.

A doctor, clad in white, spoke to her grandfather, "She may experience moments of deliria. For the most part, she's alright, but she's not out of the woods yet. She'll need lots of rest and a healthier lifestyle to prevent this from happening again. She's young. She shouldn't work her body so hard." He held a clipboard, writing down notes.

The sky outside the hospital window was clear. Pigeons flew by in flocks, and the room smelt strongly of disinfectant.

Kai studied her grandfather's ageing profile and how bright his frosty blues were. The lines and sunspots that covered his cheeks and the more brilliant white streaks in his already grey hair.

Her gaze slid to Stace, the bags under her dark eyes, the spots from stress on her forehead. Stace hadn't let go of her hand since she had awoken. A leg shook with concentration as she listened to the doctor, as well.

"This is real…" Kai mumbled out, catching everyone's attention.

A nurse rushed in. "Doctor Scuttle, we have two more patients who have woken!"

The doctor nodded, eyes back on Kai. "Get some rest, kiddo." He nodded to Kai's grandfather as he followed the nurse quickly out the door.

She mumbled again, "I'm back…" Tears of her own lined those eyes.

Her grandfather hobbled over to her left and kissed Kai's forehead. "You shouldn't push yourself so hard… If you're struggling, tell your pappy. I'm always here for you, child." His trembling hand rubbed the back of her head.

The last few weeks broke forth from Kai's restraint. The tears kept coming as everything tumbled out. She tried to explain the events that had happened, catching the looks shared between her two companions. Kai didn't care; she just needed someone to listen to her, to hear what she went through.

By the time she was done, Kai had nearly lost her voice again, and a throbbing headache snuck up on her.

"It must have been terrifying." her grandfather said, pulling the quilt higher to Kai's chest.

Stace's phone began to ring as she shuffled from her spot. "It's my dad. Excuse me a moment." Stepping out of the room to answer.

Kai's grandfather scooped up her hand, rubbing it with his thumb. "She's a good friend, that one. Been here every day, stayed with you whilst I travelled down." His eyes dragged back to her after Stace had left. "I was so shocked when I got that phone call," his voice broke. He kissed the back of Kai's hand and stared at it. "It was like receiving your father's call all over again… I thought… I thought…" His head laid on her hand, and his shoulders shook.

After getting permission to walk around, Stace and Kai's grandfather escorted her around the hospital to stretch her legs. Stace was running Kai up to speed on things when noises down the hall caught curious looks.

People were shouting erratically to get back in bed.

With the help of her companions, Kai wobbled and turned to glimpse at the commotion.

A familiar face staggered out of one of the rooms – hooked up to a machine. The brown-eyed boy's features were slightly different from what Kai remembered, sickly looking in comparison. People herded around him, trying to usher him back inside.

Charlie Flounder.

They just stared at each other for a moment as if confirming whether or not they indeed went through what they had.

"Kai?" the boy's words were clear, save for the hoarseness in his throat.

She nodded quickly to Charlie, her hands trembling within the two engulfing hers.

Her grandfather looked between the children. "A friend of yours?" Then scanned over the machine hooked up to the boy.

Kai's grandfather stepped out the next day, gunning for the college. He planned to ring out the headmaster for yet another student who had collapsed due to extreme pressure – leaving Kai in Stace's care.

"I didn't know you were friends with that Charlie lad?" Stace had asked her.

Kai had already tried to explain, but she could tell by the look on her and her grandfather's faces that they didn't believe her. And how could they? Saying all that had happened out loud sounded ridiculous, even to her.

You would have had to have gone through it to understand.

"We met briefly at the pub once. I just didn't put the name to the face at the time," Kai lied, offering her best friend a tight smile.

She watched as Stace struggled to open the Jello packet, not allowing Kai to lift a finger to do anything for herself.

Reaching out, she stopped her. A hand rested on Stace's. "I… I missed you."

Brown eyes softened as Stace gripped that hand back. "I missed you too, bitch. Don't ever scare me like this again!"

A phone rang again, interrupting the moment. Stace's family had been ringing every couple of hours since she texted of Kai's update.

Waiting until Stace left the room to take the call, Kai confronted her thoughts. She was beyond relieved to be back, yet a part of her still stung with pain.

A gnawing feeling ate away at her gut, slowly but surely.

She pulled her phone from the little moving table at the side, removing the white charger. The screen was cracked from when the phone hit the ground, spiderwebbing all across the screen. It was still usable, and Kai was thankful to whoever the bystander was to hand it in.

A small smile was on her face as she read all the texts of well wishes from colleagues to aunts and uncles.

She squinted at the one unsaved number between them, a message saying, 'Get well soon, Redsi!' Followed by three kisses.

Kai guessed it was Zachary, as he was the only one who ever called her by her surname. A nose scrunched up in thought – having no idea how he had her number.

She swiped away all the notifications, bringing up her Android's browser, and googled when the book was published.

Only the book did not appear.

Kai searched and couldn't find any links about The Cursed Rose.

She googled the author's pen name and then her first, hoping to find something, but the browser found nothing. There were just recommendations for books with similar titles or authors with similar names.

She pulled up her grandfather's number, ringing him next. Asking him to bring the book when he collected some clothing for her.

Later on, when her grandfather arrived empty-handed, she turned to Stace. "Do you know where my book is?"

Stace was folding Kai's clothing, ridding them of the wrinkles from being shoved into a bag. "Which one?"

"The Cursed Rose, the one you said had seen better days. We were talking about it after we went to Starbucks?"

Stace gave her a funny face. "Never heard of it." Continuing with her task.

When Kai was allowed to wander again the following day, she and Stace visited Charlie—surprised by yet another visitor already there.

Ava Sebastian.

Like Charlie, she, too, was hooked up to a machine.

She glared at Charlie, her voice also hoarse as she asked who the women were. When he explained who the red-haired girl was –Ava's eyes widened, and she whipped to Kai in disbelief.

The four made idle chat, carefully avoiding how they *really* knew each other to Stace.

They headed outside the hospital for fresh air, casually talking about the stress of grades. The sky had clouded over, the scent of rain on the air as the four made themselves comfortable in an alcove near the smoker's pit.

Stace jumped right in as she and Ava kicked it off. The girls seemed to have instantly clicked, talking about niche trends to social media celebs they both looked up to. Stace was also drilling Ava about what school she attended and what products she used that made her skin so soft-looking.

Leaving Kai and Charlie to the side in quiet conversation.

Kai explained the strangeness to Charlie at her left, careful not to catch Stace's attention. Even Charlie was in the same predicament, as he sent his sister for his copy.

To his utter surprise, it wasn't there.

"Ava said she couldn't even find the book online." Charlie leaned in and whispered to Kai, "Like the book never existed."

It was nice that Kai could understand Charlie for once and didn't rely on Ava's translations.

The boy's soft voice reminded her of another's smooth and velvety tone.

Kai nodded in thought, shaking away the manifesting faces. She watched as Stace's head tipped back with laughter at whatever Ava told her—reminding herself that it was finally over.

"Maybe it's for the best..." she mumbled to Charlie.

As the days passed, Kai was finally discharged, and the doctors were satisfied with her recovery. She inquired about Ava and Charlie, only to hear it would be another week before their doctor's approval.

Their cases were much more severe.

Kai had learned that she was in a coma for just over two weeks. She couldn't even remember the days within the book, as time seemed to go at a snail's pace.

It had felt like another lifetime.

"Look at this..." her grandfather moaned, plucking one of the books that riddled Kai's cover table. "I gave that school's head a mouthful for not looking out for its pupils," he continued muttering and cleaning up the place.

Kai stood at the door, gaping at her stupidly expensive apartment. A part of her was convinced she wouldn't ever see it again.

"You okay, sweetheart?" Her grandfather turned, worry pulling down his face. His years of lines and creases deepened.

"Yeah, it just feels like a dream... being back," lamented Kai.

She settled in, touching everything and questioning whether this was real. All the while, she searched for that book.

If it hadn't been for Ava and Charlie confirming they were there and that they remembered everything just as she had done, Kai would have believed she was going mad.

The day's light was devoured by the dark clouds rolling in. Kai offered her grandfather the bed for the night, but only the old goat refused.

He lectured her for the second time today that she had just been released from hospital and needed proper rest. So, her grandfather stayed on the couch, refusing to go home until he was sure Kai wouldn't have another episode. Still muttering for her to drop out of school and come home with him, even as he laid down to get rest, too.

Kai was in bed, blankly staring at the white ceiling, consumed with dubiety at what had happened to the book. Red lights from somewhere outside her window reflected inside the room, casting glares on her bare walls.

It reminded her of those red, teary eyes staring at her, fear adamant in them. She speculated on what happened to them. If they were still trapped, or if their souls were freed and finally at rest.

The visualisations continued to degenerate, getting progressively worse. Kai quietly cried to herself and prayed to whatever god, deity, or space being may have been listening – for them. Until she finally fell asleep.

CHAPTER FORTY

It had been six months since Kai woke in that hospital bed — one hundred and eighty-two days since that strange dream of being trapped inside her once-adored book.

The days returned to normal, mostly. Save for the fact that Kai's grandfather and Stace harassed her to take vitamins and breaks where she could. School progressed as usual, and she returned to her job, working late nights again. Stace's father, however, increased her wages and took away shifts, balancing it out so she didn't end up back in the hospital.

Even Mr Humperdink was different, always mothering Kai during their odd shifts together. He began this routine of dragging her to his car and driving her home, even if she claimed she wanted to walk for a change. He also tried to become more involved with her in school, striking up conversations and opting to sit with her.

The longing glances he threw made Kai downright awkward around him.

She did her best to avoid the man at all costs to save her sanity. But failed, as the man seemed to be around every damn corner.

Though life had returned to normal, a part of Kai was forever changed. Whenever she heard a ticking clock, she found her head snapping to see if some shadow appeared on the walls. Or if a voice whispered into the air.

Kai also developed a fear of reading fantasy books; an abstraction in the back of her head chased the enthusiasm away whenever she opened a novel. A voice would whisper in her head, wondering if they were characters at all, or were they, too, were once like her?

She spent most of her days working, studying, or hanging with Stace, Ava and Charlie.

The four of them had developed a bond since the hospital. From jointly catching films to going shopping, the quad spent most free weekends together.

Charlie even joined Stace, Kai, *and* Zachary during lunch breaks while they all attended school.

Kai's small friendship circle had flipped overnight.

She couldn't complain; life was relatively easy. Kai even sought professional help to ease the dreams chasing her awake at night.

Though she always felt slightly frustrated after each session, knowing the woman didn't believe her story, no matter how often she told it. Her educated diagnosis was just like everyone else's.

One spontaneous day, Kai dyed her hair back to red, waiting for the natural colour to grow. Something she learned to cherish every time she looked in the mirror.

She was grateful for the thoughts of her parents and how they kept her sane inside the book when it used to drive her into depression before. She thanked the once sad memories for grounding her when that fictional world sent her soaring into the lines.

As the days passed and exams neared, Kai was so busy studying and preparing that her graduation crept up without realising it.

She passed her final exams and gained her long-awaited business degree.

The day was filled with joy and tears as Kai closed yet another chapter of her life.

TEN YEARS

LATER

Chapter Forty-One

Many people were sharply dressed outside; some were awed by the romantic scenery as music cascaded outside the venue. Violins, pianos, and cellos played a swaying tune as groups slowly filed in.

"Listen, Glen, just pen the appointments in. I will deal with it when I return from holidays... Yes..." Kai pinched the bridge of her nose, listening to her assistant brief her about upcoming meetings. "Glen, I have to go. I'm going to be late!" she expressed, pulling the phone away from her ear.

Her green acrylic fingernail hit the call-end button while the voice continued to murmur, and her other hand knocked on the window.

The car door opened, and a tall, bulky man dressed in a sharp suit stepped to the side. "All ready, miss?"

Kai nodded, and the chunky earrings at her earlobes swung. "Yes, sorry about that, Stuart. Glen likes to talk even more when he's not with me," she apologised while stepping out of the car. Her four-inch black heels adjusted her footing as her dress spilt out of the vehicle.

In the last ten years, Kai had worked her butt off for Stace's dad. Eventually, she landed a gig as director of one of his companies.

She took over a whole new world of stress and responsibilities.

She also got the opportunity to travel the world, representing Core-Edge and securing a few multi-million-pound deals, which included hefty bonuses for her.

With the stupid amount of money she made from all of it, Kai didn't mind enduring these new stresses.

During those days, Kai opened a mental health clinic with the money she made and saved, which focused on helping struggling individuals from all walks of life who couldn't get in with their NHS providers sooner than the waiting lists could offer. Its main focus was assisting them in finding their feet and coping with the stresses that plagued them, from PTSD to depression.

Her centre thrived, and with the support and funding from many other private corporations, she opened up two more clinics across the United Kingdom.

As CEO and Founder of TranqWell.

Straightening out her silk green dress, Kai received the gift her driver presented for the event.

"I will return at eleven fifty-five, miss. Unless you wish to leave sooner, just ring, please."

Kai smiled, thanking Stuart as she walked towards the impressive venue, her dress kicked back with each step. She had her elegant wedding invite in hand, approaching a massive sign. Kai surveyed the bold words, and a sense of pride swelled in her chest.

Mr and Mrs Flounder.

Pictures of Ava and Charlie were all within the block letters. Some photos she recognised, as she and Stace were on that holiday with them. A giggle slipped past her lips, one photo in particular catching her attention.

One of her and Ava – half pissed and totally off their rockers.

"Oh, my goodness, you took sooo long!" Stace complained, stomping red heels right up to her.

A sigh released from Kai's painted lips. "Sorry, work has been hectic. I barely just got Glen off the phone." She had a feeling Stace was going to be in a huff over her tardiness.

Stace linked arms with Kai, and those brown eyes rolled. The gold eyeshadow on Stace's eyelids glittered profusely from the action. "That's it. I'm done. If it's not one thing stealing your time away, it's another. Just tell my dad straight away and quit. You don't need so many jobs!"

Kai's attention slid away from the extravagantly dressed Stace in golds and reds to the cute photos. "I like the money, Stace. So, I don't mind."

"You can marry my brother and still have money pouring in, woman!"

Kai squeezed the arm linked with hers, giggling at her friend's complaints.

It didn't matter what she said. Stace was going to argue back.

Now that she and what's-his-face were broken up, Stace was back to being Kai's clingy, money-spending best friend. Who just wanted to shop, party, or watch serious trash TV.

They entered the hall together, chatting about fashion and galas approaching while finding their respective seats.

The venue quieted down as the wedding party took their places. Charlie's big brown eyes were already full of tears when they landed on Kai, slyly waving a hand.

Music flowed into the room as all guests rose for the bride, her eyes in wonder as she scanned all those in attendance, a smile blossomed on her face when they landed on the groom.

As the wedding proceeded, and the groom kissed the gorgeously dressed bride, Kai and Stace were gibbering messes, padding the tears away before they could ruin the hours of makeup on their faces.

Kai had congratulated Ava and Charlie, and she stood at the bar, sipping from a drink. Observing as Stace threw her hair over a shoulder, chatting up a blonde gentleman, she was finally able to corner.

It had nearly been eleven years since that strange dream before waking up in that hospital. But still, to this day, Kai would wake panting at night, wondering if any of this was real. She occasionally drifted away from reality, thinking about that strange, winged fellow and his tear-filled eyes.

"Well, that was embarrassing..." Stace plodded up and collapsed on a bar stool, her upper body leaning over the counter.

Kai sipped from her cocktail again and swallowed the burning liquor. "He's gay," she explained, distracting herself before the thoughts could fossilise.

Those brown eyes cut to Kai, and Stace's face frowned deeply. "And how do you know that, hmm? Do you know him, too? Been out making more friends without me?"

Kai rolled her blues, landing on Stace's pouting lips. "How many guys do you know to walk around saying 'Yes queen' to every girl?"

Stace considered it. "He could be trying to be hip, using all the slang nowadays."

Kai downed the rest of her drink, swallowing back her reply. She might have believed that too if it wasn't for the fact he told her that her dress was a *statement*. His arm was linked with another man's, who Kai believed to be his partner, as they blew each other kisses and called each other babe.

That solidified her assumptions.

"I haven't seen you try lately. It's been like, what, three years since you broke up with Zachary."

Kai's nose scrunched. "Hmm, please, don't remind me."

Stace straightened, ordering rounds. She watched the young barman pour the shots; her eyes barely glanced at Kai. "I thought you two were doing great. It was obvious how in love he was with you... You dated for a year, and the man looked ready to lock it down."

Kai tucked the dress under her, settling into a bar stool. "I just wasn't all there, Stace... he was great, both physically and-"

Stace turned her chin, giving her a look. Her drawn-on eyebrows sky high, wiggling.

"That's not what I mean... but you know!" Kai grabbed the shot the moment it was placed down, downing it. Her voice strained, "He deserved better, someone who could give him one hundred percent back. I was a shit girlfriend. I can admit that."

The two of them drank and talked and drank even more.

Chatting mindlessly about men.

Kai's phone rang on the counter, catching Stace's attention mid-convo. "Oh my god!" She snatched the device, frowning at the name displayed on the screen, and even went as far as answering it.

Kai was dancing in her spot, enjoying the buzz she was catching. "What's wrong?"

She wondered who Stace was talking to and why Stace's phone looked a lot like her new one.

"Seriously, Dad! She quits. Stop calling her!"

Kai sobered up, realising that it was *her* phone.

She snatched the mobile back, a hand shoved away Stace's frantic ones. "I'm so sorry, Mr Williams! Please give me a moment to go somewhere quieter." Kai got up from the spot, dashing quickly towards an exit.

She tucked herself away from the noises of people coming and going, plugging her one free ear. "Again, I'm so sorry about that, Mr Williams!"

He responded on the other line with his thick Italian accent, "It's fine, Kai. I know what my daughter is like..." A strange noise followed his words.

"Is everything alright, sir?" Kai asked, noticing the weird grunt he made at the end of his sentence.

That grunt usually indicated that he was peeved off with something or someone.

He sighed, the microphone making an absurd sound at Kai's ear. "Do you have family within the elites?" he interrogated.

Kai watched as the moon peered out from behind a cloud, replying, "Uh, no. Not that I'm aware of."

Mr Williams grumbled again, then followed with another deep sigh. "Listen, kid, I need you to come back earlier. This, Mr Redsi, has been a pain in my backside. He won't sign the papers until he meets with someone more eloquent and on his *level*."

"Mr Redsi?"

Stace's father hummed on the other line, "Yes, Mr Redsi, that's what I'm being told. He holds major stocks with...." He then began briefing Kai on her target and what he wanted from her.

"Get me his signature, kid. I'm counting on your skills."

"Yes, sir. You can count on me." Curiosity festered as she hung up the phone. She stared at the number displayed across the screen until her background image appeared.

A photo of a photo, an image of her and her parents she had found while digging through her grandfather's boxes. The photo never failed to make her smile, which is why she snapped a pic of it and made it her background.

Small Kai was making a funny face while her mother was holding her pigtails up like long ears, and her father was laughing, holding his wife from behind.

"So, what did he want?"

Kai twisted to a swaying, arms crossed, frowning Stace. "I have a meeting with Mr Redsi. I'll be heading back to the UK earlier than planned."

Stace was mid-eye roll. "Wait... Redsi?"

Kai nodded with confirmation.

"Do you have a family with the big guns?"

Kai shook her head this time, putting the phone into her bra, closest to her heart. "Like I told your dad, not that I'm aware of..."

Her best friend swayed excitedly. "Maybe this is like one of those k dramas!" Her face lit up. "The hidden son from your uncle's side comes along trying to steal your wealth! Oh! Maybe someone in your family had a secret affair!"

It was Kai's turn to roll her eyes, stepping forward to Stace still swaying. "You, my friend, watch too much television." Laughing as she helped Stace inside.

Kai wanted to dance the night away and not worry about anything else before tackling the reality she would return to.

CHAPTER FORTY-TWO

"Good morning, Miss Redsi!"

"Morning."

"Good morning, Miss Redsi!"

Kai nodded respectfully, wishing everyone a good morning as she walked by, "Good morning, Joanne."

With a briefcase in one hand and a newspaper in the other, she headed for the office across the top floor of Core-Edge. Each employee sat at their desk, glanced up and smiled, or wished her a good morning.

Glen was already inside, scurrying around with piles of paperwork as she entered. His long blonde hair was in a man bun, and his groomed facial hair reached his sideburns. "Good morning, Miss Redsi!" He turned with a smile; his hazel eyes sparkled as they landed on her. "Thank god, your back!"

Kai reviewed the local headlines, giving Glen a brief glance. "Good morning. Did you bring the reports up from finance, as I asked?" Immediately diving into her position of leadership.

"Yes, ma'am!" He stepped up to her desk, handing over the two top files. "I've also brought Mr Williams's files about Revive Energy."

Kai mumbled a thank you, flipping the file open. "Can you bring up a tray of hot drinks and some refreshments for the meeting at ten?"

"Yes, ma'am!" Glen smiled wide and dashed out of the office.

"Not now, I mean-" Kai sighed as the door closed. Still in wonder, after these last few years, how that man had so much energy.

Glen was four years older than Kai but acted a decade younger with his over-the-top personality. She used the man's stamina to do errands for her, as he had a habit of talking too much, which caused her to lose focus on tasks.

Kai paused on the information below, reading over what they had gathered about this potential partner.

She reviewed the notes about Mr Redsi being a heavy investor and a major stockholder in the gas and electric industry. Baffled by the three sheets that followed, going into specific details on the man's corporate path.

Surely making a deal with Mr Williams should have been 'up to his level?' Considering her boss's list of companies under his impressively long resume, she read on in deep thought.

Kai sat back, eyes drifting out the stretched floor-to-ceiling window covering an entire section of her office.

How could someone like me persuade this big shark?

Clouds congested the skies, threatening to rain down. Cars zipped by like little ants below, and little moving blobs of people carried on about their days. Her attention was snagged by the statue on the fountain in the distance—a bronzed mermaid all alone in the sea of people around her.

Kai's long fingernail tapped the polished wood of her armchair, thinking about this mysterious businessman.

She had called her grandfather when she landed to see if they had distant relatives who still carried the name, as it was a very uncommon, nearly impossible surname for just anyone to have.

To her dismay, her grandfather was just as shocked to hear. So, that idea of getting some background or some dirt was a dead end.

All Mr Williams said to her was that he was a prominent tycoon who came out of nowhere and started monopolising the big corps.

He even had his fingers in some of the big banks globally. Striking a deal with him was crucial to protect their assets.

Kai placed the file aside and opted to get the one she requested out of the way. She would deal with the matter when the time came. Meeting the gentleman first might reveal something she could use.

A head peeked into Kai's office. "Ma'am?" Green eyes blinked, waiting to proceed. "Mr Redsi is here to see you now."

Kai placed her pen down and swiftly glanced over to the computer screen.

The time showed nine, fifty-nine, right on the dot.

"Thank you, Joanne. Send him in." She shuffled her papers and removed the glasses from her nose.

In the background, she could hear the secretary speak to the gentleman, "Right this way, sir." Her pitch was higher than usual, indicating that Joanne found the man attractive.

Kai straightened out her dark green blazer, then ensured the white turtleneck was neatly tucked into her green trousers as she stepped away from the desk.

As the door opened wider, a gentleman swaggered in, hands in trouser pockets.

Kai noticed he was wearing a dark suit designed by Alexander Amosu, implying this man was no joke. If that was the real deal, he spent a lot of money to purchase it and then had to pay even more to clean it. The suit was a perfect fit for his well-kept, sturdy frame. Kai's scrutinising stare continued to drag up to the man's sharp jawline, a five o'clock shadow of dark hair coming in.

Not exactly clean-shaven, she said to herself. Her investigation ceased as her icy blues clashed with browns, which glinted red from the sunlight that began to peek from behind the clouds pouring into the office.

Kai's steps halted, eyes widened, taking in that profile.

Dark lashes protected those eyes, so thick it appeared like he had a thin coat of eyeliner on the edges of his waterlines. Thick dark eyebrows adorned his enviously flawless face. His dark hair has slight waves, gelled back at the top and sides, showcasing those familiar features.

Her breathing became laboured as she couldn't suck air in fast enough. The sinfully tempted man standing inside her office was strikingly identical to the one that surfaced in her mind occasionally.

Joanne nodded; her cheeks were pink as she excused herself from the room, her eyes unable to remove themselves from the man's backside.

The gentleman glimpsed, offering the exiting woman a pleasant smile.

As he faced Kai again, that gentleman's grin dropped. His eyebrows raised as his stare scanned Kai head to toe, then trailed up deliberately slow.

A smirk climbed his sculptured cheeks. "Agapi mou."

Even his voice sounded similar to the man in her imagination.

Kai rapidly blinked, waking herself up from fumbling this meeting any further. "My apologies, Mr Redsi. Please have a seat." She gestured a shaky hand at the couch, very much aware of his presence.

Mr Redsi tilted his head to a side, that smile wiped clean. "So... that's what your actual voice sounds like, then. Sounds even prettier in person."

Kai had taken one step and froze again, wondering what she had heard.

A brief thought pinged in her mind, like a notification on a screen. Telling her she needed to call her therapist and set up another session. Clearly, it had been too long, as her mind seemed to be playing a trick on her.

The man removed his hands from his pockets, showcasing dark tattoos on their backs. His voice dropped low, "I wonder what your voice will sound like when it's screaming *my name* later." Hands reached up, one undoing his blazer button, the other loosened his tie.

Kai's toes curled inside her white heels, and her back suddenly heated. Normally she disliked a straightforward man, but this one... It's like his mojo oozed from every pore.

His voice became huskier with her silence, "Agapi, have you forgotten all about me?"

"It's not possible..." she mumbled, seized still, and staring. So many emotions were coursing through Kai.

The room began to feel light as if she was finally aware of how far off the ground this floor was.

That man took nine significant strides, closing the gap between them. His polished shoes gleamed with each swift step.

"I haven't forgotten about you for a second in this last decade." He halted right in front of Kai, toe to toe, towering over her. A hand paused just before her face. His eyes locked on her lips. "It took a while for me to get the gist of this new world. So, I apologise for being late."

His hand gently touched her cheek, and his eyes sparkled with reassurance as if he was sure that she, too, was real.

"Oh, I've missed you."

His other hand reached, pulling Kai flat against him.

Kai's soul had left her body, just gaping at him. All those moments she doubted what she went through flooded in.

"Can't say I enjoy this downgrade." Eros's eyes darted between hers. "What's on your mind, tell me?" he spoke tenderly, a heavy emotion weaved into his tonality.

"H-How?" was all Kai could stutter out.

That fear returned to that heated gaze but then gone within moments. "I'll tell you after, but please... Please tell me you missed me, too. Please give me more than that?" Eros's Adam's apple bobbed, swallowing down nerves.

Kai's hand twitched as it rose from her side. Her fingers hesitated just centimetres from him.

Eros closed the gap again, pushing his cheek into it. Her hand was now flat, touching his warm skin, feeling the roughness from his stubble.

Her eyes welled up, comprehending this wasn't a fabricated scenario her mind created.

"It's okay," he assured her, his hand slipped to the back of Kai's head, bringing it to his chest. "We're okay."

Kai could hear a strong heartbeat within. The warmth of his body cascaded onto her; a clean scent of evergreen wafted into her senses.

Her hands slid up his back, clutching onto his suit. Her chest finally gave way, weeping onto the man as all those unanswered questions rose.

She could register his fingers flex, shoved right into her hair, rubbing the scalp. His chest vibrated into her ears as he hummed, just holding her.

"Coffee, tea-" Glen froze at the door, pushing a tray of refreshments Kai had asked him for. His words stopped as he observed his boss and Mr Redsi embracing each other near the massive window.

A dark head shifted and angled Glen's way. A robust masculine nose peeked at him with red glaring eyes. Hostility barred.

"Get out," the man ordered.

Glen sucked in a sharp breath, backtracking with great speed. The door closed just as quickly as it had opened.

Eros placed his chin on Kai's head, patiently waiting. The poor woman continued to cry; those small shoulders trembled constantly. He didn't offer anything else, as he allowed Kai this moment.

After the tears had dried up, and Kai couldn't squeeze another out – even if her life depended on it – she pulled away.

She was embarrassed with herself over that mental breakdown.

Kai put some distance between her and the gentleman, concealing her face. Her eyelashes were lowered, and she was unable to look at the man. "I apologise… again." She searched the surfaces of the furniture, looking for a tissue box.

Eros refused to allow her the space and stepped in her way. He grabbed her arm gently, a tissue in his other hand from his blazer pocket. "It's quite alright." Immediately, he started wiping away the lines gleaming on those flushed cheeks.

Kai tried to step back, but he refused, taking a step with her.

"We… We have a business to discuss," she tried to explain. "If you just give me a moment…"

Eros waved a dismissive hand. "I'll sign the contract." His other hand reached again for her. "We have other things to deal with."

A thin red eyebrow rose as Kai's confusion furthered. "Deal with?"

Before she knew it, Eros had backed her up to the desk. Kai's thighs collided, and seconds later, Eros was hiking her onto it. Hands reached behind, hoisting her up.

Kai yelped from the sudden events.

"Ten years, I thought about this moment. Ten years, I thought about what I would do with you when I had you in my grasp again."

"M-Mr Redsi!" Kai placed her hands against his chest and attempted to shove him back, with no effect.

Eros offered her a smug grin. "Yes, Love?" His eyes twinkled with mischief.

The heat had exploded up Kai's spine, up her neck, and currently burned her face. "This is an office, w-we are in a meeting!"

Eros nodded, hands gripping the woman's plump bottom, sliding her closer to him. "Oh, there'll be a meeting, alright. Your body and mine meeting in glorious rhy-"

A hand stopped him from finishing.

"Have you no shame!?" Kai's face was just as red as her messed-up hair.

Thick eyebrows rose as teeth began to nip at the smooth hand that covered his mouth.

Kai retracted her hand with such speed, and Eros dove straight in with that opening. Her breath hitched in surprise as their lips clashed.

Eros's kiss was demanding and needy, unlike the ones with her and Zachary.

A tongue swept across Kai's bottom lip, asking for entry. Kai parted her lips slightly, which was all Eros needed as he deepened the kiss.

He took complete control, angling Kai's head, thumb on her chin. The other pulled her closer, trying to fuse his body with hers.

"Breathe, my Love," Eros whispered against her lips.

And right on command, Kai inhaled, her eyelashes fluttering. A tingling sensation had taken over her legs, shooting for her toes. Kai hadn't even realised one of her heels had fallen off.

Brown eyes were again darting between hers, a hand pushing back the red strands in Eros's view.

His voice began, unstable at first, "You died... and then there was a big commotion. I... I thought the loop would start again, and I'd forget about you..." He took a steady breath, and that fear that often surfaced in Kai's mind was there again on his features. "But instead, we were swallowed by a blinding light. When I woke, the first thing I did was collect debts owed to me from some very, very old friends... They punished Elphaba for her crimes, and I was given a choice. I could put it all behind me and take up my position as before, or..."

Kai wasn't sure what she was hearing, but she listened. Dazed out, she continued absorbing his handsome profile. "Or what?"

"Well... I chose this. This mortal life, for this mortal woman. Who I had only known for a short time but had never been more certain about anything before her."

She was once again swaying. Her heart thumped wildly in her ears like a drum. "Certain of what?" Her head still felt dizzy from that air-robbing kiss.

Two hands found the sides of Kai's face, and his thumbs brushed underneath those vivid eyes. "I would happily give up my immortality for a mortal life then to live a long and sad existence without her in it."

A shaky smile appeared on his face, and once again, those lips found hers.

Kai reciprocated this time, pulling Eros to her. Her body erupted to life with such need, feeling the electricity between them.

Her tongue fought for dominance as she allowed herself to be greedier.

Kai's cheeks were permanently red, and her lips and chin were sore.

Eros's stubble on his chin gave her a slight irritation. She was currently trying to sort out her hair and straighten her outfit, which was in disarray. Her blazer was half discarded, and the belt she was wearing was undone. Her shirt also needed to be re-tucked from Eros's roam around within.

The mysterious man was sitting on the leather couch, leant back, head hung over as he adjusted the crotch of his trousers. His blazer was still by the desk, the top three buttons of his white dress shirt broken, lost somewhere on Kai's office floor. His chest was rising and falling hard.

"Tell me... again," Eros started between his breaths. "Why couldn't I just take you... here and now?"

Kai's head snapped to him, a mortified expression on her face. "This is a place of work. We still have things to talk about!" She inhaled a deep breath of her own, calming herself down.

She only prayed that those outside didn't see or hear anything they shouldn't have.

This was not the place for this sort of behaviour.

Eros hummed. "Give me the contract, please. I'll sign quickly, and then we can finish what *you* started."

That fluttering sensation returned to Kai as she tried to shove it down. "You haven't even read it." She tried to defuse the situation rationally, "We could be scamming you."

That head gradually rose, those eyes hungrily taking on Kai. "It was never about the contract or the company. It was about getting a moment with the director of Core-Edge and the founder and CEO of TranqWell. The famous, the irresistible, Miss Kai Redsi." A finger gun pointed at her. "I believe I'm the one scamming you guys." The corner of his mouth twitched upwards.

Kai swiped a heel from the floor, pausing. She twisted her head to Eros, her hair swung behind. "Is your surname, really-"

His twitching smirk bloomed into a full-on smile. "I would have taken it on after we got married. We didn't have surnames back then."

Her eyes blinked three times at this bold man, who winked shamelessly at her—allowing his head to fall back with a chesty chuckle.

Kai got the contract signed, making Mr Williams ecstatic to have the tycoon himself on board. But now, she had Eros lounging around the office with no plans to leave.

Kai needed a moment to wrap her head around what had just happened and what she would do moving forward.

How could she explain this to anyone when she couldn't even explain it to herself?

She was curious about how Eros could even be here and why her body still reacted the way it did, even though she was no longer inside that novel. His persona shouldn't affect her anymore.

Eros sat there and watched her as she went through file after file, trying to work through her emotions. He would never tire of watching Kai. Even if he couldn't reach for those thoughts anymore, she kept many of them on her face. Her small pink tongue peeked out from those swollen lips, trying her damnedest to stay focused.

"Do you not have work or somewhere else to be?" Kai asked, peering up from the page. Icy blue eyes squinted, half hidden by paper.

Eros had a pout stuck on his lip. "My first order of business was to act out everything I had envisioned when I found you. But the other party has prioritised other work over me. So, no."

Kai shook her head, attention on the file. Trying to ignore the arousal she was feeling whenever she locked eyes with him.

Her underwear was in serious need of changing.

She cleared her throat and fixed the glasses on the bridge of her nose. "I'll finish this, and we can go for lunch. I don't have much left."

Eros chuckled, "Are you on the menu?"

Kai offered him a pointed look. "I'm trying to work, and you're making it hard."

Another deep laugh bubbled out of him. "Welcome to my world, Love." Winking at Kai with his words.

Warmth exploded into Kai's face, and her head shook as she continued with the job at hand. Her gut was, once again, filled with butterflies as she shifted in her seat.

Chapter Forty-Three

The driver kept glancing in the mirror. His eyes asked Kai if she was alright, watching as she fidgeted in her seat. He had never seen Miss Boss Lady act so out of character.

Kai was sat, cheeks dusted pink, attention out the window. She was constantly shifting in her seat while her hand was caged into another hand.

A man refused to give it back.

The tall, dark, and handsome gentleman who sat in the back with his boss was someone Stuart had never seen before. The only fellow Boss Lady ever had had long since been gone. He had never heard her talk about seeing someone new since then.

Kai caught the questioning stare in the dashboard's mirror. "I'll explain later," she offered.

She had learned that when Stuart's eyes flickered to that mirror, he worried about her well-being.

Kai appreciated Stuart's concerns and his life lectures when she asked for his opinion. He had become vital to Kai, not just on business terms.

Years ago, she had called him drunk, blabbering about ending it with Zachary. Her driver just listened, explaining how proud of her he was for not wasting the boy's time, much like what she imagined her father might have done in that situation.

She had grown rather fond of him over the years, and Stuart was quite protective of her. She knew that.

Eros's ears perked. "Explain what?" he asked.

Her stare went back out the window, not trusting herself to look at him. "My driver is suspicious of you. I don't usually ride with men unless it's Mr Williams or Glen." Kai told herself to get a handle on her hormones.

A low snarl started, "Who's Glen?"

Eros squinted at the lady next to him, who hadn't looked him in the eyes since they left her office. Or looked at any of the gapping employees' faces as she scurried out of that place.

Kai giggled as she tapped his large hand three times. Which was currently trapping her left one. "My assistant. Heel, boy."

The driver burst out with his own puff of laughter, swiftly pulling it together. "My apologies, miss, sir." Those eyes checked out the dangerously-looking man behind. The ex-warrant officer spoke sternly, "I'm Stuart Bradley, sir." Questioning him, "And you are?"

Kai fought the chuckle, knowing all too well Stuart was pulling one of his stunts. He had done it with Zachary when she first introduced them, scaring the poor man.

"Eros Redsi, life partner to Kai Redsi," the man countered, giving his not-so-innocent grin.

Those mirrored eyes were back on Kai. "Life partner?"

But Eros answered the driver, "We're married in spirit. The ceremony and paperwork can come later."

Stuart's eyes widened with disbelief, his right subtly twitching. "I see..." Not believing the sheer gulls of this guy.

The car slowed to an idle, pulling up to a curb in front of a tall building. Eros was out the moment the wheels stopped, not giving Mr Bradley a chance to open the back door.

Kai was still sitting inside the car, only able to see their torsos outside the tinted window.

"This is my job, *Mr Redsi*," Stuart explained.

Eros's chin pointed back to the driver's door, a smile on his mug. "A driver, yes. I'll take it from here, though. You have my thanks."

Kai hardly heard the conversation but caught narrowed eyes from Stuart as he reopened the driver's door, and his backside slid in. "Good luck with him, miss." He gave Kai a firm nod in the mirror, patting his chest where he kept his phone.

A silent signal to call him if she needed to.

Her door opened not a moment later, and Kai was guided out with Eros's helping hand.

"Thank you." She offered him a small smile, attention still low.

They were guided to a table and settled into their seats, separated from the rest of the restaurant. A window over-looked the river, the London eye in the distance, up it. The restaurant displayed a mini monocular telescope upon a cushioned box at the windowsill for guests to see the historical buildings over the river.

Kai placed the cream-coloured napkin on her lap. Her icy blues collided with gleaming browns.

Resting his chin in a hand, Eros had his head cocked to a side, observing her. It reminded Kai of the moments in the Wastelands, a weird sensation of nostalgia.

"What... is my makeup smudge?" she asked coolly, a thumb swiped under those eyes.

Eros softly shook his head. "I just enjoy looking at you." Those pupils grew in size as a lover's grin sprouted on his face.

Kai thanked whatever sky being that may have been listening, glad this man could no longer hear her thoughts. So, he couldn't see or feel how much his presence had control over her.

His very existence seemed to bring every receptacle to life within her body.

"The food here is good," she bashfully said, picking up the lamented menu.

"Is it now? I could probably think of something even better."

Kai glanced up from the cuisine text, curiosity raising her eyebrow.

Eros flashed her a playful smoulder. "Or... someone better."

Even though they were sat near an open window, and the weather was beginning to cool, it did not stop the burning infernal Kai was becoming. She needed to do something about this...

"We need to talk."

His breathing paused as anxiety flickered across Eros's features. "About?"

Kai took a steady breath and straightened in the seat. "Everything. I don't even know who you are... What your real name is, or-" Her voice dropped to a whisper, "*What* you are."

Those blues spied the French doors, ensuring no one was lingering. The whole floor of tables was emptied, thanks to her reserving it.

"It's the very least, between two people, to get to know each other," she finished carefully.

The man exhaled a long breath. "Fair enough..." He scooted his chair forward. "So, where exactly should I start?" Elbows found the table as his large, tattooed hands came together.

"The beginning. Who, what are you? I mean... Immortality?" Kai's face scrunched. "That's probably a good start."

What *another story* that was...

Kai sat there reflecting on how a once-wonderful world could be so.... bad.

If she had been the twenty-two-year-old college student before the trauma of that book, Kai might have thought the man across from her was downright deranged – psychotic even.

But she wasn't that girl anymore, just as she wasn't that carefree child with both her loving parents.

Kai nodded, soaking in Eros's lengthy tale. He started with how he was once considered a god, hailing from Greece of all places. Though the novel had stayed true to his real name, it was rare for people to know it. Many within the tale had called him a demon, creature, or monster. It had been so long since hearing it that he had forgotten his name, too, as did his memories.

In that comment in her office about calling in debts with friends, Eros meant to say that he rallied up the other gods that failed to come to his aid – making them pay up and doing some of his biddings before giving up his position.

Vanessa, or Elphaba, lost her long life after the book was destroyed. The souls released from her entrapment spell were finally laid to rest. This took away the life force that was feeding hers, leaving her wretched soul to be dealt with.

"Eternal damnation."

That was what Eros said happened to Vanessa. Then, the gods just plucked the memories from reality as if the book no longer existed.

Kai stopped his story, "So, how is it we remember?" She felt closure somehow, but this one thing didn't add up.

Kai sometimes found herself googling the book's title or a similar title to it. To see if it would reappear and if more people would be conned into Vanessa's twisted scam.

Even after ten years, Kai could not shake the hanging feeling of madness that rose to the forefront. She needed evidence to prove it wasn't just a terrible dream.

Eros swirled the red wine in his glass. "Taking away the memories from someone who had gone through it is much more difficult than someone who hadn't… Consider it this way… If they took yours, we wouldn't get this chance, now." He threw her a wink and dared a sip.

Eros talked about what had happened and how the curse was broken afterwards. It turned out that Scarlett and Dexter had been the main characters all along. Dexter Ubar was actually Dexter Alus.

The original male lead of the story, and the True Love's Kiss.

"How did she expect any of us to figure that out?" Kai slammed a hand down on her armrest.

Eros paused his story, watching a new show of emotion he'd never seen with her. It had the corners of his lips twitch upwards, reminding him of an angry red squirrel.

"I read that book hundreds of times. Not once was anything mentioned between those two…" Kai paused herself, "Except… when Scarlett tried to-"

Eros nodded as he jumped in, "The foreshadowing was done quite early in the book, I'm afraid. It was poorly written, but it was an attempt, nonetheless. With every new loop, the tale strayed from its original notion…"

He proceeded to elaborate on how Elphaba made Eros the villain she perceived him to be; the story was initially his prison. Eventually, she added her son before he slipped away forever and his lover. That's when she began disguising it as a tale, enjoying her payback on Eros and seeing her son live on in another way.

He continued discussing how he was given 'mortal flesh' once freed from the novel. Kai didn't want him to elaborate any more on that. She told herself there would be another time for it.

This was already a lot to soak in.

"What happened to the other souls then? You said they were laid to rest, but what does that really mean? Was every single character there an actual person?" The food Kai managed to nibble while listening flopped in her stomach.

Eros glanced to the sky, and those pupils pinpointed. As if they could focus and gaze beyond the clouds that were congesting the heavens.

"They will no longer suffer at the hands of that witch but be reunited with those they love. Who knows, maybe they'll even reincarnate and get their second chances too…" Those brown irises glinted a red gleam as he looked back at the beautiful woman across from him. "A majority of them were *real* people."

Eros watched the horror seep into those vivid blues, wishing he could have punished Elphaba himself for putting that expression on Kai's face.

She pushed her plate further away, daring to ask, "Like… who?"

"Scarlett, that old hag that served her, her son Dexter, many of the village folk, that worm. The list goes on."

Eros explained to Kai where Vanessa had pulled these people from, each ranging from different periods, as the previous souls were insufficient to continue feeding her prolonged existence.

He explained that Scarlett, whose real name was Rosie, was Madam Jade's daughter. Dexter was someone Scarlett had met in their little village. They were separated by illness when Dexter's body contracted a disease.

No one knew what caused it, and Medieval medicine, at the time, was powerless against it.

Kai learned that Warrick was a mercenary with the unfortunate pleasure of meeting Elphaba on his travels. But getting that information was like pulling teeth from Eros. It seemed he held onto that shred of aggression towards him even after the spell had ended.

"And you?" Kai asked, interrupting again.

Eros frowned at his food, jabbing the meat on his plate. "She had come to our temples, praying for divine intervention for her son… She wasn't satisfied with the results and took matters into her own hands. You know the rest."

Kai nodded, deciding not to push it any further. She understood that dullness on his face, reminiscing about a memory he didn't want to.

It was probably best he did it on his own terms.

"So, how exactly did you become a business tycoon?" She plucked up the fork, moving on from the subject. "If it weren't for Mr Williams taking me under his wing, I wouldn't be where I am today." Kai looked at Eros, who was cutting his steak. "You did it in mere years, from nothing to something. It took me a decade, not counting my years in school. Not to mention, I'm actually from this *new world*, to begin with."

Eros brought the meat to his lips, not breaking eye contact. That gleam returned. "I have friends in high places," he said before popping it in.

Kai rolled her eyes, and her lashes stuttered with the movement.

Eros then complained about this world and their love for robotic things. From the glowing gadgets in their hands to the horseless carriages they called cars, he struggled to adapt.

Wiping the corners of his mouth with the napkin, it was now Eros's turn. "Well, that's enough about me. What's your story, then?"

Kai had finished her desert long before him, studying his movements as he ate gracefully like he was trained by the queen to fine dine in the highest class.

Her arms crossed as she leaned back in the seat. "If you were a god, wouldn't you know all about me, in some sense?"

Eros pushed his plate over, his folded napkin placed on it. "Not my department... I dealt with other matters. Besides, this is more fun." He reached into his blazer's inner pocket, retrieving his wallet. "I once saw this really intriguing pub where we can get a decent drink. I think it was called The Georges Tavern. Have you heard of it?"

Kai's gaze dashed away, her head shaking as she started to laugh.

"I want to hear your voice. Your story matters to me."

Still shaking her head, she regarded him, "Sorry to disappoint, but I lived a rather boring life in comparison."

Eros tucked a black credit card into the leather folder, not even glancing at the bill. "I find that hard to believe, Kai Redsi. How many people do you know just randomly end up inside a novel one day? Who also managed to melt the frozen heart belonging to the man of love and desire, himself." He flashed her a smile back, ready to leave.

CHAPTER FORTY-FOUR

Kai stood outside The Georges Tavern, marvelling at the scaffolding on some of the building's outer structure.

Eros was standing next to her, looking up as well. His head tilted sideways, commenting, "If this new world weren't so cheap on materials, they wouldn't need to do that so often. Our buildings lasted hundreds of years."

"Really?" Kai huffed, rolling her eyes at him. That was the second time he had commented, comparing the past to the present since lunchtime.

Her hand gripped the steel handle, pulling the door towards her. Heat rushed into her face, as well as the familiar rank of alcohol and body odours.

She had to admit, she did not miss that smell. It used to take her ages to get the stench out of her uniforms, eventually giving up as it became a never-ending cycle.

Her proceeding steps paused inside the establishment, eyes surveying how the place hadn't changed in the last eight years.

That was the last time she had been here. When Scottie pulled her aside and offered her a job elsewhere, the next part of her story began, finally putting her degree to use and chasing her lifelong goals.

Eros swaggered behind, blowing out a lengthy whistle. "Interesting…"

Kai twisted, catching a strange look on his face. "What?"

The man slowly approached, a hand gently laying on her lower back.

"You think with the money they're putting into fixing the outside, they would have done inside, too," he whispered into her ear.

Eyebrows came forward as Kai mentally disagreed.

This place had become her second home during college and was her stepping block to where she was now. Her heart was biased when it came to comments about the place. It held a special place in her heart even if it wasn't Americanised like many of the pubs were doing lately.

"By god!" a voice shouted over the music filling the chilled-out atmosphere.

Kai and Eros turned their attention to the bar, noticing three older gentlemen looking their way, sharply dressed.

"HA! I told you!" One of the men punched the other on the arm. "It's our singing lass!"

A smile blossomed on Kai's face as she quickly stepped for the individuals.

Brodie, Jimmy and Tommy.

"Gentleman!" sang Kai as she practically skipped.

Brodie howled, "Am I glad to see you again! Not the same these youngsters." His chin flicked at the blonde man behind the bar. "Don't have that same vigour you kids had. Why don't you get back there and show them how it's really done!"

Kai beamed, looking between them. Other than the inevitable ageing signs on their profiles, it looked like their spirits hadn't changed one bit.

She reminded herself not to let her emotions get the best of her as she felt the tears wanting to swarm her eyes.

"How's our little business lady doing?" Even Jimmy was smiling for once rather than grumbling off about something. "Heard from Scott you got another clinic going in Wales. Congratulations, girl."

Before Kai could reply, she noticed all their eyes cut to her left.

The grins on Brodie and Jimmy faltered. Even Tommy seemed to straighten from leaning against the bar.

Warmth settled on her back as fingers began to drum individually.

On Kai's left, Eros had approached them, grinning weirdly at the senior men. "Good afternoon, gentlemen."

Kai checked out the other three's expressions. Jimmy and Tommy had narrowed their eyes.

Brodie's head went low, then raised, checking out Eros's full height before looking at her again. "Business partner?" he asked.

Her head started to nod, only to slowly shake. She didn't know how she was supposed to answer that. Reflecting on what had happened in her office...

Kai stopped that train of thought before the heat could explode in her face. She and Eros still had to talk about *that*.

"What happened to our boy, Zac?"

That hand on her lower back twitched, and fingers halted. Then came the flat tone, "Zac? And pray tell, who is that?"

A meek smile was offered to Eros as Kai turned back to the friendly regulars. "We didn't work out... That ended years ago." Her hand raised, awkwardly scratching her neck.

Surprise replaced Brodie's features. "That's a shame..." He pulled his overly stuffed wallet out, retrieving a few notes and shoving them to Tommy. "Guess I lost that one."

Tommy unquestioningly accepted the handed-over cash, adamant with his narrowed eyes on Eros.

Kai blinked, stunned as she watched the exchange of cash. *Did they seriously bet on us staying together?*

"Whiskey, is it?" Eros asked suddenly, eyes flickered to the untouched drinks behind the guys. "My kind of men." His browns then cut to the boy behind the bar. "I'll take one as well, and-" His hand gently rubbed Kai's lower back. "What would you like, Love?"

"A glass of red..." Kai hesitated, "please."

She knew there would be questions about Zachary and wasn't looking forward to that awkward conversation either. There was some strange feeling of guilt clenching her gut.

"It's on us." Tommy threw the bills Brodie had given him onto the counter. He turned back towards Eros and Kai, nodding as he sauntered to a seat, leaving the other guys behind for once.

Brodie let off a deep chuckle, quickly recovering with a feigned cough. "Was lovely to see you, lass. Don't be a stranger." He winked, following Tommy.

Jimmy was the last to linger, his eyes still locked in place. He was silent, carefully taking his drink and following his mates to their usual spot.

Even after all these years, the three still sat near the middle of the pub, each facing the front door.

Kai's cheeks puffed up with air as she steadily rocked on her high heels. Her attention crept to Eros, who was silent next to her.

He forced a smile; one eyebrow raised up. "So…Who's Zac?"

Kai was on her fourth glass of red, feeling her cheeks permanently heated. The first was nursed as she explained her life to him. The second had constantly touched her lips as she sipped it back, trying to avoid answering the same question Eros would revert to. By the third, she had let go of her worries and insecurities, enjoying the taste and the expressions the man offered her.

Kai was trying her hardest not to laugh at the man sitting across. Who was still sulking over the fact she had a *boyfriend* before he arrived.

"Hey…" Her lips twitched as she bit the inside of her cheek.

Brown's eyes refused to look at her; with arms crossed, a long finger tapped a bicep. Eros's blazer was folded and discarded on the bench rest behind him. The three missing bottoms of his dress shirt gave her a peek at his squished-up chest.

"Eros?"

His tight-lipped mouth threatened to turn downwards. Still, his attention remained on something at the colourful bar.

She really wanted to laugh at how adorable his pout was, hiding her smile behind her glass of red. Kai took a deep breath before trying again, "Mr Redsi?"

Eros's eyes finally met hers.

"He was a distraction. I ended it because he deserved better, and to be perfectly honest with you... I don't have time for men nowadays. My schedule hardly allows it."

Those eyes dared to glare at her words as Eros quickly downed his glass. His lips smacked together, never breaking eye contact as he swallowed the liquor.

His Adam's apple bobbed profoundly. "Oh, so if your schedule allowed it, you would have?" his strained voice replied. Before she could open her mouth and respond, Eros continued, "I see how it is..."

She tried with all her might and failed miserably. The giggles spilt out, causing the man to frown even more, dashing his stare away.

Tears welled in Kai's eyes, and her belly ached from the prolonged laughter. A hand laid on her stomach as she calmed herself down. The other hand dabbed her corners, stopping the tears from falling.

She drew in a wheezy breath, trying to soothe him, "Or maybe I was waiting for someone to make me want to make the time to date again." Kai observed.

Eros's eyebrows twitch, his ear perking up with her words.

"Maybe... I was waiting for someone to come along and sweep me off my feet... like you."

His eyes again cut to her as hunger seeped into his pupils, expanding them.

She couldn't stop herself even if she tried. Liquid courage pushed her truest thoughts out. "I thought about you a lot, you know. Even when I was with him..." Kai's eyes lowered, and her voice quieted, "It felt wrong... We would be doing something, and suddenly, something would remind me of you. That's why I ended it."

Kai focused on picking at the acrylic on her nails, pulling them away from the cuticles, recalling the one big argument between her and Zachary.

When Zachary asked her why she would pull away sometimes, forcing her into a corner, he tried to get her to admit she was seeing someone else by how she acted. How guilty she felt at the time for not telling him the truth.

She heard Eros clear his throat and peeked at him.

Colour had risen to his face. His eyes stared at his empty glass. "Maybe you should have just started with that."

A smile twitched on Kai's face once again. A mischievous idea popped into her mind. "I could have, but I kinda like when you pout. It's cute," she teased.

His face dropped as he met her stare. "Men aren't supposed to be cute, Love." Then the man crossed his arms once more, shaking his head away.

Kai stifled the laugh, her gaze studying his side profile.

Whether smiling, smouldering, or pouting, Eros was charming. Her grumpy, prince charming.

The laugh slipped from her lips at that thought, earning her a look from him.

Chapter Forty-Five

The upper floor was dark as Kai stepped up the stairs, hand gliding along the swirling rail. "Babe?" She peeked into the first dark room, not spying Eros inside. His computer screen was the only thing left on within.

She closed his office door and headed down the long hallway towards their shared bedroom.

A light illuminated from within it.

"Babe?" She pushed open the white door, still not finding him. "That's strange...." Pulling her phone out, she went over the message a second time. "He said he was already home," she mumbled.

Walking inside the room, she tossed the mobile device onto the massive circular bed. Immediately beginning to change into some comfy clothes laid to a side.

Kai paused, hearing running water come from the en-suite. Her head angled to the closed door, overhearing Eros singing faintly.

She smiled as she undid her yellow dress shirt. *So he is*, she thought to herself.

It had been two years since Eros appeared inside her office and two years since he followed her everywhere like a shadow. Anywhere she went, anything she did, Eros was there.

For the first little while, he was inseparable from her. Eventually, he relaxed when he came to terms with the fact that Kai would always come back and wouldn't vanish before his eyes.

The first six months were the hardest for Kai, trying to balance her social life, job, and new, very needy life partner.

Stace had a hissy fit when Kai invited her over for the first time since she started officially seeing Eros, wanting to introduce her new boyfriend. Her best friend was thrown into a bigger huff when Eros repeatedly referred to himself as Kai's husband.

Two years later, Stace still hadn't forgiven Kai and did not like Eros. Constantly throwing Kai's boyfriend shade whenever the three were together, or low-key jabs saying Kai was to marry her brother.

Eros learned to ignore Stace, accepting that she was important to Kai. But he never held back when he argued with the woman, which sometimes went on for many minutes until Kai dragged one away from the other.

While Eros had to catch up with meetings during those days because he prioritised Kai over most things, she called Ava and Charlie to inform them of the situation.

However, she didn't tell them the whole extent of Eros's tale, believing it wasn't her story to tell.

Both Ava and Charlie were equally stunned. Neither was ready to meet Eros when she offered, which Kai respected wholeheartedly.

Ava had finally recovered from the nightmares at the time about losing her sight. She was a regular patient at one of TranqWell's clinics, so Kai knew the ins and outs of all her sessions.

With their first baby then, too, Charlie didn't want to risk Ava relapsing after all that therapy and putting their child at risk.

It had taken a year till her other companions met Eros, both equally as awkward around him. Even though Eros, himself, could not remember them.

She tried not to laugh during their interactions, with Charlie peeking behind Eros's back, looking for those wings. Ava wasn't nearly as awkward as her adorable husband; she at least conversed with Kai's boyfriend.

Kai threw a dark cashmere cardigan around her shoulders, her attention delayed on the photo of her grandfather and Eros on the oak dresser. She picked up the image, softly smiling at it.

The two men smiled wide, both holding a large fish in their hands on open waters. She shook her head at her two silly boys, their funny fishing hats full of funky pins. One of those funky pins was beside the spot where the picture frame lived. It was a giant tacky thing that said '*Keeping it Reel*' with a silhouette of a man fishing.

Her grandfather was the only one who welcomed Eros with open arms.

The first time they met, he lectured Eros on sex and marriage. Then her pappy did a one-eighty and commented about their future children having the best genes and constantly calling the man a handsome devil, which satisfied Eros's ego all the while.

It went from zero to a hundred quickly with those two, a bromance of the ages sparked.

Whenever she had the chance to speak to her grandfather, she was never surprised when he asked to speak to Eros. With Eros's permission, Kai passed his number along. Now, she hardly heard from her granddad at all.

The man usually called her boyfriend first. She became an afterthought.

Kai knew her grandfather always wanted grandsons, so she didn't take it personally. With his three kids being too old for children now and giving him seven granddaughters, letting them bond was fulfilling.

She wanted the man who raised her to have what he wished, as he had always tried to grant hers.

Kai enjoyed seeing them together; a spring always returned to her granddad's wobbling steps, and Eros seemed to enjoy having an elder's undivided attention.

The two things those men bonded over were fishing and their confusion over technology. Eros hated mobile phones and computers just as much as her granddad.

An old man in spirit, Kai laughed to herself.

Steam rushed out of the bathroom as the en-suite door opened.

Fresh out of the shower, Eros prowled with a low-hanging, white towel wrapped around his waist. Water droplets still riddled his body. Some streamed down his shoulder and legs.

"Agapi, when did you get back?"

Water dripped off that black hair, gliding down his sculptured chest. The black and red tattoos up his arms popped with colour even more now that they were saturated.

Kai placed the photo down, angling towards his voice. "Not long, I did shout for you..." her words got quieter, watching the droplets travel over his flesh.

One, in particular, glided down his left pectoral and appeared to bounce as it skimmed down his chiselled six-pack.

Eros hummed, biting back the smile as her pupils dilated hungrily. He casually walked past and headed for the closet. His tattooed back to her.

Kai swallowed, suddenly feeling anxious. "What... Um... What did you want to talk about?" His attitude was strange and out of character.

He hadn't even given her a kiss like he usually did when she got home from work.

Eros's back muscles rippled as he began pulling clothing out, making that tattoo of the black wings move. "Did you complain to Stace that I was *needy*?"

Kai straightened like a board, immediately picking at the sleeve of her cardigan. "Well... I said... You see..."

Eros threw a white shirt on, turning to the stalling woman. "You said I couldn't possibly think of having a baby right now. Eros is far too needy. He's—" His fingers came up, air quoting. "Baby." Then those arms crossed as his lips pursed.

The look he gave her was not one she liked. He usually returned it to Stace when she frowned at him.

Kai chewed on her lip and cringed. "You heard all that?"

A nod. That's all he gave her as he shifted his weight to one hip.

She began rocking on her heels, guilt festering in her conscience. "I'm sorry... she was in my ear complaining we would have babies soon, and she'd still be all alone… I didn't mean it in a nasty way. But I see now that it wasn't very nice saying that behind your back."

Eros hummed and shot her a look. "Remind me, which of us is crying like a baby to God when I'm bending you over?"

Kai scoffed, "First off, I do not cry!" Her finger shot up, counting as her cheeks bloomed with colour. "Secondly-"

The man laughed, cutting her off, "Oh yes, you do."

A mouth flopped open and closed, and no words came from Kai's lips. Her hands waved in front, dismissing the conversation as she twisted for the bedroom door.

Eros rushed after her departing figure. "Where are you going?" Arms encircled her up by the waist. "We're having a conversation here."

"J-Just get dressed. We can talk downstairs!"

He chuckled into her ear, tightening his hold on her. "Or you can soothe your *needy* boyfriend, whose feelings are *very* hurt."

Kai allowed herself to be dragged backwards, and then Eros turned and twisted, pushing her onto the bed.

She could have gotten out of his grip if she wanted to, as he had never once forced his true strength on her.

As she landed flat on the bed, her mind began wondering how that towel Eros had on was still in place. The towel dipped, hanging dangerously low, showing that robust v-section. A dark treasure trail dived beneath that towel.

"Eyes up here, Love." Eros winked from above, pinning her hands above her head with just one of his.

"Look, I said I was sorry… Please…" Her eyes pleaded with him, doing her best at puppy dog eyes. "Please don't do this?"

He shook his head. "I've been insulted, so you *must* be punished." His free hand came down and hovered over her already tensed stomach. "Any last words?"

Kai began trying to wiggle her way out as Eros's hand descended, beginning his tickle assault.

Her punishment quickly escalated to another round of steamy sex, much rougher than their morning session before work. Her clothing was discarded all around the room, a sock slung over that picture frame she had earlier.

Kai rolled over to a side as her bottom lip stuck out. The once clean hair sticking to her face from sweat. "You beast..." she huffed, trying to find the energy to search for her discarded underwear.

Eros chuckled, arms going around her waist, keeping her from leaving him. "Let that be a reminder the next time you think of calling me *baby*," he growled into an ear before nipping at it.

Kai rolled her eyes, letting herself relax into his chest.

She wanted to get up and sort dinner out, but now she had no energy to do so. She wasn't even sure if her legs would function adequately to make it downstairs.

"Babe?"

Kai hummed as a response.

"Did you book Friday off, like I asked?"

Kai nodded meekly, suddenly feeling drowsy. "Mhmm... yea... I did," she managed to say as her eyes fluttered shut.

Eros nuzzled in closer, his chest rumbling as he said something she didn't catch.

Friday came, and Kai was exiting a plane, her stare squinting at the cloudy skies above through the boarding bridge windows. "Why are we here again?" she turned, asking her travel partner.

Eros was carrying both their carry-ons, unaware of all the women's ogling eyes on him.

He had dressed down for once rather than sauntering around in a fitted, expensive suit. But the black hoodie and grey sweatpants didn't dull down the ooze of sex appeal he seemed to radiate to those around him.

"I told you. You'll see when we get there." He leant down and rubbed his nose to hers, throwing a carry-on over one of his wide shoulders.

They strolled hand in hand through the airport, making their way for the rest of their things. Kai's suspicion was in hyperdrive, wondering why they needed to pack so much for a simple visit.

After collecting the rest of their luggage and exiting the airport, Eros opened the car door of the waiting taxicab for Kai.

Ushering her in while he privately spoke to the driver.

She looked out the window, examining how much this place had changed in the last ten years. She had a sneaky feeling they were going to her grandfathers to celebrate her birthday with him.

She couldn't think of any other reason they would visit Ireland, as neither had business to tend to here.

Eros seated himself in the back, offering a smile that mischievous glint flared. "Get some rest. We should be there in a couple of hours." His arm extended, going around her shoulders.

Kai's nose scrunched up in thought. *It doesn't take that long to get there.* Her eyes narrowed on her partner, observing his face for answers.

Eros's smile only grew as he pulled Kai to him. "Rest, Agapi. We have much to do."

And Kai did, surrendering to him yet again. She laid her head on his lap and let sleep claim her.

It was easy to fall asleep around Eros, as his warmth and scent always lulled her into a comforting peace of mind.

She had been worn down as of late, with constant meetings and department reviews – Kai looked forward to her birthday weekend with some much-needed time off.

Within moments – or so it felt like – Kai was gently woken by Eros, kissing her face. "Wakey, wakey."

"What time is it?" she asked, scratching her scalp.

It had felt like she was sleeping for only minutes, wishing she could have had another five. She blamed Eros for her lack of sleep for the last night, *exercising* extensively before bed.

"It's time for your surprise."

Kai sat up, double-taking the scenery outside the car windows.

Tall evergreen trees lined a gravel road, steadily ascending a hill—her headshot to Eros, who only offered a grin.

"We'll walk from here, sir."

Money was handed over, and then Eros exited the vehicle without any explanation.

Kai's head whipped to that road. Images of walking that trail after exiting the school bus played out before her.

Her chest felt like it was tightening, wondering if she was still dreaming or if she was truly here.

She never dared to come, at least not alone.

Eros opened the car door, offering a hand while a swirling pool of emotions consumed her. Kai's hand trembled, laying hers into his as she crept out of the vehicle.

Her stare was locked on the homely scenery.

Though the flowers weren't there anymore, the memory of their scent still hung in her nose. She sniffled up the mess that threatened to drop.

Kai could somewhat see the house through her now blurring vision. They kept the home's original colours, repainting the wear and tear.

Tears swelled, ready to spill over as she dropped her hand luggage. "I... I grew up there..." She turned to Eros, sniffling more. "What's going on?"

"Yes, you did," Eros said the bare minimum, gathering the luggage. He pivoted for the road, heading up the slight ascend.

Kai could only cautiously pick up her handbag, her steps hesitant as she followed with a headspace of questions.

Her heart rate increased as the cosy little cottage idly got closer, that same green door beyond the wooden porch closing in.

Eros finally paused, reaching into his grey sweatpants, and began to dig something out. "I once remembered a dream you had..."

Pulling out a jingling item.

"Of a cosy homely estate, far away from the weird world of gadgets. I vividly remember the longing I felt through you as if it were my own." He gently grabbed Kai's empty hand and placed keys into them.

He curled her fingers around them with his own. Holding her hand as he locked eyes with her.

"This was your home... and is, once more. Happy birthday, my Love."

Those tears overflowed from Kai's eyes as she looked at those keys, droplets falling onto both their hands. Her attention wobbled to the handsome face before hers and swayed to the house not far off.

"Come on, then." Eros flicked his chin. "I'm dying to see what my *baby's* room looked like." Throwing her a wink, he grabbed her bag and continued walking forward.

Kai wobbled, taking in the house, the yard, the trees... the man walking up to the porch.

This was where her heart had *always* been.

Home, her home.

A smile blossomed on her face as the best childhood memories played out.

Her dad, with his backwards cap riding the lawn mower, the three of them decorating the yard for the holidays, putting up crazy rainbow lights. She even envisioned her mam picking the flowers from around the house and spraying her father with the garden hose in the summers.

Kai let the tears out, basking in this new feeling. This hope and anticipation for the future - where she would make new, happy memories just as precious as those.

Where she and Eros would live happily ever after.

THE END

ACKNOWLEDGEMENTS

First and foremost, I want to thank the *readers* who have made it this far, whether you enjoyed the book or not. Thank you for taking the time to read and taking a chance on this small author.

Secondly, *to my alpha, beta and ARC readers,* a heartfelt thank you to you, as well. I appreciate the feedback and the constructive criticism from each of you. Thank you for pointing out errors and things that didn't make sense or, quite frankly, didn't fit into the plot. Authors really owe it to you behind the scenes for being the fresh eyes when ours have been staring at the words for far too long.

To *Moonchild* from *fantasybookdesign.com,* thank you for your time, patience, and a massive applause for that stunning cover. Your customer service skills were appreciated, and the talent behind your many years of work really shows!

I wish to thank my family for their patience and support during all my writing, as I could be busy at times and not fully there when my mind ran wild with new story ideas. Thank you for your unconditional love and continued support as I chase this dream of writing.

I would also like to thank all the folks from Booktok and the My Indie Bookshelf community for a wide range of support. These communities welcomed me, as well as other Indies, with open arms. There had been a few days, even weeks, where I had struggled *big time* with imposter syndrome. Going over the material and thinking I was a rubbish writer, I often asked, "Why do I do this!"

I would take days - sometimes weeks - off writing and focused on simply growing my following. Then, the guilt would set in, and I criticised myself for not working on the novel. Some days, my mind became a game of tug-a-war. Write, don't write, edit, don't edit. Personally speaking, they made me feel a little better about myself, to know I was not alone in this struggle. It resonated with me hearing some of your similar experiences and just the kind words of acknowledgements that helped give me that positive kick in the backside to keep on going!

I'm not very good at this section of the writing process and hope my short and sweet words of acknowledgments doesn't come off as insincere, but I have soaked in so much from each of you mentioned and wish to thank you all again.

– So, thank you.

PAULINE S. FLYNN xx

<u>OTHER WORK(S) BY THE AUTHOR:</u>

MISERY (BOOK 1 OF THE ILL-FATED SERIES) PAPERBACK.

BOOK 2: PAIN

  DUE WINTER 2023

BOOK 3: RISE

  DUE 2024

Visit The Author's Website: https://paulinesflynn.com or

@p.s.flynnbooks   **@P.S.Flynn Books**

Stay current on future releases, other works, and sneak peeks.